Manwhore

By

Bonnie Rivera and Clyde Hudson

A BONNIE AND CLYDE BOOK

Manwhore

By

Bonnie Rivera and Clyde Hudson

Manwhore

ISBN 978-1-7350415-2-0

Cover Design by Jesse Baker
Interior Graphic Images by Daniel Yader

Disclaimer

This book contains sexually explicit scenes and adult language which may be considered offensive to some readers. The content of this work is fiction. While it contains references to historical facts and existing locations, the names, characters and situations are fictitious. Any resemblance to actual persons, living or dead, existing businesses, or local events is coincidental and is the fruit of the imagination of the authors.

Table of Contents

Chapter One

Born to Fuck

My name is Michael Stephen Grant and I was born to fuck a whole lot of women.

Ever since I reached puberty and discovered that my pecker was in good working order, my main mission in life became to nail as many women as possible regardless of what shape and size their figures materialized in. Looking back on a lifetime of erotic encounters with the opposite sex, at the age of sixty-five, I can honestly say that I've been to the moon and back. Despite having been physically intimate with enough women to populate a small city, there is still a shitload of firepower left in my joy rocket. If it wasn't for me getting sick, I would pack up my stuff and volunteer for another trip in a heartbeat.

So, how does a cool cat like me who's had enough women land on his bed to fill nine lives get a name like Michael Stephen Grant? Actually, it's a rather amusing story. My mother, may she rest in peace, was a bit promiscuous. Who am I kidding? She was a ravenous man eater whose best friend was Jack Daniels. That's right folks—the apple doesn't fall far from the tree. Melody Ann Grant happened to be juggling and riding two raging broncos at the same time when I was conceived. One was named Michael and the other Stephen.

Since back in those days DNA testing wasn't so readily available or affordable for that matter as it is now, my mother had no idea which one of the two broncos had knocked her up. According to her, the plan was to wait and see which one of them had the balls to make a personal appearance at the hospital after giving birth to me. The one who showed up would automatically be declared my father by default and I'd be named after him. Well as it turns out, neither of them bothered to show up so my mother had no choice but to name me Michael Stephen Grant. There you have it. I was clearly named after my two deadbeat dads. The funny thing is that no one really addresses me by my full given birth name. Most of my male friends call me Michael. Women in general clamor for me while I'm screwing their brains out by using either one of two nicknames, "OH GOD!" and "OH BABY!"

At this juncture you may feel inclined to ask: Why on earth would a highly successful skirt chaser like me want to bare his heart and soul about a lifetime of erotic behavior, especially now at my age? This may surprise you but scoring with women is not the only thing I've excelled at in life. I've spent decades developing a biography that's second-to-none. While you may find it a hard pill to swallow, I could very well be the most disciplined man on this planet and that has been the key to my success in every facet of my life. Being a master of discipline has allowed me to accomplish 100 percent of my professional and personal goals. The word failure has never been in my vocabulary.

People who know me well describe me as being self-centered and narcissistic. These are the individuals who actually like me. Can you imagine what people who have a strong disdain for me think? While I can't deny fitting the perception others have of me, I will say that I also possess good characteristics like being self-driven and positive. The key differentiator between me and other men who have charm, intelligence, decent looks and a nice physique is my methodological approach toward life. With every passing moment, I live life with a sense of urgency. Not a day goes by that I don't wake up with a clear-cut purpose.

Since this approach has served me well in my professional life, I use it to engage women only for the sake of pulling off another conquest of the fleshly kind. Unlike other men, my brain never turns into mush or goes south between my legs. No matter how beautiful the woman is, I never lose my wits. I've always been way too disciplined for that. Make no mistake: It has never been about wanting long-term female companionship. That does very little for me. The bottom line has always been to get in and out as quickly as possible, but always leaving them something memorable so they never forget MSG.

On a professional level, nothing pumps my adrenalin more than the planning and execution that goes into getting a woman under my covers. I've successfully accomplished hundreds of major and minor goals without one failure throughout my entire life. My accomplishments speak for themselves. At the age of nineteen, I purchased my first home in the San Francisco Bay Area. Two years later, I graced the cover of *Hot Rod Magazine* with my prize-winning car and boat. I went on to start and operate multiple successful businesses which ultimately led to me owning about a half-dozen homes, without mortgages I might add.

By the time I hit forty, I was already a self-made multi-millionaire. However, that still wasn't enough for me. To keep boredom at bay, I took it upon myself to write a book. Then I wrote another and another until eventually one day I found myself running my own imprint of IT management books for one of the biggest publisher's in the world. To date, I have authored and published more than forty books. On top of all this, I have exercised religiously seven days a week for over four decades and I only sleep four hours a night.

Before people start arriving at the conclusion that I accumulated my wealth the easy way, I'll have you know that I am one of the world's leading organization and personal mentors. That's right people, Michael Stephen Grant is recognized as being the foremost authority on providing practical guidance for solving management issues and challenges. For more than thirty years, I have devoted myself to helping professionals build competitive organizations. My client list reads like a Who's Who of American and International Business. Suddenly, I don't seem to be that shallow after all, do I?

Besides doing the horizontal mambo with women, my passion is to help people excel in their professional and personal lives by helping them develop the self-discipline skills needed to combat the top issues that can sabotage them which typically are severe procrastination, poor time management, ineffective goal management, lack of focus, no sense of urgency and lack of motivation. I am also highly effective in helping individuals improve their communication, relationship management, interpersonal, and leadership skills. My system has worked so well that it is now widely known as the *Discipline Mentoring Program.*

Now if I had to identify what my greatest assets are, I'd have to say my caring demeanor, incomparable energy, and a genuine desire to help people manage their lives efficiently. What I do on my own downtime is an entirely different story and really nobody's business.

I work extremely hard so I deserve to have my playtime. Most people would consider my daily routine to be crazy and downright unhealthy. Even though I'm sixty years old now, since my early twenties, I have mastered the ultimate level of discipline. I am a firm believer that the body and mind should be pushed to the max every single day.

So, why would I potentially taint all the good things I've accomplished by airing truckloads of dirty laundry? Well for starters, I just found out today that I have stage four lung cancer and don't have much time left to raise Cain. Doctor Campbell says that if I'm a lucky bastard and he is of the opinion that I am, I will still be in heat for at least another year. Apparently, I am in the throes of the most advanced stage of lung cancer there is. The cancer has already spread to both lungs and is high-tailing it at this very moment to my liver and other key internal organs. In the coming months, I can expect to have serious fluid build-up around my lungs and that's just the beginning of my slow, torturous demise. My main airways will also get obstructed and eventually I'll start to cough up blood. The real fun will kick in when I start to suffer from excruciating bone pain, headaches, seizures, weakness, speech problems, and dramatic weight loss.

What is absolutely mind-boggling to me is that of all the diseases known to man that I could have contracted, a health nut who doesn't drink or smoke, I end up with lung cancer. This goes to show that karma can have a wicked sense of humor when it wants to. Considering my proven track record of having reckless and uninhibited sex with countless women from around the world, some of which were from third world countries, I thought that AIDS would eventually rear its ugly head and bite me right on my large sculpted white ass but apparently it had no interest in doing so.

In essence, I've been a bad and naughty man for the most part of my life. But I'm a far cry from being the criminal type who commits felonies and eventually gets incarcerated. Women have always known to be on the lookout for these types. I am a lady-killer of the highest order and women never see me coming. I've turned preying on unsuspecting women by manipulating their minds and winning over their hearts into a science. The more innocent, naive and conservative they are, the more exciting the hunt is for me.

Virgins in particular have always been the biggest turn-on for me, especially the ones who are reared in a strict culture. I am especially drawn to those who have to marry before giving up that pot of gold between their legs. Yeah, I think most men would agree with me that there is nothing quite like rosy pink, tight pussy that's never been penetrated before. Crude . . . I know, but it's the way my mind operates. In retrospect, I have probably plucked and deflowered as many virgins as they are bluebonnets in Texas. Okay, so maybe I'm exaggerating just a bit here.

Other women who intrigue me are the ones who give out a strong vibe that they are unapproachable and impossible to get—you know those really *hot ones*. They have a chip on their shoulder and love to tease and manipulate the guys who hit on them. They've heard every lame pickup line in the book, but it doesn't compute with them. Because they are so desirable these women have heard that rhetoric for years and have become immune to it. They can spot inexperienced pick-up artists coming from miles away. Sometimes it takes more than a predator merely being easy on the eyes, intelligent, ruthless, cunning and relentless in his quest to conquer. This world is filled with men with these credentials. The key differentiator between myself and the competition is that I, Michael Stephen

Grant, am the undisputed *Master of Self-discipline.* All those younger playboys have nothing on me. Not even a tsunami can stop me once I catch a whiff of fresh pussy, tits, and ass.

During my teens, twenties, thirties and early forties my priorities were money, gym and sex—in that order. My life now still revolves around these three pleasures. Everything else is secondary to me. Money and the gym have always been my two greatest loves. Exercising seven days a week rain or shine is the reason I have a tighter and more sculpted body than most of the young bucks who live in the Dallas metropolitan area. While most men in my age bracket are walking around looking like their nine months pregnant, I'm parading my 6 ft, 2-inch frame of solid steel and sex appeal all over town. Back in my more glorious days, I had thick, wavy brown hair and eyes as blue as the Mediterranean Sea. Nowadays, I have salt and pepper hair, character lines in all the right places, and my eyes haven't lost their sparkle. A good number of women have told me they think I'm a much dapper version of Richard Gere. Whatever, the point is that I am the total package.

In my career, I have always been structured; constantly strategizing to improve efficiency, developing action plans with tasks, milestones and due dates, and always holding myself accountable. Since this way of thinking and operating is what has made me thrive professionally why not mimic this winning formula with the opposite sex? Well, that's exactly what I've been doing all these years and let me say it works like a charm. I strategize, develop a plan, conquer, and then move on to the next victim. Easy as pie!

Back in the day when I was in great demand as an international motivational speaker, my *modus operandi* was pretty much the same wherever I happened to be in the world, whatever the situation, or whoever I was with:

1. *Locate target:* I was always on the prowl for fresh meat. I was never satisfied and I had this strong sense of urgency to nail as many women as possible. It sounds horrible, but I was addicted to success in every facet of my life including sex. Some would say I was just overly horny. Okay, I'm guilty as charged. But in my defense, what normal hot-blooded male isn't? For me it was all about the hunt and accomplishing another goal. The climax was secondary and merely the cherry on top of my desert.

2. *Befriend target:* One of my cardinal rules was to never approach women with a heavy dosage of bullshit. Believe me, they seem to have this built-in tracking device that enables them to smell you coming a mile away. The trick is to come off as being a genuinely nice guy. I made it a point to always act timid, not aggressive. Pretending to be innocent and shy was a real stretch for a cocky *sonofabitch* like me but I managed to pull it off every time. If you show them that you genuinely care about them as a person and not a piece of meat, it will go a long way in getting them to trust you.

3. *Evaluate target:* My next step was to figure out all of the logistics like was she married? Did she have a fiancé or a boyfriend that I would have to factor into the equation? I can't stress enough how important it is to gather all the Intel you can about your intended target.

4. *Determine category:* The next order of business was to put the woman into a box and label her. Obviously, if the woman was highly intelligent versus being a naïve virgin the level of

difficulty and the resources required would be much greater than the promiscuous/unintelligent ones.

5. *Determine level of difficulty:* Once the woman who happened to be on my radar was properly categorized, I paused to determine just how much effort it was going to take on my part to gain access to that pot of gold between her legs. If I happened to peg them as being easy and low maintenance with their being minimal to no risk, then there was really no need to over think it. In these cases, I just unzipped my pants and went for it. On the other side of the coin, if the woman in question was of the untouchable sort and it seemed as though it was going to take nothing short of an Act of Congress to get her to spread-eagle her legs for me, then I had to make the tough decision whether it was worth moving forward with this particular endeavor or not.

6. *Win over their mind and heart:* Once my nine-inch dick pointed to a woman and said, "I want to fuck your brains out for hours on end" then I would not waste any time in strategizing to determine the best approach to ensure success while minimizing any risks. Believe me there are always different options to get inside a woman's panties but you must plan as though the life of your cock depends on it because well it does. The objective is to make the woman think that you truly care about her and you want to be in a long-term relationship. You gotta make her believe that, "She completes you." That's right you have to make them feel special and this can only be done by feeding them a load of crap. But you have to be a total gentleman about it. Buy them roses, be courteous and attentive, otherwise there ain't no way in hell you're getting any blow.

7. *Determine resources required:* Once I got this far in the process, I really had to put my dick on ice and figure out just how much effort it was going to take for me to score. You have to calculate the costs to see if you can afford it. There's no point in starting a relationship if you don't have the time or money to finish the job properly.

8. *Develop an action plan with key milestones:* After deciding that I was willing to bankroll the acquisition of a fresh piece of ass, I rolled up my sleeves and identified the small steps I would have to execute to ensure a successful outcome. At this point, I was willing to alter my daily routine so that I would be ready to fuck at a moment's notice? Sometimes the devil is in the details.

9. *Execute and conquer:* The last and final step was to have fun, pure and simple. All of the steps had been worked and a small fortune had been spent. Finally, I could get buck naked and treat myself to hours and hours of all-you-can-eat-pussy.

Whether I was at the corporate office, travelling for business, at the gym or shopping, I was always on the prowl for fresh meat. Heck, I was even on the make when I took my young daughter on walks to the park to feed the ducks. Sex was the desert I was entitled to have after every meal. I loved the challenge whether I was single or married at the time, which even made it more exciting. Yes, many of my titillating escapades were pulled off while I was married. Most of my time was spent at work or in the gym when I wasn't at home, so naturally many of my conquests emerged from these places.

Here's a case in point. On several occasions I used to see this pretty lady on a second-floor balcony of an apartment complex located on the way to a pond near my home. I could tell she was checking me out every time I passed by holding my daughter's hand. The first time I saw her she was wearing a blue flight attendant uniform. She looked damned sexy in it too. I don't remember her name; however, what I do know is that she worked for the now defunct Piedmont Airlines. From my vantage point, it seemed as though she had just gotten home from work and was leaning over her balcony enjoying a beautiful day in the San Francisco Bay Area.

The woman gave me a hard-on at first sight. I had to let go of my daughter's hand to cover up my impropriety. She was 5'6, probably weighed 135 pounds, and had long blonde hair and a firm round butt. I found out later that her eyes were a beautiful blue-green color. They were the kind of eyes a man could easily get lost in, especially with his cock inside of her. I looked up to say hello. I even coached my daughter to say hi and wave adoringly to help my cause. Although she didn't know it at the time, my little girl helped me nail the mystery woman on the balcony a few weeks later.

From that day forward, I made it a point to take my daughter to the park more often with the hope of getting another opportunity to speak with the hot flight attendant. To my credit, I never tried to rush an encounter. I did not want to make it look like I wanted to get into her pants. After a few weeks I saw her again and we had a longer conversation. Actually, she invited my daughter and me to her place for water and soda. At that pivotal moment, I knew this woman liked me and the chances that she'd eventually want to suck my dick were looking pretty good. During that visit, she intentionally recited what her schedule was going to be for that entire week. I took it as a sign from the sex gods that this fine piece of ass had my name written all over it. If I played my cards right, it would only be a matter of time before I got to taste her sweet nectar.

Later that same week, I stopped by her apartment alone. She was there and invited me in. That's when we spoke candidly and I gave her full disclosure that I was married. However, I quickly followed up that startling confession with, "I think you're drop dead gorgeous and I would like to go out with you." Since I was on a roll, I went on to say, "I travel a great deal for work. Would you be interested in taking a trip together so we can get to know each other better?" This feline was in heat because without the slightest hesitation she replied, "Sure, I would love to."

As it turned out, her airline flew to Boston from San Francisco on a daily basis. I lied through my teeth and told her I had never been to Boston before. Truth be told, I wanted her to get me on a flight for free so I would not have to use my own miles. I also wanted to make it seem as though she was going to show me the sights of the town and that excited her. So, we planned a two-night, three-day excursion to Boston. I will never forget the limo driver picked me up first on the day of the excursion. Then we picked up the young lady who only lived a few blocks away and off we went to the airport. I was oozing with confidence and sex appeal.

The foreplay started on the flight over to Boston. We were sitting in our first-class seats and had covered ourselves up with a few blankets since it was a bit chilly. In one fluid move, she unzipped my pants and began stroking my penis with feather light touches. I reciprocated by fondling her tits and rubbing her crotch. It was blatantly obvious to everyone who passed by what we were doing under the blankets. But we didn't give a shit. We were so hot for each other.

We had built up so much sexual tension during the flight that we fucked like rabbits as soon as we got to the hotel in the afternoon. A few seconds after entering the room, we dropped our luggage and began tearing each other's clothes off like wild animals. The sight of her naked body really revved my engine so I lightly pushed her onto the bed and immediately went down on her. Her pussy smelled and tasted good, better than most. She had light blonde pubic hair and it was short and well-maintained. My tongue went to town inside her vagina with the same enthusiasm of a starving kid slurping a bowl of hot Spaghetti-O's. Her nipples, which were a light-tanned color, quickly pointed north. She was the real deal. I made her cum several times and then she forced me to stick it in—by that time—I was so horned up that I came in seconds.

After having defiled the hotel bed, we went out to dinner. She wore a tight-fitting red dress that accentuated her curves in all the right places and made me horny. In the middle of our meal, she slipped off one of her red stiletto pumps and started to massage my penis with her toes under the table. It's a miracle that I didn't explode in my pants right then and there. When we finished having dinner, just to kill some time, we painted the town red which was merely a prelude to more mind-blowing sex. When we arrived back at the hotel after experiencing a bit of Boston night life, we were pretty much ready to taste each other's erogenous zones again. We stepped into the elevator hand in hand. If there hadn't been other passengers along for the ride, I would have started fucking her in the elevator like a madman.

When the elevator doors opened up and deposited us on the ninth floor, we practically sprinted to our hotel room. I ushered her inside, locked the door, and headed straight for her like a heat seeking missile. A part of me wanted to prolong the fuck as much as possible, but she didn't give me much of a choice. Wearing a killer smile, she unzipped her dress, seductively pulled it off her shoulders, and let it fall to the floor in one dramatic sweep. The sight of her lacy scarlet red push-up bra and matching thong set my loins on fire. I approached her and picked her up in my arms. She reacted by wrapping her succulent thighs around my waist. I tossed her on the bed and she struck a seductive pose while I undressed. The whole time she looked at me with those beautiful blue/green come-hither eyes and it made me feel like I was King of the Jungle.

Unable to restrain myself any longer, I slowly crept onto the bed and immediately went down on her. She moaned with pleasure. "Oh my God! You give a whole new meaning to the term silver-tongued devil," she purred. Her praise only egged me on so I flicked my tongue inside her back and forth in perfect rhythm until she started to spasm out of control. After a medley of delicate cries, she had an orgasm and out came her sweet juice for my lips to taste. We ended fucking for hours and finally collapsed from exhaustion around midnight. I woke up after my usual four hours of sleep ready to go again. While she slept, I slithered my rock-hard cock inside of her and pumped it up and down as gently as I could so as not to wake her. It didn't take long for me to hit that high note.

The next morning, we got up and had a hearty breakfast. We did some more sight-seeing then went back to the hotel and exchanged bodily fluids several more times. She was a fantastic kisser and loved sucking dick. On the flight back to San Francisco our conversation went something like this.

"Thanks for an unforgettable weekend," I said to her right before we landed. "When can I see you again?"

She flashed me a confident smile and replied, "I would love to see you again. But you have to leave your wife and be mine exclusively."

After mulling it over in my head for a split second, I gave her a roguish grin and said, "Thanks, but no thanks."

All the color drained out of her face immediately. "You're kidding, right?"

"Nope," I replied rather nonchalantly, as if she had just offered me a breath mint.

Her eyes shifted and focused on the nearest exit door. I could tell that the gears in her mind were cranking a hundred miles an hour. After a few moments of awkward silence, she looked me squarely in the eye and said, "You're an asshole. You totally used me. I wish we were still up in the air so I can kick your ass through the exit door."

That was the last time I ever saw her. At first, I was disappointed that she didn't want to continue seeing me. She had such a great body, beautiful facial features, and a nice personality to boot. But the disappointment only lasted about an hour. When I got home my daughter wanted to play so that consumed my time for the rest of the day. As soon as the sun came up the following day, I had already moved on to my next spicy adventure.

This is merely a small sampling of a lifetime of carnal encounters. Stick around and I'll tell you some more of my crazy sexual antics while I wait for the Grim Reaper to come take me away. I've got nothing else better to do. Just keep in mind that I have logged in over four million airline miles over a span of fifteen years. So, come fly with me around the world in 365 days. But fasten your seatbelts because it's going to be a hell of a bumpy ride.

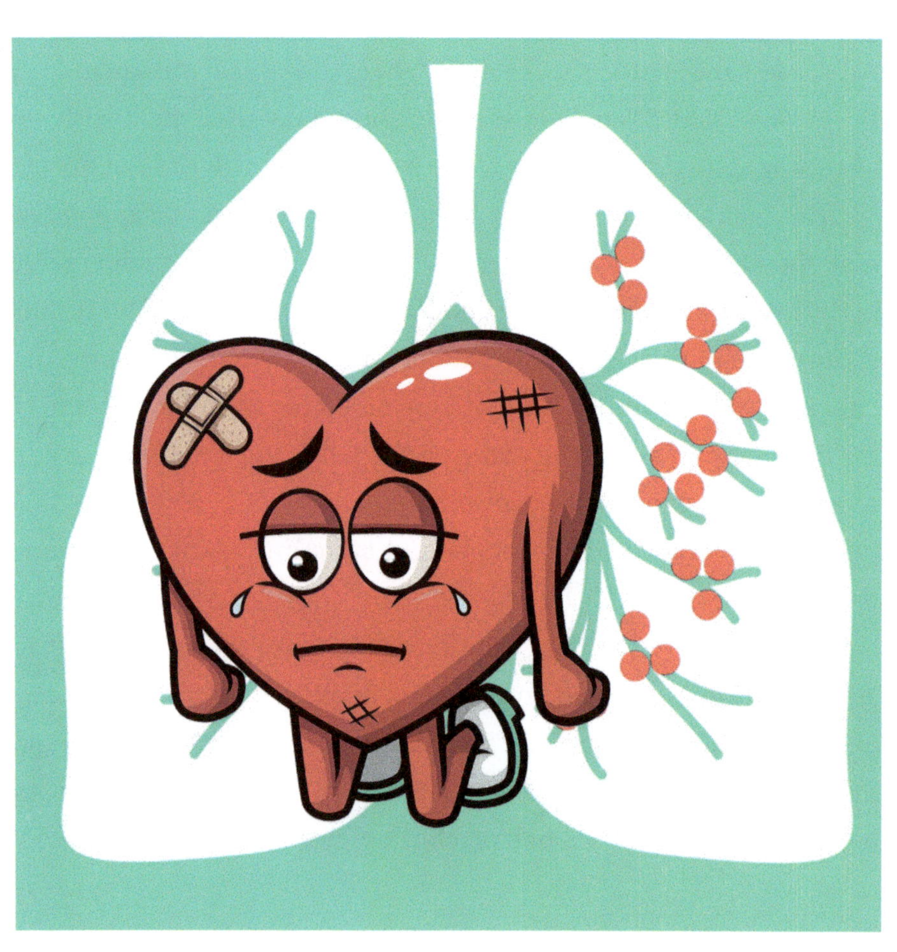

Chapter Two

Achy Breaky Heart

"So, are you ready to place your order? What's it going to be MSG? Radiation or Chemotherapy? Better yet, may I suggest our Special of the Day—Clinical Trials?"

This is what Dr. Joseph Earl Campbell, the man who delivered my death sentence a few weeks ago, said to me during my follow-up visit with him earlier today.

"I've given it a lot of thought doc and the way I see it is that none of these treatments are going to cure me. They are just going to mask the symptoms," I said, leaning back in the comfy chair he had provided me to sit on. "Thanks, but no thanks. I'm just going to let nature take its course."

Dr. Campbell stopped jotting down notes in my medical chart and looked up at me with a frustrated look on his face. "So, that's it? You're just going to ride off into the sunset like some crazy *desperado* and not do anything to help yourself?" he asked point-blank.

"Affirmative," I answered without the slightest hesitation.

He picked up his pen and began writing again. "Your participation in one of our clinical trials could help save the lives of future lung cancer patients. You would receive the best care and we'd make sure you are comfortable until the end if things don't work out."

"I appreciate the sales pitch doc, but I'm not buying into your propaganda."

I could tell my biting sarcasm was not well-received by the good doctor. He pushed back his chair and got up abruptly. "You are impossible to deal with," he blurted out.

"That's not the first time I've heard that," I quipped back, grinning from ear to ear. "Look, Dr. Campbell, I appreciate your concern, I really do. I'm not gung-ho about dying, but if I must, then I want to do it on my own terms. Is that too much to ask for?" I added on a more serious note.

Doctor Campbell remained silent for a few seconds then he softened up a bit. "I guess not," he said. "I would still like for you to come in on a regular basis so I can check you out and prescribe some painkillers."

"I'll think about it."

"Toward the end, if you feel the need to be hospitalized, call my office and one of my people will arrange it for you," he said.

"I appreciate the offer, but I'd rather take my chances at home," I replied. "There are only three places in the world where I would want to die and the hospital sure isn't one of them."

Doctor Campbell closed my chart and stared at me with curiosity written all over his ruggedly handsome face. "Oh yeah, and where might these places be?" he inquired.

"When it's my time to go, I want to be either inside a woman's vagina or at the gym."

"That's only two. What's the third place?" Dr. Campbell probed.

"INSIDE A WOMAN'S VAGINA AT THE GYM," I answered with a devilish smile plastered on my face.

Doctor Campbell chuckled a little which gave me an indication that there was a sense of humor lurking somewhere underneath that crisp, white lab coat of his. "Are you still living alone?"

"Yes, I am."

"Then I suggest at some point you hire a nurse to take care of you. If you'll see Linda at the front office on your way out, she can give you some referrals."

I made the handgun finger gesture and pointed it right at him, "Now that Doctor Campbell is an interesting proposition."

"Do you have any more questions before I release you from this visit?"

"Actually, I do have one last question."

Doctor Campbell crossed his arms and braced himself for what was about to come. "Shoot."

"Is there going to be sex in the afterlife?" I ventured to ask.

Again, he shook his head at me. "I have no idea," he replied candidly. "That's for you to find out my friend and report back to me. Now get out of my office. I have other patients who do wish to help themselves that I must attend to."

"Thank you, Doctor Campbell," I said before walking out of his office and heading for the comforts of home.

***

On the way home from Dr. Campbell's office, I decided it's time for me to start living like I am dying again, the same way I used to in my younger glory days. Ever since my third wife divorced me, packed up the kids, and moved to Corsica, France several years ago without real probable cause, I have been slacking off in this department. To deal with the heartbreak and loneliness, not to mention the huge dent it left in my bank account, I have been pushing myself to the limit and sleeping only two to four hours a night. But starting today, this is going to change. The prospect of a premature, agonizing death in my near future isn't going to stop me from getting more tail, taking care of my life coaching clients, and living in the lap of luxury. With that in mind, the first thing I did when I walked through the front door was run up the stairs to change into my swimming trunks. Then I went into the kitchen, cut up some fresh fruit, grabbed a cold bottle of water and high-tailed it to my outdoor hot tub which seemed to be calling my name on this beautiful spring day.

So here I am soaking in my jacuzzi, relaxed as can be, with 80's music blasting in my ears. As much as I hate to admit it, I find myself confronting my biggest fear of all—being alone. Isn't it ironic that the idea of dying doesn't bother me all that much, but spending the rest of my days alone scares the shit out of me? Up until this point in my life, I have never lived alone. But here I am living in a spacious five-thousand-square-foot home with six empty bedrooms in a suburb north of Dallas, Texas, with no friends or family around me. Since I'm relatively a newcomer to the Dallas area, I can't say that I know anyone here except for my real estate agent Todd Morgan who has become a good friend. The truth is I've kept too busy to socialize with others. Hey, there comes a time in every man's life when he has to do whatever it takes to mask the pain. For yours truly, this consists of working, exercising, and having sex or at least thinking about it because quite frankly lately I haven't been able to rise to the occasion. This scenario is far worse than Paris Hilton being spotted at fat camp.

Although I like it here, I do miss traveling all over the world, speaking before thousands of people and keeping up with my executive responsibilities. It sure was a charmed life. Back then the name

Michael Stephen Grant was synonymous with Information Technology (IT). I swear my ego got so inflated that I have no idea how I managed to fit into the many planes I flew in. Even though I had it all, I still wanted more. Young, beautiful women swarmed around me like flies on shit and I didn't have the willpower to resist all the carnal temptation. Being away from home a great deal sure did make it easy for me to play the singles scene. Every time I boarded a plane, the ole' wedding ring came right off and my marital status magically disappeared.

The fun continued for almost two decades. I had girlfriends all over the world, but it still wasn't enough. Lying became second nature to me. Not only did I lie to my first and second wife, but I also deceived all the women I encountered along the way. To quench my never-ending thirst for sex, I pretty much used every pick-up line in the book to weasel my way in between a woman's legs. The goal of course was to get each one to hop into bed with me. The more notches I had on my bed post, the more macho I felt. Some of these unsuspecting women actually became my steady girlfriends. There was always a girl waiting for me in every port I visited, and this is not an exaggeration.

Right about now, you're probably wondering if an unscrupulous skirt chaser like me is capable of falling in love. Well, as difficult as it may be to fathom, this heartbreaker has in fact had his heart broken. So, the answer to this question is a resounding YES! In my life, there has been only one woman special enough to have really gotten under my skin and that is my third wife who I refer to as my "Puerto Rican Goddess." As I mentioned earlier, she left me a few years ago and it really turned my life upside down. Up until then, I had never cried before. The truth is I didn't know how because I've always been more machine than man. But the day my "Puerto Rican Goddess" walked out of my life, this heap of strong metal was reduced to a pile of rusty old bolts.

There are times I still cry like a baby because I miss her and the kids so much. Living alone in this monster of a home only adds salt to the wound. One of the first things I did when I moved in was hang up all of our wedding pictures. I rigged the house so that from an outsider's perspective it looks like she is still at home taking care of our children, but it's just an illusion that I've created for my own delusions of grandeur. No one is home but this stupid asshole. In a way, I guess you could say that I haven't lost hope that she will come back to me someday.

I met my "Puerto Rican Goddess" back in 2000. She was working as a front desk manager at at a four-star hotel in New York City. It was a small boutique style hotel on the upper east side of Manhattan. I used to travel frequently to Manhattan on business, but always stayed at the former Marriott Hotel next to the World Trade Center prior to 9/11. One day a friend of mine suggested that I stay at her hotel because it was physically attached and associated with one of the best gyms in Manhattan—The Equinox. The first time I saw her was during one of my first stays. She checked me in at the front desk and from that moment on I was totally bewitched by her remarkable beauty. That day she seemed to be having a bad hair day. It was long, curly, and messy but that didn't stop me from wanting it splayed all over my naked chest. I was easily fifteen years her senior. When she opened those perfectly shaped and thick sumptuous lips of hers and spoke to me, I knew right then and there that I had to have this woman or die in the attempt.

The next day, I put my seduction plan into motion. After my workout, I went by the front desk to say good morning to her, but only for a minute. She was busy and I didn't want to appear too desperate. Then I went upstairs and got ready for work. Before leaving my room, I called the front desk knowing perfectly well she would be the one to answer the phone. When she did, I asked if ten large empty FedEx boxes could be delivered to my room while I was away at work.

"Did you say you need ten FedEx boxes?' she asked. Her voice sounded so angelic and it really brought out the devil in me.

"Yes, please. I need to ship out some books," I explained.

"Okay, I will make sure they are delivered to your room this afternoon," she promised.

Of course, I didn't really need ten boxes, but I wanted to make an impression and stand out from the rest of the businessmen who were probably trying to hit on her all the time. Yeah, she was that hot. The next morning, after my workout, I decided to go the extra mile and I purchased a protein drink and took it to her at the front desk to say thank you for the boxes. She absolutely loved the drink, so I continued to buy her one daily for the next several weeks.

For the first time in my life, I felt intimidated by a woman's personality and beauty. I have no idea how she was able to pull it off so quickly but Maribel turned this master seducer of women into a shy schoolboy. Just about every morning I would stand and hide behind the wall of the front lobby and take a peek at her while she was working. She on the other hand knew exactly what I was doing. As it turned out, Maribel thought it was awfully cute and she never called me out on it. Finally, I got the nerve to ask her out for dinner. Lucky for me she said yes.

My first date with Maribel turned out to be the most memorable night of my life. It was a cold wintery evening in Manhattan—in the thirties. We decided to meet up on the west side for coffee and cheesecake instead of having a full-blown dinner. Afterward we just talked and walked for the next four hours from the west side of Manhattan to the east side. In total, I'd say it was probably fifty blocks—but who was counting? We held hands and talked the whole time. Occasionally, I would put my arm around Maribel to try to keep her warm. For a guy who was used to fucking a woman on the first date, this was totally uncharacteristic of me.

That night I learned that my dream girl had some major issues to deal with. It turned out that she was a single mom with two children fathered by deadbeat dads. She was single-handedly parenting and supporting her son and daughter. Maribel went on to tell me she was in way over her head in credit card and student loan debt. At this juncture, most men would have jumped off this sinking ship. After all, why would any single man getting all the pussy he could handle want to deal with this kind of excess and undesirable baggage?

At the time, I was in between wives and single again, driving a brand-new black on black Mercedes SL500, seeing multiple beautiful young women—pretty much had it all. In retrospect I was living the kind of life a gigolo would envy or so I thought. Normally, I would have bolted right out of there in a New York minute, but this "Puerto Rican Goddess" was too spell-binding and irresistible for me to be able to make a clean getaway. Somehow, she had rendered me breathless and incapable of leaving her side so my size thirteen shoes stayed cemented right next to hers. Every fiber of my being wanted to take care of Maribel and the children, not out of pity, but because I had fallen head over heels in love with her. Although it was just my first date with Maribel, I stopped seeing other women immediately. My heart was taken that quickly.

While eating dinner during one of our first dates, I reached out for both of her soft, delicate hands and raised them up to my lips.

After kissing them gently, I gazed deeply into her eyes and asked, "Maribel, what are some places that you've always wanted to visit but have never had the opportunity to do so?"

After giving it some thought, Maribel gifted me with one of the most radiant smiles I've ever seen and replied, "I've always wanted to go to Las Vegas and Hawaii."

"How would you like to drive to Las Vegas with me?" I asked her.

At first Maribel was at a loss for words. But after a few seconds, she was able to articulate what was on her mind. "How? When?"

With the confidence of a Roman gladiator, I spelled it out for her. "I'll arrange for you to fly to Los Angeles. You can spend the night with me at my home and from there we'll drive to Las Vegas."

Maribel agreed to fly to Los Angeles. I arranged everything and I picked her up from the Burbank Airport in Southern California and brought her to my home. I put her luggage in the guest bedroom and left it there. "This is going to be your room for the night. We'll leave for Vegas early in the morning," I told her.

That evening we went to dinner, saw a movie, and walked around the mall afterwards. I decided to buy her these really nice pair of designer sun glasses because I thought they would look really cool on her and they did. It was a great evening. When we got back to my place, we decided to call it a night. Instead of trying to hit a homerun with her, I gave Maribel a big manly hug, kissed her, and said good night. I went to my master bedroom and she retreated to the guest bedroom. It took every ounce of willpower I had not to make any sexual advances toward her that night. It was one of the hardest things I've ever had to do. She was so fucking desirable. I wanted her so badly it hurt.

In the morning, I woke Maribel up by presenting her with a home-cooked breakfast. We were on the road by 5:00 AM to make sure we would avoid all that horrible Los Angeles traffic. As soon as we hit the road it was nonstop talking and believe it or not, I held her hand pretty much the entire drive to Vegas. I wouldn't let go of it. She loved it, but so did I. Okay, so the cat's out of the bag. Let the record show that Michael Stephen Grant is a romantic at heart.

Unbeknownst to Maribel, I had made reservations at the beautiful Venetian hotel. She had no idea how truly magnificent it was. I reserved one room with a king-size bed hoping that she would not protest. She didn't say a word. When we stepped inside the hotel room with our luggage in tow, she was completely taken aback by how beautifully decorated it was.

"Let's get cleaned up and go have some dinner," I suggested. "I'm starving."

"Okay, let me take a quick shower and get dressed," said Maribel.

Let me tell you that the wait was certainly worth it. Maribel was a vision of loveliness dressed in an elegant form-fitting red dress which came about two inches above her knees. Since I already knew that she had a taste for Italian cuisine, I took the liberty of making a reservation at a fine Italian restaurant located inside the hotel. It turned out to be one of the most romantic restaurants I had ever had the pleasure of dining at. Our entire dining experience must have lasted three hours but the time just flew by. The whole time I couldn't take my eyes off of Maribel—not even for a moment. I couldn't believe I was falling majorly in love with this woman. Suddenly, the carefree, sex-filled lifestyle I had been living no longer seemed appealing to me at all.

After dinner we took a leisurely stroll to see more of the hotel. We got back to our room around three o'clock in the morning and

I offered to give her a back massage. Her beautiful eyes lit up. "Do you mind?" she asked.

"Of course not! I love giving massages. I've been told that I have strong hands for it," I boasted. "Why don't you change into your pajamas and come lie down," I suggested.

Maribel complied and before I knew it my hands were roaming all over her sexy body. I could tell by her body posture that she was enjoying the massage immensely. What can I say? I happen to have a sensual touch that gives women great pleasure. Maribel fell asleep while I was massaging her which didn't bother me in the least. Even though we were in the same bed together, I still did not try to make an advance. For some crazy reason, I was perfectly content just having her warm body snuggled next to mine which was a first for me. That just goes to show how truly mesmerized I was by this incredible woman.

We got up late the next morning and headed back to L.A. On the drive back, I immediately reached out for Maribel's hand and held onto it for dear life. Before entering L.A. city limits, I pulled off the highway and parked on the shoulder. There was something I had to tell her that just couldn't wait. "I want to take you to Hawaii next," I blurted out, staring at her like a lovesick puppy.

She looked at me and smiled, "You're serious, aren't you?"

"You know I am," I said to her with conviction.

Two weeks later it was *déjavu* all over again. I picked her up from Burbank Airport but this time I had a different game plan in mind. Like before, I put her stuff in the guest bedroom and then we went to dinner. When we got back to the house, Maribel and I decided we wanted to unwind so we snuggled on the couch and began to watch TV. I started rubbing her shoulders and the next thing I know we were kissing passionately. In a matter of a few seconds, we went totally out-of-control.

Maribel was wearing tight-fitted jeans that really accentuated her great ass and a short-sleeved blouse. My hands went ballistic all over her entire body. There wasn't a square inch of her figure that I didn't explore. Feeling that old familiar spark inside of my pants, I got up and grabbed her by the hand. Our lips were gridlocked as we made our way up the stairs—not even a crowbar could pry us apart. It must have taken us a good twenty minutes to climb ten steps. When we finally made it into the bedroom, I unbuttoned her blouse and removed her bra. Then with tender loving care, I maneuvered her onto the bed and immediately got on top of her. Before proceeding full speed ahead, I stopped for a moment to reflect on just how much this woman meant to me. Right then and there, I decided that I wanted this to be the most memorable night of her life.

I unbuckled her jeans and slowly slipped them off. To avoid having an unfortunate accident prematurely, I left my pants on. The truth is I was so excited and horny beyond belief that I could have easily exploded at any moment. My tongue was desperate to taste the most intimate part of her. It needed to know if her juices were bitter or sweet. Before taking that plunge, I took her perfectly manicured feet in my hands and rubbed them gently. Then one by one, I sucked her toes ever so slowly and sensually.

After nibbling all of her toes with my lips, I found my way back up to her luscious mouth and kissed her amorously for at least five minutes. When we finally came up for air, I started heading down south but made a pit stop long enough to shower her perfectly shaped breasts with tantalizing butterfly kisses. In seeing that her large brown nipples were aroused, I moved on to her belly and began leaving a trail of kisses all over it. I could feel her body move in slow rhythmic waves as my lips edged closer and closer to her white cotton mini-briefs which really pushed me over the edge.

At last the moment of truth had arrived. Just to tease Maribel, I began kissing her pussy while her panties were still on. They were already moist to the touch. Her breathing started to feel and sound labored and pretty soon cute moaning sounds were coming out of her mouth. My right hand cupped her butt as I started to pull of her panties with the other. Once they were completely off of her, I then started to kiss around her naked pussy and went right for the clit. My eyes opened wide after having savored that unforgettable sweet and clean taste.

"Your pussy smells so great and it tastes delicious," I managed to say to her.

I wasn't kidding. It was by far one of the best smelling pussies I had ever tasted in my life. After sucking on her clit for a few minutes, Maribel had her first orgasm of the night. She didn't know it yet, but I wasn't coming back up for air anytime soon except for taking a brief intermission to kiss her fervently on the lips after each orgasm. After each kiss, I immediately went back down on her again. It didn't take me long to figure out that this was going to be my new high-water mark for pussy-sucking orgasms in one encounter. My previous best was four. I had the perfect woman and perfect pussy; nothing was going to stop me from breaking my own record.

As I continued sucking on her clit, my right-hand fingers penetrated her pussy occasionally. To heighten Maribel's pleasure even more, I used my left-hand fingers to hover over her butt hole ever so gently and occasionally press inward. I was careful not to go in too deeply though. I was in Seventh Heaven and I didn't want to scare her. I didn't want to take that chance and end up killing the mood— not with her anyway. Based on all my past sexual experience, I knew that some women were a bit weird about having anal sex. Some were scared to death of it and tried to avoid it as if it were the Ebola Virus. My *modus operandi* worked because Maribel had her second orgasm.

Maribel continuously tried to pull me up. "I want you inside of me," she kept telling me.

"In due time," I said to her. "Please trust me, I know what I'm doing down there." This went on back and forth for quite some time. She continued trying to pull me up by any means necessary. Maribel tugged me by the ears and hair but I wouldn't budge. She even pressed her thighs tightly against my head and tried lifting me up with her muscular legs. Let me tell you something, Maribel had strong and shapely legs. All her efforts were in vain because I had every intention of beating my personal best.

After orgasm number three came and went, I knew Maribel wasn't going to be able to take much more. I, on the other hand, was willing to push the envelope. This time not even a forklift could force me to come back up and she knew it perfectly well. In the throes of heated passion, I began sweating profusely but I had to keep on going. In a way it was a risky move on my part because I didn't want her to think that this scenario would be the norm everytime we made love.

Right after Maribel had her fourth orgasm I stopped and took a short breather. Just to buy me some more time, I actually teased her a bit by penetrating her vagina with my penis but pulled it back out after a few strokes. Then I went back down on her to work on making the next orgasm happen which eventually came to pass. I turned her over and started kissing the backside of her legs and around her butt hole but my mouth never made contact with it—that would come later. I flipped her back over and went right back for the clit.

Once the sixth orgasm was in the bag, I went back up and placed her in my arms. I was a bit winded so I took a much-needed ten-minute break. For a few minutes, I just laid there holding and caressing Maribel while my hands roamed up and down her body. After a while I felt a strong urge to kiss her lips and neck passionately so I did. In that instant I made up my mind quickly. I wanted to make her cum for the seventh time badly. For some reason that number stood out in my head, I thought it would be easy to remember later in life. This orgasm took a long time to achieve—for me it felt like an eternity. By my count, it must have taken a good thirty minutes but in the end a new record was born. Adding to this crowning moment was the satisfaction of knowing that I, Michael Stephen Grant, had made love to the woman I cherished like a true champion.

The entire rendezvous between her clit and my tongue took more than two and a half hours. I was totally wasted and so was she. After all that intense lovemaking, I was drenched with her sweet bodily fluids. It was all over my hair, face and even chest which made me a really happy camper. My sheets were all wet from a combination of sweat, her juices and my semen. But it was far from being over. "Look into my eyes," I said to her.

Maribel complied right away.

I, in turn, gazed deeply into her lovely eyes and then confessed, "I love you PR." Those initials were short for Puerto Rican. Then I turned Maribel over to her side and slithered my penis inside from the rear. She let out a soft cry and within seconds I was ready to explode inside of her. Surprising, somehow, I was able to hold it together until she had one more final splurge of pleasure. That was a night I will never forget and as for Maribel well let's just say that my name was engraved permanently on her pussy. I pretty much owned it. From that day forward I nicknamed her Lucky Seven. Although technically she had experienced eight orgasms in total, for me, the ones that truly counted were the ones provoked by my skillful tongue. Besides, Lucky Seven had a much better ring to it than Crazy Eight.

The next morning, we were on our way to Hawaii. It was like being on our honeymoon—only much better. I was determined to leave an indelible mark on this woman's heart as a lover and I did. But I wasn't done yet. Now I wanted her to see the softer side of MSG. I wanted to show her how much I truly loved her.

We stayed in a suite which had a breathtaking ocean view of Waikiki. There was a stretch of pristine blue ocean water for miles and miles. The other side offered an unspoiled view of Diamond Head. Once we got settled into our suite, Maribel and I decided to take a shower before going out for a meal. Instead of individual showers, we opted to take one together. We kissed and kissed like two teenagers in heat. I even went down on her in the shower with a heavy stream of water going up my nostrils. I kissed her lips, breasts and eventually made my way down to my favorite spot. I simply couldn't resist the urge to taste her sweet-smelling pussy again and I did just that. Maribel had an orgasm just like I knew she would. After she stopped shuddering from the pleasure, I turned her around so that she faced the shower wall and I placed her hands on it as I inserted my excited dick inside her from the back. I placed my hands-on top of hers and passionately had intercourse. After we both climaxed, Maribel and I stepped out of the shower, got dressed and headed for the beach.

We stayed on the beach for about forty-five minutes. Neither of us wanted to get too much sun exposure on the first day. We returned to our suite and changed into shorts before heading into town. During the excursion we ended up at this outdoor mall and happened to walk by a jewelry store. Upon seeing a beautiful white gold necklace with multiple strands and a few dozen sparkling diamonds scattered throughout being prominently displayed, I stopped dead in my tracks. It was absolutely stunning.

"Wow! Look at that," I said to Maribel. "Now that would look awesome around your neck."

"No! Please that's way too much. I know you MSG," she pleaded with me.

"C'mon. Let's just go inside and try it on you. There's no harm in that," I suggested, pulling her by the hand. As it turned out the necklace had a hefty price tag. I don't remember the exact amount but it was somewhere close to 5K. I didn't give a shit. I had to get it for her. It wasn't like I was trying to buy Maribel's love. At that point, I knew that I had already engraved my name in her heart. Buying Maribel the necklace was just as much a gift for me as it was for her. It made me happy seeing the necklace on her. The minute we stepped out of the jewelry store, I embraced her close to me and said, "I love you Maribel."

She was completely blown away by the gesture. "I love you too," she said with tears in her eyes.

After four months of dating, I surprised myself and everyone who knew me by doing the unthinkable, I asked Maribel to marry me and she accepted. Perhaps all those years of non-stop sex with multiple partners had finally taken a toll on me. For the first time ever, I was perfectly content having only one woman in my heart and bed. I couldn't believe it but this adventurous lady-killer was finally putting in for retirement. Once Maribel became my wife, I took her all over the world with me: Hong Kong, Australia, Singapore, Amsterdam, and many other great places. We had so many unforgettable memories together.

One of the most beautiful evenings we spent together as husband and wife was in Hong Kong. On this occasion, we booked a suite overlooking the infamous Hong Kong Harbor. The view was absolutely spectacular and so was Maribel. After having a late lunch, Maribel and I headed back to the room to take a nap. Not long after we had gotten comfortable on the bed, we started making out passionately. We got so lost in the moment that we never bothered to get under the covers.

After a while, I gently grabbed her hand and instructed her to follow me. I guided her into the living room and leaned her up against the huge window overlooking the harbor. We were still kissing with our clothes on. I snuck my hands under her dress and slipped off her panties. Then I knelt down and went straight for her clit to make sure she had an orgasm in Hong Kong. Once my mission had been accomplished, I brought Maribel down to her knees—she still had her skirt on. I positioned her hands on the glass and gave her a deep, intimate kiss.

"Look at that view. Isn't it breathtaking," I asked?

"Yes, it is baby," she replied.

For the grand finale, I moved behind Maribel and lifted her skirt again. I penetrated her with a sense of urgency and proceeded to make love to her as we both stared blissfully into the beautiful harbor.

Once the honeymoon phase was over, I made the monumental mistake of reverting back to my workaholic ways and put my "Puerto Rican Goddess" and step-children on the back burner. To make a long story short—fifteen years later, Maribel ended up leaving me, and it was such a rude awakening. She accused me of seeing someone else and given my proven track record of infidelity, there was no way I could convince her otherwise. While I wasn't guilty of cheating on her with another woman, I did neglect her and the kids bigtime. Now five years after our divorce Maribel is still *numero uno* in my heart.

Chapter Three

The Deflowering of an Indonesian Flower

It's six o'clock in the morning on what looks like is going to be a beautiful Monday and I just got back from doing my daily work-out feeling like I could kick Spartacus's ass—without a sword. I like to hit the gym in the wee hours of the morning while the world is still sleeping. Believe me, it's the only way to avoid all the annoying drama that goes on at any given workout facility in America. Sometimes I get approached by fellow gym goers, male and female, who want me to train and work out with them. So, a couple of days a week, I grace the gym with my presence later than usual for the purpose of helping those poor souls who have no fucking clue what they're doing on all of the state-of-the-art exercise equipment. I know, I know, I'm such a great humanitarian.

The truth is I've been a workout and health freak since the age of thirteen. Unlike other people who constantly need someone to pat their behind and cheer them on, I am totally self-driven when it comes to taking care of my body. At the risk of sounding like an egotistical jerk, I must say that I'm doing a fantastic job because I look like a modern-day gladiator. Honestly, just the other day, before leaving the gym, a cute blonde with perky breasts stopped me and said, "Excuse me Mister, but I have to tell you that your body is to die for."

I couldn't help but laugh before saying to her, "No sweetheart, you're totally wrong. I have a body to live for." She flashed a seductive smile and then gave me a piece of paper with her phone number on it.

Another time I happened to be working out by a group of younger guys who all seemed to be in their late twenties. One of them walked up to me and waited to be acknowledged. "Hey man, can I ask how old you are?" he inquired.

"Sure, I just turned sixty years old," I replied candidly. "Why do you want to know?"

The young guy turned back and pointed at his group of buddies. "We were all just wondering because boy do you look great for an old-timer," he said. "I hope I look as good as you when I'm your age."

I immediately put my weights down and grabbed a nearby towel to wipe the sweat off my forehead. Then, I started chuckling and nodding my head at the same time. "What are you talking about son? You don't look half as good as me NOW. Get your bony ass back to your friends and keep working on those spaghetti arms."

The poor lad didn't know what hit him. He slowly walked back to where he came from with his head tucked between his legs. Hey, there's one thing everyone should know about me and that is I'm always brutally honest. Don't think for a minute that being a celebrity at your local gym is easy because it's not. Everyone who goes there wants a piece of you. The men all want advice and the women just want to screw your brains out. That's why I like to keep a low profile and avoid going in during peak hours.

When it comes to my overall health regiment, the three most important words in my vocabulary are discipline, consistency and management. These are the three key areas I focus on religiously. For more than four decades, I have pushed my body to the ultimate level in every conceivable way possible. My work outs are gruesome and not for the weak. This is why I prefer working out alone most of the time. My daily workout routine consists of weight training and cardiovascular exercise which is great conditioning for having mind blowing sex with women half my age every time the opportunity arises.

Regardless of how I'm feeling that day, I always try to outperform my previous best workout. It's so much fun to manage by the numbers. I always try to beat those numbers whether it's one more repetition, five more pounds pumped, ten more calories burned. Am I always successful? Hell no! But that doesn't mean I stop trying. As I sit here in my home office and spit in death's face, I'm proud to say that my body looks great in the here and now. It certainly wouldn't surprise me a bit to hear later in the afterlife what women who came to pay their last respects at my funeral said about me. I can just hear them now as they're secreting juices in their black panties. "Damn! He looks so hot lying there in his coffin. If only there was a way to raise his penis back from the dead."

Now that my day is off to a great start, the next thing on my To-Do-List is to write an ad for a live-in nurse to post on Craigslist. The beginning of summer is just a few weeks away, which means it's been more than two months since Dr. Campbell practically handed me my death certificate. You would think by now that I would be feeling like total shit, but surprisingly I'm not. Actually, I feel pretty good. Sure, I get headaches once in a while and have trouble sleeping which is nothing earth-shattering. Just the other day, Dr. Campbell called to ask how I was feeling.

"I hate to disappoint you doc, but I feel like a million bucks," I bragged over the phone.

"Well, I'm certainly glad to hear that," he said. "But don't be fooled by this false sense of security MSG. Make no mistake, this organ-eating bitch is very much alive inside you and she isn't going to stop feeding until she has her fill. I really wish you would revoke your No Treatment Policy."

For a few fleeting moments, I actually thought about accepting Dr. Campbell's advice but my pig-headedness won out in the end and so I lied. "I'll give it some thought, I promise." Feeling a bit guilty about lying to him, I decided to throw Dr. Campbell a bone. "Hey doc, on a positive note, I decided to take your advice and hire me a live-in-nurse. I'm beginning my search today."

"That's certainly a step in the right direction," Dr. Campbell said. "Call Linda at my office and she will give you some names of qualified and competent nurses that we highly recommend."

"Thanks, but that won't be necessary, I've got that covered."

"One more thing before I let you go," Dr. Campbell said. "Are you experiencing any depression?"

His question kind of rattled my cage a little. "Uh, uh, not really," I lied again.

"If you do, please call me and I'll write you up a prescription for a strong anti-depressant." That was the last thing Dr. Campbell said to me before ending our conversation.

I hate to admit it but Dr. Campbell kind of hit the nail on the head by asking if I've been experiencing depression. Lately, I have been feeling a bit indifferent about having female companionship and that is practically the same as hell freezing over. Even though during these past few months a few attractive women have made passes at me and in an indirect way hinted they are willing to present me with their pussy on a silver platter, I haven't gone for that dangling carrot. At this point I'm guessing that my lack of interest in having sex is due to my dangling carrot. Even though I'm feeling lonely, especially at night, I am solely focusing on my work and exercise routine.

If I had to pinpoint when these gloom and doom feelings first started to well up inside me, then I'd have to say it was a couple of weeks ago when I confessed to Maribel over the phone that I have stage four lung cancer. Much to my surprise, she was devastated by the news which in turn rekindled my hope that I still had a chance with her. The conversation between us became overly sentimental quickly and we both ended up crying like babies. Maribel told me that she still loved me and I saw this as an open invitation back into her life.

"Oh, Maribel, you're the love of my life. I will love you til' the day I die," I professed in between my sobbing. "There will never be another woman who can take your place."

"That's very sweet of you to say," she replied.

"How fast can you pack up and come home?" I asked her.

After several seconds of awkward silence, I knew I was in deep shit but pressed on anyway. "Maribel, are you still there?"

"Yes, I'm still here," she finally said. "MSG, I'll make arrangements to go visit you for a couple of weeks."

"Did you say a couple of weeks?"

"That's about as long as I can get off from work."

I could hardly believe my ears. The woman had just declared her love for me and now this load of crap. "You mean you're not leaving Corsica and coming home?"

Once again, she delayed her response. Her prolonged silence was a dead giveaway. Maribel had no intention of coming home for good and it pissed me off big-time. In retrospect I wasn't angry at Maribel. I was mad at myself for letting this woman use her wrecking ball to crush my heart for the second time. Maribel's flat-out refusal to return to me permanently really hurt so I went ballistic on her.

"If you're not going to stay for good, then don't come at all. Just stay there in fuckin' CorsiFUCKA," I yelled into the phone right before hanging up.

After that dramatic episode I decided to treat myself to a live-in nurse. But she's got to be young, sexy, and have a wild streak in her, the kind you would see on a *Nurses Gone Wild* video who is willing to take my temperature the old-fashioned way—with her tongue. Hey, I think I already feel a fever coming on. I'm even prepared to import her from Indonesia if I have to. I want to enjoy my last days to the fullest so the last thing I need is some fat middle-aged woman named Helga or Mildred coming to my bedside in hideous looking orthopedic shoes to pump me up full of meds. That's not my idea of getting PUMPED UP. The question is: Where am I going to find my dream nurse? There is only one place that comes to mind and that's Craigslist but first I have to write an attention-grabbing Nurse Wanted Ad. In my lifetime, I've written over forty books, so this should be a walk in the park for me.

***

Well, it took me about an hour to come up with an ad, but I'm happy with my deliverable:

Seeking Live-In Nurse Built Like a Brick House with Naughty Bedside Manners

Destined-to-die handsome, mature man with a great physique, the sexual stamina of a raging bull, and money to burn seeks live-in nurse to pamper him for the rest of his days. Must be between the ages of 21-35, brunette with shoulder length or longer hair and weight must be proportionate to height. All female parts must be natural, no artificial tits or butts please. A nursing degree would be nice but not required, so long as you possess a basic knowledge of tender loving care and are an incurable nymphomaniac. You should be a decent cook in the kitchen and an explosive chef in the bedroom. Must have a sexy sounding voice and an extensive collection of sexy lingerie. If you don't already have such a wardrobe, one shall be provided for you if you're the ideal candidate. You absolutely positively must have a valid Passport and the ability to drive a car on the street and ride patients in bed. I'm offering an attractive salary, free room and board, 24-hour access to state-of-the-art jacuzzi, swimming pool, and theatre room, plus all the mind-blowing sex you can handle. If interested please contact me at msg1954@hotmail.com.

Isn't this a masterpiece of an ad? Now all I have to do is post this baby on Craigslist and it will only be a matter of time before I start getting bombarded with responses. That's right, come to papa! To avoid getting red-flagged the second this ad goes viral, I'm going to post this in the Men Seeking Women section because if I was to actually place it in the Jobs section, my ad would never see the light of publication. If you think that I was only kidding when I said that I'm willing to import my live-in nurse from Indonesia then you don't know MSG at all. I happen to be a real softy when it comes to this beautiful country and its delectable, bite-size women.

One of the most challenging women I ever met was from Indonesia. What I mean by this is that I had to practically move heaven and earth to gain access into the Promise Land between her legs. In retrospect she was probably the most beautiful girl I've ever seen in my entire life and since I have seen legions of women, well that in itself is a monumental statement. On my degree of difficulty scale with a 10.00 being the highest, she registered a 9.0, which didn't happen very often.

Not long after I got separated from my first wife, I found myself facilitating a presentation for one of my new books at the Hilton Hotel in the capital city of Jakarta. After my talk, I went outside of the ballroom into the hallway for a breather and there she was manning some kind of promotional booth. I thought I had died and gone to heaven. She was a total vision of loveliness in a long, white dress fit for a goddess. This woman was gorgeous—stunning—with an hour-glass figure and long, shiny jet-black hair. By my estimates, she was about 5'4" tall and weighed approximately 120 pounds. She was the perfect new toy for MSG and I couldn't wait to play with her.

From the first moment I saw this girl, I was completely mesmerized by her large brown eyes, tiny nose, and beautifully structured chin, a rather uncommon physical trait for an Indonesian. It was a given that wherever this woman walked, heads turned. I asked my personal guide if he knew anything about her. He told me her name was Hanny and she came from a devoted Muslim family. He also stressed the fact that she was a virgin who was engaged to be married to an extremely rich oil tycoon in Jakarta. Apparently, Hanny's incomparable beauty made her a celebrity amongst her own people. It took but an instant for me to decide that this precious rare Indonesian gem had to belong to me, and I was willing to do whatever it took to add her to my extensive collection of pretty things.

Landing this beauty was going to take a major sting operation. It wasn't going to be easy—how badly did I want her was the question *de jour*. How was an Israeli Jew supposed to capture the heart and virginity of a heavily guarded Muslim girl? There I was in my early forties and technically still married and she only nineteen years old, caught right smack in the middle of being an impressionable young girl and a fully developed woman. After analyzing the situation, I quickly realized this was going to be my greatest challenge yet and so I started to formulate a plan of attack in my head. These were the milestones I came up with:

1. ***Introduce myself and ask for her name:*** The first order of business was to put MSG on her radar by introducing myself. Although I already knew it, I approached this Indonesian flower, introduced myself, and asked for her name. Once the ice had been broken, I moved on to the next step.

2. ***Have at least two mini-conversations with her throughout the day:*** Although, I was flying out the next morning it was important for me to make it clear to her that I had every intention of coming back to Indonesia multiple times for business purposes. Throughout the day, I made it a point to engage in mini-conversations with her. In between being introduced to executives and dignitaries, my mind was hard at work trying to think of interesting topics to discuss with her.

I asked her to recommend restaurants that served authentic Indonesian cuisine, and places of interest I should visit the next time I blew into town. Hanny was very shy, which only added to her charm.

3. ***Ask for permission to write:*** By the end of the day, I had succeeded in establishing a good rapport with her. Feeling pretty confident, I went out on a limb and asked if I could write to her. I didn't want to be too forward and ask for her phone number—not just yet anyway. Besides, I knew that every Tom, Dick, and Harry within a one-hundred-mile radius was trying to get her phone number and I wanted to stand out from the pack of hungry wolves. I wrote her a letter every day from wherever I was in the world. If I happened to miss one day, I made up for it the next by writing her multiple letters. One time I even wrote and sent her a total of ten letters in one day just to shock her and her ultra-religious Muslim father. Like I said before, I was willing to do anything to deflower this Indonesian flower.

4. ***Begin using the 'L' word:*** After a few months of continuous letter writing, I started to use the 'L' word with her like it was going out of style. I also told her over and over again that I thought about her all the time which was far from being the truth. Actually, it was a downright lie. The whole time I courted Hanny, I continued to fuck all of my other girlfriends in different ports. To keep her from getting suspicious, at least once a month I sent her flowers and fancy lipsticks and perfume from different countries around the world. By this time, I already had her number and so I called Hanny three times a week from wherever I happened to be. This was all part of keeping up with appearances. I had to prove my

unconditional love and devotion to her even if it was all one big farce and I did with flying colors.

5. ***Ask to meet her for lunch:*** It pretty much cost me a small fortune just to meet up with her to have lunch. I had to fly from Los Angeles to Singapore or Hong Kong and from there catch a connecting flight to Jakarta which turned out to be a grueling twenty-hour endeavor. Although I had no further business in Jakarta, I would fly there just to meet Hanny for a few hours at a restaurant. That's how much I was obsessed with her. I would sit hours and hours in my hotel room just in case she called to make sure I wasn't out playing the field. Even though it was a big sacrifice on my part, it's a good thing that I did because she actually called to check on me several times.

6. ***On my third trip to Jakarta spend serious alone time with her:*** After having played my cards right for about a year and a half, I finally decided the time had come to move in for the kill. I went ahead and made arrangements to visit Jakarta for the third time. When Hanny agreed to spend an entire day with me, I really had no expectations. My goal was to hang out with her for the afternoon in my hotel room and see where that would take us. By this time in our so-called relationship, I knew that her heart was engulfed by me and this is how things played out from this point on.

It was super-hot and humid in Jakarta on the day that Hanny and I were supposed to spend together. I planned to stay in town for a few days with the hope of getting some serious alone time with my young Indonesian Goddess. There were so many naughty things I wanted to do to her. All along since I had first decided to make the long haul there, I couldn't wait to see that beautiful face of hers. I guess you could say that I was infatuated with her beauty and innocence. Was I in love with her? That's really difficult to say. By then, I had told her that I loved her numerous times. But it was all part of my mode of operation. I told a lot of women the exact same thing. Hanny was drop-dead gorgeous, intelligent, and had a caring demeanor as well. What man in his right mind wouldn't be in love with her? Wherever we went together, heads turned.

After we had lunch that day, I asked her to come back to the hotel with me to relax, cool off, and watch a movie. I had a large suite with a king-size bed, executive desk, and two large lounge chairs. When Hanny came into my room, I gave her one of my signature manly hugs and she immediately sat in one of the large chairs while I lied down on the bed with my head propped up against the headboard. Although she started chatting in an animated way about this and that, I could tell she was tired.

"Hanny, do your parents know you're here with me now?" I asked her.

"No, I'm meeting with you in secret," she replied softly.

"If your father finds out, he'll probably have both of us hunted down," I said in a half-joking way.

At that point, I flashed her one of my killer, debonair smiles. "Come lie down on the bed next to me and close your eyes for a little while. After you take a short nap, we can watch a movie."

Hanny got up and proceeded toward the bed. I took her willingness to join me as being a sign that all systems were go. Perhaps this was going to be the day she would give me what so many others had tried to get from her and failed miserably. I got up, grabbed her hand gently, and lured her toward the bed. I sat Hanny down, took off her shoes, and then gently scooted her back so she could recline her head against the pillows.

After making sure she was comfortable, I lied down next to her. Just to make things more interesting, I put my arm around Hanny ever so slowly and rested her head on my shoulder. At first, I just held her closely. A part of me wanted to savor every moment with her. A few minutes later, I started rubbing Hanny's left arm to warm her up in more ways than one. The air conditioning unit in the room was on full blast and she complained that it was getting chilly.

Being so dangerously close to uncharted territory was starting to make me horny. "I'm going to give you a small kiss there before you fall asleep," I said pointing at her forehead.

Hanny looked at me with those gorgeous, big brown eyes of hers. I swept in and planted a sensual kiss on her forehead just like I told her I would. Her eyes grew even wider which was all the encouragement I needed to give her another stirring kiss. After that, we gazed deeply into each other's eyes. There was no denying that we had reached the point of no return. I extended my hand and touched the bottom of her chin. Then I slowly guided her lips toward mine until a connection was finally made. The next thing I knew we started to kiss with wild abandon.

That day Hanny was wearing a blue skirt that hung a few inches above her knees. She always dressed conservatively which left a lot to the imagination. She wasn't wearing any pantyhose as her skin had a natural caramel colored sheen to it that drove me bonkers. I remember she also had a silky white blouse on with buttons in the front. To complete the ensemble, she had on a pair of black high-heeled shoes which made her legs look so fabulous that I could have easily sucked on them non-stop for hours and hours.

As we continued to kiss passionately, I started raking my right arm gradually down the left side of her body. When I finally reached down to the bottom hem of her skirt, I deliberately made a U-turn and started creeping up north. With my hand still underneath her skirt, I caressed Hanny's soft nineteen-year-old skin with the intention of getting her all worked up. As I inched my way closer and closer to the Promise Land, which no man had ever boldly entered before, she parted her legs ever so slightly giving me full access to her virgin pussy. It had taken me more than one year, hundreds of hand-written letters and phone calls, expensive gifts, flowers, not to mention several trips to Indonesia to win this beauty's heart. There was no way in hell that I was going to rush this moment in Shangri-La. I fully intended to savor this pivotal moment as long as possible and this meant lots and lots of foreplay.

When I reached her wet pussy, I gently rubbed my fingers all around it. Although it was beckoning me, I didn't want to go for the clit just yet. Knowing this was going to be Hanny's first time, I wanted the experience to be a truly memorable one for her. After I teased her blossoming rosebud, I retreated and focused on her breasts. I massaged them for a few seconds from the outside of her blouse. Her nipples quickly became erect and I started to unbutton her blouse. In one quick fluid move, I skillfully removed her blouse and began nibbling the top of her breasts. Within a matter of seconds, I removed her bra and started sucking on her sexy bronze colored nipples. Hanny had nice sized breasts, not too big and not too small. I went from one to the other like a real pro.

By this time, I had a bulging and throbbing hard-on that desperately needed to come out of the black spandex tights I was wearing. My rock-hard cock was suffocating and, it needed to be liberated immediately. I pulled off my tights but still left her skirt on. I wasn't done teasing her. I turned Hanny over to her side so that I could feast my eyes on that great ass of hers. She had a pair of expensive silk white panties on. As long as I live, I'll never forget the erotic image of Hanny's skirt half-way hiked up her butt and that picturesque posterior view featuring those silky, white panties of hers.

Just for kicks, I left them on for a while longer because it felt so gratifying stroking her butt cheeks against the light airy fabric. Finally, I couldn't take the heat any longer so I pulled them off with a sense of urgency I had never felt before. Her pussy was already dripping wet and ready for my cock to pay a friendly visit. It was nicely trimmed with black pubic hairs. I took my sweet time brushing my finger gingerly over her excited clit. I could tell by Hanny's body posture that she couldn't wait for me to put it in.

"I want you so badly," she kept telling me in between her deep breathing.

"If I put it in now it's going to be over in a matter of seconds. I've been waiting for this moment for over a year. There's no way I can hold it," I warned her.

"I don't care. I just want you inside of me. Now! Please, put it in."

"Let me go down there and kiss you for a while longer so I can make you feel amazing," I pleaded.

Hanny shook her head vigorously. "No. Please just put it in. I'm begging you."

Taking into consideration that she was a virgin and already nervous, I decided to comply with her request. I slowly raised myself above her in the traditional missionary style and slithered my penis inside of her tight cunt. The friction I felt making my descent into the very core of her was out of this world. When I entered all the way I had an orgasm immediately, within seconds.

"What happened?" Hanny asked.

"I told you I wasn't going to be able to hold back," I replied. "Give me twenty minutes and it will be fine."

"I don't understand," she tossed back with a puzzled look on her face.

You could tell sex was foreign to her. I pulled out and snuggled next to her. She fell asleep as I held her closely in my arms. I dozed off for about fifteen minutes which is all it took for my batteries to get recharged. I went ahead and let her sleep for about an hour before starting to fondle her butt again. It didn't take long for me to get hard again but I continued to let her rest. Maybe I was in love with her. Perhaps I was in denial. I couldn't really be sure. When Hanny woke up, she looked at me with an undeniable flicker of desire in those big brown eyes of hers which made my dick stand at attention and salute. I maneuvered my way behind her and glided it in. I thrusted back and forth for the next fifteen minutes while kissing the back of her neck. One way or another, MSG was going to leave his mark on her—permanently. Judging by her facial expressions, I could tell Hanny was thoroughly enjoying the moment. She no longer seemed to be in pain from my initial penetration which caused her to bleed some.

After we had both climaxed, Hanny and I decided to watch a movie. About an hour into it, my penis got hard again and was ready for Round Two. I went on top of her missionary style this time and pleasured her for about half an hour, changing positions every so often. I even kissed every inch of her butt. In seeing that she was enjoying it immensely, I stuck my finger in to heighten her pleasure. It was the right move because after that she gave me that backstage pass I so desperately wanted. Once Hanny gave me permission to take her in that way, I didn't procrastinate one bit. Carefully, I slipped my hardened cock into her small aperture. It hurt her but she seemed to like the bittersweet pain. Within a few seconds after having fully penetrated her for the second time, I had an explosive orgasm. Once that happened, I was pretty much done for the night. We got up to take a shower and order room service.

Her parents never knew that I had taken their sweet daughter's virginity. If they had known that at the time, it would have destroyed them altogether. Hanny insisted on keeping it a secret because she wanted them to accept me as their son-in-law one day. As for the filthy rich oil tycoon they wanted her to marry, he showed up one day at their home and officially asked for Hanny's hand in marriage. She turned him down on the spot and this really disappointed her parents because they had devoted their entire lives to making sure she would marry well. Hanny's outright refusal to marry the highly revered oil tycoon was a shameful experience for them. So, you can imagine that they didn't exactly warm up to me at first. But once I turned on that ole' Michael Stephen Grant charm, in time I was able to win them over. From a financial standpoint, I wasn't exactly chopped liver. Their main gripe with me was that I wasn't Muslim. Ironically, this is precisely what Hanny liked most about me. She was very westernized and did not want to marry a Muslim. "If I marry a Muslim man, he'll just put me in a cage and never let me out," is what she once told me.

Taking Hanny's virginity felt awesome, but at the same time the guilt ate away at me day and night. For once in my life, I actually felt strong remorse for having tarnished this wonderful human being who was madly in love with me. In the end, my culpability made me cave in and I ended up marrying her. The marriage lasted only two years. As it turned out, I wasn't really in love with her. The only reason I married her was because of the unrelenting guilt. I was also infatuated by her traffic stopping beauty. Hanny was that trophy wife every man wanted to have in his bed. It really stroked my ego when men would look at her with lust in their eyes. Everyone wanted a piece of this hot property, but it belonged exclusively to me.

Realistically speaking there was no other motivation for me to be with this woman other than the fact that she made me the envy of other men. She was nowhere near in the same intellectual level that I was. Hell, we were in two entirely different stratospheres. When we made love, she preferred missionary style and nothing else which made her boring sexually. No matter how hard I begged, she would never let me go down on her and everyone knows how I feel about that. I didn't realize it at the time but in her religion and culture practicing experimental ways of having sex was largely frowned upon. So, you tell me, what good is it to have a piece of forbidden fruit in your hands and not be able to take a bite out of it? To be totally honest, after I nailed her the first time, I pretty much lost interest in having sex with her. It didn't help matters either that she was extremely jealous.

Hanny also wanted to have children with me badly, but I wasn't about to let that happen. There was no way I was going to be stuck in purgatory for the rest of my life. So, on one of my week-long business trips, I secretly had a vasectomy done and she never found out. As long as I'm being brutally honest, I must admit that I cheated on her before we got hitched and throughout our entire marriage. Yeah, that's how committed I was to this gorgeous woman. On the other hand, I knew she would never cheat on me. I could count on her to always be there waiting for me to come home from my business trips. Every part of her life revolved around me and I felt an immense sense of power knowing that.

Even though I realized early on that marrying Hanny was a huge mistake, I honestly believed that somehow things would turn out okay. At least I was hopeful they would. However, it was foolish on my part. No matter from what angle you looked at it, MSG was royally screwed and needed to find a way out of bondage. I continued cheating on her hoping I would get caught and eventually I did. One day, Hanny went through my e-mail and discovered that I was having affairs with at least a half-dozen women. That evening when I got home from work, she went ballistic on me and held a knife to my stomach. I really thought I was going to be a goner because no matter how criminally insane Hanny got, I couldn't retaliate against her. Striking a woman regardless of the situation is something I could never bring myself to do. To escalate the situation, she also violently tore up all the pictures of my two biological children.

I'll never forget that night for as long as I live. My beautiful, desirable, trophy wife was totally out-of-control and I had to break down and call the police. The police arrived at our home and managed to calm her down. After that brutal domestic violence episode, I started to plot in my head how to ship Hanny back home to Indonesia without having her touch my fortune. For the next six months, I plotted and calculated how to get her to go back home and forget this whole nightmare of a marriage ever happened.

To keep the peace, not to mention my super exciting cheating life, I patched things up with Hanny and promised her I'd never lay my eyes or hands on another woman ever again. I had to rely heavily on my acting abilities and pretend to love her, which was all part of my master plan to get my wife-free life back. Lucky for me, she was caught shoplifting three times in three different states. I will never understand why she did it. We had lots of money. My guess is she did it out of sheer frustration and lack of attention.

After the third arrest, I convinced Hanny that she would never get her Green Card with her tainted identity. The only way to solve the problem was to get a divorce so that I could remarry her under a new identity. That meant she would have to spend some time in Indonesia to establish that new identity and then return to the U.S. Since she really didn't have much of a choice, Hanny agreed to follow the plan. I did an excellent job of making her believe this was the only way to clear her name. So, I escorted her back to Indonesia and promised I'd be back for her which of course I had no intention of doing. After a few months, she came to the grim realization that MSG wasn't coming back to get her.

This ugly chapter in my life taught me two important life lessons. First and foremost: Be extremely careful what you wish for because you just might get it. The second thing it made me realize that I have never been and shall never be marriage material. Up until recently, I used to brag that I was the total package and any woman would be damn lucky to land me in bed and in her life. But that couldn't be further from the truth. In theory and on paper, I appear to be the catch of the century. This just goes to show that appearances can be downright deceiving. It should be against the law for workaholics and serial cheaters like me to get married. Because all we do is end up making a mockery of the institution of marriage. It just isn't fair for women. And if by chance an irresistible hot number comes along and we decide to break the law, then guys like me should just be charged for Involuntary Woman Slaughter the second we say "I Do." Another option would be to sue us for collateral damage and causing great emotional distress to the opposite sex. So, while I may undeniably be the "Fuck of the Century", I don't foresee any "Husband of the Year" awards in my future.

Truth be told, I should have quit right after my first marriage went sour. At that point I should have just accepted that fact that

I was toxic for all women. If only I had remained true to myself, a lot of women would still have their egos and hearts fully intact. Now that I really think about it the only viable reason I got married is because I didn't like being alone. The irony is that whether I married or not, the bottom line is that being alone is what has been written in the stars for me all along. Then Maribel came along and for the first time I ended up being on the receiving end of pain. I fell hopelessly in love with her and the two children. Perhaps one of the reasons I married her so quickly was because in some crazy way I wanted to replace the first family I lost, especially my son and daughter. This is where I went wrong and now, I'm paying a hefty price for it.

Chapter Four

Down Under in the Land of Under

The one undeniable fact I've learned in all my years of being an international playboy is there is no such thing as free pussy—easy maybe—but never *gratis*. Fucking a beautiful woman is pretty much equivalent to test driving a high-dollar luxury car. Both of these extravagant toys require high maintenance in order to keep them performing at an optimal level. The only difference between the two is that your dream ride will never emasculate you like a fantasy woman can and will if you don't have a strong enough grip of the steering wheel. I know this because in my lifetime, I've test-driven all types of women who can be compared to the most expensive and fastest flash cars in the world—the McLaren FI, Ferrari, Lamborghini, Hennessey Venom GT, Porsche Carrera GT, Saleen S7, and the list goes on and on.

Sure, it's an intoxicating feeling when you first step inside the vehicle and fire up the engine. The sensations you begin to experience only intensify when your footsteps on the gas pedal and that first surge of lightning bolt speed is felt. After a while, the smooth ride at top speed starts to build up more and more until it happens—an orgasm of epic proportions. Then it's all downhill from there. Once the initial pleasure of riding the car of your dreams subsides, one of two things is bound to happen.

1. You'll start to feel bored and the overwhelming urge to test drive another car will hit you like a demolition wrecking ball.
2. The car will run out of gas and leave you stranded out in the middle of nowhere thus becoming a totally useless high-dollar piece of equipment that can no longer take you to all the exciting places you still wish to go.

Take it from a man who's been there and done that: Pick the damn car over the woman. Based on extensive first-hand experience, in the end after you've had your short-lived fun with them, gorgeous women will only drain you of all your energy, money, and testosterone level. God help you if one of them falls hopelessly in love with you. Then you're stuck with a clingy blood-sucking leech that you'll have a hard time getting rid of.

So, why the sermon regarding the evil machinations of alluring women with killer bodies made for sinful acts on a beautiful April spring afternoon? Well, here's a startling revelation for you, MSG has had a change of heart about wanting a live-in nurse who's willing to degrade herself by entering a state of indentured servitude where she will be expected to fuck on command. After having read the dozens and dozens of responses I got from the ad I posted on the Internet, making this decision was a real breeze. You would not believe some of the messages and pictures I received. I had no idea just how low women are willing to stoop in pursuit of the high and almighty dollar.

One of the responses I received was from an over-the-hill Russian dominatrix who was willing to come out of retirement for me. She sent me a photo of herself all decked out in full dominatrix gear in a seductive pose and with a leather whip in her right hand. She was a dead ringer for the American actress Angelica Huston. I might have actually ordered the total package had she not sent me a waiver to sign which would absolve her of all blame in the event of an accidental strangulation.

I also received an e-mail from a so-called high-dollar call girl from Thailand professing to look like Lucy Liu that read like it had been written by a first grader:

Pick me. I make ya holla for a dolla! I suck you dick til' you blue in da face. We make sex day and night.

One of the most eerie messages came from a woman in Transylvania, Romania, who claimed she was a three-hundred-year-old vampire princess and could make me immortal by sucking my cock and blood at the same time.

I wrote her back and said, "No, thank you! The last thing I need is a blood-free cock which would make it impossible for me to have an erection ever again—even in the afterlife."

This now brings me to the point I'm trying to make. MSG has had his fill of these kinds of women. I'll be damned if I am going to spend the rest of my life dealing with emotionally draining BIMBO DRAMA. So, this is why I decided to scrap the whole idea of hiring a live-in nurse and begin my search for a legitimate

Personal Assistant (PA) who comes with no strings attached, unless of course I feel like being tied up.

After giving it a great deal of thought, I've concluded that the PA I hire should have the following characteristics which are non-negotiable. First and foremost, she must be a true-blue Latina. I'm sick and tired of hyper-sexual Asian women, overly dramatic black girls, and goal-digging white females. It's been my experience that Latinas have a naturally inbred caring demeanor and when they fall in love it's real and eternal.

The PA of my dreams must have a fantastic sense of humor. Since major pain is what awaits me in the near future, I will require heavy dosages of humor. Laughter will be the best coping mechanism against misery. I suspect that toward the end, I'll start getting philosophical about many things in life and will want to converse with someone intelligent who can give me a fresh perspective. I've had nothing but sexual stimulation my entire life and look where it's gotten me. What I desperately need before leaving this world is the kind of intellectual stimuli that only a highly intelligent, creative, and witty woman can provide. I need so much more than a woman whose favorite catchphrase is, "I make ya holla for a dolla!"

Since I have the attention span of a high-level executive which is about three minutes tops, if that much at all, a prospective interviewee is going to have to captivate me with her charm, wit, and intelligence in record-breaking time. Although she doesn't have to be traffic stopping gorgeous, I should at least be able to look at her without feeling the impulse to put an appropriately sized brown paper bag over her head. For the first time in MSG's history, I am not going to judge the book by its cover. In the past, physical beauty alone has bored me easily after a period of time. I'm not going down that ugly road again. Now that I've come to the tail-end of my life,

I need and want a female hero to save me from myself. Oh, and did I mention she has to be a creative genius as well?

That's right, even with death nipping at my heels I'm never going to stop strategizing to improve. MSG isn't going down without a fight. The only way I'm leaving this fucked up planet is in a blaze of glory. I plan on coaching my clients and writing until I take my last waking breath and I'll need my PA to help me brainstorm new ideas. Not just any run-of-the-mill concepts will do. She must have the never-ending ability to shock me with off-the-wall brilliance. In other words, she has to be a Think Tank and having a decent ass won't hurt either. Yeah, I know perfectly well this is a pretty tall order. But there's only one MSG and soon he'll be gone for good. This whole experience is going to be a two-way street. My PA, whoever the lucky girl turns out to be is going to get just as much out of this relationship because of my knowledge, wisdom, and discipline. Who knows, if she plays her cards right, I'll even give her the most explosive orgasms she's ever had as an added bonus.

***

Surprisingly, it didn't take long to find her. The moment I started reading her profile on the Personal Assistants for hire website that my friend Tom recommended to me, I was completely hooked and reeled in.

I'm an extremely witty, high-energy, super intelligent thirty-something Latina author who is down on her luck seeking asylum from this insane world I can no longer afford to live in on my own. This Jack-of-all-trades with the heart of Mother Theresa and fighting spirit of Spartacus will work for a roof over her head, decent meals at least twice a day, quiet place to write, and relaxing atmosphere to take frequent and drawn-out baths. In return, I will bring an explosion of sunshine and fresh, never-before-heard-of perspectives every single day of your life. I've been gifted with the kind of charming personality and sense of humor that can practically raise anyone from the dead. I also have mesmerizing almond shaped eyes that can lift your spirits or condemn you in a heartbeat—it's your choice. I am a walking encyclopedia of out-of-the-box ideas which makes me highly entertaining and have a pair of shapely legs that have intoxicated more men that Jack Daniels. The best thing you can do for yourself is open up your home and let me manage your life, no matter how messed up it is. This genuinely caring PA with an endless supply of tricks in her arsenal will light that much needed fire in your pants and have you running like a well-oiled machine in no time.

She signed at the end of her profile: *The PA you simply can't live without, Raquel Lopez.* Well that pretty much sealed the deal for me. Right then and there I was ready to sign on the dotted line, with either my blood or semen, whatever the woman wanted of me. This mystery PA's profile pushed all the right buttons for me. She had a way with words and her personality just oozed right out of them. So, I sprang into action immediately and sent her a SKYPE interview request which I figured would save me time and money. About twenty-minutes later, I received a one-liner e-mail from her which read: "There's no time like the present" followed by a SKYPE address.

This woman was no procrastinator, which turned me on in a big way. She was the REAL DEAL and MSG wanted to move in on the action before anyone else did. With an open mind, I switched over to my SKYPE account and added the address she had sent me to my contact list. A few minutes later, she accepted my invite. My right index finger reacted by enthusiastically tapping on the video call button. I sat back in my chair and waited. A few seconds later, her image came through loud and clear on my computer screen, and I immediately felt like my insides had been sucker-punched by Floyd Mayweather, Jr. Yes, the impact she made on me was that well . . . impactful.

Raquel Lopez was not the most gorgeous woman I had ever seen but there was something about her that deeply moved me. Don't get me wrong, it didn't hurt to look at her either. The first physical attribute about my prospective PA that I zoomed in on was her long, raven black colored hair. She had the kind of hair that a man could easily get wrapped around in if you know what I mean, the kind that screamed FUCK ME NOW!

Right after we got the formal introductions out of the way I said to her, "You have the most remarkable hair."

She flashed an adorable lopsided grin and replied, "Thank you. I grew it myself."

I laughed out loud. "You also have beautiful eyes. Did you grow those yourself, too?"

"Nope! These peepers were a gift," she replied.

We had only exchanged a few words but the chemistry between us was off the charts. She intrigued me and I wanted to know everything about her.

"So, tell me about yourself," I said.

"Would you like to hear the truth and nothing but the truth or a watered-down version?"

Once again, I couldn't suppress the urge to laugh out loud. Raquel's sense of humor which seemed to come so naturally and easily to her was just what the doctor ordered. She was sharp and quick-witted.

"I want to hear all the juicy stuff."

She smiled again and batted her pretty eyes at me. "If I tell you all the juicy stuff, will you still respect me in the morning?"

"Of course I will!"

"Well that's a relief to hear. Otherwise whether you end up hiring me or not, I'd have to kill you in your sleep," she quipped back.

"You are something else," I said to her, grinning from ear to ear.

She didn't say anything for a few seconds and the look on her face became more serious. "Mr. Grant, I must apologize for the direction this interview has taken. I didn't mean for it to transpire this way. I must seem unprofessional to you which is not true."

"Please don't apologize," I said. "Are you kidding? This has got to be hands down the most entertaining interview I've ever conducted. You're exactly what I'm looking for. And please call me Michael."

Raquel became silent, but only for a moment. Then she proceeded to tell me about herself. As I kicked back and listened attentively to what she had to say, it struck me that this woman was genuine and had a caring demeanor. She was a rare, flawless diamond that isn't unearthed every day. Unlike so many women from my past, there were no superficial airs or nothing pretentious about her.

In the midst of our conversation, I realized that we were clicking on all cylinders. The best part of all is that I didn't have to censor what came out of my mouth. Raquel took everything I said to her in stride. She seemed to be so comfortable in her lovely caramel colored skin and that made me feel totally relaxed in mine. We ended up speaking for more than an hour but that was long enough for me to conclude that Raquel was the one for me. Somehow my manly intuition, if there is such a thing, told me that her face would be the last one I'd look at before taking my last breath here on Earth. Once this message registered in my brain, the most honest-to-God feeling of peace and tranquility came over me. I hired Raquel on the spot.

***

Today is the day my new PA is supposed to move in. She is scheduled to arrive at any moment now and I have to admit that I'm nervous and excited all at once. So here I am killing time by day-dreaming about one of my favorite places in the world—Australia. What a country! The people are extremely friendly and genuine there. The sights are pretty incredible too. Australia's ocean water is so blue and eye-appealing and, its inviting powdery white beaches are second-to-none.

I spent quite a bit of time working and doing speaking engagements in Australia, namely in Sydney and Brisbane. When I travelled there, I always made the effort to taste the local cuisine and by this I certainly don't mean the kind of food you put into your mouth for sustenance. It didn't matter where I was in the world, my never-ending craving for fresh pussy could never be fully satisfied.

There was no greater feeling for me than latching on to a local clit and tasting that sweet nectar that makes us men see stars in 3-D and high-defnition. Honestly, I didn't care whether I penetrated the woman or not—that was irrelevant. It was all about leaving my mark behind. I wanted each and every woman I fucked to never forget Michael Stephen Grant. The only way to do that was to make them have multiple, spine-tingling orgasms which can best be achieved by stroking their G-Spot with your tongue. Take it from an expert in the art of fucking who has seen more clits than a team of working gynecologists, using your dick alone will not get the job done. Sticking your hardened cock into a woman before she's had multiple orgasms just isn't cool. You've got to light that fire inside of her first before putting out your own. One of the most important life lessons I've learned is the way to a woman's heart is through her vagina.

Since I truly wanted to stand out as an Alpha Male, my goal was to always stay down on a woman as long as humanly possible before moving on to the act of intercourse. The objective was to push the woman to the brink of reaching Nirvana and having her beg me to stop. I wanted her to squeeze her thighs against my head and try to pull me back up by tugging on my hair. It turned me on to the point of no return to see them squirm and claw out of sheer desperation. The more they begged me to penetrate their soaking wet pussy, the more I felt like a powerful Modern-Day Sex God.

Most of the time, I played a numbers game in my head. Making a woman cum three, four, and even five times before penetration became my signature trademark. As you know, my all-time high was seven orgasms in one night. No woman in her right mind can ever forget a man who cares enough to make her cum seven times in one love-making session. This my friends is how you properly suck a woman dry. Sure, you may be dead to the world afterward but rest assured that once the woman in question gets those juices of hers flowing again, she's coming back for seconds.

When it comes to eating pussy, hygiene has really never been that important to me. Totally satisfying a woman and making her feel ecstasy to the highest degree is what matters most to me. In the grand scheme of things, all I've ever cared about is sexually pleasing women because they truly deserve it. So, what if I contracted a sexually transmitted disease along the way. In my mind there's no better way to go. Tell me, what man wouldn't love to have the following message engraved on his tombstone: Here lies (insert name), who died of a pussy overdose. May he rest in peace!

Anyway, back to my original topic. Every time I went to Sydney, I stayed at the finest four and five-star hotels the city had to offer. On this particular trip, I had a week-long workshop to IT executives. Due to being a frequent visitor at this one exquisite hotel, I was typically housed on the concierge level where free breakfast and delicious snacks were made available throughout the day for the taking. Actually, it was enough food to fill you up for dinner. It was a rather cozy setting with comfortable sofas, recliner chairs, TVs, and a nice dining area as well. One night I was ransacking the place for something to eat when a pretty, young blonde woman walked in and made my penis throb with desire.

She made her way to the area where the food was being served. My eyes became fixated on what I knew would be my next conquest. No longer hungry for food, I got up and walked right up to her for the purpose of making small talk.

"Hello there! My name is Michael Stephen Grant," I said to her.

This vision of loveliness smiled at me in a friendly way. "Hi! I'm Susan. It's nice to meet you," she said in one of the sexiest Australian accents I'd ever heard.

"The food here is awesome. I've tried just about everything at least once," I ventured to say. "Are you here on business or pleasure?"

"Business. Actually, I'm from Auckland, New Zealand."

"How long are you in town for?"

"The whole week. I work as a human resource specialist for a large retail firm and my parent company is headquartered in

Sydney. I spend one week a month here and the rest of the time at home in Auckland," she explained.

"Would you like to join me at my table?"

"Sure, I'd love to."

Susan had shoulder-length, dirty blonde hair that was nice and full. The way she applied her makeup really made her sparkling green eyes stand out. She was wearing jeans that looked like they had been painted on her and a light-turquoise colored blouse with a plunging V-line. From my vantage point, I could tell that she was not very well-endowed in the breast department, which I could care less about. She could have easily traded in her bra for a band-aid, which is all those small fun bags of hers needed for support. I had absolutely no hang-ups about screwing flat-chested women so long as they had a viable and penetrable ass and pussy.

As we nibbled on some finger foods while speaking about her job, all I could think of was having Susan's legs wrapped around my face while I cradle her butt in the palms of my hands. Although it was hard to do, I pretended to be genuinely interested in her career.

"So, tell me Susan. What would you say is the toughest challenge you face at your job every day?" I asked her.

"That's a no-brainer. Definitely the heavy dosage of politics," she blurted out.

"Really? Are you telling me corporate politics is just as bad in the Land of Under as it is everywhere else in the world?"

"That's precisely what I'm saying."

After listening to Susan talk about some of her pain points for a while, I offered up some recommendations, which she was grateful for. We ended up talking about her job for a few hours. The whole time, the sexual tension between us began to build, minute by minute. When we were finished eating, I suggested that we go for a walk so she could show me some of the most interesting sights since we were staying in a popular tourist area. After walking around the city for hours, we got hungry again and decided to find a nice restaurant to have dinner.

During the course of our meal, Susan asked me a ton of questions about what I did for a living. I could tell right off the bat that she was intrigued by my career and the fact that I was a highly accomplished IT business consultant, self-help author and international motivational speaker.

"Listen Susan, I'm giving a presentation to a large group of CEOs' at the hotel tomorrow morning. Would you like to come hear me speak?" I asked her in the middle of having dessert.

"I would absolutely love that," she replied bubbling with enthusiasm.

I smiled because my strategy to get her into bed was working like a charm. Having Susan present at my CEO forum and having her watch me in action was going to clinch the deal for sure.

To give her something tangible to mull over before saying good night, I wanted Susan to know that I was seriously thinking about moving to Sydney permanently for business reasons which of course was an outright lie. Chances were if she felt that I was eventually going to move there then she'd be more willing to open up her legs for me. I used this line a lot. Actually, abused it is more like it. Women don't ever want to feel as though they're only going to be a one-night stand. It was my job to outsmart them, which I did every time.

When we got back to the hotel, I gazed into her beautiful eyes and gave her a small peck on the lips. We hugged and said good night. Although I was super horny, I decided to play it safe and not make any hard-core advances toward her. I returned to my room and put on a porn flick, jacked off, then took a shower.

In the morning, she came down to the hotel ballroom where my event was being held wearing the hell out of a classy, black dress and matching high-heeled pumps. I greeted her professionally and politely suggested that she take a seat while I welcomed my other guests. As I interacted with others, I could sense that she was watching me closely from the back of the room. She was sitting there with her divine, athletic looking legs crossed in a lady-like manner. I was going bonkers but couldn't show it. It was really hard to concentrate on my presentation with Susan sitting in the back, looking so hot. My mind simply could not stop conjuring up impure thoughts.

After the presentation, I proceeded to thank everyone for coming, including Susan. Judging by the look she had on her face, I could tell she was impressed.

"Did you enjoy the presentation," I asked her.

"Immensely," she replied right away.

"Susan, I know this is a long shot, but would you like to meet up with me around 5:30 PM in the Concierge Lounge so we can talk some more?"

"I think that's a great idea!"

Susan and I met at the hotel's Concierge Lounge just like we had agreed to. After sharing some light snacks, I decided it was time to put my plan to get laid into motion so I insisted that we have dinner together. She happily accepted, which was all the validation I needed that the odds of her wanting to screw my brains out later on were strongly in my favor.

"Oh shoot! Do you mind if we stop by my room for a moment? I need to send out an urgent email before we got out to dinner? I totally forgot about the time difference."

"Not at all," Susan answered with a sweet smile.

Susan was a pretty smart cookie and I'm certain that she knew perfectly well this was just a pick-up line to get her into bed. She didn't resist one bit so this only meant that Susan wanted to do the horizontal mambo with me. When we stepped inside the room, I told her to please have a seat.

"I'll only be a few minutes," I said to her. I walked over to the desk and booted up my computer. As it fired up, I inquired about how her day at work was.

"It went well. Thanks for asking," she answered.

After discreetly sending an e-mail to myself, I walked to where Susan was sitting and helped her up out of the chair. I looked deeply into her eyes and planted a sensual kiss on the lips. Then I kicked it up a notch and French kissed her but was mindful not to shove my tongue too deep down her throat. Instead of being overly aggressive, I let her take the lead because a considerate male lover should always adapt himself to what the woman likes. Our tongues seemed to be totally in sync with one another.

Sensing that she wanted more of me I pulled away long enough to add fuel to the fire. "I'm sorry for French kissing you like that so soon. I just can't help myself. You looked absolutely gorgeous this morning and I haven't been able to stop thinking about you since we met yesterday at the Concierge Lounge," I confessed.

Susan inched closer to me and I kissed her again. Then we started to kiss passionately and from that moment on, our body temperatures rose quickly. I slowly eased both of us back toward the bed. I sat down but told Susan to remain standing for a while longer so that I could admire her beauty. Within a few seconds, I placed my hands behind her knees and started sliding them up ever so slowly. Her legs felt silky smooth to the touch. My hands made a pit stop right behind her quads and began to gently massage the hamstrings instead. This subtle movement was pure ecstasy for the both of us. At this point, I stopped teasing Susan and sat her down on the bed next to me. I kneeled on the floor and slipped her shoes off. Before coming back up I instructed her to lie down on the bed.

With the agility of a jungle cat, I crawled my way back to the bed, but stopped at Susan's dainty feet. I started massaging them and graduated to kissing her toes, one by one. To spice things up, I started sucking on each one slowly. When I finished making love to her toes, I began to inch my way back up again and headed straight for the pleasure island between her legs. Alternating between both legs, I left behind a trail of tongue kisses. By the time I reached her heavenly thighs and the hem of Susan's dress, my penis was throbbing out-of-control. I pulled her dress up only two inches but went no further. Instead of doing the predictable thing, I switched gears and started to venture back down to her feet with my tongue. The goal was to drive her insane before my tongue reached its final destination.

After more arousing foreplay, the time had finally come to really heat things up. I slipped my hands under her buttocks and squeezed gently. I tugged at the back of her panties and in one fluid move pulled them down. Susan was wearing a skimpy pink thong, which to be completely honest didn't impress me much. What can I say? I've never been a fan of anal flossers. Her pussy was nicely trimmed and dotted with short blonde colored pubic hairs. The sight of her naked pussy ignited a burning inferno inside my pants.

"Stop! Let me help you out of your pants," Susan pleaded.

While the idea appealed to me a great deal, I wasn't ready to expose myself just yet. "Patience my dear!" I said to her. "Good things come to those who wait. Besides, I've just gotten started with you."

Once again, I kissed Susan passionately and unzipped her dress. I turned her over gently so she could lie flat on her stomach. While she relaxed, I pulled off her dress slowly and savored every moment of the unveiling. Then I undid Susan's bra and flipped her back over. At that point, I hit the pause button and took off my V-neck T-shirt. Susan gasped at the sight of me.

"Oh my God! You're so ripped and beautiful," she cried out.

Without saying a word, I leaned in and started to caress her small breasts with my fingers. Eventually, I got around to sucking on her nipples and this really turned Susan on. Since I was on a roll, I decided to migrate down south again with my tongue and stopped when it made contact with her mouthwatering pussy lips. Just to see what kind of reaction I would get; I gave Susan's vagina one giant lick just like you would do with a lollipop. She went ballistic and her pussy became soaking wet with desire. Sweet moaning sounds came out of her mouth a few seconds after I started to pepper her clit with butterfly kisses. Then I latched onto her G-Spot with the tenacity of a pit-bull. Her moans became louder and more pronounced, but I refuse to let go. I continued to suck on her clit with wild abandon and it didn't take long for Susan to have her first orgasm. When she reached that sweet note, her entire body quivered and then tightened up.

After taking a quick break, I began to finger fuck her in and out slowly. I was never big on finger-fucking but did it with every woman because I knew it turned them on. While it revved my engine somewhat as well, I always preferred to infiltrate their gateways to pleasure with my tongue. Although I had satisfied Susan like no other man had before, I wasn't through with her yet. I wanted

Susan to cum several more times before I inserted my cock into her beautiful pink mound of flesh. She, on the other hand, was trying desperately to get me to insert my penis inside her moist pussy, but I wouldn't have it. I wanted her to beg for it after a few more orgasms.

Against her will, I headed back down for more. Susan tried with all her might to hold me back, but I easily won that battle. Showing no mercy, I attacked her clit with a vengeance. Poor Susan she just didn't stand a chance against an Israeli pit bull who wanted more of that Kiwi meat of hers. In a matter of a few minutes, Susan had another orgasm, but that didn't stop me from trying to start building the momentum for another one. I continued my plight relentlessly with Susan struggling to unlatch me from her clit the whole time. This exciting as hell sexual tug-of-war between us went on until Susan finally surrendered and climaxed for the third time.

Just when Susan thought it was safe again, I turned her over and stuck my tongue into her asshole. I wanted to end this love-making session on a high note. Bracing myself for the waves of pleasure that was sure to follow, I yanked my pants and underwear down and slithered my rock-hard cock into her pussy from behind. It was extremely challenging to keep my volcano from spewing forth its hot molten lava. Susan was a beautiful girl with a great body. We both climaxed in less than a dozen thrusts. Suffice it to say, we never quite made it out to dinner that evening.

The rest of the week played out in the same manner. I ended up making a few more trips to Australia to fornicate more with Susan. I always looked forward to seeing her. She was a total blast and had a great demeanor. I found myself starting to fall in love with her. In time, Susan made it crystal clear that she wanted more out of the relationship. One day she called my bluff and asked me point-blank when I was moving to Australia. The gig was pretty much up at that point and I had no choice but to move on and now if you'll excuse me, I must answer the door because the PA of my dreams has just arrived.

Chapter Five

It Ain't Over TIL' the Fat Lady Comes

Raquel Lopez is going to be a powerful force to be reckoned with. This is the first thought that crossed my mind upon opening the door and coming face-to-face with her porn-sized tits.

"Good morning! I'm Raquel. I am here to make your life easier," she said, extending her hand out to me in greeting.

My new PA definitely had a great deal more star quality in person than she projected on the computer screen a week ago. Honestly, the web cam didn't do her justice. I was rendered speechless by her commanding presence at my front door for who knows how long before I finally snapped out of the hypnotic stupor, she had put me in and shook her hand. Don't misunderstand me, she wasn't that beautiful. I've seen and bedded far better than her. It's hard to explain but it almost seemed as though I was being visited by a divine entity clearly not of this world.

"Are you going to stand there all day and gawk at me like I've just sprouted another head, or may I come in?" she asked.

"I'm so sorry," I said stepping back to clear the way for her. "Please excuse my bad manners. I'm Michael Stephen Grant. Won't you come in and make yourself at home?"

Raquel stepped inside with a look of skepticism written all over her round, ethnic but pretty face. For a few, fleeting moments I was sure that her exotic looking green eyes had penetrated through the deepest level of my soul and saw me for the conniving manwhore I am. At that point, I half-way expected Raquel to turn her cute ass around and make a beeline for the door, but she didn't budge an inch.

"You have such a beautiful home," she said, her eyes darting in every direction. "I could see how a girl could really be happy here."

"Well, it's going to be your home now for as long as you like," I ventured to say.

Her off-the-wall yet friendly response was not what I expected to hear. "Am I going to be expected to clean this magnificent castle?"

"I'm not really sure how I mustered up the gumption to articulate my comeback but I did. "Only if you don't want to be locked up in the dungeon."

Raquel half-smiled which really put me at ease. Then a few seconds later I caved in. "Relax, I'm only kidding. Actually, I do all of my own housekeeping and chock it up as exercise."

"I can respect a man who does his own housecleaning," Raquel stated out of left field, sizing me up from head to toe with those captivating eyes of hers. "How tall are you?"

Not sure where she was going with this, I replied, "I'm 6'2."

"Now answer me this. Was it hard to find a sexy French maid uniform to fit into and more importantly will you be wearing it the next time you clean up around here?"

A hearty laugh escaped me. "Yes, it was rather difficult. I had to have it custom-made. That reminds me it's at the cleaners right now and will need to be picked up soon."

Although I was enjoying trading humorous punches with her immensely, I decided to expedite things by asking, "Raquel, where are all of your things?"

"In my car," she answered.

"Let me put my shoes on and I'll help you bring them in."

"Before doing that, why don't we go over the logistics of our living together?"

Suddenly, I became afraid, very afraid of Raquel Lopez. "I'm not sure what you mean."

"If this arrangement of co-habitation is going to work, rules and boundaries must be established and agreed upon by both parties," she explained in a more serious tone of voice.

"So how do you propose we go about doing this?"

"Why don't we talk about this while you give me a grand tour of the house?"

"Okay, fasten your seatbelt and follow me then."

The first part of the house I showed her was the living room. I stood next to her in silence while she staked out the area.

"Wow, you've got a great fireplace!" Raquel said. "Do you fire it up often?"

"I've only lived in this house less than a year so I haven't been able to put it to good use."

"May I make a suggestion?"

"Do I have a choice but to hear you out?"

"Not really. You'd be fighting a losing battle," Raquel tossed back.

"Then by all means, suggest away."

"You really need to place an inviting bear skin rug in front of it. The chicks you bring home will totally dig it," she said in a playful manner.

Just then her eyes zoomed in on the pictures placed above the mantel. She walked over and hand-picked the photo of Maribel and the children. "Is this your wife and kids?"

"Ex-wife and step children," I corrected.

"She's beautiful and the kids are both cute. Where are they now?"

"France."

Somehow Raquel sensed this was a taboo subject for me so she dropped her line of questioning altogether and instead focused on the six, twelve feet high bay type windows that provided an un-spoiled view of my beautifully landscaped backyard.

"Raquel, feel free to make use of this living space anytime you'd like. Now let me show you the kitchen."

On the way to the kitchen, Raquel noticed the pool and jacuzzi outside which were visible to the left. She let out a loud whistle. "Nice! Are they both heated?"

"Indeed, they are," I replied.

"Well, you know what they say. Some like it hot. Do you mind if I use them every once in a while?"

"Of course not! I already told you, this is going to be your home from now on. So, please enjoy all the amenities this castle has to offer you."

This time she flashed me a genuine smile which made my heart do a somersault. "I really appreciate that."

When we arrived at the kitchen, Raquel set her purse down on the counter and walked directly to my stainless-steel refrigerator. She opened the door, bent over and started to take inventory of what was inside. While she did that, I checked out her legs. Raquel was wearing a purple, mini-dress with a flared-out hem and high-heeled strappy sandals the same color. Her legs were truly exquisite. They were naturally tanned and smooth. It was a given that Raquel did not ever have to wear pantyhose. Both her calves and thighs were well-shaped and muscular and for a moment I thought about how heavenly it would feel to have them pressed against my face while in the horizontal position. My personal assistant had not been in the house more than twenty minutes and already my mind was in the gutter.

"Are you looking for anything in particular?" I asked.

Raquel stopped rummaging through my refrigerator at once and closed the door. Then she went for the cabinets, opening and peeking inside each of them. "Where's your wine?"

"Don't have any. I don't drink."

"You didn't tell me I was going to be working in an alcohol-free zone," Raquel said with a scowl on her face.

"Sorry. But you didn't exactly inform me that I had to have a current liquor license and fully stocked bar in order for you to take the job. Is that a deal breaker?" I tossed back at her.

She thought for a few seconds about what I asked for. "Guess not. It's my bad. I should have asked you from the very beginning. Would you consider adding a small stipend on top of my agreed upon salary so I can buy some? I work so much better with wine in my system so it would be in your best interest to do so."

I stood there wondering why I was allowing her to manhandle me like this. Then an illicit thought entered my mind. *It may be easier to nail her if she's tipsy all the time.* "Why not?" I finally replied.

"Great! So, what's next?" Raquel asked.

"Why don't I show you my home office?"

"Age before beauty," she said playfully. "Lead the way."

Judging by the look on her face, my home office really seemed to have made an impression on Raquel. The way she took her time looking around you would have thought she was in a world-class museum.

"So, I take it this is where all the writing magic happens for you," she stated matter-of-factly as her fingers strummed along the edge of my desk. Suddenly she stopped and gestured toward the front facing wall of which every square inch was occupied by professionally framed and glass-encased shadow boxes containing my book covers to date—all forty of them.

"Michael Stephen Grant Wall of Fame?" she asked.

"I guess you could say that," I replied. "Are you familiar with my work?"

"I won't lie to you. Up until our Skype session last week, I had never heard of you. But since you hired me, well I did some research on you and made it a point to visit all three of your web sites."

"And . . ." I prompted.

"You have quite an impressive track record. May I ask what your current work-in-progress is about?"

"Why do you automatically assume I'm writing a new book?" I challenged her.

Raquel walked around the desk and sat down in my nine-hundred-dollar chair without asking. "Mr. Grant, don't forget that I'm a writer too. The way I see it, there are only two kinds of writers, the one-book wonders and lifers. I'm willing to bet my life that you are the latter."

"Guilty as charged," I answered. "How about you?"

She leaned forward and placed her elbows on top of the desk. "I'm still too young for the final verdict on that one. Well, are you going to tell me what your new book is about or am I going to have to beat it out of you?"

"Why should I tell you? You just said I was old."

Raquel smiled demurely. I guess I did. Sorry."

"Now that smile deserves a straight answer," I said to her. "My new book is about self-discipline."

"Self-discipline," Raquel repeated out loud. "That seems to be your topic of choice. I know you're this big-shot self-discipline guru and all but don't you think you've already beaten that poor horse to death?

"What do you mean?" I asked feeling a bit offended.

She whirled the chair around and pointed to several shadow boxes mounted on the wall. You have already written several books on self-discipline. Don't you think it's time to change your tune, especially now that you are facing a painful, imminent death?

I hated to admit it, but my ballsy personal assistant had made a valid point. "Well, I will certainly keep that under advisement. Are you ready for me to show you the master bedroom and bathroom?"

"Now that's what I'm talking about," is the first thing that came out of Raquel's mouth as soon as we walked into my interconnecting master bedroom and bathroom. "I love all these windows with plantation-style blinds. And where do these double doors lead to?"

"The backyard. There's a comfy patio set out there that you're welcome to use anytime."

"Hey, that's not a bad idea. It seems like a relaxing and peaceful place to write, especially now that the weather is going to be warming up," she pointed out. "Do you ever come out here to write?"

"Not really. I usually stick to my office."

Raquel diverted her attention to the 60-inch flat screen TV mounted on the wall. Then she turned and faced my beautiful brass California King-size bed. "Nice set-up," she blurted out.

"I bet if this bed could talk, it would have some pretty juicy secrets to tell."

I chuckled at what she said. "You could say that, but it's been sworn to secrecy."

"So, this is your Pandora's Box and it can never be opened?"

"Got that right sweetheart."

Raquel then noticed the double doors to the right. "May I?"

"Please, be my guest." Instead of following her, I stayed back.

A few seconds later, I heard Raquel's reaction. "I've died and gone to heaven. This bathtub of yours totally makes up for the fact that you don't have any wine in the house. It's absolutely gorgeous. I've never seen a bathtub encased in solid oak wood before."

"You like it?" I asked from where I stood.

"Like it? I more than like it. Hell, I want to marry it," she called back.

Raquel's sense of humor was such a breath of fresh air. Practically everything that came out of her mouth made me laugh. Just having a conversation with her alone was entertaining enough. She was the kind of woman I had never encountered before. In other words, I didn't have to fuck her to have fun. That's not to say that the idea of ravaging her body didn't appeal to me because quite frankly it did—big-time. That in itself was totally out of character for me because as far as her physicality went, she wasn't exactly my type.

"How do you like the walk-in shower?" I asked her. Raquel emerged out of the master bathroom and I could tell she had something on her mind. "It's quite nice but I'm more of a bathtub kind of girl. We need to negotiate," she said flat-out.

"What are you talking about?"

"I want private access to your state-of-the-art bathtub at least twice a week, maybe three."

"Well, that depends on whether or not I can watch you bathe," I countered.

She flashed me a dirty look and crossed her arms. "Only if you double my salary."

I walked up to her and leaned in too close for comfort. The point was to make her feel uneasy and I think it worked. "Listen up sweetheart. In my lifetime, I've seen more naked women than Hugh Hefner and Larry Flint put together. I ain't about to start paying for something I can get for free."

Raquel took a defensive stance with me right away. She held up one hand in the air and said, "Excuse me, I had no idea I was dealing with an over-the-hill gigolo. So, what's it gonna be then, two or three times a week."

"That remark you made about me is going to cost you a dip in the tub. Twice a week and that's my final offer."

"I'll take it!" Raquel answered without the slightest hesitation. "One more thing . . ."

"What now?"

"Is it okay if I buy some aromatic candles and place them around the bathtub?" she asked.

"How many are we talking here?"

"Just a couple . . . dozen."

"Good grief! Are you going to be taking a bath or having a séance?" I asked, grinning from ear to ear.

"Both," she replied in a smart-alecky way. "Don't you know taking a bath is so much better when you commune with the dead?"

"You are something else," I said pointing my finger at her. "Now c'mon and follow me."

"Where are we going?"

"Upstairs so you can pick out a bedroom. Plus, there is something else I want to show you," I explained.

"You mean I can have my pick of bedrooms? How many are there upstairs anyway."

"Only five."

"That's enough to house an entire harem of women," she commented.

"I know," I muttered under my breath.

When we got upstairs, our first stop was the theater room. Raquel went ballistic as soon as she saw the immaculate set-up. "This room is amazing," she said, planting herself on my spacious, black leather couch. "So, is this going to be one of the perks that comes with the job?"

"Sure, if you want it to be," I said to her. "You like to watch movies?"

"All writers like to watch movies. It helps get those creative juices flowing," Raquel said. She reached out, grabbed one of the throw pillows and hugged it which made her look adorable. "Do you mind if I watch movies in here during the weekends?"

"Not at all. But I'm afraid I don't have that great of a movie collection to choose from?"

"Why do I get the feeling that you've got nothing but porn flicks?"

"Again, guilty as charged," I admitted.

"Well lucky for you, I happen to own all four seasons of the Spartacus series and let me tell ya, it is so much better than porn."

"I've heard about that series. Is it really that good?"

Raquel's face lit up. "Let me put it to you this way. Spartacus is to women what Viagra is to men. Do I make myself perfectly clear?"

"Crystal clear," I answered a little choked up because what she said sparked both my penis and curiosity.

The rest of the tour took place without a hitch. Out of all the bedrooms upstairs, Raquel opted for the one closest to the theater room which didn't surprise me in the least. I couldn't shake off the feeling that she was going to end up sleeping there most of the time anyway. After walking Raquel entirely through the second floor, we came back downstairs and ended up back in my office.

"Are you ready to go get your things out of the car now?" I asked her.

"Yeah, let's do it. But first, let me see your daily schedule. You were supposed to have a print-out of it for me by the time I got here."

"Nothing gets past you. Does it?" I opened the top right drawer of my desk, pulled out a sheet of paper and handed it to her. I felt like a nervous schoolboy turning in a late homework assignment to the meanest teacher in school.

Raquel reached out for the schedule and our hands accidentally brushed against one another. I only felt the smoothness of her hand for an instant, but the contact was enough to produce a cold shiver down the base of my neck. While she looked over the schedule, I rubbed my neck hoping the feeling would go away. It didn't.

When Raquel was done skimming through the schedule, she looked up at me and said, "Are you kidding me? This is how you live your life day in and day out? Any nursing home resident probably has a more interesting life than you."

I plucked the schedule out of her hands. "There's nothing wrong with the way I live my life on a daily basis. It's called having structure and self-discipline. This is the reason I've been able to accomplish as much as I have.

Raquel backed off immediately. "There's no mention in the schedule about when you take your medications or go in for cancer treatments," she pointed out. Since I will probably be driving you around, I'll need to know this."

"It's not on the schedule because I ain't doing any of these things."

Raquel's jaw practically dropped to the floor. "Do you or do you not have Stage Four lung cancer?" she asked.

"I do."

"Then why aren't you doing anything about it?"

I answered her question with another. "What's the point?"

She shook her head. "Without medication or any type of treatment you're going to die faster than you should."

"I know and I'm at peace with that."

Raquel stepped away from me as if I was contagious. She raised her arms up in the air and then let them drop back down in one clean dramatic sweep. "Oh great! Now I'm stuck in a dead-end job."

I couldn't help but chuckle at what she said because I thought it was funny as hell. Apparently, my laughing was infectious because Raquel joined in. After we had our fill of comic relief, I posed a deadly serious question. "So, now that you know you're in a dead-end job, the question is: Are you staying or going?"

Her radiant smile turned into a frown instantaneously. I could tell she was really struggling to cough up an answer for me. After a while, she cleared her throat and said, "C'mon DEAD MAN WALKING, let's get my things."

It took us a few trips back and forth to bring all of Raquel's things into the house. During the last round, as I was carrying the last suitcase in; I happened to notice several small pieces of cloth scattered throughout the driveway. I set the suitcase down and picked them up one by one for closer inspection. Apparently, Raquel had been in such a heated rush to get inside the house that she didn't notice she'd lost some of her panties along the way. I scooped them all up in my hands and looked around to make sure none of my nosy neighbors were watching me. When I saw that the coast was clear, I raised the panties up to my nostrils and took one gigantic whiff. They smelled like a field full of daisies. The aroma was downright intoxicating. Before proceeding back into the house, I randomly selected a pair and stuffed them inside my jean pocket just for future entertainment.

When I walked into the house, Raquel was waiting for me at the top of the stairs. "Thank you for getting that last suitcase," she said climbing down the stairs. About halfway down, she noticed I was clenching a fistful of multi-colored small garments.

"You dropped these," I said to her.

"What are they?"

"I've seen plenty of these in my lifetime. I'm pretty sure they are panties."

The second I announced what the unidentified colorful objects were, Raquel practically flew down the rest of the stairs and snatched the small collection of panties out of my hands.

I could tell she was embarrassed about the whole thing. "Would you like me to take your suitcase upstairs to your room," I asked.

"Thank you, but no. You've already done enough. I'll get it," she replied.

"Okay. Take all the time you need to get settled in. I'll be in my office working if you need anything," I said.

Raquel nodded, grabbed her suitcase, and began to make the trek back up the stairs to the second floor. I, on the other hand, high-tailed it into my office, closed the door and sat down. Before booting up the computer, I just had to do it. I fished out the pair of panties I had held onto for my own sick demented pleasure. I unfolded the lone panty and raised it up in the air. It was bikini-style and bright turquoise with silver-colored lettering on the backside. I flipped the panty over, and it read: I Want You! These had to be one of the cutest pair of panties I had ever seen and trust me I've seen just about as many of them as you can see stars in the heaven on a beautiful, clear night. And let me tell you something, not all panties are created equal which reminds me of the time I fucked a woman whose underwear could have easily doubled as a camping tent for a family of four.

***

At the time, I was an executive at a major technology firm in Silicon Valley, responsible for managing their global computing infrastructure, which included field offices throughout the world. The pressures were immense, but the job had a few perks to make up for that fact. My position afforded me the opportunity to travel a great deal and with that came a lot of fringe benefits including meeting hordes of women. There was one lady who worked out of our Atlanta Sales office. Her name was Stephanie and she had an incredible personality.

Aside from being one of the nicest people you could ever speak with, Stephanie was also remarkably beautiful with long blonde hair, blue eyes, a perfectly shaped nose, and white-as-snow straight teeth. Her awesome smile could have lit up the Dark Ages. She was one of those southern belle types you hear so much about. Stephanie had the accent, personality and good looks. There was only one tiny problem—she was obese. By my estimate, Stephanie was at least fifty pounds overweight, maybe even seventy-five. It was difficult to tell. Mass is mass and she had a ton of it. All my life, I had always been turned off by fat people. I thought they were all undisciplined and lazy. After all, I exercised daily and managed my eating habits to have a nice physique, so why couldn't they do the same? I never bought into that whole "maybe they have an unmanageable thyroid problem" spiel.

For a period of three weeks many issues with the networking equipment in this particular office cropped up that needed my attention. The problems were intermittent so that made it all the more difficult to troubleshoot. Stephanie would call me directly to complain in the nicest way possible when things weren't going smoothly. She was extremely respectful and genuinely nice and I liked that. Pretty soon I started asking myself: Could she be a potential victim for MSG? I grappled with that very thought for weeks.

Based on all my interaction, I could tell Stephanie liked me. She was mine for the taking. All I had to do was take one trip out there and I could nail her, but that extra weight . . . ugh. I had always considered myself quite the connoisseur of women, especially ones with sexy bodies. The thought of me fucking a fat woman was totally out of character, especially since I had never been with one before. I remembered what my best friend Marcus always used to say, "There's no greater feeling than having a big, juicy booty." That got me to thinking how many men like screwing girls who are plump. Maybe there was something to be said about being able to grab all that surplus flesh during intercourse. Personally, I thought it was a major turnoff, but everyone has to try something at least once, right? Well . . . at least that's what I kept telling myself. It was just another whole to plug, another notch on my belt. Sure, I was married to my first wife at the time, but these extra marital affairs were a blast so why not try it just once.

The next day, I picked up the phone and called Stephanie. She was happy to hear from me but that was no surprise. I informed

Stephanie that I was scheduling a flight the following week to meet with her to review the problems with the telecommunications equipment. The plan was to catch the first flight out and arrive in Atlanta on Monday afternoon. I made it a point to tell Stephanie that I was going to be on a tight schedule and I wanted her to meet with me that same afternoon in her office. If needed, we could continue our discussion over dinner as I would have to fly out the very next morning. In the back of my mind, I wanted to have a quick getaway plan in place just in case I became totally disgusted with what I was about to do.

Stephanie was really excited to hear that I was coming to Atlanta. The flirting between us got pretty hot and heavy in the days leading up to my trip. In anticipation of my arrival, she asked to see a copy of my trip itinerary so she could pick me up at the airport. When I arrived at the airport, her pretty face and radiant smile was present and accounted for as expected. But then there was all that extra flab hanging around—it looked far worse in person. That day Stephanie was wearing her business attire, a LARGE conservative white dress. All of the previous hype building up to this encounter went down the toilet in a matter of a few seconds. Of course, I couldn't show it but I was truly disgusted being near all of that fat. She drove me back to the office and for several hours we reviewed all of the problems and decided on a game plan to resolve the issues.

Throughout the afternoon, I acted in a very professional manner and so did Stephanie. Around 5:30 PM we decided to call it a day and go out for a nice sit-down dinner. There was no denying that she had an awesome personality which made it easy to converse with her. After having our desert, I knew the time to move in for the kill was drawing near. For months, I had been preparing for this moment and I was super horny because I hadn't had sex for a week.

So, I decided to cut through the chase by asking her, "Where do you live?"

"Not far from here, just a ten-minute drive," Stephanie replied. "Would you like to come over for a cup of coffee?"

"Sure, that actually sounds great," I said.

After picking up the tab for dinner, Stephanie and I got into her black Pontiac Firebird and headed to her apartment. About halfway there the weirdest thing happened. We were driving along when suddenly it started to smell as though something in the car was burning. A few seconds later, we saw smoke coming through the dashboard. Before we knew it, the car had caught on fire. I should have saw this for the bad omen that it was but never underestimate the stupidity of a man who is so horny that he's willing to get caught in the midst of a burning inferno just for the sake of getting a piece of ass, even if it is a fat one.

Stephanie pulled the car over onto a side street and we got out and watched it go up in flames. Lucky for us, the fire department showed up in a timely manner and doused the fire. Shortly after that, the police and tow truck came to haul the car away. The whole freakish incident upset Stephanie terribly and I really felt bad for her as well. I tried my best to comfort her as we rode back to her house in the back seat of a taxicab.

When we got there a defeated Stephanie pointed at the couch and said, "Please have a seat while I make us some coffee. It's been an extremely long day."

"Thank you! That would be nice," I answered.

We continued to talk while she brewed the coffee. I repeatedly told her how genuinely sorry I was for what had happened to her car. Stephanie waved it off and said it was time for her to get a new car anyway. She brought my coffee over to where I was sitting on the couch and nestled right next to me. Finally, she was mine for the taking. The question was: Did I want her? After mulling it over for a few seconds, I decided what the heck. I was horny enough that a fat piece of ass was better than no piece at all. At the end of the day, it was just another cave for my dick to explore and besides I needed to report back to my friend Marcus about the whole experience.

To get the foreplay going, I put my arm around Stephanie and started to rub her wide back. As I was rubbing, she turned her face toward me and looked deeply into my eyes. Caught up in the moment, I reached over, grabbed her chin and brought it close to my face. I kissed her delicately on her normal sized lips. Then the kissing intensified, and tongues were swapped. In hindsight, she was an excellent kisser. You could tell our encounter made her happy and it was obvious that she wanted to please me. For a moment, I totally forgot how fat she was because we all know when a man's dick gets hard, well he pretty much stops thinking altogether. Stephanie grabbed my hand and led me into her bedroom. Despite being overweight, she had both the initiative and self-confidence to instigate our fuck session.

In anticipation of what was to cum, we got on top of her bed and continued kissing. At this point I was so horny that I didn't think about all that extra territory I would have to cover. I started to unbutton her blouse—so far so good I was still hard—so maybe in the grand scheme of things her fatness wasn't all that bad. I continued my seduction of this super-sized southern belle beauty by taking off her bra and once I did it started to hit me because too much of her protruding stomach and massive chest was exposed. I could feel myself starting to get turned off, but I was still horny and hard. All I had to do was avoid looking at the massive amount of blubber lying before me in all its glory. Ironically her breasts weren't humungous, and they didn't sag very much at all. Her nipples, on the other hand, were rock hard.

Out of the blue, Stephanie decided to hit the pause button so she could get up and turn the light off. I've always preferred having sex with the lights on so I can really feast my eyes on a woman's body. I also like looking deeply into their eyes when I'm in the throes of climaxing. In this case it was best to turn the lights off. I remember her telling me, "Let's pull the comforter off and get under the blanket." I knew exactly why she said that because of what was coming next.

Determined to go through with this, I started to unbutton her pants at the waist. Let me tell you it wasn't easy to find because of all that surplus flesh spilling over her pants. A desert camel would have had better luck getting itself through the eye of a needle. But being the fuck trooper that I was, I found the zipper and pulled down her pants, ever so slowly, all for the sake of special effects. That's when I started feeling more and more of her fat, but I was still horny, so I pressed on. When I grabbed her XXL-sized panties and removed them that's when I woke up and smelled the coffee. Stephanie was wearing granny style panties—ugghhhhhh!—oh was I turned off in a major way. Her underwear was bigger than the ones I was wearing and, I weighed 210 pounds, still do. The thing is I had already reached the point of no return and couldn't back down now. My reputation as a master seducer of women was at stake. So, I decided to suck it up, be a man, and fuck Stephanie's brains out anyway.

Just because Stephanie was easily three times a lady, I wasn't about to forget about my number one rule of going down on a woman before penetration. A man's got to do what a man's got to do—right? So, I ventured down south like I had done hundreds of times before. However, this felt radically different as typically I straddle a woman's ass with my hands while I munch away on her clit. Well, obviously two man-sized hands weren't enough for that much girth. Still, I reluctantly performed my duties but let the record show I just wasn't that excited about it. Right then and there I decided that I would do the bare minimum—one orgasm prior to penetration.

I kept my eyes closed the entire time. I was too chicken shit to get a glimpse of anything. The good news is that I was able to pinpoint her G-spot easily and when I did Stephanie went absolutely bonkers. She jolted and moaned like a fat cow, like it had been a really long time since another human being had ventured to the large southern hemisphere that was her vagina. Not to be mean, but anyway one looks at it there simply weren't ANY sexy parts on this behemoth. I couldn't help but wonder how on earth any man can get turned on by all that blubber. I'm not kidding when I say that moving her girth around was like trying to steer the Titanic away from that giant iceberg before crashing into it.

When Stephanie climaxed, I was sure her next door neighbors knew about it. Actually, I was expecting much louder noises but, her moans of pleasure were quite subdued, which was nice for keeping a low profile. She did however tense up quite a bit during the climactic moment. Now it was my turn to have whatever fun I could and put this chapter in my life behind me quickly. It didn't take me more than a few minutes to cum and once I did it was like someone had dumped a bucket of ice down my pants. That's how turned off I was! Knowing she was lying there naked totally grossed me out and I wanted out of there as fast as my legs could carry me. Stephanie tried her hardest to entice me into having more sex by putting in a lot of effort into trying to turn me on. Granted, she was a VERY willing participant but once I shot my load and realized where I was and who I was with, my first inclination was to run for the border.

Even though she went down on me and swallowed my cock whole to keep me hard, it simply wasn't enough to make me want to stick around for another round.

Even though I had never been that grossed out in my entire life, I didn't want to be downright disrespectful either. But when she turned the light on in her bedroom and I saw her body in full living color and the size of her underwear, I got the overwhelming urge to kill my friend Marcus. Of course, Stephanie wanted me to sleep over but, I told her that I had urgent work to do for an overseas customer back at my hotel room, which was a total crock of shit. However, I did promise to call her in the morning. I then asked Stephanie if she could call me a cab and she obliged. I couldn't wait to get the hell out of there. I made good on my promise and called her back the next morning to thank her for a good time. There I was still unable to stop feeling disgusted by what had happened between us, but still I didn't want to hurt her feelings. When I returned back to my office, I also sent her an e-mail thanking her for everything.

In one of our subsequent conversations Stephanie asked me when I was coming back to Atlanta. I lied and said that I would in the very near future. Of course, that was all bullshit. There was no way I was going back there unless I absolutely had too for work related reasons. I didn't feel guilty at all because I gave Stephanie something very few men would have and that was to suck on that clit until she climaxed—probably like never before. She got the five-star royal treatment and I know beyond the shadow of a doubt that it was a highly sensual experience for her. So, I brushed aside the sexual encounter with Stephanie as a Good Samaritan act and moved on to more physically fit women.

Chapter Six

Banging in Bangkok

Personal Assistant Extraordinaire Raquel Lopez has been living under my roof for about a month now and I'm having the time of my life. She and her crazy, fun-loving antics is a much easier pill to swallow than any anti-depressant or painkiller Dr. Campbell could have prescribed for this dying man. She is unlike any other woman I've ever met before. For the first time in my life, I am toying with the idea that perhaps it is possible for an unscrupulous manwhore like me to go radical and become a one-woman man. But it would take a remarkable woman to make me give up an entire universe of pussy. Could Raquel be the cure for this die-hard womanizer? Honestly, I can't remember when I ever enjoyed the company of a woman more—with my clothes on. It's a true-blue miracle I tell you.

Everything about Raquel intrigues me. I find myself wanting to know every sordid detail about her life even if it is mundane. I can't get enough of her. Some days I totally forget the fact that I'm dying. As far as her PA duties goes, she's detail-oriented and somehow is able to perceive what my needs are before I even know.

This young, beautiful Latina, who happens to have a heart the size of the Grand Canyon, is taking better care of me than my own mother ever did and I'm loving every minute of it. Hell, I wouldn't give a shit if she never lifted a finger in this house again. I just want, need, her companionship and I'm willing to pay through the nose to have it. Isn't it ironic? All I ever wanted from women was sex. I could never get enough of it. But with Raquel it's an entirely different story because she is an ENDLESS STORY that will never stop interesting me.

For instance, the other night, Raquel and I had just finished having dinner. She's actually a pretty decent cook. I watched her like a hawk while she cleared the table and proceeded to wash the dishes. It was poetry in motion. There I sat, fascinated by every minuscule move she made. Suddenly, I felt the burning sensation to be close to her but not in a sexual way. So, I did something the old MSG would have never done. I offered to help. She graciously accepted my offer and assigned me to rinse duty.

"So, what was your childhood really like? Was it a happy one?" I asked taking a plate off her hands.

"I was raised in a strict, religious home with three older protective brothers always keeping a close eye on me. It was like having my own secret service detail," Raquel said with what sounded like a bit of resentment in her voice. "Let's just say being the fourth child of a low-income family did not entitle me to too much. Both my wardrobe and toys were handed down to me. I never really got anything brand-spanking new."

"It sounds like your family went through some pretty tough times," I commented.

"Growing up, I may not have had much in the way of material things. But there was one thing this little Mexican-American spitfire did have plenty of, and that was IMAGINATION! Believe me when I say that I used it quite often, especially when it came to entrepreneurial pursuits," Raquel said with a reminiscent look in her eyes.

"In what ways did you use your imagination?"

"Well since my parents couldn't afford to give us an allowance or lavish gifts, my brothers and I had to rely heavily on our resourcefulness. While other kids in the neighborhood wasted their time on bogus activities, we spent the days brainstorming ways to make money."

I took another soapy plate off her hands. "Actually, it sounds like a great way to grow up. I'd say you had a character-building childhood."

Raquel paused and looked at me as if a light bulb had just been turned on in that cute head of hers. "You know, I've never thought of it that way, but hey, I think you're right."

We spoke about her wonder years long after the dishes had been washed, rinsed, and dried. I enjoyed our one-on-one interaction so much that now I'm going to make it a point to help her clean up more often after having dinner. Spending time with Raquel is so much fun and it comes effortlessly. I don't have to work hard to impress her and she's so easy to talk to. There's no sexual cat and mouse game needed here because the relationship we have started to build is not based on lust, at least not on my end. If it was, hell I would have already tried to nail her, FAST and FURIOUSLY. Going that route would end the relationship with her too quickly and I don't want that to happen.

There's an old saying that goes: The bigger they are, the harder they fall. Well, when it comes to matters of the heart, I think this adage is applicable: The older they are, the harder they fall. Ever since Raquel moved in, I've started the process of undergoing a complete transformation. Before she arrived at my front door, I was nothing but a hard-core, hard-nosed, hard-assed workaholic living a baneful existence. Realistically speaking, I had already thrown in the towel and quit living a long time before being told by Dr. Campbell that I had stage four lung cancer. Then Raquel stepped into my world and she has breathed new life into me. Don't get me wrong, I'm still a money-hungry workaholic. That will never change. The difference now is that work is no longer the only thing on my mind. Now it's her I think about most of the time.

I hate to admit it but, Raquel has made me forget all about the high and mighty dollar. I always used to ask myself, "Where is my next buck coming from?" Now I keep asking myself, "When am I going to get to spend more time with her?" Like now for instance, while she is out of the house running some errands for me, I should be working on my new book. It should have been finished by now but somehow the writing isn't flowing all that well. Maybe Raquel's right about me penning another book on self-discipline. I've written so many books on the topic, perhaps Michael Stephen Grant has covered this ground pretty well and the time has come to move on to new terrain. The question is: What else can I write about?

Instead of focusing and trying to come up with some fresh ideas, here I am sitting at the kitchen table with Raquel's laptop in front of me. She accidentally left it powered on before leaving and I'm about to poke around in her business. So, what if it can be construed as invasion of privacy? The woman should have thought about that before hightailing it out of here without making sure her laptop was turned off. I'm sure she would do the same thing if I inadvertently left my computer on. The temptation is just too great and lately I've been wondering if she is seeing anyone. Okay, okay what I really want to know is if she's fucking someone. So, here goes nothing!

***

As it turned out, I only had about an hour to go through all of Raquel's laptop files before she walked into the house with two large bags full of fresh groceries. The second I heard the garage door opening and closing, I quickly exited, pressed the sleep button, and went into my office hoping she wouldn't suspect any foul play. Even though my time on her laptop was short, I put it to good use. While sticking my nose where it didn't belong, I came upon two interesting files and of course I clicked on both.

One of them was a file that contained dozens of images of Raquel and a rather attractive woman who had a great ass on her. They were smiling and embracing one another in most of the pics. The funny thing is that Raquel and this mystery woman seemed to be really into each other. *OMG! Can it be that Raquel is a lesbian?* The mere thought of it makes me cringe. I can literally feel all the blood draining from my face. If she really is a lesbian, I don't stand a chance with her.

Up until the point I discovered the photos, in my eyes Raquel was the epitome of womanhood and now that perception I had of her is pretty much shot to hell. Or is it? One way or another, I have to find out the truth but, this isn't exactly the kind of thing you can bring up on the fly. Am I supposed to ask her if she prefers fucking women over men point-blank? Or is this the kind of investigation that requires more of a direct hands-on approach if you catch my drift? While I try to figure this out, let me tell you about the other file I stumbled upon. Apparently before leaving to go run errands, Raquel was working on her current work-in-progress and being the conniving son of a bitch that I am, of course I couldn't resist helping myself to a sneak preview.

After having read only a few paragraphs, I was hooked. Man, is there anything this woman can't do? Her novel is about an extremely successful and heavily sought out beautiful literary agent who has become disillusioned by how superficial her life and relationships have become. After doing some heavy-duty soul searching, the literary agent decides to leave her charmed existence behind by faking her own death and signing up as a volunteer for the Doctors without Borders program in a third world country under a fictitious name. I was just getting to a juicy part of the novel when I heard Raquel's footsteps in the garage. As much as I wanted to continue reading, I had to abort the mission and make a beeline for my office before getting caught.

I waited for Raquel to make her way into the kitchen with the groceries before poking my head out of my office and asking her, "Do you need help in there?"

"Nope, I got it," she said, dismissing me with a wave of her hand. "You keep right on working. I'm just going to put away the groceries and fix us something to eat. In case you haven't noticed, it's almost dinnertime."

"Yeah, it sure is," I concurred after checking my watch. Suddenly, I saw the perfect opportunity to do some probing into her personal life. "Raquel, you don't have to make dinner for us. It's Friday night. Don't you have a date or something?"

Raquel paused and thought about what I asked. "Not tonight," she replied casually.

I could pretty much tell that was going to be all the intel I'd be gathering up this Friday afternoon so, I dropped it by saying, "Oh, okay. Dinner would be nice. I can eat."

"Well, don't be getting all these great expectations about dinner. I'm just opening a bottle of wine and preparing some finger foods for us to snack on," Raquel explained.

"Beggars can't be choosers," I quipped back. "Sounds good to me."

Raquel gifted me with one of her sweet, radiant smiles. "I'll call you when it's ready."

About forty-five minutes later, Raquel called me into the kitchen. I walked in and found an opened bottle of wine, two glasses, and a full spread of goodies artistically arranged throughout the counter. The sight of it all made my stomach growl and I'm sure my eyes gleamed as well. The thought that she would go through all this trouble for me went to my head and quickly.

"This looks amazing," I said. "Thanks for going through the trouble."

"Oh, it was no trouble at all," Raquel corrected me. "Sit your ass down and dig in while I pour you a glass of wine."

"I don't drink, remember?"

"Well, tonight you do," Raquel said with authority. "I want to drink and I'm not doing it alone. Besides, I think you'll like this kind of wine."

"What is it?"

"It's an Italian Sweet Moscato," Raquel said as she poured some into my glass. "It goes great with some of the cheeses I've laid out for you."

Raquel gestured at the empty plate she had placed in front of me. "Go, ahead and fill up your plate."

While I filled my plate with cheese, bread, grapes, and cold cuts, Raquel poured herself a glass of wine. She came around the counter, sat down next to me on the other barstool, and went to town filling up her plate. She was wearing a cute denim skirt which she had to hike up a bit when sitting down and my eyes couldn't help but zero in on her nicely sculpted olive-colored legs.

"Someone is ravenous tonight," I said jokingly. "Hey, why did you pour a lot more wine in your glass than mine?"

Raquel took a sip of wine, closed her eyes, and let out a soft, sexy moan. "Because I'm a professional wine drinker and you're not," she claimed.

"Guilty as charged," I admitted. Right then and there I decided to toy a little with my gracious hostess. "Oh, I see what you're trying to do."

"What are you talking about?" Raquel asked after taking another sip of wine.

"Don't pretend you're not trying to get me drunk so you can have your way with me," I ventured to say.

"You haven't even taken a sip of wine yet and already your judgment is warped. Besides, the last time I checked; you can't rape the willing." Raquel said to me. "Somehow you don't strike me as the kind of man who needs to be pumped full of alcohol or drugs to want to have sex."

"Oh no, then what kind of man am I?"

"You're the kind who will have sex at the drop of a hat with anyone, anytime, anywhere," Raquel said, wagging a finger at me as if it were a miniature windshield wiper.

I smiled demurely at her and confessed. "Guilty as charged. So, if you want to arrest me, go right ahead. I won't object if you want to frisk or strip search me either," I said.

"Nice try. I'll give you an A for effort," Raquel tossed back. "Now shut up and take a sip of your wine before it ages another year and we have to wish it Happy Birthday."

Somehow Raquel had a knack for getting me to do whatever she wanted. She barked out commands and I obeyed like a faithful dog. That's how things worked since the day she moved in with me. I listened to her about everything, don't ask me why. Thinking about how much I respected her, I tilted my head back a little and took a sip of the wine. The Moscato tasted so pleasant that I let it swirl in my mouth before swallowing.

"You ain't kidding. This shit is good," I blurted out. "Hey, I wouldn't mind drinking this once in a while."

Raquel reclined further back into the barstool and shook her head giving me an indication that I said or did something terribly wrong. "Don't ever refer to fine tasting wine as shit," she said. "All you did was spoil a perfectly sophisticated moment for us."

"Uh, sorry?"

"Since you're a newbie, I let your wine blunder slide, just this once," Raquel said.

We continued to chat, snack on munchies, and drink our wine without any regard for the passing of time. I had just finished my second glass and was starting to feel tipsy and horny, which rather surprised me considering that my ability to launch had been inconsistent for months now. As for Raquel, she was like on her fourth or fifth glass. The woman wasn't kidding about her ability to consume alcohol without losing her decorum and good judgment. There was no doubt in my mind that even though I was probably two and a half times her size, she could easily drink me under the counter. I felt sorry for any man, myself included, who thought he could buy her a couple of stiff drinks and wait for her to keel over stinking drunk with her succulent looking legs wide open. That shit was never going to happen, but still, you can't blame a guy for trying.

One thing about Raquel that I did learn was that the more she drank, the more confident and flirtier she got. The whole time we were talking, laughing, and having a good time, I couldn't help but wonder if she found me attractive at all. In a way, my heart would be broken if she didn't. It would be a first. All women found me attractive or at least that was what I was led to believe. The only reason Raquel would not find me sexually appealing would be if she was a lesbian which was a strong possibility. Still, the chemistry between us was undeniable and electric. At least that's the way I felt.

The entire time we were sitting next to each other, our body posture seemed to naturally gravitate toward one another and there were a few times Raquel touched my knee softly. Let me tell you her touch spiked my blood pressure on the spot or maybe it was the wine. The point is that we were so into each other. We were completely alone without any outside interference. I had her all to myself and wanted this night to never end so I kept making conversation with Raquel and she didn't seem to mind.

"Tell me a story Michael Stephen Grant," Raquel requested as she poured herself yet another glass of wine.

"What kind of story?" I asked her.

Raquel raised a finger in the air and said, "I know, I know, tell me about the wildest twenty-four hours you've ever had in your life."

"Are you sure? It's going to be a triple X-Rated story."

She encouraged me by saying, "You go right ahead and don't worry about shocking me."

"Okay, I'm going to tell you about my first visit to Bangkok, Thailand. After a sixteen-hour flight I arrived in the city around midnight."

"Did you go there on business?" Raquel inquired.

"Yep. After clearing customs, I grabbed a taxi and asked to be driven to my hotel, the Grand Hyatt. It was about one o'clock in the morning when I finally got there. Due to the time difference, I was really wired up and decided that I didn't want to be alone. So, after unloading my suitcase and freshening up a bit, I ventured out on the town."

"Where did you go?"

"Well, prior to my arrival, I had already done my homework about which areas were safe and which ones to stay away from. I ended up in an area that was just a five-minute drive and then a short walk from the hotel. As I was walking to the main tourist area, I encountered a young Thai girl and her two friends who were walking toward me." I let out a loud whistle. "Man was she tiny and beautiful, the ultimate spinner. She had shoulder length jet-back hair and was wearing shorts that accentuated her pretty legs."

"So, Michael Stephan Grant has a fetish for bite-size women," Raquel commented wearing the most adorable sarcastic smile I'd ever seen. "What happened next?"

"I approached the girl, showed her a piece of paper with a name on it, and asked her if she could point me in the right direction."

"It's two blocks straight ahead on the left-hand side," the girl replied politely.

Thank you and by the way you are very pretty," I said to her in return. "Where are you and your friends going?"

"We're going home. We just watched a movie and had dinner together," the girl answered. She was the one I had set my sights on from the get go.

Then the cute girl asked me where I was going. I explained to her that I had just flown into the city from Los Angeles and was looking for a restaurant to get a bite to eat. Then I decided to go out on a limb and ask her if she and her friends cared to join me as my guests at a nearby restaurant. They all looked at each other and nodded their pretty heads in agreement. "Okay, but we can only stay for a little while. It's getting late and we have to go to work in the morning," the one that I was really horny for said.

The four of us walked across the street and into a restaurant. I ordered my usual diet Coke and got each of them a soda of their choosing. I also ordered an assortment of finger snacks. As we sat there and ate, they cross examined me about what I was doing in their country. I told them I was giving a presentation at the Grand Hyatt to a group of several hundred executives. They knew exactly where it was. Being the smooth operator that I am, I made it a point to converse with each of them. As it turned out one of the girls was twenty the other nineteen and the one I wanted to bang the most was eighteen years old. She could have been younger, but that's what I was told.

After about an hour of talking and snacking, I could tell they were all getting comfortable with me. My little spinner's name was Daeng and she was sitting next to me on the right. I wanted to hold her hand, but thought it was in bad taste to do it with her two friends sitting at the table as well. I waited for the right moment and it came when she put her left hand down by her side for a few minutes. When I saw that it was up for grabs, I helped myself and she didn't protest in any way.

"It's getting kind of late. We should probably call it a night," I said to them. "But do you girls want to meet me at the lobby of my hotel tomorrow night for dinner? They have great food with a wonderful atmosphere."

"This is getting more interesting now," Raquel said, biting into a piece of cheese.

"It gets better," I replied. "They happily accepted my invitation to dinner and, I was all set up to have company the following night. Down deep inside, I knew Daeng was mine for the taking. But one woman wasn't going to be enough for me. After all, this was Bangkok and I had heard all the stories. I wanted the entire package, all three girls in my bed at the same time. I wasn't about to settle for anything less."

Before continuing on with my story, Raquel interrupted me by saying, "Well, duh! Of course, one miniature doll wasn't going to satisfy that sexual appetite of yours. I can see how it was going to take three of them instead of one."

In realizing that I had an enthusiastic listener in Raquel, I pressed on with my account. "It was 3:00 AM when I parted company with the three girls but instead of going back to the hotel, I hailed a taxi and directed the driver to take me to the world-famous red-light district known as Patpong. I wanted to see one of the wild, sex-filled shows I had heard so much about."

Raquel chimed in again. "Yeah, I've heard about those shows."

"Since I didn't exactly want to see the show alone, I asked the taxi driver to stop several blocks from the area so I could walk the rest of the way. The night wasn't over yet and I thought perhaps I could still get lucky."

"Did you?" Raquel asked.

"I came upon two older women who were walking with a much younger one who definitely caught my eye. She had long black hair, an adorable face, and a great little body on her. I thought she'd make a tasty appetizer before my main course the next night."

I paused only long enough to take another sip of wine then went on. "As our paths were about to cross the young girl looked at me and said hello. I quickly knew that she was for hire but I wasn't about to break my golden rule of never paying for sex regardless of how horny I get."

"Oh, I see, it is beneath Michael Stephen Grant to pay for pussy," Raquel interjected.

"Damn straight," I reiterated.

"Anyway, not one to give up so easily, one of the older ladies accompanying the girl spoke English, so I told her I was going to see a show and then head back to my hotel room. I stressed to her that I was a very nice man and would take good care of her young friend if she accompanied me."

"What did the lady say?"

"She told me it would cost me 600 *baht* which was equivalent to twenty bucks here in the U.S. Again, I said to her that I was just looking to see a show with someone, nothing else."

Raquel giggled. "I can't believe she couldn't smell the bullshit and standing so close to you."

"Then the lady lowered the price on me. She said 300 *baht*. I smiled politely, then thanked them, and got ready to leave."

"Then what happened?"

"After the older woman finally got the hint that I wasn't going to pay for sex, she turned to the younger one and said something to her in Thai. As I was about ready to leave, she said something to the young lady again and they both smiled. Then the lady I had been negotiating all along with turned to me and said, 'Her name is Nan. She will go with you.'"

It looked like Raquel was about to fall off the barstool when I relayed that part of the story to her. "You are one lucky bastard," she blurted out, her speech a bit slurred now.

I paused to help steady her and then went on with the story. "Nan and I walked hand-in-hand to the one show I had to see. I can't remember exactly what it was called but I'll say it was The Flying Fuck Show. There was a one drink minimum so, I ordered a Diet Coke and a regular one for Nan. Before us there was a stage with a table on it and a nude girl bent over grasping the sides of it. Approximately twenty-five feet above the stage was a large platform. On that platform was another nude girl but this one was strapped into a harness hooked up to some kind of pendulum device. She also had a dildo attached to her. Let me tell you this was no small dildo either. It was easily nine inches and fairly thick."

"This is getting more interesting by the second," Raquel interjected.

"All of a sudden the music started up and there was a countdown in English, FIVE, FOUR, THREE, TWO, ONE, and the girl on the platform jumped down in the direction of the other one who was bent over the end of the table. Unfortunately, she missed on the first attempt. The device pulled her back up to the platform for a second attempt. She adjusted everything, raised her hand, and the countdown began once more. THREE, TWO, ONE, and within a second or two—BANG—she nailed the girl bent over on the table who screamed. The high flyin' girl unshackled herself from the pendulum device and started fucking the girl grasping the table, who appeared to be loving every second of it. I was totally blown away."

"I'm sure you were. How about your date? Did she like it?" Raquel asked.

"Nan seemed to enjoy the show as well. After we finished our drinks, I decided to bring her back to the hotel room with me. Although she didn't speak a lick of English, she was a real sweetheart. Like the other young girl Daeng I had met earlier, she was also tiny, probably five feet tall and 100 pounds."

"What's the matter MSG? Afraid to pick on someone your own size?" Raquel teased.

I laughed a little then continued. "When we got back to the hotel room, I politely suggested that she sit down and make herself comfortable. She smiled and complied. I also asked her if she wanted to take a shower before coming to bed. Nan did and when finished, she came out with a towel around her body. I took a shower as well. It was getting to be 4:30 AM and I needed to get a few hours of sleep before getting to the gym and doing my presentation."

"So, what happened next?" Raquel demanded to know.

"Since I picked up this girl from the red-light district, I wasn't about to take any chances. I put on a condom and did not go down on her. I slowly took off her towel and mounted her in the quick and traditional missionary position. I used my right hand to guide my penis inside that small opening of hers. I thrusted in and out several times until we both had an orgasm then we both quickly went to sleep. I got up after having gotten a few hours of sleep and found that she had already left the hotel room."

"How did your presentation go that morning?" Raquel asked me as she popped another bite-size morsel of cheese into her mouth.

"Surprisingly, it went rather well, especially considering the fact that I hadn't slept all that much," I replied. "But I didn't care because I was all revved up about the possibility of having three beautiful Thai girls in my bed that evening. "

"Did the girl's show up?"

"They sure did. All three of them were wearing dresses too. I greeted and escorted them to where a large buffet-style dinner was being served in the hotel. The dinner wasn't cheap but it earned me quite a few brownie points and I planned to cash them in later. After two hours of laughing and having a good time, I told them that I didn't feel like going out on the town again. Then I asked them if they just wanted to come to my room and watch a movie with me."

Raquel shook her head in disbelief, "They actually fell for that line?"

"Hook, line, and sinker," I quipped back with biting sarcasm. "When we got to the room, I instructed Daeng and her friends to take their shoes off and make themselves comfortable. My suite had a spacious living area equipped with a sofa bed and large flat screen television. I told the girls to open up the sofa bed so we could all cuddle up together and watch the movie. They complied and suspected nothing."

"Oh my God! These girls were so fucking naïve," Raquel yelled out.

"We found some action flick to watch that neither of us had seen before. So, there we all were huddled up in the same bed and I of course was lying next to Daeng. The time had come for Michael Stephen Grant to try and pull off one of the biggest accomplishments of my life, me and three other women."

"So, what came next?"

"About twenty minutes into the movie, I put my arm around Daeng and started rubbing her shoulder softly. She didn't resist and actually got closer to me and put her hand on my lap. I reached over and turned Daeng's head toward me and kissed her right on the lips. She reciprocated. Two minutes later, I did it again, but this time we remained locked for a longer period of time. After getting up to go to the bathroom I came back and purposely lied between Daeng and the older friend to my right. As I was kissing Daeng, I started touching the other girl's leg and she didn't push it away. Then I grabbed her hand and brought her closer to me and Daeng. In turn, the older girl grabbed her other friend and brought her closer. Soon all of us were much closer."

"I gotta hand it to you. You're a smooth operator with the young chicks," Raquel commented. "And I do emphasize, young chicks."

"Are you through chastising me? Do you want to hear the rest of the story?" I asked Raquel a bit annoyed.

"Sure, go right ahead," she said.

"So, then I asked Daeng if she would mind if I kissed her friend too."

"How did she respond?"

"She said it was up to me. I'll never forget those words. It was clearly an open invitation to turn the heat up. These girls wanted to please me because I had taken good care of them. Actually, I had spent almost $200.00 on dinner for the four of us, which is a lot of money in Thailand."

"This coming from the man who said he never pays for sex," Raquel was quick to point out.

"I couldn't stop kissing Daeng, but at the same time, I started moving my left hand up her dress. My right hand went up the other girl's dress. Oh, what a feeling! They had that beautiful soft Asian skin. Finally, I stopped kissing Daeng and started in on the second girl for a few minutes while my hands travelled up her skirt. Then I stopped kissing Girl #2 and focused on Girl #3. I kissed her hard and took things even further. I laid the girl down and pulled her dress all the way up. Then I began grinding her while looking straight at Daeng. I could tell she was getting even more excited. Then I stopped the grinding and gently positioned Girl #3 closer to Daeng and went back to kissing my youngest sweetheart."

"Sounds like you were about to score a triple homerun," Raquel said.

"You got that right. At this point, I started feeling all of the girl's pussies and they were wet as can be. They still had their dresses on and that was perfectly okay with me. I wanted it that way. One of the girls, I can't remember which one, took off my pants and underwear. What I do recall is kissing all three of them passionately. Then I grabbed Daeng and brought her closer to the oldest girl."

"Did she get the hint that you wanted what every man wants—some girl-on-girl action?" Raquel asked.

"She did. So, I brought Daeng and the older girl close to one another. Then I pulled back and started to rub each one of their pussies. Immediately after they had locked lips, I went after Girl #3, bringing her closer to the action. I grabbed her hand and motioned for her to lift the skirt of the oldest girl and together we pulled her panties off. I went down on Girl#2 and after a short while I recruited Girl #3 to take over and she did. Then I went down on Girl #3 and all hell broke loose. She had an orgasm within minutes."

By this time, Raquel's face had skepticism written all over it but I went on with the telling of my story. "Then I went over to Daeng, lifted her skirt and slipped off her panties. With the intention of giving her a mind-blowing orgasm, I went down on her. At this point, there were pussies and lips everywhere. Everyone's clothes were off by now and none of us were watching the movie. We were having our own little orgy and it went on for hours."

"Went on for hours . . . I find that hard to believe," Raquel said, rolling her eyes.

"Really! We were all kissing lips and pussies. Not only did each of them suck my dick but at some point, two of the girls blew me at the same time. I actually thought I had died and gone to heaven. How I wanted the night to never end. I kept going down on all the girls and giving each one of them multiple orgasms. But I didn't want to cum yet. Actually, I was hoping that I wouldn't cum at all. I wanted to keep going and going as long as humanly possible."

Raquel leaned back in the bar stool and crossed her legs. "When did it finally end?"

"Several hours later Daeng climbed on top of me. Like I said before, she was the ultimate spinner. She wanted it hard and deep and of course I obliged. But I still wasn't ready to cum. While Daeng was on top of me the other girls were still kissing on her and each other. I wanted to fuck all of them badly. After Daeng had another orgasm, I pulled her off and put the other girl on top of me. We were going crazy until she had an orgasm, but I was still able to hold out. There was one more girl to go. I put the last girl on top of me and she climaxed quickly. As soon as she did, I exploded in a MAJOR way. And that Raquel was the craziest and wildest twenty-four hours, I've ever experienced in my life."

Raquel got off the barstool and gave me a standing ovation. "I have to hand it to you MSG. That is one hell of a story. I'm going to name that story Banging in Bangkok."

I cracked up on the spot. "That's hilarious!"

"Tell me something. Do you have more stories like that?"

"A whole bunch more, why?"

"Instead of writing another book about self-discipline, you should try your hand at writing about your sexual escapades," Raquel suggested matter-of-factly.

"That's an interesting idea! "I blurted out with bubbling enthusiasm.

"Now if you'll excuse me, I'm gonna clean up and go to bed. It's late," Raquel announced.

"Hey kiddo, why don't you go on up to bed? I'll clean up around here?"

Raquel flashed me an appreciative smile. "Really? That would be great. I'm really tired."

"Sure. Get outta here. But first answer me this question. Does this story make you think any less of me?"

Raquel fell silent for a few seconds then she scrunched her eyebrows. "So, you're a manwhore. Big deal! You're not the first and you certainly won't be the last. You were just doing what comes naturally to a man."

I must say her response really surprised me. A part of me expected her to be judgmental and critical, but instead she listened to my story objectively and may have even found it to be highly entertaining.

Before I could say anything in response, Raquel quickly added. "Personally, I could never fall in love with a manwhore. My type is something entirely different."

Having said that, Raquel turned around and headed for the stairs leaving me alone with my thoughts. *"Shit Shit! Shit! She is a lesbian."*

Chapter Seven

Cowboys and Indians

Is she, or isn't she a lesbian? This question has been driving me crazy for the past month or so. My gnawing curiosity about Raquel's sexual preferences keeps growing and growing by the second and has now become a dark, gloomy cloud of epic proportions that hovers over me day and night. I curse the day that I stumbled upon those suggestive photos of her and the mystery woman. Every time I think I'm ready to ask her if she's batting for the other team, I chicken out. Another equally perplexing question is why do I give such a flying fuck about it? Perhaps the Olympic-sized torch I am carrying around for my trusted PA is starting to show big-time. Whatever the true underlying reason is, this itch of mine has got to be scratched. I can't stand it anymore. One way or another, tonight I am finding out if Raquel likes dick or pussy.

For the past four weeks, Raquel and I have had a stand-in dinner date and it all started that Friday evening when we drank wine, snacked on appetizers, and I told her my *Banging in Bangkok* story. Ever since then, on Friday nights, Raquel cooks up something special, then we sit and talk up until the wee hours of the morning. In the process, not only have we bonded in a major way, but she's turned me into a lover of sweet tasting wine. What else can a dying manwhore ask for? Raquel is a beautiful package and I'm more than ready to unwrap it, if only I can somehow muster up the courage. I've had plenty of chances to do so but every time I think the magic moment has arrived, I let my older male insecurities get the best of me and the golden opportunity simply passes me by.

As much as it pains me to admit it, I don't feel 100 percent confident that I can nail Raquel Lopez for various reasons. First there is the unanswered question about her sexual preference. If in fact she is a lesbian, there ain't no swinging dick big enough in Texas that's going to make her defect to the other side. On the flipside of the coin, if she isn't one, then the question becomes: Can I produce enough fuel to launch my rocket straight into what perhaps could very well be the final frontier for me? There is nothing worse, no greater upset or humiliation for a man than having a "failure to launch."

Another reason for my fear of not being able to perform optimally is that lately I haven't been feeling all that great. Some of the symptoms that Dr. Campbell warned me about have started to surface and these days I've been feeling fatigued and short of breath. I also get headaches more frequently and sometimes moderate pain keeps me up at night. We are now in the midst of summer, approximately four months since my diagnosis. I know it's going to get far worse but, I'll cross that bridge when I get to it. For now, I'm on a mission to boldly explore what promises to be an exciting new galaxy and nothing is going to stop me tonight.

Honestly, I can't remember the last time I felt so psyched out about something. Despite the fact I'm not feeling so hot on the inside, on the outside I'm still a total hunk, at least that's what my full-length mirror in my bedroom confirmed earlier. In preparation for this much anticipated Friday evening, I quit working early enough for me to do some personal grooming and take a long shower. I decided that if I'm going to impress Raquel right out of her clothes, I have to pull out the heavy artillery which is my favorite pair of jeans that I fill up quite nicely and snug black muscle shirt that really shows off my canons. These two old trusted friends of mine have never let me down before and I'm certainly counting on them tonight to get the job done. I'm topping all of this off with a splash or two of my expensive French male cologne guaranteed to drive any woman mad with passion.

One of the things I enjoy the most about our weekly "eat and chat" sessions is that Raquel is giving me some really interesting viable book ideas. As a result, I've been able to finish my current-work-in-progress which really had me stumped for a long time. With her help, I've been able to start writing two new books simultaneously and my goal is to finish them before I kick the bucket. One of the books is about me being a lifelong workaholic and the hefty price I've paid for living this kind of self-destructive lifestyle. The other work is a collection of all of my sexual escapades and let me tell you this is the project I am most "excited" about, in more ways than one.

Life sure is full of surprises. I used to be the kind of man who exploited women for their anatomy. Yet, at the end of the day, after having had my fill of pussy and ass, I was still left feeling hungry and unsatisfied. But with Raquel it's entirely different. All I seem to want to do is exploit her for her genius. Raquel feeds me intellectually like no other woman ever has. She is the only one who has been able to complete me and. she's done this without once having to remove her clothing or bend over. Now that's what I call pure, unadulterated talent.

Don't get me wrong, our relationship is not all one-sided. Raquel is also reaping the benefits of my talents as a world leading life and organization mentor. I'm coaching her on how to develop better self-discipline and time management skills and I am beginning to see a great deal of improvement. I'm also trying to help her reduce some of that credit card debt she's accumulated from having to live from paycheck to paycheck for many years. I genuinely care about my larger- than-life personal assistant and want nothing more than for her to be successful long after I'm gone.

Now between us, I really do think that Raquel enjoys listening to my erotic adventures every Friday night. Tell me, what girl needs a vibrator when she's got MSG to tell her bedtime stories? Personally, I think my racy accounts and how I tell them make her horny and in just a few hours I am going to put that theory to the test. Last week, I told her about the time I screwed a Human Barbie Doll which turned out to be one of the most regrettable sexual experiences I can remember having.

The woman in question was a trainer at the gym where I went every morning for fifteen years. All the other women envied her and thought she was in fantastic shape. However, the men, including myself, thought she was an anorexic bitch, except for the ones who loved HUGE knockers. Her name was Laura and she had these size 36DD plastic boobs that were clearly way too big for that anorexic frame of hers. She had long, wavy blonde hair and green eyes which contributed to her human Barbie doll looks. What I remember most about Laura is that she babbled non-stop while others at the gym were trying to work-out and she had a flat-as-a-pancake ass.

One day, I ended up next to Laura on the elliptical machines. Out of the blue, she started talking to me about an incident being featured on the Fox News station, which we happened to be watching at the time. At first, I was only being cordial and politely responded about that incident and then we started talking about a few other topics. I quickly realized that she was no blonde bimbo. Actually, Laura was rather intelligent and, we had quite a bit in common. Her political world views were similar to mine. She was extremely disciplined when it came to her exercise routine and she also happened to be a writer just like me.

From that day forward we chatted more frequently. Although her body looked pathetic, she had a nice personality and we seemed to click. She was married and had a teenage daughter. She also knew that I was married as she had seen my wife at the gym with me on several occasions.

"Where has your wife been? I haven't seen her for a while," she asked me one day.

"We just bought another home out of state. She's there trying to get things situated," I replied. I don't know what possessed me to do so but I quickly added, "She's going to be there probably for the next three to six months."

"Congratulations. I hope all goes well with the new purchase," she said to me.

A week later, Laura asked me if I wanted to have coffee with her one morning after our work-out.

Being the serial cheater that I was, I accepted her invitation. Then I said, "I make some really good Latin-style coffee. Would you like to stop by my house before going to the gym and I'll make you a cup?"

"Yes, I would love to try some," Laura responded.

Laura came over for coffee two mornings later at precisely 3:00 AM. For my viewing pleasure, she was wearing her typical workout clothes, long tight spandex pants and short T-Shirt with a sports bra underneath holding back those man-made large boobs of hers. We were sitting in the kitchen sipping coffee when I leaned over five minutes into our conversation, placed my right hand on her shoulder and moved in for a kiss. She was an excellent kisser. I took her coffee cup and placed it on the counter then I grabbed her hand.

"Come with me," I said to her in a commanding voice.

I took her into the guest bedroom. Then I picked Laura up and gently laid her down on the bed. She wasn't as light as I thought she'd be. I had forgotten that she had quite a bit of muscle mass and besides those puppies of hers had to weigh at least five pounds each. Once I was able to get her situated in an ideal fuck position, the kissing intensified and I felt a strong impulse to feel those big implants. Up until that point, since I wasn't much of a boob man, I had never felt implants before. Since the opportunity had presented itself, I figured I'd see what all the fuss was about. So, I reached out and gave those lemons a squeeze. What a major let down it was. They felt like hard plastic, but I was still horny and, the Human Barbie Doll knew how to use them.

Laura showed me no mercy whatsoever. She teased me with those big melons by rubbing them all over my body. She even took the initiative to go down on me before I had the chance to work my magic South of the Border. She began by kissing the head of my penis and then sucked on it slowly. In a matter of a few seconds, she had swallowed it whole without gagging. She was definitely a highly experienced cocksucker. Something told me she had done this probably a hundred times before—Laura was that good. When she was finished sucking, she took my wet penis and rubbed it between her huge melons.

Then it was my turn to perform. I pulled my penis from her mouth otherwise I would have shot my load right then and there, which has never been the MSG way. Without the slightest hesitation, I went down on her. As skinny as Laura was, she had an orgasm in less than a minute. Then I came back up and slid my penis into her wet pussy and after five or six strokes we climaxed together. It actually felt pretty good. As gross as her flat-ass was, her pussy still served its purpose in a functional way. Right after our sex romp we cleaned up a bit and headed to the gym to get our work-out in. This casual sex affair of ours went on for a few months until I moved out of town.

***

"A penny for your thoughts?"

It isn't the sound of a small copper penny landing on the island counter, but rather Raquel's voice that brings me back into the present. I turn around and am stunned by what I see. My PA is standing before me wearing what can best be described as a Pocahontas costume. The sight of her makes my cock swell up a little, which gives me an indication that all systems are going to be a go for this evening. Raquel is a vision of downright sexiness and I now want her more than ever.

"Why didn't you tell me we were dressing up for dinner tonight? I would've whipped out my sexy French Maid costume?"

"Don't be silly. I'm actually going to a summer costume party." She takes a couple of small steps back and strikes up some seductive poses. "You like?"

"Me like."

Are you kidding? My eyes are the only thing I don't want to take off her tonight. Raquel looks absolutely yummy and with her features can easily pass as a beautiful Native American maiden and I sure would like to stick my arrowhead into her, well, you know . . . I don't know where she got her costume, but it's stunning and revealing.

The upper part looks to be a bustier of some kind and is made of suede. Even though breasts are not my favorite part of a woman's anatomy, Raquel's babies look mouthwatering and ready to burst out of the small garment. The matching fringed mini-skirt she's wearing, also made of suede with multi-colored beads on it, shows off her shapely and flawless legs nicely. What really completes her ensemble though is the pair of knee-high moccasin boots she's sporting. Her usual voluminous, black hair is being kept in place by a heavily beaded headband with a turquoise and red feather attached to it. Raquel in that costume is certainly capable of taming the Wild West in Michael Stephen Grant. Shit, not even an entire tribe of Cherokee Indians can stop me from moving forward with my plan to ambush Raquel and ravage her body later on.

I'm so wrapped up in the vision of loveliness, when Raquel says to me, "So, are you hungry?"

"Famished," I respond but food is the furthest thing from my mind right now.

"Great, I made you my award-winning chicken enchiladas. They are in the oven keeping warm. When you're ready all you have to do is take them out and serve yourself."

At first Raquel's instructions don't quite register because I'm too busy feasting my eyes on her. Then suddenly it hits me. "Wait a minute! Aren't you joining me?"

"No, I told you. I'm going to a costume party," Raquel replies.

"When?"

"As soon as my date picks me up," she says rather nonchalantly.

Her outright statement makes me go ballistic. "What? You have a date?"

"Yes, and why do you seem so surprised?"

"Well, you haven't mentioned it to me all week," I fire back defensively.

"I didn't know I needed to advertise it or get your approval for that matter."

Even though I know perfectly well that Raquel has a valid point, the intense jealousy I happen to be feeling at the moment won't let it go. "Who's the guy?"

Raquel huffs and puffs a little then crosses her arms. "His name is Kit Pettigrew.

"What kind of stupid name is that?"

"He's a professional horse buyer and trainer."

"Where did you meet him, at the local honkytonk bar?"

"At the grocery store," Raquel corrects.

Things are starting to heat up between Raquel and me but not in the way I had hoped it would. I wag my finger at her and say, "That's it. From now on, I'm doing all the grocery shopping around here."

Raquel's eyes grow larger than what they already are. "MSG, what's wrong with you? Are . . . are . . . you jealous that I have a date tonight?"

Great! Now I'm being put on trial. It wouldn't be so bad if I wasn't guilty of being jealous and mad as hell that the object of my desires is spending the evening with another man. Just then I get the epiphany I've been waiting for. *Raquel is going on a date with a man. She isn't a lesbian after all. She does like dick and now all*

I have to do is get her to want mine. MSG ain't afraid of a little competition. Bring it on! Suddenly my demeanor changes and I put on a brave face.

"Of course, I'm not jealous. Concerned is more like it," I say to Raquel. "How well do you know this Kit Pettigrew?"

"About two weeks' worth."

". . . And you met him at the grocery store?"

"Yeah, it was in the middle of the day. We both happened to be browsing in the wine section at the same time," Raquel volunteers.

"Wait a minute! I thought cowboys drank beer or whiskey, not wine," I point out.

"Most of them do, but not Kit. He's an exception to the rule. A rugged, handsome cowboy who drinks wine, now that's definitely for me," Raquel confesses with a naughty look in her eye and lopsided grin.

Once again, the green-eyed monster known as JEALOUSY rears its ugly head inside of me. "Cowboys smell like cow manure and aren't very smart."

"Not this one," Raquel tosses back.

Right on cue, the doorbell rings and interrupts our debate. "That's him now," Raquel whispers. "Be nice."

She straightens up and starts to adjust her Pocahontas miniskirt while I look on—thinking how easily I could swipe it off with just one single, fluid move. How is a man, especially one who has so much manhood to offer, supposed to think straight in a situation like this? Only one word comes to mind and that is CASTRATION.

So many thoughts run through my brain as I watch Raquel walk to the door with the rhythm of a quarter racehorse. Then it occurs to me that perhaps this Mystery Cowboy is not going to be so hot after all. Maybe there will be a bald spot underneath his cowboy hat and I don't have anything to worry about. Holding on to that vision, I stand my ground and with bated breath wait to meet the competition.

A tidal wave of disappointment swoops in on me when Raquel walks into the kitchen hanging on to her date's arm. Just my luck Kit Pettigrew happens to be a real man's man. I hate to admit it but if I was a woman, I'd definitely want to do him. He looks to be about 6'1" and in really great shape or maybe his attire is really flattering on him. Judging by the large bulge in the crotch area of his painted-on jeans I can tell he's definitely male porn star material. The best way to describe him is a hybrid between Paul Newman and Matthew McConaughey and what's killing me the most is that Raquel is practically undressing him with her eyes. Why the hell did she have to bring home a Greek God in cowboy boots?

In seeing that she's totally distracted by Kit Pettigrew's dreamy looks, I take a few steps forward and extend my hand out to him in greeting. "Hello there. I'm Michael Stephen Grant. It's nice to meet you."

Kit Pettigrew reacts immediately by reaching out and shaking my hand. "Of course, you're Raquel's boss. It's a real pleasure to meet you, Sir."

The fact that he called me Sir makes me want to go for his throat and strangle him with my bare hands. The nerve of him showing me the proper respect you'd show someone who is a lot older. I swear he's trying to imply that I'm old enough to be Raquel's father and not young enough to be her lover. In my mind he's just declared war. Or could it be that I'm overreacting? Maybe my lust for Raquel has blinded me so badly and is making me have outrageous thoughts.

As if reading my mind, the cowboy who looks like he just stepped out of a men's underwear ad says, "Raquel tells me you're a writer, just like her."

Again, I feel offended. "Published author," I correct him on the spot. "There's a big difference between the two."

Realizing the error of his ways, Kit Pettigrew flashes an easygoing smile. "Yes, of course," he concedes.

"I don't suppose you read much," I ask him flat-out, hoping to prove my point to Raquel that cowboys from Texas are not intellectual human beings.

"Actually, I've been an avid reader since I was a young boy. Mark Twain and Louis Lamour are my absolute favorite authors," he announces. "As you can see, I much prefer compelling fiction versus self-help books with all their psychobabble and mumbo jumbo," Kit Pettigrew adds. His easygoing smile has made a sudden disappearance and seems to have been replaced with one that telepathically conveys: I know what you're up to old man, but I'm taking the woman you want, TONIGHT. At least that's the message I'm getting loud and clear.

Raquel chimes into the conversation by saying, "Kit, shouldn't we be going?"

The cowboy takes his eyes off me and focuses them on Raquel, no correction, her cleavage. "Whatever you say gorgeous." Then he glances back at me and asks, "Isn't she the most beautiful Pocahontas you've ever seen in your life?"

At last, the cowboy and I finally see eye-to-eye on something. The trouble is we both seem to want the same thing. "So, you kids are off to some kind of summer costume party? That's interesting."

"In my circle of friends, it's kind of a tradition. I can't wait to introduce Raquel to everyone," Kit Pettigrew says with bubbling enthusiasm. "Shall we?" he says to the lovely Pocahontas standing and doting at his side.

"I'll just get my purse," she answers. Before walking off, Raquel looks at me and says, "There's no need to wait up for me. I've got my house keys."

"Don't worry Mr. Grant. I'll bring her back home safe and sound. Tonight, Raquel is in good hands," the cowboy assures me.

As soon as they exit the house, I rush to the front door after them to see what he's driving. Just as I thought, he's got himself one of those high dollar pick-up trucks, the kind where hot looking cowboys like him can comfortably bang any chick they want without having to fork out money for a hotel room. Fuck! Now my whole evening is ruined.

***

It's a quarter past one o'clock in the morning and I'm wide awake after having gotten my customary four hours of sleep. I'm all dressed up in my exercise clothes and ready to head out to the gym to work out. There's only one small detail keeping me from leaving the house. Kit Pettigrew's monster truck is parked in the driveway right behind my silver Toyota 4-Runner. He and Raquel drove up about half an hour ago which really surprised the heck out of me. I thought they'd be in much later than that but I'm glad he brought Raquel back home where she belongs at a decent hour.

The bad news is that after raiding my fully stocked refrigerator, they went upstairs with a bottle of champagne in tow. I was straightening things up in my office when I heard them come in through the front door. Not wanting them to know that I'm up, I quickly closed the door and laid low until they were done ransacking the kitchen for food. My dilemma now is should I somehow make it known to them that I'm not asleep anymore and kindly ask the cowboy to move his big-ass truck out of the way so I can get to the gym or do I continue to lurk in the dark and spy on them? I think I'll go for the latter. I just have to be careful not to get caught. And if I am, what are they going to do? Accuse me of being a Peeping Tom in my own house?

I can't decide what I'm more pissed off about, the fact that I can't get to the gym or that Raquel has taken a man, who isn't me, up to her bedroom. As soon as I reach the top of the stairs, I can hear the cowboy's voice and it seems to be coming from the Theater Room. A surge of relief comes over me because they are not in Raquel's bedroom. Seconds later that feeling is gone and replaced with thoughts of them doing illicit things on my exquisite, black leather couch. Slowly and softly, I make my way to the Theater Room and find that the door has not been closed all the way and I'm sure if I stand here quietly, I can make out what they are saying. Although the cowboy is speaking to Raquel in a low, controlled voice, it is still audible and from what I'm able to hear, he's really laying on the charm pretty thick.

"Raquel, I really like you. When can I see you again?"

"I bet you say that to all the girls," she answers in return.

Kit Pettigrew laughs softly then says, "You're right! I have said that to a lot of girls before. But this is the first time I'm saying it to Pocahontas.... he pauses for effect, then continues "... a real woman, in every sense of the word."

There is a brief period of silence after that. My guess is he's trying to get physically closer to her so he can move in for the kill.

"Honestly Raquel, I think you're the most fascinating woman I've ever met."

"I just love the way you say my name," Raquel compliments him. "That inbred Texas drawl of yours is such a huge turn-on. It should be banned in the state of Texas."

"Beautiful and funny! How did I get so lucky?" he says.

"Hold on cowboy! Don't you think you're pulling the trigger a bit prematurely?" Raquel asks him.

"Maybe, maybe not," he replies. "Raquel, I've been dying to kiss you all night long. If I don't get to do it soon, I think I'll die of heartbreak on this very spot. "May I?"

Raquel chimes in immediately. "An over dramatic cowboy who looks like an Adonis. How lucky can a girl get? Or is it still too early for me to be calling myself lucky?"

"Oh no! See the difference between you and I little lady is that I have absolutely no will power to speak of. You want me? Hey, I'm yours, right here, right now. Take me. I ain't going to put up a fight. What you have on your hands is a willing participant."

"If you're not going to put up a fight, then where's the fun in that?" Raquel tells him with a hint of playfulness in her voice.

The very next thing I hear is a sexy sounding moan followed by, "You are simply irresistible. Now, how about that kiss?"

"A real man doesn't ask. He just takes," Raquel says with an alluring and seductive tone in her voice, which up to this point, I had never heard before.

Again, there is a dead silence and its sheer torture for me. Unable to resist the suspense a moment longer, I quietly push the door open just wide enough for me to step inside the darkened room. If I can manage to breathe easily and make my way to the edge of the hallway that leads to the main sitting area, perhaps I can take a quick peek around the corner wall and see what is going on. Inch by inch, I am able to position myself where I need to be in order to get a bird's eye view of what is happening between my Pocahontas and the cowboy.

Just as I suspected, there is monkey business on the verge of taking place and instead of making my presence known by barging in and raining on their parade, I freeze and watch the whole scenario play out. First of all, I silently exhale a deep sigh of relief in seeing that Raquel has been mindful enough to drape her queen-size red satin comforter over my black leather couch. But that only means she has every intention of doing the tango with the pretty cowboy. Ouch! I also happen to notice they have made themselves more comfortable by removing their footwear. They are looking at one another with such wanton desire that I could easily step into full view and still I wouldn't be noticed at all.

Kit Pettigrew looks like a jungle cat ready to pounce on his prey. From where I'm standing, I watch him pluck what looks like one of them overly priced chocolate covered strawberries Raquel is always bringing home from the supermarket out of a bowl sitting on the table. Slowly and deliberately he takes a bite then brings it dangerously close to Raquel's lips and offers it to her. She leans forward and takes a small bite, then chews with a great deal of sexual innuendo implied. Raquel and the cowboy continue exchanging bites until the strawberry is stripped bare to its green core. Then the inevitable happens, their lips still moist from the strawberry juices meld together and they both moan at the same exact moment. I hate to admit it but this whole Adam and Eve reenactment thing they've got going on here is making my penis come alive inside my sweatpants against my will.

In a smooth velvety voice, the cowboy latches onto Raquel's right earlobe and says something to her. He nibbles on the earlobe for a while before planting butterfly kisses down the right side of her neck. She in turn has wrapped her well-manicured hands around the back of his strong neck and is pulling him toward her with a great sense of urgency. Everything about her body language is screaming, "I want you too."

The cowboy continues to explore every centimeter of her neck with his lips. Raquel is gasping, as if she's not getting enough air to breathe. After teasing her senseless, he finally kisses her passionately and Raquel reciprocates as if her life depends on it. Perhaps with the intention of adding more fuel to the fire, Kit Pettigrew starts to trace a long imaginary line right down the middle of her breasts with his index finger. When he gets to the outer ridge of her belly button, the cowboy pauses and waits for Raquel to protest what is next on his agenda. But judging by the fiery, glazed over look in her eyes, she has reached the point of no return and is well on her way to the brink of nirvana.

One by one, gingerly and deliberately, the cowboy unfastens all three snaps in front of her bustier. The small garment gives way and paradise is unveiled before his very eyes. The full-frontal view of the natural rise and fall of her naked breasts seems to have taken him aback. At first, he tries to offer some kind of praise but is rendered speechless for several moments. Finally, once the cat has let go of his tongue, he gazes into her eyes and manages to say, "Those are the most incredible breasts I've ever seen."

In response, Raquel smiles and opens up her arms, clearly an invitation for him to roam freely in paradise. The cowboy cups both breasts with his hands and takes his sweet time massaging them and nibbling her erect nipples. For the first time in my life, I can clearly comprehend that there is greater happiness in giving than receiving because Raquel is acting as though she's having an outer body experience. In the heat of the moment, she sits up and suddenly turns the table on her lover by tearing apart his taut denim shirt with a vengeance and quickly burying her face deep into his impressive looking pectoral muscles. In the beginning she starts to plant soft kisses all over his bare chest but gradually they become more needy and intense. The cowboy tilts his head back and allows for all hell to break loose.

After she's had her fill of the cowboy's bare chest, Raquel pulls his dangling shirt completely off of him. Then she drops down to her knees and goes straight for his zipper. As she gazes up at him with the most dishonorable of intentions, her long, lean fingers quickly unsnap his jeans and pull down the zipper without much effort. She slides both of her hands inside his jeans and underwear and pulls them down to his ankles in one clean dramatic sweep. The cowboy steps out of his jeans and underwear and kicks them aside. His cock becomes rock-hard and ready for action in the blink of an eye.

"OH MY GOD! You're beautiful!" Raquel cries out, unable to take her eyes off his poised instrument which happens to be aimed directly at her sensuous mouth. Before he can counteract her next move, Raquel reaches around and gives his buttocks a hard squeeze. "You've got a masterpiece of an ass," she purrs.

"It's all yours baby," Kit Pettigrew lets her know.

Raquel moves her face in between the cowboy's muscular thighs and starts to alternately kiss and lick his pelvic and scrotum area ever so softly while one of her hands tugs his penis lightly. In feeling the vibration of his throbbing erection against her lips, Raquel's pussy begins to ache for the same kind of stimulation she's giving. Ignoring her own desires for the moment, she starts to draw a circle around the ridge of his penis with her tongue. When the circle is complete, she takes all of him into her mouth and begins to thrust back and forth rhythmically.

Within a matter of seconds, the cowboy begins to produce deep guttural moans of pleasure. "Oh baby, please stop! You're driving me crazy," he pleads.

Raquel pauses and releases his penis from her mouth. "That's the whole idea."

The cowboy pulls away from Raquel. He takes a hold of her by the forearms and raises her up to his eye-level. "We can get back to that later. But right now, I have special plans for you." Having said that, his strong fingers tug at her mini-skirt zipper and don't stop until the small garment is split open. All on its own, Raquel's mini-skirt falls to the floor and she is left standing before him totally vulnerable. Kit Pettigrew takes a few steps back probably to admire the view and only then am I able to see that she's wearing a suede tan colored G-String. As if unwrapping a present on Christmas morning, he unties each side and with a quick flick of his wrist tosses the G-String onto the couch. The sight of Raquel's exposed pussy makes me super horny on the spot but there is absolutely nothing I can do about it but just keep on watching in secret and let nature takes its course. Besides I'm too physically invested to just walk out of the Theater Room. A pack of wild horses couldn't drag me away now. Even if I get caught, I'm staying put and seeing this thing through.

Kit Pettigrew lifts the naked Raquel up and places her on his six-pack abs. She automatically wraps her legs around his chiseled hips and starts performing her rendition of mouth to mouth resuscitation on him as he walks both of them over to the couch. Suddenly without warning, he tosses Raquel onto the couch as if she's a sack of potatoes. She lands right smack in the middle of the red satin comforter, wild-eyed. The cowboy raises his index finger to his lips and shushes her.

"Lay back and get comfortable pretty lady," he tells her. Then, it seems out of nowhere, he pulls out a single long-stem rose and places it in Raquel's hair right above her right ear. The cowboy looks around and pinpoints what he's looking for, his black cowboy hat which he grabs and props up against Raquel's pussy. Again, he steps back to admire the view and I'm able to get the total picture and I must say he's created a true work of art. The portrait he's created of Raquel is breathtaking. There she is, lying in all her naked splendor against a red satin backdrop, her gorgeous black velvety hair splayed out artistically. Kit Pettigrew's cowboy hat strategically placed over her vagina area certainly adds an air of mystery. It is the ideal final touch.

After studying his artwork for about a minute or so, the cowboy lies down next to her and props himself up on one elbow. "Tell me Pocahontas, are you the kind of woman who is not afraid of making bets?"

"Bring it on cowboy," Raquel answers without the slightest hesitation.

He leans in closer. "I bet I can make you cum without laying a single finger on you."

"Now that's one I haven't heard before."

"Buckle up Pocahontas and enjoy the sweet-smelling ride." Kit Pettigrew reaches over and pulls the rose out of her hair. After giving it a quick whiff, he proceeds to caress Raquel's face with it tenderly. Then he slides the rose down her neck and goes on to trace the curvature of her breasts with it. He pauses long enough for the soft petals to brush and then punctuate her nipples. With the rose still in hand, the cowboy draws a trail down her tummy and makes it a point to tickle inside her belly button. Raquel's body seems to be responding to the aromatic stimulation. I can see her flinching especially when the rose makes its way to her hips.

In what appeared to me an unprecedented move, Kit Pettigrew removes the cowboy hat and places it on his head with dramatic flair, leaving easy access to Raquel's gateway to pleasure. He gazes into her eyes and in a seductive voice instructs her, "No matter how much you want to, don't touch me."

Once he's laid out the rules of engagement, he uses the rose to do the same things his erect penis would do. At first his strokes appear to be long and sensual but then they become shorter and more pronounced. By the sounds that Raquel is emitting, I can tell he's doing a good job of building momentum inside of her.

"This feels so good. I can't take it anymore. Ditch the rose, I want to feel your cock inside of me now," she pleads.

The cowboy doesn't even consider her proposition. He simply laughs and continues on his mission. After several more minutes of pleasuring Raquel's pussy with the rose, he finally inserts the soft petals inside her and explores inside until rosebud meets clit. The moment the connection is made, Raquel releases a cry of sheer ecstasy unlike I've never heard before. The sound of her having a rose induced orgasm shakes me to the core. For as long as I live, I'll never forget that sound. What comes next also throws me for a loop. From my angle, I see him dip his index finger inside Raquel's vagina. After letting it linger inside for a few seconds, he pulls it out and takes a lick.

"Oh darling, you taste as sweet as you sound," he says point-blank.

"That was such a mind-blowing experience," Raquel manages to say in between her heavy breathing." She collapses back onto the couch and he on top of her. They don't say anything for a while until finally Raquel breaks the silence between them. "Okay, it's my turn cowboy."

"What do you have in mind?"

"An eight second bull ride," Raquel suggests. "Now it's my turn to place a bet. I bet I can make you cum in eight seconds flat."

"You're on," the cowboy replies removing his hat from his head and placing it on hers.

"Lie back and get ready. It's going to be a tough and bumpy ride," Raquel warns him. With a sharp quickness she mounts him and lowers herself slowly until his hardened dick is way deep inside of her. Lightly slapping his left hip for good measure, she starts to sway back and forth at a steady pace. For the first time, I'm able to get a good look at her perfectly round ass. Watching it work its magic has a hypnotic effect on me. Suddenly it occurs to me that I should start a mental countdown to see if Raquel is going to hit her mark or not. I'm about ready to conjure up the number two when the cowboy lets out a loud pent-up cry of sexual release which easily puts mine to shame.

Even in the dark, I can see that their bodies meld together beautifully. Their lovemaking is a work of art and poetry in motion all wrapped up into one. And even though a large part of me feels bitter because it wasn't me on the receiving end of all the pleasure Raquel has dished out this evening, I am happy that she's been sexually satisfied in one of the most creative ways I've ever seen. She truly deserves that.

At that point, I pivot and start to make my way out asking myself: How the hell am I supposed to compete against that? What I just witnessed was no ordinary fuck session. It was eroticism to the highest degree. This night is certainly going down in the history books. It's the night MSG got schooled in the art of lovemaking by a good ole' boy from Texas. As I make my way down the stairs, I can feel drops of semen trailing down my leg. I look down and see that the entire crotch area of my sweatpants is soaked with my cum. "Shit, tonight I've been fucked not once but twice by a Greek God in cowboy boots. First, he fucks the woman I want, and now me."

Chapter Eight

Navigating through the Panama Canal

"Of all the hospitals, in all the cities, in all the world, you just had to be rolled into mine on a gurney, didn't you MSG?"

Even though I feel unhinged and my eyes are still trying to adjust to the light of day filtering through the blinds covering up the only window in the room, I know perfectly well where I am and who has just laid one hell of a corny line on me. Both Dr. Campbell's imposing silhouette hovering over me and the nauseating antiseptic smell of Baylor Medical Center is unmistakable. The severity of the predicament I'm in has just registered in my brain. Foolishly, I try to sit up abruptly. The sudden movement triggers a sharp pain in my chest that knocks me back down and renders me defenseless.

"Stand down soldier!" Dr. Campbell says as he draws closer to my bedside. There is an undeniable look of concern etched all over his face.

"What happened to me? Why am I in this hellhole? How long have I been here?" All these questions come out of my dry cotton mouth in rapid succession.

Dr. Campbell crosses his arms and strokes his chin. For as long as I've known the man, this has been his signature move which makes him the epitome of masculinity and authority. I'm sure he's a big hit with his female patients. "You don't remember what happened?" he asks.

"Nope."

"What's the last thing you recall?"

I close my eyes, take a few deep breaths, and search my memory banks high and low. After a few moments of silence, it all comes back to me like a torrential downpour of rain. Of course, I'm not going to confess that recently I was a "silent partner" in a full-blown pornographic production. That part is better left unsaid so, I fast forward to the G-rated stuff.

"Let me see, I was driving home from the gym after one of my grueling work-outs. My all-time favorite song *Mony, Mony* by Billy Idol was playing on the radio."

"That's a damn good song. It never goes out of style," Dr. Campbell interjects. "Sorry, please go on."

"I was singing along and, I pulled into the driveway. I'd say it was around mid-morning. I turned off the ignition and that's when I started to feel shortness of breath, as if I was being suffocated by King Kong."

"So, what happened next?" asks Dr. Campbell as he grabs my chart, opens it, and poises himself to write.

"Before trying to get out of my SUV, I sat there for a few minutes hoping I could catch my breath. I figured I had just overdone my work-out. I tend to do that a lot. But then, I started to sweat profusely and, my face began to twitch. I had no control of my facial muscles."

Dr. Campbell continues to listen as if his life depends on it. "So, then you were able to get out of your car, okay?"

"Yeah, but it took a great deal of effort on my part. When I got out of the car, I suddenly felt really weak. The moment I stood up to a full upright position, my legs felt as though they were going to give out on me."

Dr. Campbell stops me right there. "Tell me, did you feel pain in your bones?"

"Hell yes!" I yell out. "What does that mean?"

"It means MSG that the cancer is spreading like wildfire and it's now affecting your bones and other vital organs. Pretty soon nearly every bone in your body is going to start to feel as though it could snap at any given moment."

"Gee Doc, thanks for sugarcoating it for me. That's mighty comforting to hear, "I toss back with biting sarcasm.

"Go on, tell me what happened next," Dr. Campbell says.

"I recall struggling to fit my key into the lock and I was able to let myself into the house. When I got inside, I headed straight for my bedroom to lie down and that Dr. Campbell is where the story ends."

Dr. Campbell stops writing in my chart and puts his pen away. "Are you ready to hear the rest of the story?"

"Do I get a soft drink and hot-buttered popcorn first?"

"Sorry, I'm fresh out," Dr. Campbell replies. "But how about some H2O instead?"

Dr. Campbell reaches for the pitcher of water placed next to my bed. He pours some water into a medium-sized Styrofoam cup and hands it to me carefully. "So, here is the rest of the story," he begins. "You never actually made it to your bedroom. An eyewitness has come forth, a beautiful one at that, and she claims that you collapsed on your living room floor."

"Raquel saw me hit the floor?"

"Indeed, she did. Your lovely assistant said she was coming down the stairs at the exact moment that you lost consciousness," Dr. Campbell goes on to explain. "The good news is that she is going to be fine and will be able to go home today. You on the other hand, will have to stay here a few days so we can do damage control."

"What do you mean Raquel is going to be okay?" The thought of her being hurt makes me lose my cool. Actually, it pushes me right over the edge of my sanity, so much that I somehow muster up the strength to sit up but not without looking like a giant uncoordinated fish out of water.

Dr. Campbell leans in and forces me to lie back down. "Relax, MSG. Your personal assistant is going to be just fine. She dislocated her shoulder trying to keep you still so that you wouldn't injure yourself any further while waiting for the ambulance to arrive. I can only imagine how difficult it was for her to keep you still."

"I don't understand. Why would she have to work so physically hard to control me?"

"After hitting the ground, you weren't exactly dead weight. You started to have a seizure which led to a temporary paralysis of the face. This is a common occurrence in patients suffering from NSCLC."

"English please, Doc."

Dr. Campbell is quick to elaborate. "Sorry about that. Force of habit. What I meant to say is Stage Four Non-Small Cell Lung Cancer."

"So, give it to me straight, Doc. Is the end near for me?" I ask, bracing myself for the worst.

Dr. Campbell flashes me a sympathetic smile which speaks volumes about his caring demeanor. "Not quite. But the disease is progressing rapidly and without any kind of treatment to counter strike its attack, well it's just going to continue on its path of destruction until it totally annihilates you. Am I making myself clear?"

A rather uncomfortable silence fills the room which creates a sense of gloom and doom. In a way, I'm thankful for the much needed moments of reflection Dr. Campbell is giving me. For the first time since this whole insane nightmare began, I can honestly say that I'm not ready to die. Now I have something to live for and she's somewhere in this hospital with a dislocated shoulder on my account. "When can I see her?" I ask Dr. Campbell.

"Soon, I promise. Her shoulder is still being tended to. She is also being prescribed some medication by the attending ER physician."

As much as I'm aching to see Raquel, it's better that she gets the medical attention she needs, so I ease up on Dr. Campbell but, he does the exact opposite with me. "You know MSG, it's not too late," he says.

"For what?" I counter back.

"To sign up for the clinical trials." Dr. Campbell pauses before explaining further. My guess is that he's giving me more time to warm up to the idea.

"Didn't you just say the disease is progressing quickly?"

"The randomized study I have in mind is geared specifically for stage four patients who have not received prior chemotherapy and are not candidates for curative surgery or radiation therapy."

"I am not saying I'm interested, but how does this study work?" I ask as I press the automated button that raises the bed so that I am more at eye level with Dr. Campbell.

"This study combines chemotherapy and other targeted therapies using new innovative drugs that are showing great promise in slowing cancer progression in previously untreated stage four NSCLC patients." Dr. Campbell lets out a spontaneous cough before continuing to build his case. "Granted, the type of cancer you have is usually considered to be incurable, however these ground-breaking treatments are prolonging survival and reducing cancer symptoms well beyond what was expected merely a few years ago."

I have to admit what Dr. Campbell is pitching here appeals to me in a big way. "How long would the clinical trial last?"

"You can continue the treatment until the disease is in remission or it has progressed to the point of no return. If the treatment begins to cause unacceptable side effects then you can stop immediately. You are also free to withdraw from the study anytime you wish."

Dr. Campbell cracks a smile and shakes his head. I get the sense that he wants to say something but is holding back his thoughts. "What is it Doc? You got something to say? C'mon now, don't be shy. Spit it out! I'm a grown man. I think I can handle whatever you wanna dish out," I insist.

He caves in without putting up a fight. "Very well then. The only criteria I think you will have a problem complying with is male subjects must practice true abstinence or agree to use a condom during sexual contact with a pregnant female or a female of childbearing years while participating in the study and for six months following study discontinuation."

"What if I've already had a vasectomy?"

Dr. Campbell is quick to shoot me down. "Doesn't matter, you still have to follow the criteria."

Now I'm the one shaking my head. "That's a deal breaker for me."

"I thought you might say that," Dr. Campbell fires back. "Look, I didn't say you couldn't have sex anymore. You just need to use a condom. No glove, no love. Simple as that."

Dr. Campbell keeps quiet for a few seconds. My guess is he is waiting for me to protest some more. "So, shall I get the paperwork ready for your signature?"

"Not just yet," I reply quickly. "Let me give it some more thought."

"It's your funeral," Dr. Campbell remarks with a scowl on his face. "MSG, if you won't to this for yourself, then do it for that hot little number being treated in the ER."

I'm really surprised he has dragged Raquel into the conversation. "What does this have to do with her?"

Dr. Campbell scratches his forehead then says, "I'm not sure what the attraction is but it's obvious that she cares about you."

His unprecedented comment stirs a warm and fuzzy feeling inside of me that I can't help but smile. "What makes you so sure?"

"The woman dislocated her shoulder and worked through the pain to save you," Dr. Campbell is quick to give his opinion. "The giddy way you've reacted just now tells me you feel the same way about her. Well, I'm certain that you are not going to stand a chance with her if you're dead."

I let out a spontaneous laugh, "Ha! I don't stand a chance with her, dead or alive."

"Not with that attitude you don't." Dr. Campbell is about to make another comment but a knock at the door keeps him from doing so.

"Am I interrupting something?" Hearing the sound of Raquel's soothing voice evokes many emotions in me all at once.

"Well, if it isn't the lady of the hour," Dr. Campbell calls out. "Come right in."

Raquel walks into the room and smiles demurely. Seeing her shoulder all wrapped up and, in a sling, breaks my heart. What Dr. Campbell failed to mention is that she's got one hell of a shiner and several other nasty bruises on her face.

"What happened to you my dear? You're all banged up," I ask.

"You happened to me, MSG. You pack a good punch," Raquel replies in her usual sassy way. "Next time you want to wrestle, pick on someone your own size, you big galut!"

"I'm so sorry," are the first words that fly out of my mouth. A feeling of guilt and sadness overcomes me and I force myself to look her in the eye. "Thank you for taking care of me. You're my hero."

Raquel's expression softens and takes on a whole different aura. "Ah, it was nothing," she says. "Don't mention it."

I like it when Raquel lets her guard down. Unfortunately, it doesn't happen too often and when it does it's always at the most inopportune time like now when I'm physically unable to act on my feelings. So, the only thing I can do is lie here like a bump on a log and savor these moments of tenderness with her. Leave it to Dr. Campbell to speak up and ruin this romantic interlude for me.

"I hate to break up this love fest but, I have other patients to see," he announces. He then looks over at Raquel and says," Ms. Lopez, may I have a word with you in private?"

Raquel is quick to answer, "Of course!"

"Why don't we step outside for a moment?" Dr. Campbell suggests. He directs his attention toward me. "Excuse us for a moment."

"Do I have a choice?" I blurt out.

"Not really," he replies calmly.

I shake my finger at him and say, "Don't run off with my personal assistant."

He chuckles. "We'll just be right out the door. You stay calm and try not to blow a gasket. Think about what we discussed earlier."

Before I can do any more chastising, Dr. Campbell and Raquel walk out of the room away from my prying eyes and ears. To kill some time, I fumble for the remote control and turn on the mounted television set. It happens to be set on *The Discovery Channel* which is one of my favorites. I drop the remote, recline my head back, and try to relax. About fifteen minutes later, Raquel walks back into the room alone. My heart melts at the mere sight of her.

"Hey kiddo," I say in a feeble attempt to break the ice between us. "If you can, why don't you grab that chair over there and sit with me a while?"

Raquel turns around and locates the chair. With her good arm, she manages to slide it right next to my bedside.

I'm so sorry about your dislocated shoulder," I apologize. "I'll make it up to you somehow when we're both back at home."

Raquel's fiery response followed by her killer smile startles me a bit. "Hell, yeah you will!"

She's like a chameleon that can change personas from one moment to the next which could very well be what keeps me interested and makes me forget there are other women in the world I could be banging.

The doctor who treated me in the ER says I'm going to be half-way out of commission for several weeks," she volunteers. "So, hurry up and get better because I'm going to need you."

Raquel's outright declaration perks me up on the spot. The notion that she needs me has ignited the desire to want to live forever and on a whim my decision is made but I keep it to myself. "So, are you going to be seeing the cowboy again?" I ask trying my best to act nonchalantly but the suspense is killing me inside.

"Nope," Raquel replies with a dismissive wave of her uninjured hand.

"What do you mean no?" I spit out. "The guy looks like a fucking Greek God and . . . . Before I can finish my train of thought, Raquel interrupts me. "Kit is really nice and, I enjoyed my time with him. But realistically speaking, he's not exactly my type."

My jaw cracks wide open. "Really?"

"Yeah, really," Raquel reiterates. "I told him I would like to see him once in a while, but I wasn't looking to enter into any kind of exclusive relationship with anyone," she goes on to explain. "Sure, Kit Pettigrew is definitely the kind of guy every girl wants to have on stand-by whenever the urge strikes and her vibrator is fresh out of batteries. But he's not a keeper."

I am completely shell-shocked by Raquel's rationale for kicking this poor guy to the curve.

"Don't you think that's a bit cold-hearted?" flies out of my mouth.

Raquel is quick to take offense. "What, a woman can't indulge in a one night stand every once in a while?"

"Correct me if I'm wrong but don't most women loathe one-night stands?"

"Maybe fifty years ago," Raquel answers. "If men are allowed to have as many one-night stands as they want, then why should it be any different for women?"

I let out a loud sympathetic whistle. "Wow! I can't believe you used the cowboy for sex," I blurt out but am quick to regret it thinking I just incriminated myself.

Raquel picks up on it right away. "What makes you so sure I had sex with Kit Pettigrew?"

"Ah, ah, I just assumed." I swallow hard and then decide to play dumb. "Well, did you?"

A true lady doesn't climax and tell," she quips back.

"I'll take that as a yes. You're a real heartbreaker Raquel Lopez. God help the men of this world," I say, shaking my head.

Raquel relaxes and smiles. "We have unfinished business Mr. Grant."

"We do?"

"Shall I have Dr. Campbell draw up the paperwork for the clinical trials?"

I take a leave of my senses for a few moments before gazing deeply into the illuminating eyes of the woman I have come to love deeply and saying totally defeated, "Yes dear."

Raquel's face lights up with a sheer radiance that takes my breath away. "Great, then it's settled." She reaches over and places her small hand over mine. "You're doing the right thing, MSG." Clearly, we are having a moment but, it ends much too soon for my liking. Raquel directs her attention to the T.V. and asks, "What are you watching?"

"I think it's a documentary about the Panama Canal."

"It looks like it could be interesting," Raquel comments.

Just then a light bulb goes on in my head. "Hey, have I told you about the time I travelled to Panama for business and ended up on a yacht with a beautiful Latina?"

"No, you haven't. Is this going to be another one of your graphic sexcapade stories?" Raquel wants to know.

"Does MSG tell any other kind?"

"Silly me. Point well made," Raquel acknowledges. "Since we've got the time, go ahead and tell me the story. And don't skimp on any of the details."

It happened more than twenty years ago and I still remember every single detail. I was contracted by the Panama Canal Commission's (PCC) IT department to deliver a speech on how to build a world-class organization and help the executive team implement their strategic plan by facilitating a workshop to motivate the team and hold them accountable. I was taken to my hotel in a private car.

When I got there, I was given specific instructions by the front desk to call Javier Mendoza. He was going to be my sponsor and guide for the next few days.

A few hours later, Javier picked me up and we proceeded to dinner. He was very courteous and such a gracious host. During dinner, he briefed me on how the PCC operated. He also explained how his department functioned and what the key initiatives were as well as who the main players were. The next day, I was greeted by the head of the PCC who took me on a personalized tour of the Panama Canal. What a truly spectacular sight that turned out to be. I was totally blown away by it all.

Lucky for me that day one of the canal's waterways was drained for maintenance and I was taken to the engine room which operated the entire canal. Although the facility, its technology and equipment all looked antiquated, everything still seemed to operate like a charm. After spending some time touring the bottom of the canal, they surprised me by taking me into the control room where I was shown how everything worked. They even let me operate the valves that raised the water levels as each ship came through.

After the special tour, I got down to the business at hand. I met with the leadership team and listened intently to what each member had to say. They had some pretty aggressive goals to meet and challenging technology issues to resolve. By the end of the day, I was totally wasted. I was driven back to my hotel room so I could freshen up for dinner. An hour later, I was picked up by Javier and Franko who was the CIO of the PCC. They took me to this upscale Panamanian restaurant that served authentic local cuisine. The food was awesome and we all hit it off beautifully.

After dinner, the three of us went to a night club which was no ordinary establishment. Both the music and atmosphere were electric. The three of us were sitting around a table that could have easily accommodated up to six people. Little did I know that equation was about to change. A few tables over, we noticed two breathtakingly beautiful Latinas sitting alone and they seemed to be enjoying the music. After a few minutes, Javier got up and excused himself from the table. "I'll be right back," he said. Franko and I watched him walk over to the table where the two hotties were sitting. He leaned in, said something to them, and then pointed over to our table. In a matter of a few minutes, Javier walked back to our table accompanied by the two women.

Javier wasted no time in introducing them. "Maria and Yolanda, please allow me to introduce Señor Grant and Señor Franko from the Panama Canal Commission," he said in a cavalier way. Up close both girls were absolute stunners. As it turns out, they were both in their late twenties and dressed in a rather classy way. One wore a white dress and the other a blue one. There was nothing sleazy about these two beauties. The one named Yolanda sat to the right of me and her friend Maria on my left. Javier then motioned for the waiter to stop by. He ordered the most expensive bottle of champagne on the menu. The waiter filled up five glasses and we toasted to my first visit to Panama.

Both women were drop dead gorgeous, highly educated, and spoke English rather well. When they eventually went to the restroom to "powder their noses" like all women do, I saw that Yolanda had the most beautiful round ass of the two. She is the one who really made an impression on me and there was no way I was going to go back to my hotel room without her. I wanted her ass so badly and I told that to Javier when they were in the bathroom. Javier said, "Let me handle this in Spanish." The challenge was how to separate them and get Yolanda to come back to the hotel with me.

When the ladies came back from the bathroom, Javier positioned himself on the other side of Yolanda. From time to time, you could see him whispering things to her in Spanish. The next thing I knew Javier looked over at me, smiled, and nodded his head. Yolanda did the same. Thirty minutes later, we all decided to call it a night. I whispered in Yolanda's ear and told her to meet me at my hotel lobby restaurant for a cup of coffee so we could speak further.

It was around midnight on a Thursday evening, relatively early for that part of the world. Javier and Franko dropped me off at the hotel which was only ten minutes away from the nightclub we were at. Fifteen minutes later, Yolanda walked through the lobby and saw me sitting in a sofa waiting for her. I got up and started walking toward her immediately. The lighting in the hotel lobby was much better than the night club. She was more beautiful than I originally envisioned. I gave her a hug and thanked her for coming on such short notice. Then I put my hand around her waist and guided her to the restaurant.

We ordered coffee and some Panamanian desert that Yolanda had seen on the menu that she thought I would really enjoy. I started the conversation by talking about my business and future growth plans. We talked non-stop for at least an hour and sipped on our coffee while sharing the desert. The conversation shifted to a more personal one by design of course. Yolanda asked a lot of questions. I told her I wasn't married and didn't have any kids, which was all a pack of lies. As we talked about each other's personal lives, I kept feeding her spoonfuls of dessert and she reciprocated. It went back and forth for a while and then I kissed her. "I know it's getting late, but I don't want this evening to end," I said, gazing into her eyes. "Would you like to come upstairs with me? I want to spend every moment I can with you on this trip." Sure, I was being overly aggressive, but I sensed she liked it that way.

Yolanda stood about 5 feet 6 inches tall and must have weighed approximately 130 pounds. She had beautifully shaped legs to go along with that top-rated ass of hers. When we got upstairs, I sat her on the bed, and we started kissing passionately. I knelt down on the floor and took off her shoes. Then I moved my hands upward toward her thighs. Her skin was soft as silk. I stood up and pulled her onto the bed so she could get more comfortable. I grabbed one of the pillows and gently maneuvered her head on it. After making sure she felt relaxed, I got on top of her gently and continued to kiss her passionately.

I began the foreplay by caressing her averaged-sized breasts which was the detour I would have to take before being able to move onto that voluptuous butt that had my dick on overdrive. After a few minutes of kissing and grinding, I slowly turned her over for the purpose of pulling up her dress slowly for a rear-view look. As I slowly pulled up her dress, I practically started to foam at the mouth. Talk about being a dog in heat. I knew perfectly well that I would cum in my pants if I actually touched that beautiful ass that had slowly come into plain view. But what choice did I have, especially pulling her panties down. I was bound to touch it sooner or later. To avoid having an accident in my pants, I had to think about something gruesome instead of my throbbing dick inside of that gorgeous butt. So, I did what any other man would have done. I thought about bodies being blown apart in an all-out bloody war. Boy that did the trick! It kept me from having a premature ejaculation. Yolanda's ass was a true masterpiece and I wanted it so badly.

At this point, I flipped Yolanda back over and started to kiss the back of her neck, shoulders, and breasts. Eventually, I worked my way down to her V-shaped nether region. I started munching away on her pussy and within forty-five seconds she had an intense orgasm. Yolanda was a screamer and you could tell she loved getting fucked. I, on the other hand, was going absolutely insane as I had my hands coupled under her butt, trying my best to hold my composure. I wanted her to have at least three orgasms before I penetrated her ass. Her pussy was not the bull's eye I wanted to hit. The real target was that butt of hers. She kept begging me to stick it inside her pussy after the first orgasm, but I wanted her to remember MSG for the rest of her life, so I didn't.

She still had her dress on after the third orgasm. I wouldn't let her take it off her hot body. I simply pulled it back down and this drove her crazy. Finally, I took pity on Yolanda and unzipped the side of her dress and pulled it down slowly as I feasted my eyes on her plumb butt staring back at me. I went from nibbling the back of her neck to making my way down south to her butt hole which I munched on for several minutes. Once she was naked, I retrieved my trusted small container of Vaseline from my amenities bag in the bathroom and rubbed some all over my hard-on. All greased up and ready to go, I mounted Yolanda's butt and slowly slithered my penis in. In the beginning, she moaned as there was some discomfort, but within seconds I made full penetration. Yolanda changed her tune and I exploded while a display of tiny stars danced above my head.

Yolanda ended up spending the night in my hotel room. We slept back-to-back in the fetal position. When I woke up the next morning, I turned over and saw that perfect round ass right in front of me, ready for the taking. I couldn't help myself so, I reached out and touched it. I became hard immediately. She was still sleeping so I just lay there and rubbed her ass softly. Since I didn't want to wake up the entire floor by fucking her in the ass again, I decided to slip my penis into her pussy from behind. My gentle thrusts woke her up and it didn't take us long to have an orgasm together. Yolanda went right back to sleep after that while I hit the hotel gym.

A few hours later, we both showered and had breakfast in the hotel restaurant. I really liked Yolanda so, I promised to call her Friday after work. We decided to meet for dinner and go see a show on Friday night. During our date, Yolanda was doing it to me again. She wore a beautiful turquoise colored dress that really accentuated her ass. I couldn't help but stare at it every chance I got. The night ended on the same note as the previous one, with her sleeping over and us making love.

The next morning, Javier arranged a fishing and sight-seeing boating excursion on a private yacht for Franko and me. At least that's what I was made to believe. It was all so cool. We would get to enjoy a panoramic view of the canal and surrounding waterways and do a little deep-sea fishing. There were three yacht crew members plus three of us.

While the crew was loading the yacht with food and alcohol, we were on the dock waiting. The next thing we heard and saw was this car driving onto the large dock area honking its horn with three hands waving out the window. To my surprise, it was Yolanda, Maria, and another friend they had brought along. I looked over at Javier and whispered "Thank you!"

At first, it all seemed too good to be true. I honestly thought I had died and gone straight to heaven. As soon as we got on board the yacht, Javier told me that the master suite was all mine. Yolanda and I went in there and put our stuff down. We couldn't have asked for a better romantic weekend getaway than this. It was a beautiful morning in the seventies. The girls were all wearing shorts with their bikinis underneath. We set sail around noon. Yolanda and I went back into our private suite and didn't come out for the next hour. I just had to have her ass right then and there. But Yolanda knew she would get her delight first. However, it was going to have to be a quickie. I went down on Yolanda with a vengeance and didn't stop until I made her see fireworks. After being pleasured, she knew what was coming next and had no problem complying with my demand. Off course I had my trusted Vaseline on me. I never left home without it. I lubed up my cock and stuck it in the most gorgeous piece of meat I'd ever seen. I had Yolanda bent over the bed and instructed her to look at the views while I plowed her ass like there was no tomorrow. She was digging it as much as I was.

The sex continued for the entire weekend. On Saturday afternoon the crew took us to a deserted island and we fucked our brains out on this private beach. The other couples went to different secluded locations and also fucked like crazy. When we had our fill of uninhibited sex, everyone swam around in the buff underneath the warm afternoon sun.

When it was time to go back Sunday afternoon, I hated to say goodbye to her. I promised her I would come back to see her and I actually did several times. She was definitely special. In fact, I might have even married her if I wasn't already spoken for.

***

"Wow! That's quite a story," Raquel says. "You certainly have lived a charmed life, MSG."

"I sure have," I concur.

We became strangely quiet. Suddenly, a rather uncomfortable feeling overwhelms me and if I have to identify it my guess is it would have to be FEAR. It also hits me that of all the women who have come into my life in the past, none of them can hold a candle to the one sitting before me in the present, the only one I can be my true vulnerable self with.

"What's wrong?" Raquel asks.

Goddamn it! I swear the woman can read my mind. The question is, should I lie or tell the truth? In an instant I make my mind up to lie like a dog, but my heart betrays me and I tell the truth instead. "I'm scared."

Raquel's exquisite eyes become watery. "I know," she whispers back. She takes a deep, cleansing breath and with a half-smile goes on to say, "If you're able to navigate these clinical trials the same way you did Yolanda's canal, then you have nothing to worry about. You're going to be just fine Michael Stephen Grant."

Chapter Nine

Paradise in the South Pacific

"Happy thoughts! You need to think happy thoughts," is what the cute nurse with adorable dimples tells me as she puts in an IV into my right arm with great precision.

"If only it were that simple," I answer back sarcastically.

She flashes me a sweet smile and says, "You're going to be here for several hours Mr. Grant. So, imagine you're on a beautiful deserted island and . . ."

I cut her off before she's able to finish her train of thought. "Thanks sweetie! I'll definitely do that."

"Do you need anything before I go?" she asks. "Perhaps some magazines to read?"

"No thanks. My personal assistant is due to arrive any minute now with my laptop. I'll be just fine."

The petite-sized nurse with an equally petite-sized ass crosses her arms and is quick to show me how disappointed she is in me. "Mr. Grant, this is the first day of your clinical trials. You should not

"

be working," she scolds me. "There's no telling how you're going to react to the medication. This is some pretty potent stuff getting pumped into your veins. You really need to forget about working and . . ."

"I know, I know. Think about being in paradise," I finish for her. "I'll do exactly as you say."

The nurse who I imagine would be fun to bang looks at me with skepticism stamped all over her forehead. "If you need anything, just press the Call Button on your left."

"Got it."

As Nurse Dimples makes her way to the door, I call out to her. "Does that shake come with some fries?"

She stops dead in her tracks, looks back over her shoulders, and repeats, "Imagine you're on a beautiful, deserted island . . ."

As Nurse Dimples was kind enough to point out, here I am on my first day of clinical trials. To say I'm nervous as hell is an understatement. On the bright side, apparently, I'm the only newcomer today so I get the treatment area all to myself. Everyone else participating in the trials is ahead of schedule so they come in on a different day which suits me just fine. I'm in no mood to make small talk with other cancer patients. They just ain't sexy, except for yours truly of course.

Actually, I'm rather surprised by the whole ambiance of it all. This treatment area certainly doesn't appear to be a place the "Walking Dead" would frequent on a regular basis. It has the look and feel of a spa of relaxation and serenity. And if this place offers a deep tissue full body Swedish massage administered by an Uma Thurman look alike on the side, then I have no problem becoming one of the regulars. OH MY GOD! She was so smokin' hot in those *Kill Bill* movies. I've seen them more times than I care to admit. The whole time I sat there and watched, I just kept thinking to myself, *If Uma Thurman can fuck as good as she can slaughter whoever crosses her path, I want her to screw me until I die. I can think of no better way to go.*

I think the hardest part about these clinical trials for me is having to come to this place three times a week and sit still for hours on end while I get pumped up full of experimental drugs. This is why I specifically instructed Raquel to bring me my laptop. I'm not about to just halfway lie here and twiddle my thumbs. There's no reason why I can't do life coaching and writing while fighting for my life. This being my first day and all, Raquel wanted to drive me here and stay the whole time. Sometimes she can be such a real sweetheart. While I could have used her moral support, there were some errands that I really needed her to do for me today. So, I took a cab instead. When Raquel is done running my errands, she'll swing by to take me home.

In retrospect, it's hard to believe that six months have gone by since the diagnosis. It's autumn here in Texas, a time for new beginnings. The other day, I received an unexpected call from Maribel in France. She mentioned that she missed me and was starting to feel homesick. Surprisingly, it had no effect on me whatsoever. This time, I spoke to Maribel with indifference. I didn't break down and beg her to come home like before. But I did go ahead and tell her that I had enrolled in the clinical trials and she seemed to be relieved that I am finally taking action. I also mentioned to her in passing that I had hired a live-in personal assistant. Being the typical woman, she wasted no time in firing away a barrage of questions about my new hire.

Of course, the first thing Maribel asked was if my PA was a man or a woman. So, I told her the truth and nothing but the truth, so help me God. "My PA Raquel Lopez is a masterpiece of a woman in every sense of the word," I stated boldly.

"You're just saying that to make me jealous," Maribel was quick to say.

"If you don't believe me, why don't you come see for yourself?" I suggested to her.

"Is that your way of telling me that you want me back?"

"Not really. But if that's the way you want to interpret it, then knock yourself out, baby," is the next thing I said. "It's true, six months ago I did want you back so badly that it hurt worse than a full-frontal blow to the nuts, but that was then and this is now. You don't have to feel sorry for me anymore Maribel because I'm in good hands.

"Is that so?" Maribel asked. "Have you slept with her yet?"

"Only in my mind. I'm practicing for when it happens for real which is just a matter of time." I have no idea why I said that. Maybe down deep inside I just felt the need to hurt Maribel a little for divorcing me in secret, breaking my heart, and taking half of my fortune. Whatever the true underlying reason is, it's too late to take it back.

The next thing I heard was Maribel clearing her throat. "Well, it looks like Michael Stephen Grant is back to his old tricks again."

"Think what you want Maribel," I said. "Look, I appreciate you calling. It's good to hear your voice." Then I softened my stance a bit and proceeded to tell Maribel that I still cared about her very much and that seemed to put a soft lilt in her tone of voice.

"I just want you to be happy," she said to me.

"I know baby," I answered back. Our conversation ended shortly after having made these declarations to one another. Maribel promised to call me again soon and I told her I would look forward to that.

Ever since I was released from the hospital three weeks ago, things on the home front have been running smoothly. Since Raquel and I have had our own handicaps to deal with, we've actually been able to work in synchronicity to get all the chores done. Of course, I've had to pick up most of the slack in the cooking and cleaning department, but considering all she has done for me, I don't mind one bit. Actually, it's been kind of nice having her depend on me. Hopefully it paints a picture in her mind that I'm a strong, virile man who can rock her world in bed if she would only give me half a chance.

Another thing Raquel and I have discovered during this harrowing chapter of our lives is that we make a damn good writing team. In the early morning and late evenings, we've been helping one another with our literary projects. She's got one of the most creative minds I've ever come across. If Raquel stays in my life like I hope she will, I'll be able to crank out more books because her ideas never stop coming. She can sit in my office and pitch one brilliant idea after another. This woman can structure a book in record time which is something I've always struggled with. My avid reader fan base doesn't have to know that she's my secret weapon so long as I agree to share my royalties with her which I've already done. So really, in a manner of speaking, I'm already in bed with Raquel figuratively. I just have to find a way to take it to a physical level. All I can say is that Rome wasn't built in a day and I'm working on it.

While I waited for Raquel to arrive, I decided to take Nurse Dimple's advice about envisioning myself being in paradise. The funny thing is that I won't have to imagine or fantasize about being on a beautiful deserted island with a sexy woman because this really happened to me, more than once. But this particular time I'm thinking of what happened in the Philippines after having pulled off a presentation for hundreds of CEOs in the capital city of Manila. It was one of the most incredible excursions I've ever been on in my life and here's how it went down.

***

My sponsors were grateful that I agreed to headline their event on such short notice; they rewarded me with a weekend getaway to one of their plush island resorts. The area was called Palawan and the resort Club Paradise. To get there was an adventure in itself. It was one of those types that could have come straight out of an Indiana Jones movie. My newest girlfriend, a twenty-year-old beauty from Manila and I chartered a twin-engine airplane that sat four people. It was a really bumpy flight. Several times we both felt like we were going to puke our guts out.

The island was remote and desolate. We landed on an old dirt runway and what looked like a shack immediately came into view. There was a sign on the shack that read: Welcome to Club Paradise. We decided to go in and buy a soda and snacks. After a few minutes a jeep arrived. Our guide climbed out and said: Welcome to Club Paradise. My date and I got into the jeep and for the next forty-five minutes we bounced around like ragged dolls through the mountains in the back seat. Then we came to a giant crater—it was as far as the jeep could go. From that point on, my girlfriend and I had to walk around the crater and then we followed our guide to this old walking bridge made out of bamboo. As the bridge swayed gently from side to side, in a single file we crossed over some desolate land until we reached a river with an old small boat waiting there for us.

As we approached the boat, the two-person crew already on board said to us, "Welcome to Club Paradise." Apparently, this was everyone's favorite catchphrase. After handing us sandwiches and a Coke, they pushed the boat back and we started going upstream. Twenty minutes later, the river widened and transformed into this beautiful, dark blue ocean. It was a bit nerve-racking to be in this tiny boat in the heart of one of the deepest waterways I'd ever seen. However, the trip was absolutely breath-taking—some of the most beautiful scenery I have ever witnessed. Imagine if you will, pristine blue water surrounded by large mountains on either side—unspoiled by mankind, just like you would see on a postcard.

Up ahead in the distance we could see there was an island. We were headed right toward it. I asked the guide, "Is that Club Paradise?" He smiled and nodded his head up and down. When we arrived, the boat went right up on the beach. We were instructed to jump out and the crew once again said, "Welcome to Club Paradise." The water was crystal clear and, the beaches were powdery white, extremely soft and gentle on the feet. It was like no other sand my feet had ever felt before.

There were several dozen cottages sprawled out along the beach. They were decorated in a romantic tropical atmosphere—dreamlike. I was with a beautiful twenty-year-old brunette bombshell. You couldn't ask for anything else except . . . there was no Internet or telephone service. I had no access to the outside world except if there was an emergency. I didn't know any of this until after I arrived.

Her name was Agnes. She was approximately 5'2, 115 pounds with shiny long hair and typical beautiful Asian brown eyes. She had a wonderful personality too, an absolute sweetheart—a pure joy to be with. This was our first excursion away together. Up to that point, we had only been on two dates. We still hadn't had sex yet, but as soon as we checked into our bungalow on the beach that storyline changed quickly. The setting in our cottage was luxurious, private, with a romantic atmosphere. I went over to Agnes, picked her up in my arms and said, "Isn't this place gorgeous?"

"It is beautiful," she agreed.

I gave her a giant bear hug. Then I looked deeply into her eyes and gave her a sensuous kiss on the lips. She kissed me back and that's all it took to heat things up between us. We kept on kissing. Our lips were locked as I picked Agnes up and placed her on the bed. She was adorable. Although she was a fully-grown woman, Agnes had the face of a teenager. She also had that beautiful olive-toned Asian skin and her arms and face were smooth as silk. I couldn't wait to feel the rest of her anatomy. Her boobs were practically non-existent, but that didn't bother me in the least. My hands went right for that cute ass of hers. It was tiny but round.

As we were kissing, I pulled down her shorts and then slipped mine off as well. I couldn't wait to feel my skin rub up against her naked body. Oh, that skin of hers was incredible. She was wearing standard white panties—nothing sexy. The moment I touched her ass, I almost shot my load. It was one of the smoothest butts I have ever touched. Her thighs and legs were as well. I rubbed every square inch of her. My hands must have roamed freely for a good five minutes, passing over her pussy several times.

The time had come for me to venture south. I turned Agnes to the side and held her tightly in my arms. A few seconds later, I started kissing the back of her neck and then moved on to her shoulder blades on both sides. I flipped her over and started to kiss her tiny breasts and suck on her miniature brown nipples. She tried to stop me from going down on her but, I wouldn't have it. I went right for Agnes's pussy to find her G-spot. For being such a tiny person, she made quite a few loud moans from the sheer pleasure. She told me afterwards that no one had ever done that to her. Within a matter of seconds, Agnes had her first orgasm, but I still wouldn't come back up. I wanted her to cum once again. During her first orgasm, I held her really tight so she could feel the full joy of that explosion. After a few minutes, I gently turned her over and began to play with her butt, using my fingers to get her aroused again.

As a result of my finger handiwork, Agnes started to make some cute moaning sounds. That was my cue to turn her back over, put both of my hands under her butt, and go right for her clit. This time it took me five minutes to get her to another state of ecstasy. I came back up and planted a big wet kiss on her lips so she could taste her own juices. I then lied down next to Agnes, lifted her up and brought her back down right on top of my penis. As it slowly slithered in, I held on to her beautiful butt cheeks. She was light as a feather. I had her moving all over the place with great ease. She was definitely a spinner. When I exploded inside of her, she knew it. But even so, I made sure she had one last orgasm before putting our shorts on, getting some food, and heading to the beach.

Later that day, Agnes and I fell asleep on the exquisite powdery sand. We were so exhausted from all the love-making that we were both out in less than ten minutes. Then as it grew hotter, we woke up and went into the water. Agnes was so happy and playing like a child. She was on top of the world and so was I. Every time I went to the Philippines, I would spend time with Agnes. She always waited for me with open arms. I saw her off and on for about a year, but when she became too clingy and wanted a full commitment from me, it was time for MSG to move on to his next seduction.

***

"Gotcha!" followed by a series of annoying clicks serves as a sobering reminder of where I am and what I'm doing. I shift my eyes toward the front entrance of this fine establishment and see Raquel taking pictures of me with her cell phone.

"Stop that!" I yell out, trying to block her view by putting up my Sasquatch-sized hands.

". . . and miss a great photo op? No way. Now put your hands down," Raquel tells me. "I want to take more extorsion pics of you."

I refuse and keep my hands up until she finally gives in and puts her phone away. "It's okay, I've already got some cheap shots in anyway," she declares with a flirty smile.

"Are you finished doing all the errands?" I ask with an air of authority, a poor attempt on my part to establish who really wears the pants in this relationship. The naked truth is that it's her. It has been since the very first day she stepped inside my house. But one day soon that tide is going to turn. Sooner or later, I am going to remove those iron-clad pants she wears and dominate her completely. She just doesn't know it yet. When that much anticipated moment arrives, it will be truly glorious.

"Never mind about the errands," I retract. "Just hand over my laptop."

"You didn't say the magic word," Raquel is quick to point out.

I huff and puff out of sheer frustration. Then I see it, a pained look on Raquel's face and it occurs to me that her shoulder must hurt from all that driving and extra weight she's carrying. And just like that I cave in. "Pretty please."

Raquel walks over to me and unburdens her load by handing over the bag that has my laptop in it. "Here, knock yourself out."

I didn't waste any time in getting my laptop out and powering it up.

"Has Doctor Campbell stopped by to see you yet?" Raquel inquires.

"Nope."

"I'm sure he will soon."

"Hey kiddo, why don't you take a load off," I suggest, gesturing for her to sit down next to me.

"Actually, I'd love to," Raquel admits.

"Good. You can help me write the next chapter in the workaholic book."

"Sure, why not," she agrees.

Raquel sits down and snuggles next to me, which is precisely where I want her to be. Her hair always smells so wonderful. We're in the middle of a highly productive brainstorming session when we are interrupted by Dr. Campbell and a colleague of his.

"Good morning to you both," he says. Then he looks directly at me and adds, "I'm so glad you came in today, MSG. You won't regret it."

"That still remains to be seen," I reply.

Dr. Campbell totally ignores my negative comment and presses on with his agenda. "Allow me to introduce my distinguished colleague. This is Dr. Adam Lancaster from London. He is the brainchild and leading doctor of the clinical trials you're participating in. He has joined our staff temporarily to oversee the trials and he's taken a special interest in your case."

Dr. Adam Lancaster, who incidentally is extremely good-looking and appears to be physically fit steps forward and extends his hand out to me in greeting. "It's a pleasure to meet you Mr. Grant."

His interest in me wanes the moment he gets a full view of Raquel's face. "May I ask: Who is this divine looking creature sitting next to you?" he asks in his thick British accent. Shit! He kind of sounds like Sean Connery as James Bond.

Raquel immediately stands up and introduces herself. "My name is Raquel Lopez. I am Mr. Grant's personal live-in assistant."

Dr. Lancaster reaches out for Raquel's hand and instead of shaking it, he slowly raises it up to his lips and gently kisses it like only a true gentleman would do. After laying out a heavy dosage of charm on Raquel, he glances over at me and says, "You're a lucky man Mr. Grant to have a personal assistant with such intoxicating eyes."

Raquel blushes on the spot and rightly so. Dr. Lancaster is a dead ringer for Clive Owen, right down to the deeply-rooted cleft on his sculptured chin. Her body language reveals to me that she's attracted to him. Hell, a woman would have to be blind from birth not to be.

The British hunk in a white lab coat points to Raquel's left shoulder and arm which are still in a sling. "What happened?" he asks. "How did you get hurt?"

Raquel smiles coyly. "Let's just say I got into a wrestling match with someone a lot bigger than me."

Dr. Lancaster's face lights up. "Ah, a woman after my own heart. I've always been a firm believer that it's not the size of the dog in a fight that truly counts, rather it's the fight in the dog that makes all the difference."

His statement seems to boost Raquel's confidence to a sky-high level. "You should see the other guy," she offers.

The man she is working so hard to impress laughs out loud. "You really crack me up."

She comes back with a quick witty comeback. "Please don't fall apart on me now. I need you to take care of my boss or else I'm out of a job."

"I doubt a girl like you would ever be out of a job," he quips back.

Oh brother, this flirting between Dr. Lancaster and Raquel is getting rather hard to stomach. By the look on Dr. Campbell's face, I can tell it's also making him uncomfortable. I've got to do or say something to put a stop to this love fest and quickly. I look directly at Dr. Lancaster and say, "Do you plan on standing there and gawking at my personal assistant all day long or are you going to give me a play-by-play commentary of what I can expect from your clinical trials?"

Dr. Lancaster's demeanor changes immediately. I'm pretty sure I've humiliated the poor bastard but, he had it coming for "coming on" to Raquel so strongly.

"My apologies Mr. Grant," he says. "I'll be happy to walk you through the clinical trials step-by-step."

Up to this point, Dr. Campbell has kept quiet which is uncharacteristic of him. A surge of relief sweeps over me when he decides to jump into the conversation. "Raquel, why don't you and I take our leave and let Dr. Lancaster and MSG get better acquainted?" he suggests.

"Sure. Let me just grab my things," Raquel says.

"Come my dear, allow me to treat you to a cup of coffee and delicious pastry in our private doctor's lounge," he adds.

Raquel perks up. "That actually sounds terrific, Dr. Campbell."

As they both start walking away, Dr. Lancaster spins around quickly and says, "I'll join you both after Mr. Grant and I have had a chance to get to know each other better." After announcing his intentions, he winks at Raquel which pisses me off royally. As he goes into his spiel about the clinical trials, I start to psyche myself out mentally to go to war with this British son of a bitch. If Dr. Lancaster thinks he can just waltz into my life and take away my reason for living, he's got another thing coming. All I've got to say is that his clinical trials better do the trick and restore my health so that I can kick his ass afterward.

Chapter Ten

Don't Ask, Don't Tell

Ever since British Doctor Extraordinaire Adam Lancaster entered the picture, I have been losing ground with Raquel and these days I'm too busy puking my guts out to do anything about it. Now I know first-hand what a living hell being pregnant and having morning sickness truly is for women. Since I began these God forsaken clinical trials several weeks ago, I've been crawling around the entire house on all fours, trying to get to what has become my main domain—the bathroom—in time to wrap my arms around the toilet so that the tsunami inside of me can spew forth and dissolve everything in its wake.

If I had concrete proof, I'd swear that Dr. Lancaster is deliberately fucking up my treatments so that all of my dignity and manhood is stripped away from me, giving him free reign with Raquel. While I may be down on my knees at the moment struggling to keep all of the vital organs inside of me from coming out of my mouth or rear end, the battle for Raquel's love is far from being over. In the end, one way or another, she will be mine—heart, body, and soul.

At this moment, Raquel is upstairs getting all dolled up for Dr. Lancaster who is coming to pick her up and whisk her away to some fancy restaurant in the downtown area. That British son-of-a-bitch has some nerve kicking a man in the nuts when he's down-and-out with stage four lung cancer. Since lately I've been feeling extremely fatigued and I'm having to take things more in stride, there's not much of a fight left in me. I'm pretty sure the side effects of the clinical trials are literally killing me.

The last complete work-up I had revealed that the number of healthy white blood cells, red blood cells, and platelets in my body are at an all-time low. Both Dr. Campbell and Dr. Lancaster keep telling me that I have to hit rock bottom before the experimental drug treatments they are dishing out can start to work. This makes me more susceptible to getting infections and feeling extremely fatigued. After more than four decades of being a dedicated womanizer who never took a day off, I can't believe it's come down to this. MSG is too damned exhausted to nail the woman of his dreams. There is nothing worse for me than not feeling sexy and that's precisely where I am at now. I wish someone would just drive a wooden stake through my heart this very moment and put me out of my misery.

To be completely honest, I guess what I'm most upset about is that I have become the underdog in this fight. Of course, I'm not talking about my battle against cancer. What I am referring to is my fight for Raquel and all the cock-tingling physical attributes that come with her. As much as I hate to admit it, I'm totally being upstaged by Adam Lancaster in the manly department. Even when I was in my prime, right before the cancer, on paper Dr. Lancaster is the better man on so many levels. How can I say that with great certainty? Well, let's just say MSG did all the painstaking research on the good doctor necessary in order to educate myself about what I am really up against. The odds are clearly not in my favor.

The more I read up on my new FRENEMY, the more emasculated I started to feel. I've given him this nickname because here's a guy who's trying to save my life, and at the same time steal the woman I am deeply in love with from under my nose. If that's not a clear definition of the word then I don't know what is. My research has revealed that Adam Lancaster had the audacity to be born into one of the wealthiest families in London. He grew up in a castle much bigger and elegant than mine, surrounded by all the ridiculous luxuries his family's money could buy. On top of all this, Adam Lancaster was known for being a boy genius with a huge philanthropic heart. He graduated at the top of his class at the University of Oxford where obviously he studied medicine.

Now here is the really insane part. The guy has everything going for him, killer good looks, money to burn, a medical degree from the University of Oxford, and access to the best pussy in all of England and what does he do? Instead of living a life of debauchery like any self-respecting guy with endless resources at his disposal would, Adam Lancaster, or maybe I should start referring to him as Father Theresa, blow's a large chunk of his trust fund traipsing all over the world, rendering free medical care to children in great distress. The thing is he just doesn't pay a quick doctor's visit to places like Yemen, the Philippines, Ethiopia, Syria—locations where the worst humanitarian crisis are taking place, Dr. Lancaster actually pitches a tent and stays for months on end. Many of the places he regularly frequents are war zone areas. His main focus in life seems to be saving children from dying of thirst, starvation, diseases, or in some cases from being riddled with bullets or blown into tiny little pieces. The clincher is that he does all this in his spare time. I guess from someone else's perspective the man could actually be revered as a hero.

In retrospect, if I had a vagina instead of a penis, perhaps I may feel inclined to get butt-naked for the man. This makes me ponder if women would rather fuck a humanitarian doctor over a hard-core self-discipline guru who is terminally ill. Really, there is only one woman's opinion that I care about. If given the choice which I'm sure is going to happen soon, which door is Raquel going to choose—the sick guy or the one trying to cure him? I'm not going to lie and say that Dr. Lancaster is not a formidable opponent and that Raquel is taken with him. Lately, her mind has been preoccupied when we are working on our book projects.

You should see how her lovely face lights up when the name Adam Lancaster comes up. I can tell she's smitten and enjoys her interactions with him. As far as I know they've only had a few casual outings together, mid-morning coffee and a quick lunch at an Italian bistro near the hospital. Tonight, is supposed to be their first evening date and its tearing me up inside because chances are that Dr. Lancaster is planning on giving Raquel a thorough physical before the night is over. The mere thought of him trying to bed her has sent me into a psychological tailspin, but I'm far too tired and nauseated to do anything about it.

Oh shit! Here comes Raquel now. I can hear the unmistakable *CLICK CLACK, CLICKITY CLACK* sound of her high-heeled pumps coming down the spiral staircase.

"MSG!" she calls out to me in her usual demanding, yet endearing way. "Where are you?"

I stop breathing for a few seconds. I really don't want her to see me this way but what choice do I have. "In here! I'm in the bathroom," I finally yell out, trying my best to achieve normal breathing status.

"What are you doing in the bathroom? Admiring yourself in the mirror again?" Judging by her voice, I can tell she's just a few feet away from entering the bathroom and seeing me crawling and drooling on all fours. Oh great! These stupid clinical trials have transformed me into a giant-sized toddler with a large swinging dick that is now doubling as a floor sweeper everywhere it goes. This clearly is not the image I want to project right before she goes on her hot date with Father Theresa.

"There you are!" Raquel blurts out as she makes her grand entrance into the bathroom looking like a million bucks. She stops dead in her tracks when she sees me on the floor, helpless and vulnerable. I can tell she is completely shell-shocked. "Oh my God, you look like hell!" she says to me.

"Well, I feel like hell," I'm quick to respond. "You on the other hand look remarkably beautiful. That's quite a dress you've got on," I point out, secretly wishing she was wearing it for my sake and mine alone.

Raquel nonchalantly waves away my insinuation with her hand. Her dislocated shoulder has completely healed now and a couple of weeks back she was able to stop using the arm sling. She runs her hands through the too low-cut-for-my-comfort purple slinky dress she's wearing and asks, "This old thing I found packed away in my closet?"

"You could have found that thing in the dumpster. The point is you look amazing in it," I say while trying to suppress the bout of nausea I feel coming on. Damn, if I wasn't on the brink of death, I'd pick myself up and take what I want. Instead of whisking Raquel off to my bed and slipping that hot little number she's wearing right off, I find myself channeling and feeling a whole lot like Tantalus did.

Tantalus, for those of you who have no clue, was a Greek mythological figure infamous for his eternal punishment in Tartarus. This fool was invited to dine with the Gods on Mount Olympus which nowadays would be tantamount to being asked to break bread at the White House. Well depending on your perspective, Tantalus turned out to be a rotten guest. After gorging himself at the feast, he stole ambrosia and nectar thinking he could take it back to his people so they too could partake and become immortal themselves. The way I see it is he was merely stealing from the GODS to give to the UNGODLY.

In an attempt to make amends, Tantalus decided to sacrifice his son Pelops to the Gods so, he carved him up into pieces and served his flesh up for them. Of course, they knew about the deception and did not eat. Because he had angered the Gods in such a profane way, Tantalus was thrown out of Olympus. After his death, the Gods made sure he was punished for eternity. To atone for his grave sins, Tantalus was made to stand in a pool of water, right under the branches of a fruit tree. However, when he tried to reach for a fruit, the branches would go higher and out of reach. When he tried to drink a sip of water, the waters of the pool would recede. Tell me I'm not in the same boat with Raquel, right here, right now.

The rapid succession of finger snapping brings me back to the situation at hand. "MSG, are you okay? You look like you're dazed and confused," says Raquel who's standing right over me.

With concern etched all over her lovely face, she puts her phone and purse on the bathroom counter and directs all of her attention to me. "Let me help you up and into bed."

Ordinarily, hearing these words fly out of her mouth would have made my dick stand at attention, but no dice. "No!" I yell out in agony. "I don't want you to dislocate your shoulder again. Besides, I think I'm going to . . ." Before I'm able to complete that thought, a tidal wave of nausea hits me, travels up my throat, and unleashes with a vengeance. Luckily, I'm able to cradle the toilet bowl in the nick of time. The vile looking shit that spews forth smells like, well shit.

Raquel instantly scowls her face and pinches her nose. "I'm calling Adam right now," she announces, reaching for her phone. For a second, I forget about my suffering long enough to say, "Oh, are we on a first name basis with the good doctor now?"

"MSG, I'm about to go out on a date with the man," she cruelly reminds me.

"Put the phone down. I don't want to see that bastard tonight. There's really nothing he can do anyway."

"He's your doctor for God's sake. Of course, there is something he can do," Raquel argues.

I try to challenge her but am stopped by a second round of nausea. While I get busy filling my toilet to the rim with nasty looking puke, Raquel starts tapping her phone. She waits for Dr. Lancaster to answer.

"Hello Adam, it's me, Raquel. I'm sorry this is such short notice but can you possibly come over earlier than you planned to? MSG is not doing well at all tonight. I'd really appreciate it if you could come have a look."

I start protesting while she's still on the phone trying to have a conversation with Dr. Lancaster. "I said I don't need to see him. I'll be fine. I just want to be left alone," I plead.

Raquel asks him if she can put him on hold. She distances the phone away from her and says to me, "MSG, be reasonable. Maybe he can give you something to help with the nausea so you can get to bed and go to sleep. How long have you been hiding out in the bathroom anyhow?"

I scratch my head and try to think clearly. "I would say about a couple of hours. But that means the worst is probably over. I'm starting to feel better now that the Green Blob Monster is out of my system." I put on the most irresistible puppy dog eyes a man in my condition can and say, "Please cancel. It's not necessary for him to come see me."

I notice Raquel is indecisive about what to do next. She mulls it over for a couple of seconds and then pulls the phone closer to her face. "Adam, it looks like you don't have to come early after all. MSG just threw up an entire country and he's feeling a bit of relief now."

She pauses again for a moment and with a pained look on her face goes on to say, "I'm really sorry Adam but I think it's best that I stay home with MSG tonight. He's going to need my help later on to change his clothes and get to bed. I was really looking forward to our first date. May I please have a raincheck?"

Honest to God, I can't believe what just happened. Raquel is deliberately choosing the sick man over the doctor. Suddenly the sweet smell of victory masks the putrid odor of my puke, but it's short-lived as feelings of guilt start to rain on this parade. I know perfectly well just how psyched out Raquel was about having a romantic dinner with Father Theresa. Maybe there is still time to salvage this and make her happy. "Please don't cancel your date on my account. I'll be okay. I promise," I say, half-heartedly.

Raquel lays her phone down again and draws closer to me. "It's too late to change my mind. Besides, good things are worth waiting for, right? If Adam really wants to get to know me better, then he'll ask me out on another date. If he doesn't, then it's a sign that he wasn't that into me in the first place. Right now, you're my responsibility kiddo," she reasons.

She takes off her purple colored pumps and tosses them aside. "Move over! Make some room for me."

"Wait." I reach over for a towel and spread it out on the floor for her to sit on. "I don't want you ruining that dress. It looks so good on you."

Raquel gifts me with a sincere smile that just melts my heart. She hikes up her dress and slowly slithers down to the floor next to me. For the first time during this whole ordeal, I notice that she smells so intoxicating. I also realize that I really want and need to be with her tonight, not sexually, but in a human kind of way.

We sit in comfortable silence for a few minutes trying to catch our breath and gather our thoughts. Then out of left field, Raquel lightly bumps my shoulder and says, "It looks like we may still be here for a while so tell me another one of your sex stories."

***

I was going back to my homeland Israel for the first time since I left at the age of six. It had been three decades since I was last there. My mom actually purchased the ticket for me because she knew that I would never take the time out of my busy schedule to visit with family. She always did know me inside and out.

When I arrived in Tel Aviv her brother was waiting at the airport. He brought me over to his apartment to freshen up and spend some time with his family who lived in a rundown part of the city. I could never understand how a family of six could live in such an old decrepit tiny two-bedroom apartment. I didn't even want to go to the toilet—heck there was no toilet seat to speak of. I also remembered seeing these huge cockroaches and other creepy crawlers. This was hands down one of the worst living domains I'd ever seen. After I showered and spent some time with the family, my uncle took me to see some of the local sights.

The first excursion on the list were those beautiful white-sandy beaches overlooking the Mediterranean Sea and of course the best scenery of all were those babes enjoying the sunshine. The beach front was breath-taking. It was a very hot day in the dead of summer. There was much to see. The beach and the babes were beautiful, but something else caught my attention as we were walking on the beachfront. It was an Israeli soldier—a woman holding an Uzi sub-machine gun. It turned MSG on like you wouldn't believe.

She had long brownish/black hair, a nice mouth, full lips, and as I got closer, she had these large beautiful turquoise-colored eyes. She definitely looked like a cross-breed—a mixture of Arab and Israeli, which is quite common as there are over one million Arabs living in Israel. The clincher was that she also had a perfectly shaped ass. Her uniform fit nice and snug around her butt. A female soldier carrying a machine gun wasn't rare in Israel, but her exotic look and those eyes were special.

As we passed the soldier, I said to my uncle: "I want to stop and speak to this woman."

"No, you cannot, she is on duty," he replied.

"I must, she is stunning," I insisted.

Her look was mesmerizing. My uncle had a feeling that I wasn't going to leave until I found out what her name was. We stopped and as we turned around my Uncle spoke to her in Hebrew. I understood Hebrew as my mom and dad always spoke it around my brother and I back home.

My uncle said to the soldier, "Excuse me but my nephew is visiting from America and he wanted to say hi to you. What is your name?"

She stopped and said, "My name is Talia." When she spoke, I was speechless, but my uncle did all the talking for me.

He told her, "His name is Haim." Then out of the blue he asked her if she was married.

"No. I must finish my military duty and then start my career. There is plenty of time to get married later," Talia replied. She was probably in her early twenties but handled herself in a very mature manner.

After a few moments I chimed in and said, "*Shalom, Ma shlomekh*?" That means how are you in Hebrew.

"*Tov*," she replied politely. Of course, that means good.

We were conversing back and forth in Hebrew for a few minutes. "I am in the reserves and have weekend duty. I am just patrolling the beaches." You could see that although she was speaking to us, her eyes were roving everywhere. She never relaxed for a second. She was extremely disciplined, but also courteous and friendly.

"What do you do for a living?" she asked.

I didn't waste any time in replying. "I wear many different hats. I am a writer, publisher, business management consultant, speaker and life coach."

She then chimed in and said, "I can see you are also very fit."

I felt like she was impressed with what she saw and heard and quite frankly so was I. Right then and there I made the decision to go for it—I had nothing to lose. She also spoke English fluently. I asked in a confident voice, "Are you available to have lunch together Monday on this beautiful beach?"

She said, "*Ken.*" *Ken* means yes in Hebrew.

"Can you meet here around 11:00 AM on Monday?"

"*Ken,*" she replied again.

At that point we all said *shalom.* She went back to patrolling the beaches and we headed to a *falafel* stand. There's nothing quite like freshly cooked middle-eastern *falafel.* I turned back to take one last look at her ass. The funny thing was she also took a quick look back to check me out. Our eyes connected so I waved—she smiled back.

It was Saturday afternoon, still very hot and muggy in the city so my uncle decided to take me up north to the mountains where it was cooler to spend a night on a Kibbutz. It was an incredible experience working off the land for your food. I met many wonderful people and the experience of being part of a close-knit community was second-to-none. A humbling experience for MSG, however my mind kept reflecting on Talia holding that sub-machine gun and her perfectly shaped ass, but I also loved her confidence and discipline. Yup, I was on a mission to nail me an Israeli soldier on the best impromptu bed I could find in the city.

We drove back to my uncle's apartment on Sunday. Oh, how I didn't want to sleep in that apartment, not even for one night, but I had no choice that first weekend. I didn't want to be disrespectful and rude. I slept maybe one hour due to the jet lag and afraid that rodents would be all over my body when the sun came up. Somehow, I survived the night and I woke up to see the sun rise. I began counting down the minutes/hours until I would meet up with Talia. This was also going to be my last night sleeping here in this nasty place.

I packed my garment bag early in the morning, had breakfast with the family, and around 9:00 AM I decided to leave. I walked a few blocks to one of the main streets to grab a taxi and asked the driver to head toward the beach area to find a nice hotel. Within fifteen minutes I was there and found a nice hotel about a block from the beach. I checked in for two nights until I was supposed to meet my other uncle who lived in a much nicer part of town. After an early check-in, I headed down toward the beach. I was there early around 10:45 AM. Within ten minutes a car pulled up and there was Talia.

She said, "*Boker Tov*," which meant good morning. "Hop in so I can find a place to park somewhere near the beach."

"Why don't we just park at my hotel? It's free for guests and only a block away?"

Talia smiled and said, "*Tov*."

OMG, she looked stunning! She had a pair of cute shorts on, makeup perfectly applied and wearing her bathing suit underneath. She was ready for a day off at the beach and I was ready for her. We parked the car at the hotel and grabbed a blanket and picnic basket from the trunk. We walked toward the beach with great expectations.

We found a nice quiet spot away from a lot of the tourists. Once we laid everything out, we decided to take a quick dip in the Mediterranean. It was already extremely hot. Thank goodness she brought some sunscreen. After our dip we went back and lied down on her large beach towel. She rubbed sunscreen all over my back and I did the same for her.

We talked about many things especially when she wasn't doing weekend military duty and what I did for a living. Our personalities were clicking on all cylinders. We were feeling comfortable with each other and that's always step one in being able to get a woman in the sack.

"You are very beautiful with your uniform and without it, actually downright gorgeous," I told her.

She had packed us a lunch and some drinks, which I thought was extremely nice of her. She was really genuine.

She asked me, "How long will you be staying here in Israel?"

"Nine days on this trip and then I have to get back to work," I answered.

"I am very disciplined myself and I want to accomplish great things in life, perhaps even write a few books like you," she came back with.

This is what I was waiting for. Up to that point, I couldn't think of an IN with this girl until she made that comment. There was no way to bullshit this woman, she had her crap together and besides I didn't feel comfortable doing so with that Uzi of hers.

I made her an offer and hoped she wouldn't refuse. "If you like I can provide you with a professional analysis of your life and design a strategy to help you fulfill your goals and be successful. This is what I love doing as a life coach."

"Really, if you don't mind, I would love that."

"No problem at all," I said. "Back in my hotel there is a desk and a side chair. It will take me about two hours to evaluate you, design a strategy, and even develop a life plan for you."

After almost two hours on the beach talking and having lunch, we decided to go back to my hotel to develop that life plan for her.

I stopped by the front lobby asking for about ten pieces of legal-sized paper. This way it looked totally legit—that I had no ulterior motives, although she knew I wanted her—she was one bright cookie. Believe it or not I was actually planning to facilitate a real-life coaching session with Talia—the same process I've done for hundreds of people and dozens of organizations throughout my career.

When we got to my room. I pulled the chair out from the side of the desk and said to her. "Please have a seat. Let's order some water. This will take at least two hours, maybe more. Please take off your shoes and make yourself comfortable. Do you mind if I take a quick shower, I am still pretty sweaty?"

"Please feel free," she replied.

I took a quick ten-minute shower then I suggested to her, "You are welcome to take a shower too while I prepare what I would like to ask you for my evaluation."

"*Ken*," Talia replied.

Twenty minutes later she came out of the bathroom. Her hair was still wet. I said, "Please have a seat."

I wanted to be a perfect gentleman every minute with her and come off in a professional manner. I started asking dozens of questions (probably closer to 50) to understand her strengths and weaknesses. Once I understood them, I provided a synopsis of my findings. I then inquired about her goals and what the best strategy would be to accomplish them. During our discussion I could tell she was listening to me closely and I think that my intelligence was attractive to her.

"For you to be successful with this strategy, we need to develop a detailed roadmap. In other words, a HOW-TO..." I started to say.

Before I could finish Talia interrupted me by asking, "You don't mind doing this?"

I answered her query with the truth and nothing but the truth. "I love helping people achieve their goals. For each goal we will need to establish detailed milestones. Achieving these milestones are the key to success. In other words, I want you to focus on accomplishing these small steps first every day. Don't worry about your goals. If you achieve these milestones every day the goals will take care of themselves."

I could tell Talia loved what I was saying. She was listening intensely and taking notes. I also noticed that she got a bit closer to me on the desk.

Once I saw that I was making good progress I pressed on, "In order for you to be efficient we need to establish a morning and evening routine, seven days a week." This led to another possible IN for my hopeful and throbbing cock, but a part of me was highly optimistic that I could close the deal now rather than later. "If you have time tonight or tomorrow and if you have a computer, we can do this together."

Without the slightest hesitation Talia replied, "Tonight, if you don't mind?"

"It will be my pleasure," I answered in return. At that moment our faces were very close to each other as I was trying to be very direct and clear on 'how-to' to make this happen.

I also told her, "I will hold you accountable for the first few months over email and phone calls to make sure you achieve those daily milestones, adhere to your routine, and also establish a to-do list every day of the week."

"You will do that? she asked.

"*Ken*, I take life development seriously and I don't believe in failure." I was staring right into her eyes and at that moment we came closer and kissed. We unlocked and looked at each other again and I guided her right on my lap and we kissed some more. She was sitting on my lap and I'm sure she could feel my pulsating dick-in-heat pressing against her buttocks. She was totally turned on from this process—listening to me the past few hours—she wanted to let me know how much she appreciated me. All of the sudden she took charge in a BIG way and I wasn't resisting. That image of her holding that sub-machine gun in her arms was vivid, but also very sexy.

She got off my lap, grabbed my hand, and tossed me on the bed like I was a rag doll. Then she pulled off my shorts and saw that I wasn't wearing any underwear. She didn't waste any time in putting my cock in her mouth. That in itself was reward enough for having spent all this time coming up with a life plan for her. She pinned my legs down and she wasn't letting me up anytime soon. I wasn't about to resist—not just yet anyway. I didn't want to have an orgasm this soon and if she kept on feasting on my penis, it was all going to be over within seconds. It took a great deal of willpower but, I was able to pull it out of her mouth quickly.

"I take care of you first," I insisted.

After giving her a bear hug, I gently turned her to the side so that her ass was right in front of my throbbing dick. I brought my hands down to her waist and started to unbuckle her shorts. Now it was my turn to take full control. I unveiled that beautiful

Middle-Eastern ass of hers. She wasn't wearing her bathing suit bottom, probably because it was dirty.

I untied her bathing suit top and her beautiful young and perky breasts fit into my hands perfectly. I was kissing the back of her neck and shoulder area as well as fondling her breasts. Then I switched directions. I went south. I started sucking on her toes and kissing her shapely legs up and down slowly. I went up and down several times sucking each toe at least twice until she was ready to scream. She grabbed my hair and tried pulling me up, hoping that I would dip my Israeli manhood inside her Middle-Eastern honey-filled pot. But I wouldn't have it, at least not yet.

I attacked her pussy with a vengeance. I wanted to show her that a disciplined Israeli with a nine-inch gun was far more powerful than her Uzi sub-machine gun. She found out quickly that the intensity level was out of this world. I latched onto her clit and she had an orgasm within seconds. She then tried with all her might to bring me back up, but I wouldn't let her. I came up for a brief moment to kiss her and let her taste her own pussy juices then back down I went until she had another orgasm.

I decided that since she was going to be back later, I would stop there. I flipped her over, kissed her ass, and then slithered my penis inside of her doggie style. I was fully loaded and ready to discharge. I wanted her to feel the impact. It was hard and throbbing and I was pounding her vagina like there was no tomorrow. She was loving it and I was watching my dick go in and out as I caressed her butt. When I exploded, I saw stars and I'm pretty sure she did as well. Talia had her third orgasm. After that we both fell asleep for a bit, showered again, and went out for some food.

Later that afternoon she wanted more immediately, but I said to her, "I need to finish your life plan first."

Talia appreciated that and later reciprocated the favor. The sex later that evening was even more intense than it was earlier in the afternoon, proving without a doubt that Israelis and Arabs can get along together. Of course, it helps facilitate the process when the parties involved are naked and up to no good.

Chapter Eleven

Doing the Kamasutra

Ahh! My first trip to India was quite an adventure to say the least. One that started out as an absolute nightmare but ended up with what MSG does best—nailing beautiful women.

I was on one of my patented business trips to speak at a large conference. In attendance would be mostly CEO's who were coming from all over India to hear me speak. I was traveling from Los Angeles to New Delhi with a stopover in London to switch planes. Everything seemed perfectly normal. My personal assistant Jenny, who I relied on heavily to keep track of my hectic schedule and book all of my travel needs had done another magnificent job keeping me on track—or so it seemed. She typically didn't make any mistakes, but this trip was the exception.

When I landed in London and proceeded to the transfer counter to check-in for my flight to New Delhi, I handed over my thick and almost fully stamped passport to the agent. She asked me for my Visa in an authoritative voice.

"Ahhh, what visa?" I asked her in return.

"You must have an entry visa before entering India," she replied.

I had no clue I needed a visa and apparently neither did Jenny. It was Saturday morning and I was exhausted from the long trip. There I was at Heathrow Airport with a large presentation for hundreds of executives to give first thing Monday morning looming over my head. I was in a major predicament. I had two options neither of which were appealing. One was to fly back home because I couldn't go any further and blow off all those executives in the process. The second option was to clear customs, leave the airport, and find the Indian consulate to issue me an emergency visa and hopefully continue to Delhi. Mind you it was the fucking weekend.

While at the ticket counter I posed a question to the Air India agent, "Can you please place a call to the Indian consulate in London for me?"

I was certain they had a separate number to handle emergencies seven days a week. I'm sure it wasn't the first time this scenario had played out for countless passengers before me.

The Air India agent was able to reach someone. "Someone will meet you at the Indian consulate in London in a few hours," she said.

I cleared customs, left the airport, and took a cab to the consulate. It was closed as advertised, but on the door, there was an after-hours number to call. I called and luckily someone answered. I believe it was the same person the ticket agent had spoken with on my behalf. I calmly explained my predicament and begged the person to come into the office to help me get a Visa. After another hour of sitting on the front steps of the Indian Embassy with my luggage in tow, the man came into work and within thirty minutes I paid the fee and was given a Visa to enter India. Problem solved!

I flagged down a taxi and back to Heathrow I went, straight to the Air India first-class business line. After getting my boarding pass, I proceeded to the Air India lounge. There were probably a half-dozen Indians waiting to get on that next flight to New Delhi. For me, it was a typical day in an airport lounge; writing another chapter of my latest book, eating a few snacks, and occasionally taking a short nap.

In retrospect, it was just like any other day. Nothing seemed to be out of the ordinary until about one hour before boarding time when the door to the lounge opened and standing there was an Indian Goddess that any man in his right mind would want to engage in Kamasutra activities with. OUCH! She was absolutely stunning. Unfortunately, THE GODDESS didn't sit next to me, but she was still a beautiful sight to behold even from a distance and man did she have a body on her. Suddenly people started fussing over her to get an autograph and photo of her as if she were a movie star or famous Indian model. As it turned out, she happened to be both. Talk about being at the right place, at the right time. My only hope was that she would sit close to me on the actual flight.

When the boarding began, we all headed out. I wanted to make sure I stayed behind this roving beauty. I was so tired but walking behind that ass of hers was like having virtual sex. Wow, what an incredible view! Pablo Picasso couldn't have painted on a pair of jeans that would've looked better. She fit into a pair of jeans like no one else I had ever seen before—unreal. Oh, and did I mention that this GODDESS also had the face of an ANGEL, a perfect, undeniable 10.

After we boarded the plane, luckily, she sat right in front of me. People were still coming up to her asking for an autograph. She had a radiant smile that lit up the whole Goddamn plane. Obviously, she was of the famous persuasion. At first, I thought she was out of my league, but then again it could be the ULTIMATE challenge I was seeking. I needed some major stimulation and I had just stumbled upon it. I didn't see a ring on her finger and, she wasn't with anyone so what was the harm of trying to speak with her.

Even though she was sitting in an aisle seat directly in front of me, I still needed a way in. This masterpiece of a woman was not going to be as easy as my usual "it's-up-to-you-sir" girls I was used to bedding. There wasn't anyone sitting next to her in the window seat. I, on the other hand, wasn't that lucky. Someone was sitting next to me and he wasn't pleasant to look at. I needed to get moved next to that beauty, but how? If I did it on my own it wouldn't look very cool. It would be an obvious and cheesy move if I did that. But if a flight attendant directed me to move over there then it would be destiny, divine intervention, two ships passing in the night.

I got out of my seat and in a cordial way I went up to one of the flight attendants and said, "Hi, I am the passenger in 14B. I'm trying to get some much, needed rest and would prefer a window seat so I won't be disturbed. Do you mind if I move to 13A, it's a vacant seat in front of me?"

The flight attendant replied, "By all means Mr. Grant. May I get you an extra pillow and blanket?"

"That would be very kind of you. Thank you for being so gracious!" I said playing along.

I turned my back to the flight attendant and of course I had a sinister little smile plastered on my face. Okay that was the first step, next to come was the real challenge at hand. With a newly lighted spark in my pants, I grabbed my computer bag and with all my chutzpah sat in my new seat. As I sat down, I looked at that beauty next to me and said, "Hello, how are you?"

She smiled back at me and said, "Fine, thank you."

"My name is Michael," I ventured on.

She reciprocated in kind. "My name is Aashna."

"It's a pleasure meeting you Aashna."

Despite being drop dead gorgeous, she actually seemed genuine. If she hadn't been, I would have stopped there and gone to sleep, but she gave me an opening so, I took it. I don't need to remind you how much MSG loves openings, especially to the gateways of pleasure of a beautiful woman, do I? What I was truly excited about was being given the opportunity to win this beauty's heart and mind. That was the real mountain to climb.

It was important not to come off like one of her fans who wanted to take a picture with her or go ape shit crazy over her beauty. I wanted to come off like I was more important and famous than she was, but not sound egotistical in the process. She had an undeniable radiance about her with long wavy brownish hair with a tint of blonde. Her skin was impeccable, there wasn't a blemish anywhere, and for the love of God, those lips of hers. You couldn't draw them on a face any better. Aashna had big brown eyes and her teeth and smile were perfect too. She was the ultimate Indian Barbie Doll. If I had it my way, I was going to be her Ken Doll that she'd play with all night long.

"Are you from New Delhi?" I asked her.

"Yes, I live with my father and mother. I was in Singapore on business. How about you?"

I strategized carefully before blurting out just anything. I could tell she was analyzing my every word. It was like a chess match and I needed to anticipate her next move.

"I was delivering a talk in Singapore and now I'm going to a meeting in Delhi with one of my customers. I have several of them in Delhi and Mumbai." I just gave her a little bit of information. Once again, I didn't want to come off like I was a big-shot businessman, at least not immediately. I was counting on the fact that she'd have an inquisitive nature and would ask me what kind of talk and she did.

Thinking that I had just gotten to first base with her I said, "I speak on the subjects of success and being self-disciplined."

"I read a lot of self-help books and I believe heavily in self-discipline. Were there many people in attendance?"

"Approximately 300."

Aashna had said the magic words I needed to hear, self-help books. At that moment, I reached into my computer bag and pulled out one of the many books I had written and handed it to her. "Please, for you."

She said, "What is this?"

"It is one of the books I've written and published. It's all about how to be more disciplined. I was going to present it to a customer I am meeting with in a few days but I will call my assistant and have her send him three additional books that I've already autographed," I explained to her.

"Thank you so much. I promise to read it. How many books have you written?"

"A few dozen, not really sure of the exact count."

"Wow, that's incredible! Do you have a wife and family back at home waiting for you?" she asked.

"No wife (which was a lie), but I do have a son and daughter from my first marriage. I am divorced now."

"What about you? Are you married or have a boyfriend?"

"No," she answered.

Right then and there I decided to pop the $64,000 question. "I feel like we have much in common, would you like to meet for lunch one day this week?"

"That would be nice. Here is my contact information." Aashna handed me her business card and I gave her mine in return.

"I'm staying at the J.W. Marriott where I am conducting my business."

"I know exactly where that is. I live really near there."

I should have been erotically excited by then but just because she had said yes to my lunch invitation, it didn't mean it was going to happen. I could tell this young lady was extremely busy between her photo shoots, acting, exercising, and friends.

After checking into my hotel room and unpacking, I decided to give Aashna a call to let her know how nice it was meeting her and to see if I could get a lunch date with her for tomorrow or the next day. When I called her phone, it went right to voicemail so, I left her a message. A few hours went by and she never called back. I called one more time later that evening and again her cellular went right to voicemail. This time, I didn't leave a message. I decided to forget about it for one night.

The next morning, I decided to call Aashna repeatedly until I reached her. Still after dozens of tries no luck so, I emailed her instead. Her email address was listed on the business card she had given me on the plane. After a few hours, I received an email back and she apologized for not returning my phone call as she was overwhelmed with work related things. I could tell she was very disorganized and lived an unstructured lifestyle. We set up a date for lunch at the hotel later that afternoon, but that still didn't mean anything. She was just so overwhelmed so there was a really good possibility that she could still blow me off, not intentionally but because she was extremely busy.

I wanted to make sure that she got to the hotel so, I had my trusted personal assistant Jenny help me out. Like I said before, Jenny was more than just an assistant and travel agent. She helped MSG on many occasions, all in the interest of nurturing and furthering my "special lifestyle." Jenny knew I was an incurable manwhore, but she respected me for my many accomplishments. She was extremely loyal, probably because I paid her handsomely and we genuinely liked each other, although she was faithfully married. She understood me like no other and on many occasions helped me nail chicks without batting an eyelash, knowing perfectly well that I was a married man.

I contacted her because I needed help if I was ever going to nail Aashna on my comfy hotel bed. During our phone conversation, I explained to her who Aashna was and how I had met her. I asked Jenny to call and email her from the US to make sure she arrived for our lunch date. I also told Jenny to find a local florist and order two dozen long-stem roses and get them delivered ASAP to the hotel for lunch—regardless of the cost.

When Aashna arrived at my hotel, one hour late, heads were turning which made me realize my limitations for the day. There was no way I was going to get her to my hotel room in one day, or two for that matter. This conquest was going to require more of a prolonged effort. This Indian beauty always dressed in western outfits. That day she was wearing a turquoise colored dress with high-heeled shoes that matched beautifully. We sat down, ordered lunch, and talked the entire time. Half-way through our conversation I told her point blank, "You know, you're very hard to contact. If you want to see more of me then I will continue to have my assistant coordinate our schedules."

"Yes! I am sorry about not returning your phone calls, but at times it's overwhelming and I just stop answering. The best way to reach me is via email and I will look for Jenny's emails too," she said.

Right on cue, the florist approached us with a sign that had Aashna's name on it. She was surprised big-time. You should have seen the smile on her face. Like her, it was priceless. On the card it read: "These roses remind me of your beauty. Thank you for accepting my lunch invite."

We continued to discuss both our personal and professional lives. I told her that I was thinking seriously about moving to India.

She looked at me in a skeptical manner, then smiled slightly and said, "I hope so."

I knew from the second I laid my eyes on this one it would take a herculean effort to get between those awesome legs and boy was I right.

After we were done having lunch, I said to her, "Until we meet again . . . and oh by the way, do you have plans for this evening?"

"I am just going to work out and then relax," she responded.

"That sounds good! Would you like to see a movie together? Is there a nice western-style theatre nearby?" I asked her.

"Yes, a very nice one," she replied with enthusiasm.

"Okay, I will have the concierge get the details and find out what's playing and, I will email you."

"That would be nice."

MSG was on a roll and date number two was scheduled. We held hands in the theatre and I also put my arm around her. She was having a good time and we were truly enjoying each other's company. But as promising as things were starting to look, I still wasn't going to take a chance on rushing a sexual encounter of the close kind with this priceless gem. At the end of the evening, I gave her a big hug and I planted a kiss on her lips. She kissed me back, but there was no tongue action.

The next day, I had my assistant send her three dozen roses. The card read: "It's a pleasure spending time with you. The more I get to know you the more I realize that your heart is more beautiful than your looks." Granted, I was laying it on a bit thick with this one and spending some major bucks but to me it was going to be worth it when I got her naked and in the sack.

We scheduled a third date, which was going to be dinner at a fancy Indian restaurant. Aashna was wearing a white long gown that fit beautifully around her hour-glass shaped figure. We had a great time and then I blurted out, "I am leaving tomorrow but will be back soon and then perhaps we can meet in some other country as well?"

She was working throughout Asia, including one of my favorite countries, Hong Kong. We decided to hook up in Hong Kong in the very near future. By this time, she knew Jenny and I told her that she would coordinate something for the both of us. One of the nicest hotels in Hong Kong is the Grand Hyatt in WanChai (Hong Kong Island). It had one of the best hotel gyms and the best views overlooking beautiful Hong Kong harbor. Also, the lounge floor had the most incredible atmosphere, views and food which made for a romantic setting.

Three weeks later, I met Aashna in Hong Kong at the Grand Hyatt. I actually got there one day earlier to make sure I was at the airport to pick her up. She was impressed that I was there waiting for her at the airport with a limousine. We had separate rooms of course, but I was hoping to change that on the second night, at the latest.

That evening we went to the Peek for dinner. One could see all of Hong Kong from there—a very beautiful setting. When I took her back to the hotel, I walked her to her room and, we started making out in front of the door. Despite enjoying my kisses, Aashna still didn't invite me in. She was going to make me work for it in a big way. The next morning, we worked out together, had breakfast, and then I showed her all of Hong Kong—we were out sight-seeing all day. That afternoon we came back to the hotel and she was holding my hand tighter than usual. She didn't let go of it. In fact, she brought me into her hotel room. Within minutes there were fireworks over Hong Kong harbor. She was wearing those same tight jeans she had on the day I met her. I'm pretty sure she planned it that way.

Peeling those puppies off was going to be an experience of a lifetime. Aashna played the game of seduction rather well—I have to hand it to her. I'm sure she learned how to play the game from having to deal with hundreds of men using every line in the book to try and get the hot curry that she was into bed. Even for Michael Steven Grant, it took a monumental effort to make this happen. In retrospect, it truly was a world-class chess match with two superstars opposing each other and the match lasting for months. Besides the actual moment of insemination turned out to be one of my greatest love battles of all-time. I will never forget Aashna's beauty, intelligence, and heart. She was special in more ways than one.

When I entered her hotel room for the first time and we were kissing passionately, I actually had an orgasm in my pants. It reminded me of when I was fourteen years old and had lost my sainthood status. It was embarrassing for me, but not for her. Aashna knew exactly what she was doing. She wanted to leave me with memories and that's exactly what she did. There I was, an international playboy in my early forties, and I just had a premature accident in my pants.

Aashna kissed with love on her lips and while we were swapping tongues passionately, I wasn't about to be out maneuvered by her again. The first round went to her but the next two to five would be mine. After I made a mess all over myself, I told her I had to go get cleaned up and she smiled back at me flirtatiously. When I came back out with a towel wrapped around my waist, she was sitting on the bed with her legs crossed. I took Aashna's hands and stood her up. Then, I gazed into her eyes and unbuckled and unzipped her pants, but still left them on.

No way in hell was I going to rush any of this. We kissed as I slipped my hands down the backside of her jeans—man were they tight. We got on the bed and I turned her over and started massaging and kissing the backside of her neck. Then I lifted up her T-shirt, unbuckled her bra, and continued kissing downward. When I finally got to that "world-class ass", I slowly started removing her jeans. Aashna's ass was perfectly round just like an NBA basketball. I must have kissed every square inch of it several times over.

After being aroused by that beautiful derriere, it was time for me to get to work on that clit of hers. Within seconds, Aashna had her first orgasm and she found out quickly that I wasn't like the other men who had previously come in and out of her life. She was begging me for my cock, but I wasn't going to let her have it for a good while longer. I had already decided that the minimum number of orgasms I was going to give her before going on to have mind blowing intercourse would be three. Well it ended up more like being five, from me sucking endlessly on her clit and at least once from me penetrating her. What can I say, sometimes it's good to under promise and over deliver. Despite having gifted Aashna with multiple orgasms, MSG still wanted more, I wanted to penetrate that gorgeous ass of hers. I wanted to mount it and watch all nine inches of my dick go in and out slowly. She knew that's what I wanted so after we had made love and climaxed together, we took a short nap in preparation for the cataclysmic event that was still to come.

After about twenty minutes I woke up while she was still sleeping. I started playing with her butt and that's all it took. BOING! I was hard again, just like that. There was some body lotion on the nightstand next to us, which I grabbed and slathered all over my erect penis, all the while she kept on sleeping and looking like Sleeping Beauty. I slowly began to rub the head of my penis around her hole and carefully began inching it in. She woke up and immediately made her butt more available by wiggling it in front of me until I put it all the way in. Aashna winced a bit and I could tell she was in agony, but soon thereafter she started moving with the flow. I turned on the light so I could watch that beautiful ass in motion. The time had come for me to have my third orgasm and when it happened, I saw a whole universe of stars.

Looking back, I can honestly say I was in love with Aashna and she was in love with me. But it was much more than love—it was some great companionship. If I had been living in India, I would have married her but that wasn't going to happen. It was just way too humid and dirty for me. We saw each other a few more times, once in San Francisco as my guest, and another in Sydney Australia. I will never forget her.

****

"Earth to Michael Stephen Grant! Earth to Michael Stephen Grant!"

It takes Raquel having to clear her throat a few times for me to realize she's back from her lunch date with that British asshole of a doctor. I swear I got so wrapped up thinking and writing about my unforgettable Kamasutra, code word for contortionist, sexual experiences with Aashna back in India that I didn't hear her come into the house. This horny man sure could use a working time travel machine right about now.

"How long have you been standing there?" I ask Raquel.

"Long enough to see that big hard-on you got going on in your pants," she replies circling her index finger in the air and then pointing it directly to my crotch area.

I look down and instinctively cover up my indiscretion with one hand while the other quickly saves the file I'm working on and clicks right out of it.

"Let me guess, you're writing about your sexual escapades again," Raquel says. "It must be one helluva story to have gotten you all worked up."

"Never mind about that," I answer back, waving my free hand dismissively at her. "Wait, you can see my hard-on from where you are, even though I'm sitting down?"

"Let's just say I have a very good view from where I'm standing." At that point, Raquel cracks a smile. "Don't be embarrassed MSG. I'm glad to see you're feeling better and writing again. To think, about a month ago you were crawling all over the house like a baby because you were too sick to walk or stand up straight for that matter. You've come a long way baby!"

Raquel is absolutely right. I'm feeling and looking so much better than that night she had to cancel her date with Dr. Lancaster because I couldn't get off the bathroom floor. That had to be one of the worst nights of my life. Both Dr. Campbell and Dr. Lancaster say that my body is responding remarkably well to the treatments and these days I seem to be regaining my strength. By the looks of things, it also appears as though my sexual prowess has been awakened from being in hibernation and is ready to spring into action which reminds me this is the perfect time to conduct a reality check.

"So, how was your date with Father Theresa? I ask Raquel.

"Great! And please stop calling him that," she says to me. "As usual, we had a great time talking."

"That's all you did?" I blurt out in an exaggerated way. "You mean to tell me this is like your fourth or fifth date and he still hasn't made a move on you? What's wrong with this guy?" Then I start shaking my head profusely. "The great-looking, high and mighty, Dr. Lancaster has a lousy bedside manner with the ladies."

Raquel is quick to defend him. "First of all, this is only our third date. I like it that we are taking things nice and slow. And besides, daytime lunch dates don't exactly make good precursors to intense, mind-blowing sex in the bedroom or a hotel room."

"Nice and slow never lead to volcanic orgasms. Don't make excuses for him young lady. When a man zeroes in on and really wants a piece of ass, he will do the impossible to get it, anytime, anyplace, anywhere. Maybe he's just not that into you."

The minute I see Raquel's face go from happy to sad, I start to regret the words that just came flying out of my mouth. Before I can switch to damage control mode, Raquel asks me, "Do you really think that?"

Not wanting to bruise her ego any more than I already have, I take the high road. "Of course not! What heterosexual man in his right man wouldn't want to rendezvous with you sweetheart? Maybe, he's just a late bloomer." I give Raquel a few moments to recover from the blow I just delivered to her self-esteem. "Well, did he ask you out again?"

"Yes, we have a dinner date planned for next week. Adam says he has something really important to talk to me about," she explains.

"Well, see, there you go!" I reassure her. While it's true that I desperately crave to be inside of Raquel, I also want her to be happy. Contrary to popular belief, I'm not a complete narcissistic pig.

"I'm going to give you a nice bonus on your next paycheck so that you can buy the most incredible dress you can find for this date,"

I offer. "Raquel, if you really like and want this guy, you're going to have to pull out the heavy artillery sweetie."

"What do you mean?"

"Show him some of the goods. You've got the kind of huge *tatas* that men go gaga over, so put those puppies on display. Reveal those traffic-stopping legs of yours more often. You know subtle shit like that."

Right away I can tell Raquel is not buying into my get laid propaganda. "Other women may not have a problem putting out all the stops, but I don't feel comfortable with this kind of branding and marketing program. First and foremost, a man has to want me because of my sheer brilliance, wicked sense of humor, and winning personality. These tools have served me well in keeping a man interested outside of the bedroom."

I am quick to agree with her. "There's no denying that you're all of these things. But you can't ignore the fact that you're really easy on the eyes, too. Take it from me, you are oozing with sex appeal. YOU'RE THE TOTAL PACKAGE. A woman who has substance and is in touch with her sexuality is a rare find. That's you, sweetheart. Own it!" As I wait for her reaction, I'm mentally scolding myself, *Why the hell are you helping out the enemy here?*

"I'll take all of this under advisement," Raquel says. "I have one question for you though."

"Shoot!"

Raquel musters up one of her radiant smiles. "Wanna go dress shopping with me?"

"I smile back at her instantly. "It would be my honor."

"Great, then it's a date," Raquel says.

We both pause and smile at one another and for a few fleeting moments it feels as though we are the only two people that exist in the universe. In the middle of fantasizing in my head that I'm Adam and she's my Eve, I have an epiphany. "Oh, shit!" I exclaim out of the blue as I start to hunt for the Post-It note with a phone message written on it.

"What's the matter?" Raquel asks as she enters the office and sits down on the chair right across from my desk.

"Someone called for you earlier. A woman. A very sexy sounding one," I explain.

Raquel furrows her eyebrows. You can tell that the gears in her pretty head are starting to shift quickly. "Well, did she give her name?"

"Yes. I wrote it down. Hold on!" I say, scanning my desk for my pad of Post-It notes. After shifting a few piles of paperwork here and there, the pad reappears. I rip off the note with the name and number written on it and hand it over to Raquel. Her whole demeaner changes the second she reads what I scribbled on the Post-It note.

"What's the matter? You look like you've just seen a ghost," I remark.

Raquel shifts a little in the chair. I can tell she's feeling rather uncomfortable right now. "Well, you could say that. I haven't heard from Stephanie in years. I wonder how she found me and why she called today of all days?"

"There's only one way to find out. Call her back!" I insist.

"It's not that simple," Raquel replies.

"Why not? Who exactly is Stephanie Trujillo and how long has it' been since you last spoke with her?"

Raquel crosses her arms and says, "It's a long story."

"I've got time so start talking," I say to her as I lean back in my chair. "Besides, you always listen to my sex stories. It's my turn to listen to you now."

Raquel regroups by uncrossing her legs and then crossing them again. "I was going through a really dark time in my life when I met Stephanie. My roommate Julie had just died in a fatal car crash and I was dumped by my boyfriend who was a fighter pilot stationed at the Air Force base located in my hometown. I had vowed to never give my heart to anyone else ever again—male or female."

"Well, that was stupid of you," I comment.

"Stupid or not, I meant it," Raquel reiterates. "But then Stephanie came into my life with her trailblazing ways and pulled me out of my zombie-like state. She brought me back to life."

So, how did you two actually meet," I ask.

"Wanting a change of pace, I decided to look for a new job. It didn't take me long to land an interview for a telemarketing position for a hearing aid clinic which happened to be located inside the local mall. Upon arriving at the interview, I was greeted by a super attractive young woman with a killer smile who introduced herself as Stephanie Trujillo. She and I only chatted for a short while but obviously I must have made some kind of impression on her because the next day she called to say the job was mine if I wanted it and this marked the beginning of a beautiful friendship."

"So, let me get this straight. You were two hot young Latinas working at a hearing aid practice, servicing old men," I point out.

A few sweet, sounding giggles escape from Raquel's mouth. "I guess you could say that." After she regains her composure, Raquel presses on with her story. "Individually, Stephanie and I each packed a pretty good punch, but together we seemed to have more fire power than the Army, Navy and Air Force put together. We were exact opposites and yet, twin souls at the same time."

At this juncture, I'm pretty hooked and want to hear the rest of the story. "So, tell me more about Stephanie," I insist.

"One of the things I most admired about her is that she wasn't afraid to be lawless when the situation called for it. She was an expert at using her feminine wiles to get what she wanted. When the need arose, and it did quite often, she could wiggle herself out of trouble, literally."

"Sounds like my kind of girl," I remark.

"We were so much more than just a couple of great looking *chicas*. Stephanie and I were two headstrong and fearless females who actually succeeded in getting the entire population to believe in us. Almost overnight we went from being two pretty faces in the crowd to icons who were recognized everywhere we went in the small town we lived in. As long as I live, I'll never forget the day we announced to anyone who would listen that we were going to start publishing our own bilingual newspaper."

I was enjoying her narrative. This prompted me to get more comfortable. "Well, that was a gutsy move!"

Raquel is quick to respond to my statement. "In the beginning, no one took us seriously. Some people ridiculed us and didn't hold back in saying that our newspaper would never amount to a hill of beans. Despite all the negativity surrounding us, Stephanie and I had big plans for our newspaper which we named *The Zia Sun Times*. It was going to be as lucrative and widely read as the *U.S.A Today*. I think we could have pulled it off had we not been crippled by serious personal issues that threatened our physical and emotional well-being."

Instinctively, I lean forward toward Raquel because I'm now emotionally invested in her story. "Well, what happened that sabotaged the whole operation?"

By the looks of things, Raquel has also become emotional. She takes a few deep breaths, reaches over, and plucks a couple of sheets out of the tissue box sitting on the corner of my desk. "In order to keep cranking out one issue after another of the newspaper, we found ourselves working fourteen-hour days. What I didn't know then was that Stephanie's marriage was on life support while I was heading straight for self-destruction. That turned out to be the beginning of the end."

"What do you mean? Please elaborate," I say with a sense of urgency in my voice.

Raquel nods her head slightly giving me an indication that she'll continue to tell her story. But before doing so, she gently dabs at the tears that are dangling from her eyelashes with the tissue. "Stephanie's marriage had reached its maximum pressure point and was about to explode into a million and one tiny fragments. She hid it from me so well. On several occasions she had asked her husband for a divorce but, he wouldn't hear of it. After putting in her request, things at home really got hostile and her military-trained husband became more and more violent with each passing day."

"Then what happened?"

"One morning before going into the office, I received a distress call from our secretary letting me know that Stephanie was gone. Apparently, Stephanie's husband had held her at knifepoint and threatened to kill her if she left him. She had no choice but to abandon the newspaper, pack up her belongings and two children, and skip town before it was too late. As I listened to our secretary's play-by-play account of the story, I stared blankly into space. Right then and there, it hit me like a ton of bricks that Stephanie was gone out of my life forever and chances were I'd never see her again. In the blink of an eye, she had practically vanished into thin air and I didn't get the chance to say good-bye."

Normally, I don't get bent out of shape when I hear a sad story. But this one just happens to be a real tearjerker. Maybe the fact that it's being told by the woman I'm deeply in love with has everything to do with my emotions being tied up in knots. "So, what happened to the paper?" I demand to know.

"With the help of a few staff members, I was able to keep publishing the newspaper for only a few months after that. It was just too much work and without Stephanie, it didn't feel right, so I ceased publication of the *Zia Sun Times*."

"That must have been heart breaking for you," I interject.

"Letting go of Stephanie and the newspaper was one of the hardest things I've ever done in my life. Together we had created something great out of nothing. Walking away from all that we had accomplished through trial and error really took an emotional toll on me. For nearly a decade I mourned this loss."

"Wow, this is an incredible story!" I exclaim. "Why didn't you tell me this before?"

Raquel pauses and I can tell she is deliberating about what to say next. "I don't know. I didn't think you'd be interested."

"How can I not be?" I stop talking as well to recap everything Raquel has told me in my head. We both sit silently across each other until we've had the opportunity to digest it all. I finally break the silence by asking, "So, is the first time you've heard from her in all these years?"

"As crazy as it sounds, it is," Raquel confirms.

Suddenly, I get the crazy idea that I somehow need to right this wrong. I pick up my phone desk and practically shove it into Raquel's teary face. "Call Stephanie right now and invite her to come visit you here. Tell her you two are long overdue for a heart-felt reunion and that it's happening in the home of Michael Stephen Grant."

Chapter Twelve

Like a Horse Trying to Screw a Chihuahua

I'm in heaven. No, wait! Let me rephrase that. I. AM. IN. HEAVEN. As it turns out, Stephanie Trujillo is a fair-skinned bombshell with long blonde hair and a booty just as delicious looking, if not more so than Jennifer Lopez's. Then there's Raquel with her seductive bedroom eyes and legs that give men whiplash. Being in the company of these two beautiful women has my dick on overdrive. All week long, I've been having to hide my full-on erections with toss pillows because I can't stop fantasizing about what it would be like to make love to the both of them—at the same time. Talk about the ultimate *ménage à trois*.

Egging on Raquel to invite her long-lost girlfriend to come visit us was the best idea I've come up with on a whim in a long time. Having a front row seat and getting to see these two twin souls reunited after so many years of being apart can best be described as a once-in-a-lifetime-experience. Aside from all the arousing sensations being around these two have brought on for me, in retrospect I can see how Stephanie's visit has done a world of good for Raquel. Ever since she arrived six days ago, Raquel has become a more fun-loving, confident, and fearless woman and I really like that. If only I could orchestrate a way to have Stephanie move in with us permanently, then I'd be the most coveted man in the world.

It seems as though Raquel and Stephanie have picked up right where they left off, talking and giggling like a couple of out-of-control, horny schoolgirls. In fact, one could say that they have defied the winds of change. Time has stood still for them which is a testimony to just how special their friendship truly is. For me, it's been a ton of fun getting to watch them catch up, but my writing has suffered because of it. What hot-blooded man with a cock in good working order after having been broken down for a good while wouldn't rather spend time with these two ridiculously hot women than write books about self-discipline? Even if I wanted to, I couldn't string two coherent sentences together. My brain has packed up all of its creativity and is vacationing down south, if you know what I mean. The writing will just have to wait.

Throughout the span of time that Raquel and Stephanie lost touch with one another, they both forged a new life for themselves. While Raquel decided to pursue a career in publishing, Stephanie got remarried again but only after having enjoyed a good number of years working in Corporate America, jet-setting to interesting places, and dating exotic men. It was only after she'd had her fill of living a fast-paced single life with lots of insatiable sex that the love bug bit her. Stephanie married a restauranteur from Uruguay and gave birth to another son. She and her husband own several restaurants throughout the surrounding Atlanta area.

So here I am, sitting on the couch, ogling these two gorgeous women working harmoniously to get dinner on the table as they reminisce and talk non-stop about their glory days of being newspaper publishers. Since this is Stephanie's last night visiting, we decided to have a quiet and intimate sit-down dinner for three. When they first proposed this idea to me versus going out to eat at a crowded restaurant, I immediately said yes. Call me crazy, selfish, or downright horny, but I want these two exquisite beauties all to myself than have to share them with a bunch of strangers.

"Michael, wake up. Dinner is ready." I open my eyes to see Raquel's angelic face dangerously close to mine and for a fleeting moment I think that I've died and gone to heaven. Then I feel the soft caress of her hand petting my arm and immediately I start to get warm and fuzzy inside—my pants. I sit up straight as an arrow, rub my eyes, and try to make sense of what's going on.

Raquel doesn't waste any time in stating the obvious. "You must have dozed off on the couch."

"It looks that way, doesn't it?"

She gifts me with one of her sweet smiles that always makes my heart skip a beat. "Well, c'mon, dinner is ready," she says to me while tugging at me to get my ass off the couch. Then she does something totally unexpectedly that sends me into a mental frenzy. Raquel grabs my hand firmly and helps me up. Then she walks me into the dining room, still holding my hand, where the lovely Stephanie is waiting for us to come to the table and be seated.

My eyes widen when I see the full spread that has been laid out before me. "Wow, you ladies certainly went through a great deal of trouble," I say, taking a seat between the both of them. "This is a meal fit for a king," I add.

"Well, Mr. Grant, tonight you are OUR ANNOINTED KING," Stephanie blurts out. "So, kick back and enjoy. Besides you totally deserve this. You have been such a gracious host. Thank you for allowing me to come visit my SISTER FROM ANOTHER MISTER."

"Believe me when I say this, the pleasure has been all mine. I only wish you could stay longer. You're welcome to come visit anytime," I say.

Stephanie reaches over and gives me a hug which makes my penis react in kind. "After you're done with your clinical trials, you and Raquel should come visit me in Atlanta. My husband and I would love to have you both. We'll have a fantastic time."

"Now that sounds like an offer I can't refuse," I'm quick to respond.

"I hope you're hungry," Raquel chimes in. "C'mon dig in!"

We stop the pleasant chitchat long enough to fill our plates. Everything looks and smells delicious so, I pile it on pretty thick. Raquel uncorks a bottle of red wine, a Malbec I think, and skillfully pours some into my glass. She does the same for Stephanie and then fills her own. "I would like to make a toast," she announces, raising her glass in the air. Stephanie and I follow her lead and gently thrust ours toward hers.

Raquel clears her throat a couple of times and then begins to speak. "First, here's to Stephanie. I have missed you so much in my life. Being reunited with you again has made my heart as full as this glass. Please don't ever leave me again." Then she pauses and shifts her gaze over to me. "Now to MSG, here's to you being cancer-free. May you live as long as you like and have all you like as long as you live."

We all click our glasses in perfect synchronicity and the sound pleasantly echoes in my ear. After taking a few sips of our wine, we get settled in, and don't hesitate in starting an engaging conversation. I'm the first one to break the ice by asking, "So, when and where was the idea to publish your own newspaper first conceived?"

The girls stop dead in their tracks and look at one another with a special fiery glow in their eyes. They seem to be communicating telepathically with one another, as if trying to decide which one of them should speak up first. "It was the week leading up to Cinco de Mayo weekend. Raquel and I were at the hearing aid office where we worked killing time by discussing what we should do to celebrate," Stephanie blurts out. "I asked Raquel if there was a local newsletter or newspaper serving the Hispanic community that we could check out to see what kinds of activities were being planned."

At this point, Raquel dives right in, "That's when I told her there was none."

"I was both stunned and upset to find out there were no existing media outlets reporting Hispanic news and events. I had always lived in cities with large Hispanic populations and every one of them had something, at the very least a newsletter," Stephanie explained. "The more I thought about it, the more pissed off I felt. So, do you know what Raquel and I decided to do? Tell him Raquel."

"We decided to take it upon ourselves to fill this void by creating and publishing a newspaper that would inspire Hispanic heritage awareness and more community involvement in our town," Raquel states with a great sense of pride. "But there was a large hurdle that we needed to get past."

"What was that?" I ask.

"Neither of us had any prior journalism or newspaper publishing experience," Raquel is quick to reply. "So, we were going to have to wing it."

"And did you?"

"We sure did!" Stephanie confirms. "Actually, we totally killed it. Within a few days, the news about our plans spread like wildfire and this caused a colorful awakening of the town's residents."

"To help us get started, I reached out to a childhood friend named Bobby Joe Cisneros who worked as a magazine graphic artist at the local university," Raquel explains. "Bobby was really smitten with our idea and he provided us with a list of equipment and supplies we would need to produce a camera-ready newspaper."

By now I'm really getting into the story and want to know more. "Then what?"

Stephanie jumps in and continues the narration. "We paid a visit to the only computer store in town and discovered that purchasing all of the items on the list was going to be extremely expensive. So, we had to improvise, yet stay within our budget which was determined by my credit score."

Raquel barely waits for Stephanie to finish her last statement before exclaiming, "The total cost for a PC, printer and publishing software took up her entire approved credit line of $10.000."

I let out a loud and clear whistle. "That's pretty steep! Hey, you girls have got me hooked. Tell me more."

Raquel takes my cue and runs with it. "While Stephanie is setting up a home office in her laundry room and learning how to use the PC and software, she orders me to dress up in a mini-skirt and high heels and throws me out into the street. She tells me not to come back until I have found a printing press and sold enough advertising to pay for the first edition of our still unnamed newspaper."

"Oh my God! Did you really do that?" I ask looking directly at Stephanie.

"Guilty as charged!" Stephanie confesses. "If you think her legs look good now, you should have seen them back then. Back in the day, Raquel's legs intoxicated more men than Jack Daniels. There was no way I wasn't going to put them to good use."

"Ha! I love it!" I let out. "And did Raquel come through?"

"Hell yeah, I came through!" Raquel affirms. "I remember returning back to Stephanie's house late in the day with a fistful of checks and a printing quote."

Stephanie's face lights up and she smiles from ear to ear. "Girlfriend, do you remember what you said?"

"No, remind me," Raquel answers.

"You said, 'I've got $600.00 worth of checks and I ain't giving them back. So, we have to print.'"

Stephanie continues telling this part of the story. "Over a couple of bottles of wine, we christened the newspaper *The Zia Sun Times* and began selecting local news and events that was going to make up the content of our first issue."

I bust out laughing. "What a great story!"

Raquel gets a devilish look on her face and says, "Oh, we've got more stories, enough to keep you entertained all night long."

"I bet you do," I respond. "Well, keep going. But first pour me some more wine."

As soon as all our wine glasses have been topped off, Stephanie immediately starts in again. "Raquel, do you remember the time you received a decent proposal from Rick Vaughn?"

Being reminded of this memory makes Raquel gasp for air. "Oh my God! That was totally insane."

"Well, spill it, every last ounce of it," I insist.

"Since I brought it up, I'll tell him the story," Stephanie says with bravado. "Raquel and I still had our day jobs and we decided to temporarily use the hearing aid office as a start-up, underground location for the *Zia Sun Times* without corporate approval."

"Oh, I already like where this is going," I remark.

"One day, Rick Vaughn, the vice-president of the company called to say he was going to be in the area and he wanted to meet the new telemarketer," Stephanie explains.

"What was the problem with that?" I dare to ask.

"Are you kidding me?" Raquel feels inclined to interject. "We had all of our newspaper equipment laid out everywhere. The place was going to be unrecognizable to Rick Vaughn. So, there we were panic stricken. We had to find a way to stop him from coming to the office."

Stephanie decides to regain control of the storytelling. "I had met Rick Vaughn previously and knew about his weakness for sexy Latinas. I told Raquel to go home and change into something more provocative. When he arrived at the front desk, we both greeted him. Then we invited him out to dinner and a comedy show at the local country saloon."

My curiosity gets the best of me so I cut in, "Did he go for it?"

"Hook, line and sinker," Stephanie answers. "Immediately overcome by Raquel's beauty and overspilling bosom, he agreed on the spot."

"So, I take it he never got past the front desk?" I make it a point to ask.

"Nope!" they both exclaim at the same time.

At this juncture, Raquel feels the need to give her two cents. "During the show, Stephanie's husband called unexpectedly to say he was home from his overseas tour and that she should go home. Well, can you believe it? Stephanie left me alone to deal with the sexually perverted Rick Vaughn and his advances."

"Why do I get the feeling that we've reached the climax to this story?" I guess.

Raquel confirms this by going on to say, "Not long after Stephanie left, Rick Vaughn didn't hesitate to make me a decent proposal that as much as I hate to admit was hard for me to refuse."

"Do tell and don't leave out any juicy detail," I egg her on.

"Rick started out by telling me that I was the most beautiful woman he'd ever seen in his entire life. He also said he strongly believed that it had been written in the cosmos a long time ago I was meant to be his."

I look at Stephanie to gauge her reaction and I catch her rolling her eyes. "Then what did he say?"

"He laid out all of his cards on the table. Rick said to me that if I agreed to become his mistress, he would take really good care of me. He would put me up in the nicest apartment my town had to offer and pay all of my bills. And the icing on the cake was that I could keep his car."

Stephanie can't help herself and she immediately volunteers, "MSG, it was a Bentley!"

"Oh my God, a Bentley?" I practically shout out.

"Yeah, all I had to do was say yes and he'd hand over the keys to me. But I would have to drive him back to Albuquerque which was where he lived at the time."

After mulling over these last details of the story I'm prompted to ask Raquel a burning question. "Well, were you not tempted in the slightest by his decent proposal?"

She is quick to answer. "I'm not going to lie. I did think about it for a split-second. I was a poor working girl, practically living in a shack, and having to skip meals because I never had any money."

"Well if you had said yes, all of your problems would have been solved." I point out.

"Yeah, maybe for a while," Raquel concurs. "But I just couldn't do it."

"Why not?"

Stephanie and Raquel exchange knowing looks and then smile. "Because he was BUTT UGLY!" they both yell out together.

"Let me get this straight. You ladies would rather become homeless or starve to death than screw an ugly man?" I question.

"Damn straight!" they both respond without the slightest hesitation.

"Women, who can understand them?" I quip back.

"How about another story? A quickie but a goodie," Stephanie suggests.

"Sure, why not? It's still way too early to call it a night," I reply.

Stephanie takes a moment to gather her thoughts and little by little, a radiant smile starts to form on her lovely face. "The name of this story is HARD NEWS," she announces.

Raquel busts out laughing uncontrollably. "I had forgotten about that. Yeah, definitely tell him."

"Shall I brace myself first?" I propose.

"Wouldn't hurt," Raquel says. "Okay, Stephanie, the mic is yours."

Stephanie doesn't waste any time in breaking it down for us. "We used to feature a Bachelor of the Month in every issue of our newspaper. In time, I became really close friends with one of them named Alex Negrete. Even though he had an out-of-state fiancée, Alex was the most coveted single man in our town. One day, he gave me a key to his contemporary decorated bachelor pad to use as a sanctuary whenever I wanted to hide from my unwanted husband." She pauses to catch her breath and then presses on. "One evening, Raquel and I were driving back from a regional newspaper industry event that had taken place a couple of towns away. We had received an award for our newspaper and were in a celebratory mood."

Raquel impulsively cuts in. "Yeah, we wanted to keep the celebration going. The problem was we couldn't go back to Stephanie's place because her husband was home."

So, what did you do?"

"I remembered Alex had mentioned to me that he was going to be out of town so we decided to crash at his pad for the night," Stephanie reveals. "We rolled into town and headed straight for Alex's loft apartment. When we got there, I let us into the apartment with the key he had given me."

Suddenly, Raquel decides to steal Stephanie's thunder. "We were at the bottom of the stairs trying to locate the light switch so we could climb up. As soon as Stephanie flicked on the switch, we came face-to-face with hard news."

"What do you mean?" I demand to know.

Stephanie doesn't mince words and she goes for the big reveal. "Alex was at the top of the stairs, buck naked with a full erection and dumbfounded look on his face," she discloses.

My hand automatically flies over my mouth. "No!"

"Oh yes! Apparently his on again, off again fiancée also had the same idea and decided to drop in on him as well," Raquel elaborates.

"You two are real ball busters. You know that, right?" I declare.

"It's a tough and dirty job, but someone's gotta do it!" Raquel professes.

We all had a good laugh about it and then decide to move on to dessert. Not wanting the night to end, I suggest to the girls that we should all work together to clean up and reconvene in the living room for more wine and storytelling. About half an hour later, we are all lounging together on the couch. "Okay girls, make yourself comfortable, kick your shoes off and get undressed. It's my turn to tell you a bed-time story, MSG style," I proclaim.

"We'll take off the shoes but keep our clothes on," Raquel counteroffers.

I make a sour face and say," I was afraid of that."

Raquel giggles and then looks over at Stephanie. "Buckle up! MSG's stories are X-Rated and pretty arousing. Hearing discretion is advised!"

"Bring it on," says Stephanie, not intimidated at all.

"Careful what you wish for, young lady," I warn her. "I'm going to tell you about my crazy sexual adventures in Singapore"

***

Back in my glory days as an IT expert speaker and international man of mystery, I traveled to Singapore for business at least a dozen times and I always chose to fly on Singapore Airlines. The customer service was awesome. The flight attendants were all young and beautiful. They always smiled and actually enjoyed their work. Oh, the form-fitting uniforms they wore was quite a treat for my roving eyes and overactive penis. I could never figure out how they could bend over in their tight outfits. It was nothing like flying in the states where the flight attendants are bitchy, unionized, and do the bare minimum. Hell, most of them should have been grounded years earlier as their average age is probably fifty.

Besides conducting business, shopping, and seeing a movie there isn't much else to do in Singapore—it's a boring little country. However, for being small it sure does have its act together in just about every area: commerce, technology, overall efficiency, not to mention that it's probably the cleanest country on this planet. Many companies like having their Asian headquarters there because of their efficiencies and Changi Airport. In my opinion it's one of the nicest and most efficient airports in the world. I used to love flying in and out of there on Singapore Airlines.

I'll never forget on one occasion I met this girl named Yi Ling through a business associate. She was intelligent, pretty, and had a warm personality. We hit it off so, I decided to make her a future victim. I started courting her long distance, calling her from the states, so when I arrived back in Singapore, I would only have to invest minimum resources in order to get her in bed. My ahead of the curve planning paid off because it only took one dinner and she was back in my hotel room. Granted, she didn't put up much of a challenge, but what made this evening memorable was the way she screamed. When she had an orgasm the entire hotel floor knew about it—no exaggeration—security actually came to our door to make   sure everything was okay. We were asked to keep the noise level down. When I plowed her in the ass, I had to put my hand over her mouth to muffle her exaggerated screams. This girl was the ultimate screamer. She was fun, but only good for a few nights. Most of the Singaporeans are westernized—especially the women. Although they may have that typical Asian (innocent) look—especially in public, behind closed doors it's everything goes and most of them take it in the ass without hesitation. There is nothing old-fashioned about them.

I met Cassandra while facilitating a talk for a company, one of many presentations on this particular three-day trip. I entered a conference room packed with about twenty people. There were only two women in attendance and Cassandra was one of them. She stood out because she was so tiny, maybe 4'11, maybe less, but she had a great little butt. It looked like an apple, one that I wanted to take a giant bite out of. I noticed it after the presentation was over. My radar picked up on it as she was exiting the room. There was no doubt that I wanted to spin that butt of hers on my cock. She was adorable, but how to befriend her without making a fool out of myself was the question.

At the end of the presentation, refreshments were brought in, and Cassandra came back into the room. I didn't want to get caught staring at her, that would not be cool at all, so I just smiled and said, "Welcome back." It was my way of breaking the ice just a bit. Cassandra smiled back at me.

This group of professionals I had just spoken to represented an IT consortium in Singapore. Every quarter they would get together and discuss different topics. Each meeting was hosted by a different company. Cassandra was ready to head out. I quickly looked at her and said, "Thank you for coming."

"Thank you for speaking to us," she replied politely.

I needed to grab her attention quickly so, I went out on a limb. "Cassandra, I don't quite know how to grab a taxi from this part of town to get me back to my hotel. Can I please follow you downstairs and you can point me in the right direction?"

Cassandra immediately fell for my traveler-in-distress act. "Yes of course! Where are you staying?"

"At the Hyatt Hotel."

"My office is quite near there. You can ride along with me in a taxi and I will drop you off first," she offered.

"Thank you," I replied.

This was the opportunity I needed. As we were waiting outside for the taxi, I got a really good view of her ass. The beige slacks she was wearing were form-fitting and accentuated it rather well. Her small size really turned me on. Cassandra was the ultimate spinner, every man's dream come true. There I was, standing beside her, picturing in my mind throwing her on top of my fully extended 9-inch joystick.

We talked for the entire ten-minute drive to the hotel. I asked Cassandra for her card and I told her that I sincerely appreciated her kind gesture. But I didn't stop there. I went ahead and asked her if I could give her a call when I got back to the states, explaining I was leaving the next day, but would be returning to Singapore in a few weeks to conduct more business. She looked a bit surprised that I would go out of my way to call her from the US.

Cassandra was well-educated and had a charming personality. That much I had gathered from our conversation. I concluded by telling her she was a very nice person and worth keeping in touch with.

She smiled appreciatively and said, "Thank you!"

In Asia it's all about establishing a friendship first and that was the goal with my future spinner. Immediately when I returned to the states, I called her and, she was pleasantly surprised. Cassandra was happy that I called to say hello. We spoke for only a few minutes. The idea was for me to just tease her a bit, leave her wanting more of MSG.

"I will call you tomorrow," I promised her

"Please, you don't have too," she answered back.

"But I want too, you are very nice and, I would like to know more about you," I reassured her.

The following day I called Cassandra and after every conversation we had after that, I got to know her more and more. My plan was to earn her friendship first and then penetrate and spin that round but petite Asian ass with my American cock. After about a half-dozen calls, we became pretty good friends and I also found out that she had a boyfriend.

I told her I was flying back to Singapore just to see her and not for business. That line earned me quite a few brownie points, but there was still a long way to go between friends and friends with benefits. There was one huge obstacle standing in my way—her boyfriend. I asked her if she could take a half day off from work and hangout with me?

Yes of course," she confirmed.

When I arrived at Changi Airport, Cassandra met me near Customs and escorted me back to the hotel. She dropped me off and said she'd be back at lunchtime and spend the afternoon with me. It came to pass just as she had said it would. So, there we were, hanging out in my hotel room, which was a suite with a large living room and separate bedroom. All I needed at that point was an IN.

For a good while, we talked about random things which wasn't getting me any closer to that lovely ass of hers. Then I changed gears and asked about her boyfriend. I encouraged her to tell me about him and their relationship. Cassandra revealed to me that she didn't like him so much because he was extremely demanding and dictatorial. He was also the jealous type. She felt like she was his property, not his girlfriend. Cassandra had been dating him for about a year. You could tell she wasn't happy with the relationship, but her parents liked him, which carried a lot of weight in her culture.

Unfortunately, Cassandra couldn't stay for dinner because she had to meet her boyfriend. She was loyal to him regardless of how she felt. That night as I sat in my room alone, I came up with a whopper of an idea. Around 6:00 PM, I sent her an e-mail with the following subject line: A SPECIAL NOTE FROM A FRIEND AND LIFE COACH. I needed to explain to Cassandra how someone who truly cared about her should treat her. She should be treated as an equal and not an object. In the e-mail, I wrote down all the wonderful attributes about her. I mentioned that she was caring, sincere, genuine, thoughtful, and beautiful. I also reminded her that she should always be respected. Sure, I wanted to get my giant Sasquatch hands all over the tight sweet ass, but all those attributes about her were true. About two hours later, Cassandra arrived home and she called me.

She said to me, "I read your e-mail. It was truly beautiful. Thank you so much for writing it and I will meet you tomorrow morning for breakfast at 7:00 AM."

The next morning, she arrived at the appointed time. She was wearing form-fitting jeans and her long, black hair was perfectly brushed. Her clear olive complexion was glowing under the hotel lighting. After breakfast we went back to my room just to hangout. It was always super-hot and humid in Singapore, so staying inside was the smart thing to do.

"Please give me a few moments to send some emails," I said to her.

My computer was on the coffee table in the living room so, I sat with my back against the couch and legs under the table. "Please come sit next to me for a bit and bring your computer here so you can do some work as well," I suggested. She always had her laptop with her.

Cassandra snuggled up next to me with her computer. She looked over to see what I was doing. When she did, I gazed back at her, smiled, and gave her a peck on the cheek. She looked at me again and I kissed her on the lips. She kissed back and the next thing I knew our lips were locked. I picked her up off the floor and carried her into the bedroom with our lips still in full locked-down position.

I put her down on the bed and gently laid on top of her. I didn't want to squish the poor girl; she was so petite and adorable. With my heart pounding nearly out of my chest, I unbuckled her jeans and slid them right off. I wanted her naked in bed with me *pronto*. As usual, I didn't even care to spend any time playing with her breasts. Quite frankly, I don't even remember what size they were. All I wanted to do was two things; eat some MSG-Free Asian pussy and when I felt totally satisfied, and only then, position her butt over my dick and go for full penetration.

Cassandra never wore makeup. The truth is she didn't need to because she was naturally beautiful with radiant, olive-toned skin that felt silky smooth to the touch. After pleasuring her to the tune of a few orgasms, I could sense that she was already starting to fall for me. She told me that her boyfriend had never pleasured her the way I had.

"He sticks it in, has an orgasm, and then takes it out. I've never had an orgasm until now. I've never felt this sensation before," she admitted bravely.

Cassandra was totally savoring our lovemaking and so was I. After having given her a couple of unforgettable orgasms, she surrendered and totally gave herself over to me. What I was going to do to her was a no-brainer. I put her on top of me and rammed the entire hardened length of my 9-inch dick into her pulsating wet pussy. Cassandra went ballistic and that made me shoot a few rounds myself. After I had an orgasm of epic proportions, we took a short nap for about forty-five minutes, and then continued to make-out and get ourselves all worked up for another round. That's when I grabbed some Vaseline from my amenities bag and rubbed it on my erect penis. Once again, I picked her up and guided her butt hole right on it. She jerked a bit. I asked her, "Are you okay?

Cassandra nodded her head, letting me know everything was good. She took it all in like a real pro. I mean all of it, not a single millimeter of my cock was exposed. I was amazed at how much she was enjoying herself. There's one thing about Asian girls, they look so shy and act so innocent in public, but behind closed doors—

SHAZAM!—they throw all of their inhibitions out the window and let loose.

It was a great morning. I even didn't mind lounging around with her. We decided to go out for lunch to this really cool market where you can pick and choose from all types of different foods from around the world. After lunch we went to see a movie at a nearby mall then back to the hotel room. Once I closed the door, I picked her up and started to kiss her passionately again. This time I went straight for her ass. I started caressing and kissing it like crazy and just about drove her insane by focusing on her butt hole.

This time I wanted her doggie style so I could watch my dick go in and out of her butt. She pretty much let me do whatever I wanted now. We both loved each other's company. When she finally left later that evening, I mentioned for her to wear a skirt the next day. I told her how much I would love to see her in one. She smiled and gave me a kiss goodnight. Cassandra lived with her parents and it wasn't cool for her to be out all night.

The next day she showed up wearing this cute denim skirt. After she came into my hotel room, I took her over to the lounge chair in the bedroom, bent her over, hiked up her skirt, slid her panties off. I munched away on her pussy like there was no tomorrow and after she had an orgasm, I plowed my penis right into her ass again. There I was loving every second of it. Suddenly it occurred to me to ask her flat-out, "How can you handle taking in my huge cock in your butt? Doesn't it hurt?"

She merely smiled at me and said, "I am happy that you are so happy Michael."

Cassandra and I continued to see each other for about a year. I knew perfectly well that she was looking to get married and well MSG already had an unwanted wife at home. Purposely, I drifted apart from her and she eventually found a man she wanted to marry. Until this day, I still shake my head every time I think about how that little cute Chihuahua took my dick in her ass each time like a true champ. She was one special young lady.

Chapter Thirteen

The Swedish Blonde, Green-Eyed Bombshell

Finally, after more than six months of living in a cold, obscure cave, a sliver of sunlight has somehow filtered through and is now shining upon my face. Could it be that my dance with the devil and his ugly sister—impending death—will soon be over? Knock on wood, the highly experimental treatments being administered to me have been declared a tremendous success and I am starting to look and feel like a well put together gigolo few women can afford to hire. Now that I am basking in the warm sunlight again, I'm all fired up and so ready to stick my impressive member inside a beautiful woman and thrust away until I see the stars up close and personal. In other words, Michael Stephen Grant, and the happy-go-lucky cocky friend that dwells inside his pants, are back with a vengeance, willing and able to partake in a whole lot of voracious lovemaking.

The first woman on my conquest list is a delicious looking Mexican dish named Raquel Lopez who at this very moment happens to be resting her lovely head on my lap. She is sleeping peacefully with her voluminous, raven black hair artistically splayed across my entire crotch area and I'd be lying if I said that all her sudden twists and turns aren't making my temperature rise. As for me, I'm riding comfortably in the backseat of a steel, gray stretch limousine courtesy of the Fort Worth-based health and nutrition company that hired me for an all-day business motivational speaking and executive coaching session.

It's been a good day for us both, albeit a long one, but we'll be home in about half an hour. My legs are starting to fall asleep from the weight of her head but I'm going to grin and take it because the last thing I want to do is wake-up sleeping beauty. She worked so hard today on my behalf to make sure everything ran smoothly since it was the first executive coaching gig that's come my way since rising up from the dead. I would also be crazy to disturb this absolutely perfect moment in time. The more I gaze at her, the more I realize how much she means to me. Since I'm coming clean now about a number of things, I might as well go on the record and admit that what I feel is way beyond just caring. I'm ready to officially declare that I am undeniably and hopelessly in love with her. But I'm also scared as hell of being rejected.

This is so ironic to me because in my lifetime I've bedded so many women that it could easily be considered a crime. Be that as it may, this is the first time in Michael Stephen Grant's philandering life that he's even considered pouring out his heart to a woman without knowing with certainty if she feels the same way about him. I'm taking a monumental risk that my declaration of love could be unrequited. The question is should I try to cross this bridge or not.

As difficult as it may be, I'm not going to grovel over the fact that I've gone from being the CHOOSER to waiting to be the CHOSEN ONE. Because I honestly don't have the faintest idea where I stand with Raquel. My relationship with her was progressing so nicely before Mr. G.Q.-in-a-white-lab-coat came into our lives. Granted, he arrived on the scene to save my life for which I am grateful for. But did he have to be so damned good-looking in the process? Before his intrusion I was pretty sure it would be merely a matter of time before Raquel fell in love and into bed with me. In the past, every woman I had set my sights on did, so why not her?

My plans to incite her into having the sweetest, mind-blowing orgasms of her life went straight out the window the minute Dr. Campbell introduced us to Dr. Adam Lancaster. It was clearly obvious to me that there seemed to be chemistry between Raquel and him. I stood there and read their body language which screamed they were drawn to one another. But she and I have also had our moments. I'm not exactly chopped liver either.

Since Stephanie left, Raquel has gone on more dates with Dr. Lancaster but, something seems to be amiss. She comes home without that radiant glow women get when they have been serviced sexually to full satisfaction, which tells me they aren't having sex yet. Believe me if they were, and he was manning up and giving it to her real good, she'd have that unmistakable after sex glow. This means I still have a shot at being able to make my grand entrance into her gateway of pleasure. Right now, I can't think of any other place I'd rather be.

Another interesting twist that has me somewhat baffled is the fact that my ex-wife Maribel has been calling, e-mailing, and texting on a regular basis. Some of her messages have been borderline flirtatious. I hate the fact that most women have this innate sixth sense that never fails them. They seem to be able to detect when another female is purposely or inadvertently trying to encroach on their territory. Hell, they could be a planet away and yet somehow; they are still able to catch the scent of another woman's pussy being in close proximity to their man. Will someone please explain this mysterious phenomenon to me?

I'm not going to lie, Maribel's renewed interest in me is really flattering and I guess down deep inside I still harbor strong feelings for her. But I can't dismiss the fact that she broke my heart, divorced me, and walked away with half of my fortune. Then she high-tailed it to a beautiful island in France to work for a rich hotel tycoon. Behavior like this has a way of turning a man into a bitter son-of-bitch who is incapable of trusting another woman, no matter how damn hot she is. For now, I'm just going to play along and see how far Maribel wants to take this. However, that's not going to stop me from trying to seduce Raquel. This is a mountain I simply have to scale all the way to the top, especially since it won't end up killing me after all. Or at least I don't think it will. But even if it does, what a way to go!

I can honestly say this whole being on the verge of kicking the bucket experience has totally changed me in many ways. Some good and others not so much. In the past when it came to getting inside a woman's panties, I never hesitated. Upon smelling or seeing an offering of pussy, I didn't even flinch, especially if it happened to be attached to an attractive woman. All of my alpha male instincts naturally kicked in on the spot and I would proceed to have my fill. After getting what I wanted, then I'd happily move on to the next offering, and the next, and so on. What can I say? I hunted pussy for sport and, I was damned good at it. Now it seems that I have become the one thing I've despised all of my life—a procrastinator. Oh, but it gets much worse than that I'm afraid. Slowly but surely, I can feel myself morphing into a monogamous human being and that totally scares the crap out of me.

For instance, the former Michael Stephen Grant wouldn't have thought twice about not taking advantage of the cozy situation he's in right now. If I were still the man I used to be during my pre-cancer days, one of my hands would have already slowly crept up Raquel's dress and started to fondle her pussy while she sleeps. These hands are just as highly-skilled as a top surgeon's and I'm pretty sure I could make her come quickly and intensely. Those lean, baby soft legs of hers have been driving me insane since day one. The absolute crazy thing is that instead of taking on the challenge of making her have an orgasm in her sleep, I find myself perfectly content with just silently admiring her beautiful, exotic looking face and watching the rise and fall of her chest.

As I stare at her, an undeniable feeling of tenderness fills me. I can feel my eyes starting to tear up. *Is Raquel the absolute love of my life? Can Michael Stephen Grant be fully satisfied with just one woman or am I destined to be a modern-day version of King Solomon for the rest of my days?* As I'm grappling with these questions, I get the overwhelming urge to give Raquel a soft kiss on her forehead and so I do. The second my lips brush her smooth, caramel skin, her eyes pop wide open and startles the both of us. Raquel sits up immediately and starts to adjust her clothing. She looks disheveled, but adorable at the same time.

"How long have I been asleep?" Raquel asks while fidgeting with the top of her dress.

"Not long after we left and got into the limousine you put your head on my shoulder, closed your eyes, and the next thing I knew you'd fallen asleep." I look at my watch to make sure what I'm about to say is close to being correct. "So, you've been asleep for about forty minutes now. I didn't want your neck to get sore so, I repositioned you into a more comfortable sleeping position.

Raquel flashes me one of her genuine smiles and I immediately start to melt inwardly. I imagine it's her way of rewarding me for my cavalier behavior. But I really wish she would reward me in more tantalizing ways and with no clothes on. Looking into her lovely, green almond-shaped eyes I say, "Kiddo, thanks for all your hard work today. I couldn't have pulled it off without you. You were so impressive and super amazing back there. Plus, I could tell that several of the male executives were really into you."

Her smile widens and brightens up even more. "You really think so?"

"Yeah, I do," I answer back without the slightest reluctance. Then I move in dangerously close to her face and add, "Honey, you have no idea what a major turn-on you are to men, do you?"

Judging by her body language, I can tell my bold statement has taken her by surprise. At first, she doesn't have a comeback for me but after mulling it over for a few seconds she says to me with a hint of sadness in her voice, "I don't think that's necessarily true. Or at least that doesn't seem to be applicable to a particularly handsome British doctor I've been spending time with lately.

Her comment crushes my spirit right away and it's a tough pill to swallow. But since she's opened up this can of worms for me, there's no way I'm not going to dig right in. "So, talk to me, sweetheart. You've been dating him for a couple of months now. What's going on?" I ask her point-blank.

Upon hearing my direct question, she lowers her eyes and stares blankly at her shoes. I'm taking this as an instant giveaway that there is something missing from the equation. Again, I silently ask myself if I really want to have this courageous conversation with her which can only have two possible outcomes. I either stand a chance with her or I don't. It's been an especially good day but what would make it even better would be to find out that Dr. Adam Lancaster has erectile dysfunction and can't get it up. This presents me with the perfect opportunity to "know thy enemy" so you better believe I'm going to do some more probing.

"What's the matter? Is there trouble in paradise?" I come out and say.

This time Raquel has an immediate answer for me. "No, but I wish that was the case. Because that would mean I've actually gotten into paradise. And by the way things are not transpiring, it doesn't look like I'll ever cross that threshold with Dr. Adam Lancaster."

Clearly the first thing I make a mental note of is the fact that Raquel wants to screw Dr. Lancaster's brains out. I suppose I can't blame her for wanting him. I have this strong feeling that most women would want to pull out their claws and rip off that white lab coat of his, mount him, and just go to town on his British dick for hours on end. Hey, I was that man once. Wait a minute, what am I saying? I'm still that man. I've just been feeling under the weather for half the year.

"Whoa! Wait a minute. Let me get this straight. After all the dates you've been on with Dr. Lancaster, he hasn't tried to fuck you yet?" I ask, feigning disappointment.

"That just about sums it up," Raquel admits.

I shake my head and throw my hands up in the air for dramatic effect. "That's unbelievable!" I blurt out. "What the hell is wrong with him? Honey, if I were in his shoes, I would've already gotten you knocked up."

Raquel laughs a little which is exactly what I hoped would happen. Wanting to keep this interrogation going, I reach out and stroke her hair which is just absolutely mesmerizing. "Just how far have you two gotten? What exactly happens on your dates?"

"Well, he does seem happy to see me every time. And he does compliment me on the way I look," she says to me. "We order dinner and then we usually have an interesting conversation."

"What do you talk about?"

"We mostly talk about his humanitarian way of life and how he'd much rather be traveling through war-torn countries saving children from fatal diseases and starvation rather than running clinical trials for the rich and shameless in the world's most state-of-the art hospitals. He's constantly telling me how much he misses that and wants to get back to it as soon as possible."

"So, the ingenious Dr Lancaster would rather be in the trenches saving displaced children from the atrocities of war and poverty than making a boatload of money and banging beautiful women? Is that what your telling me Raquel? Because if it is, I will have to concede that he's a better man than most of us."

Raquel is quick to praise him. "Yes, he's unlike anyone I've ever met before." She cracks another lovely smile and adds, "I suppose that's why I want to be intimate with him so badly. The fact that he's an incurable philanthropist turns me on like you wouldn't believe."

As unpleasant as it is to hear how much Raquel likes this man, I try my best to remain objective. "Okay, so let's fast forward things and describe for me what normally happens at the end of your dates?"

"I have to say from my perspective, which of course could be totally off, our dates do end on a positive note," Raquel begins to explain.

"What exactly does that mean?"

"Well, Adam usually offers to drive me home. Since he knows I live with you, he doesn't ask me if he can come in. We sit in his car and chat for a while before one of us decides to say goodnight."

I go ahead and ask for clarification. "Make idle banter, that's all you do?"

Raquel ignores my question and continues with her not-so-interesting narrative. "He walks me to the door. We hug and he gives me a goodnight kiss."

"Please tell me it's on the lips."

On this point, she's quick to confirm. "It is. Adam gives me these smoldering glances that make me feel like I'm the sexiest woman alive right before he moves in for the kiss. Granted, it's not a I-have-to-be-inside-you-now passionate kiss, but there is a sense of urgency to it, just enough to keep my hope alive."

"Does he moan during the kiss and do his hands ever try to roam to your erogenous zones?"

"Affirmative! Yes, Adam does let out a moan here and there. He sounds so damn sexy, too. Come to think of it, he always puts his hands on my waist and pulls me close to him firmly."

"And do you ever feel him getting a hard-on when he's kissing you?"

Surprisingly Raquel doesn't flinch at the question. I thought for sure she would reprimand me for getting too personal. "I've always been too focused on enjoying the kiss so I can't really say." She pauses and gives it a bit more thought. "There was this one time when we went back to his apartment that he did 'rise to the occasion.'"

BINGO! Raquel has finally said something that warrants further investigation. "Uh now you've got my undivided attention. Keep on talking, honey!" I insist.

"After one of our dinner dates, Adam told me he wasn't ready to call it a night just yet so he asked if I'd like to go back to his apartment for a cup of tea."

"What does it look like, his apartment I mean?"

"It's not really his place, just temporary housing being provided to him by the hospital. So, as you can imagine, its furnished just like a hospital is. It's very bright and sterile."

"Doesn't sound like the ambiance is conducive to romance and lovemaking," I'm quick to interject.

"Damn right it isn't!" Raquel remarks, obviously with a bone of contention. "Any way, when we got there Adam told me to get comfortable while he prepared the tea."

"I bet you were hoping there would be some kind of aphrodisiac properties in that tea."

Raquel concedes, "Yeah, that would have definitely livened things up. After he brought me my cup of tea, Adam turned on some soft jazz music."

"So far, so good. Then what happened?"

"We talked and laughed for a while. There we were just hanging out, having a nice, easy-going time when his demeanor suddenly changed."

"How so?"

"Adam looked deeply into my eyes and I reciprocated by looking into his. I saw a spark in them I hadn't seen before."

"In other words, he got horny," I blurt out. "Looking into those hypnotizing almond-shaped eyes of yours will do that to a man."

Raquel pauses. I think she's trying to process what I've just said. After several seconds of awkward silence, she continues to render more details about the night in question. "He put his cup of tea down on the table next to us. Then he plucked mine out of my hands and carefully set it down as well. Then Adam didn't bother mincing with words. He stretched himself out on the couch, then leaned forward and positioned me on top of him, and started kissing me ardently, like he hadn't done before."

"Oh boy! What was going through your mind?"

"Honestly? I was thinking hallelujah, it's finally happening," Raquel answered. "From that point on, things started to progress very much to my liking. His hands were all over my ass and I went from just chilling with the man of my dreams to being majorly turned on. I swear I was ready to cum in my panties. And that's when I felt it."

"His hard-on?"

"Yes, and it was magnificent."

"Then what happened?"

"His damn phone rang."

"You've got to be kidding me! Really?"

"Yeah, it was the hospital calling. One of his clinical trial patients had taken a turn for the worse and he was being summoned on an emergency basis."

"Oh wow! That was unfortunate."

Raquel agrees with me. "Tell me about it. So, we had no choice after that but to cool things down. He put his raging dick on ice and, I did the same for my inflamed pussy. It was a damn shame because he had looked profoundly into my eyes and said, 'You're so desirable.'"

"Tough break, kiddo!"

"It's all water under the bridge now. That's the closest I'm ever going to get to being fucked by Dr. Adam Lancaster," Raquel concludes.

I can't help but to detect the resignation in her voice. "Why do you say that?"

"Because Adam is leaving town soon. He told me on our last date that his clinical trial work here in Dallas is winding down. He's been asked by a highly-acclaimed hospital in Stockholm, Sweden to bring his clinical trials there for a year or so."

As soon as she says this, Raquel stops dead in her tracks and gets an I-just-got-an-epiphany look on her face. "You already know this, don't you MSG? You're his patient. He must have told you."

Feeling guilty, I lower my eyes and let out a deep sigh. "Yes, darling. Dr. Lancaster told me about his impending departure but I honestly thought that it was best you heard it from him so I didn't tell you. I hope you're not too upset at me for keeping it from you."

Raquel puts me at ease right away by saying, "It's okay MSG. I understand. I actually appreciate your sensibility. I just have to accept that it's not written in the stars for me and Dr. Lancaster."

"Don't jump to that conclusion just yet?" I say to her.

"How can I not?" Raquel quips back. "MSG, you of all people know perfectly well that long-distance relationships never work out."

"Yeah, I guess that's true." I agree.

"So, what's your game plan?" I think to ask.

"I'm just going to enjoy the rest of the time I have with him. You know, ride it out to the end. He and I are going out on another date next week."

I snuggle closer to her and lightly bump her shoulder with mine. "Need I remind you that Dr. Lancaster is not the only fish in the sea? Dallas is full of handsome, eligible men. Realistically speaking, you can pretty much have your pick of the litter. All you have to do is put yourself out there."

Raquel wrinkles her nose which lets me know that the idea of dating other men doesn't really appeal to her which makes my heart secretly rejoice. "I think after Adam leaves, I'm just going to lay low for a good while."

"Suit yourself," I say to her. Then, on a whim, I cup her chin with my hand, lean in, and give her a soft peck on the cheek. Right after doing so, I gaze intently into her eyes and say, "You still have me. Don't ever forget that." For a few fleeting seconds, I think about seizing the moment and trying to take it further. Then I come to my senses and decide this is not the time nor the place. When I finally get the opportunity to make love to Raquel, I want to take my damn sweet time and we are close to being home, so I hold back.

Raquel starts to say something back to me but, my phone screen lights up letting me know that Maribel is calling me from France.

"Whose calling?" Raquel asks.

"It's Maribel."

"Your ex-wife?"

"The one and only."

"Well, aren't you going to take her call?"

As much as I do want to, I decide against it. "We're almost home! I'll call her back when we get there. It's early morning in France so I've got time."

"Maribel has been reaching out to you pretty often lately," Raquel makes it a point to say.

"Yes, she has been."

"How do you feel about that?"

"Oh, I don't know. Why do you ask me that?"

"No reason really. Just curious. Sometimes I think there is a chance you two can reconcile and get back together," Raquel blurts out.

"Really, why on Earth would you think that?"

"It's not such a far-fetched idea. It could happen you know," Raquel pauses and then she hurls a loaded question at me. "MSG, are you still in love with Maribel?"

Raquel's unexpected inquiry makes me feel uncomfortable. It totally changes my demeanor. "I'm not going to deny that I do have feelings for her. But I wouldn't go as far as to say that I'm still in love with her. You gotta remember that she really broke my heart and I'm not sure I have forgiven her for it."

"As I understand it, you were unfaithful to her. Okay, sorry I asked," Raquel apologizes and then thinks to change the subject altogether. "So, how much longer until we get home?"

I quickly make the calculation in my head, "About fifteen minutes."

"Speaking of Stockholm, Sweden, have you ever been there?" Raquel asks me.

"Oh yes! I definitely have."

"Wait, don't tell me. You have an erotic story about Stockholm, right?"

"You damn straight I do. Would you like to hear it?"

Raquel lets out a few giggles and cracks an inquisitive smile. "Sure, why not? We've got fifteen minutes to kill any way?"

***

My first trip to Sweden was one of those bittersweet experiences. I flew from San Francisco to Stockholm, approximately a twelve-hour flight with a change of planes in NYC and London. When I arrived in Stockholm, my baggage did not. There's nothing worse than flying that many hours and not being able to change into some fresh clothes. Luckily, I arrived in Stockholm on Saturday and my presentation wasn't until Monday at 10:00 AM. At least I was able to take a shower, although I put my same clothes back on, except for my underwear of course.

I was starving so I decided to go and check out the area near the hotel and find a place that would serve me a late breakfast. I walked about two blocks and I saw this cute little restaurant with tables out front. I sat down at one of the open tables and was enjoying the sights of Stockholm, watching people walk by.

Within seconds I heard a voice say to me, "Can I get you something sir?" in this beautiful Swedish accent.

I looked up, wayyyy up, and there was this tall, blonde and green-eyed beauty hovering over me. *OMG, what do they feed these girls here?* I thought to myself. She must have been six feet tall, and was maybe in her late twenties or early thirties, with a beautiful smile to boot. Of course, I asked myself, *could this be another victim for MSG?*

I said, "Can I please have a cup of coffee and are you by any chance still serving breakfast?" as it was almost noontime.

"Yes, we still are. Would you like a menu?"

"Yes, please," I replied.

She dropped off the menu and every time she came by, I tried to make eye contact, smile, and start a conversation with her. It was discouraging at first. She was busy. I also started to think that I didn't stand a chance because she was probably constantly getting hit on by Westerners throughout the day and that had surely made her immune to all the pickup lines and other related jargon by now. But then again there was a pretty good chance that she hadn't come across someone like me before either. Believe me, Westerners who are leg men fantasize about having a Swedish Goddess like her and those long legs wrapped around their face.

It was Saturday morning. Granted, there was still plenty of time to pick up on other blonde beauties, but I wanted to improve my odds of having some company for the weekend. I didn't want to be all alone in this beautiful country without any companionship. I continued interacting with Emma, which was the name on her tag. I asked her everything I could think of, including where I could go to see the sites of the city. She gave me some suggestions, but I wasn't really paying that much attention because I was mesmerized by her green eyes, long legs, and nice ass.

I was almost done with my breakfast, but I wanted Emma to remember me after I made my exit. There had to be something I could do besides leave her a bigger than normal tip. I was sure with her being the total package, large tips were a common occurrence. Directly across the street was the answer I sought. There was a small florist on the corner. With a newly formulated plan in my head I said my goodbyes to Emma, "It was a pleasure meeting you and thanks for all the advice on where to go."

I also left her a big tip (100%) of my bill. There's no way she would forget that. Immediately upon leaving the restaurant, I went across the street and purchased a bouquet of flowers. I asked the florist to drop them off for Emma with the note I'd written for her which read: Hi Emma, it was a pleasure meeting you today. I'm the Westerner who wouldn't leave you alone. I hope you remember me...I enjoyed your hospitality and was wondering if you would like to have dinner with me tonight?"

Sure, it was a longshot, but what the heck? There are times when a man has to think outside of the box to get a fine piece of ass. I also put my phone number on the note. I decided to walk around the city for a bit before hitting the local gym. Besides working out, I wanted to check out the local talent. In Europe most health clubs don't open up until 9:00 AM or later. Europeans typically stay up later in the evenings than Westerners do. I had a good workout and afterwards I decided to go for another walk before going back to the same restaurant where Emma worked to have lunch and see if she was still on duty.

Thirty minutes into my walk, I received a call from an unknown number. I hoped and prayed that it was Emma calling me. It was.

"Hello, it's Emma from the restaurant. Thank you for the incredible tip and the beautiful flowers. It was so sweet," she said.

"You're welcome. Would you like to have dinner with me and show me the sites of your beautiful city?" I then ventured to ask.

She said, "Ja! It would be my pleasure."

When I arrived back at the restaurant, there she was, wearing a huge smile on her face. She asked in her charming Swedish accent, "Why did you get me flowers and leave such a large tip?"

"You have a great personality. You're also genuine and beautiful. I would like to know you better and hopefully earn your friendship." I threw in the word *friendship* into the conversation because I didn't want to scare her off. She was actually shy and reserved when it came to dealing with strangers, like me. I was being super careful to increase my chances of being able to take her clothes off within the next twenty-four hours.

I asked her, "What time do you get off work?"

"At four o'clock," she answered.

"Are you still willing to show me some of the sites of your beautiful city and then have dinner with me somewhere?"

Her response followed quickly, "Ja, thank you for asking."

"Where do you live?" I inquired.

"Very near! It's about a ten-minute walk from here."

"Okay, can I pick you up around 5:00 PM this evening?"

"Ja, that would be fine."

I sat down and ordered some lunch. We were still talking up a storm, which was great. I felt like she was becoming more comfortable with me as we interacted more. After lunch I decided to head back to the hotel to take a much-needed nap—jet lag was catching up big-time with me.

I slept for a few hours and then showered to get ready for my sight seeing date with Emma. She had written down her address on a small piece of paper. I asked the concierge at the hotel for directions on how to get to find it.

I started walking about 4:45 PM and arrived at her place at approximately 4:55 PM. I rang the doorbell and within a minute she opened the door and said to me, "Please give me another minute."

"Okay. I'll just wait here," I responded.

"No, please come in and have a seat on the sofa. I just need a few more minutes."

Extremely pleased with her counter offer I said, "Thank you, I will."

Emma had a tiny, but cute one-bedroom apartment. As promised, within a few minutes she came out and my eyes lit up at the sight of her. She was wearing a pair of tight-fitting jeans and a green top that really made her eyes pop—OUCH! We headed out the door and she immediately put her hand on my bicep. We definitely hit it off. Emma and I walked and walked for what seemed to be several miles. It didn't' matter to me just how many miles because I was having such an awesome time.

Emma was well-educated and spoke excellent English. This girl had it all going for her—looks, brains, and a body made for sinning. We hopped on a bus and she took me to a different part of the city where we walked a bit more. Then she took me to this awesome quaint cafe for dinner. We had already talked for a few hours when we both realized it was getting kind of late. Emma and I mutually decided it was time to start heading back.

I was actually getting really tired from the jetlag. It was nearly one o'clock in the morning and she had to go back to work in a few hours. As we walked up to her apartment, I asked her what she was doing after work the following day?

"I don't have anything planned," she confirmed.

"Would you like to see a movie?"

"Ja, that would be nice."

"Okay, let's have dinner first, then go see a movie," I suggested. When we arrived at her front door, we hugged and gave each other a nice smooch on the lips.

We met at the same time the next day at her apartment. This time Emma was wearing a skirt, which showed off those beautiful long white legs. Once I caught sight of them, I couldn't focus on anything else. I was in love! When she came out, we greeted each other with a kiss and I said to her, "You look gorgeous."

"*Tack*," she said with a smile.

We walked to a nice Swedish-style restaurant nearby and then went to a 7:00 PM showing right after dinner. I had one goal that evening and it was to get my hands all over those long legs. The way I figured it, if we arrived back at her place at 1:00 or 2:00 AM in the morning, well she might think it was too late to engage in fun nocturnal activities, if you catch my drift. But, if we were to return by 11:00 PM, then the odds of scoring with her would be greatly improved. I wanted to make sure we finished early enough to give MSG the opportunity to get his well-deserved desert.

To my advantage, the movie actually ended at about 9:30 PM. I then asked Emma, "Would you like to get a cup of coffee and relax somewhere? There's a coffee shop with a nice sitting area in my hotel lobby."

As it turned out, Emma made me a better offer I simply couldn't refuse. "I also have some good Swedish coffee back at my apartment. We can sit on my comfortable couch with our shoes off and watch TV if you would like?"

"That would be great. I can't think of a nicer way to end a beautiful evening," I said. We walked back to her place with our arms draped around each other as we had been doing for the past two days.

When we arrived at her apartment, Emma and I kicked off our shoes and left them by the door. "Have a seat on the couch and feel free to turn the TV on," she said politely. "I'm going to brew us some Swedish coffee."

Emma came back with two cups of freshly brewed java on a tray with milk and sugar. She sat down really close to me with both of her legs on the couch crossed in a comfortable position. As the dress rose further up her long, gorgeous legs the hornier I became—as if I needed additional help. Once she became comfortable, we toasted to our friendship. I looked into her eyes and told her how beautiful she was. I also made it a point to let Emma know that I hadn't been able to stop thinking about her since the moment we met at the restaurant.

She looked back at me and said, "You're so sweet and genuine."

Emma then leaned over and gave me a kiss on the lips. I reciprocated. Then we both put our coffee cups down and our lips met halfway. I paused for a moment and she asked, "What's wrong?"

"Nothing, I just want to look into those beautiful green eyes again," I said to her. Sure, I may have been laying it a bit thick but, I wanted to milk this moment for as long as I could. Realizing things were transpiring according to plan, I slowly pulled her chin closer to my lips once again.

After that slick move, I then put my right hand around her shoulders drawing her extremely close to me but leaving my left hand free. I used it to start roaming up her dress. To me, this type of foreplay was much better than the actual orgasm. I gingerly started caressing her knees and gradually inched my way to the PROMISED LAND.

Man, did it feel incredible. There was no way I was going to pull her dress off. I didn't want to. For the next few minutes, we kissed one another passionately and our hands were all over each other. Emma then stood up in front of me, grabbed my hand, and led me into her bedroom. There was a twin-sized bed that barely fit in her small room. The first thing that ran through my mind was, *how in the heck are two 6-footers going to fit into a twin-sized bed?*

We stopped in front of the bed, I was now standing behind Emma and kissing the back of her neck. At the same time, I was rubbing my throbbing dick against her backside. With dishonorable intentions, I whispered for her to lie down on her stomach. She complied right away. I gently sat over her and continued to kiss the back of her neck and shoulders. Then I started massaging her entire backside as I inched my way down to her treasure and my pleasure. I lifted her skirt up ever so slowly and watched the back of her thighs being exposed and then the bottom of her butt cheeks. She was wearing butt floss underwear, not my favorite, but who cared so long as I got my hands on the pot of gold before me.

I unzipped the back of her dress ever so slowly but didn't take it off. I wanted to continue kissing her back and shoulder area. Then I took my sweet time working my way down South until my hands stumbled upon on that beautiful butt of hers. Inflamed with passion, I started kissing those cheeks. My lips were all over both cheeks and lightly grazing near her butt hole—just enough to tease her. The poor thing was becoming all worked up. Wanting to deliver like I usually did, I decided to do what MSG does best. I turned her over, moved her butt floss out of the way and began to kiss and munch away on her pussy. Emma was going bonkers by this time and it didn't take long for her to have that first orgasm. By my estimation, it took her probably two minutes to cum. After she settled down a bit, I then pulled off that butt floss once and for all and continued licking her pussy. I clenched onto her clit with my lips so she would have another orgasm. Within a few minutes she experienced her second one. Emma kept repeatedly asking me to put my hardened dick inside of her, but I flat-out refused because I had a lot more in store for her.

"Be patient my love, all in good time," I said to pacify her desire.

After having said that to her, I went back up to kiss Emma's breasts and lips again. I also started playing with her butt hole with one finger and fondling her pussy using another. Emma was moaning and squirming like she had a dozen ants crawling up her backside. I wanted her to have one more orgasm before I penetrated that pot of *Krona*.

With a one-track mind, I went back down on her once again. For me it's always been about that clit and at this juncture I was really craving hers. I latched onto it like there was no tomorrow and Emma had her third orgasm. She then grabbed me with all her might and forced me to put my cock inside her pussy, which I complied. I gripped her butt cheeks and plowed in from behind, doggie-style and within thirty seconds it was over for the both of us. We had definitely seen the light.

Emma wanted me to stay the night so, we decided to cleanup and get some sleep. However, in a few hours, I was awakened by her butt flushed up against my dick. Needless to say, it rose to attention.

Although she was sound asleep, I gently slithered it in between her legs. This time, I decided not to go through the back entry. I wanted to save that moment for when she was wide awake and would enjoy it to the max.

It ended up being a memorable five days with Emma. During that span of time, we became quite close. I could tell she was falling in love with me and I was starting to fall for her, too. Inwardly, I knew I would come back to Sweden soon and we would spend more quality time together.

The second trip to Stockholm was more intense because I got Emma to open up about her sexual fantasies prior to my visit. One thing about me was that I always loved getting women to open up about their fantasies. We communicated back and forth while I was in the states. Every time we did, our conversations got juicier and juicier until they became X-RATED.

During one of our conversations, Emma made it clear that she wanted me to wear some silk black bikini underwear. Her fantasy was to rip them off and fuck me with a dildo up my ass. Truth be told, this wasn't something MSG was excited about. The whole idea of it did not appeal to me in the slightest. Every time I would go in for my annual physical and my doctor said it was time for him to insert his finger up my rectum, I fought it every step of the way. So, if Emma was going to be adamant about gaining full access to my virgin ass, then her virgin ass would also be mine. According to her, she had never gone there before with any man.

Not wanting to disappoint, I complied with Emma's request. I purchased three pairs of black bikini silk underwear for the next time I would be in Sweden. I told her beforehand that I was coming to Stockholm to make her fantasy come true. Within one hour of landing at the airport, I checked into my hotel room.

From there, I called Emma and we arranged to meet at her place after work.

When we saw each other, it was pure magic. We both had silly, large grins on our faces. Emma and I hugged and kissed like we were drowning and were one another's life preservers. I paused and looked at her. Then I discreetly unzipped my pants, showed her what I was wearing, and then zipped them back up. Emma was wearing a tight-fitting denim skirt a few inches above the knees.

She took me into the bedroom and shoved me toward the bed. I landed face first with my ass positioned upward. I knew what was coming next. Emma told me not to move. She opened a drawer, pulled out a brand-new strap-on dildo, lifted her skirt and strapped it on. She already had the gel ready on the nightstand. Emma instructed me to unzip my pants, but NOT to take them off because she wanted to do the honors herself. She grabbed my underwear and ripped them off without any problem. Half of the small garment was practically in shreds and the other half barely covered my right cheek. Emma grabbed the gel and rubbed some on her dildo and in my ass. In a matter of a few seconds, she had that white 9-inch dildo poking me where the sun just doesn't shine.

Damn, I was in so much frickin' pain, but she was loving it. Emma pounded and pounded me. This went on and on for what seemed like an eternity, but in reality, was probably only ten minutes. When, and only when, she'd had enough Emma yanked off the dildo. Then she turned me over, sucked my dick until it was rock-hard, and jumped on top of me. As for me, it made me happy to see that she was having the time of her life. After that carnivorous session, I couldn't sit comfortably for the next forty-eight hours.

After Emma had an orgasm of epic proportions, it was my turn to hit that high note. In anticipation of great things to come, I made sure she left her dress on. I positioned her beside me while we rested for a bit. Actually, she fell asleep for about twenty minutes. As she lay down on her stomach, I decided it was payback time so, I raised her skirt up. Much to my enjoyment she wasn't wearing any panties. I grabbed the gel, lubed my cock and her butt hole, and I turned her toward my side. Like a true gladiator, I edged it right into her ass. She gulped and screeched. It took all but four strokes for me to have an orgasm. Turnabout was fair play.

Chapter Fourteen

Uprising in the South

I can't believe it's finally happening!

After so many drawn-out days and equally seemingly endless nights of hungering to make love to Raquel, it appears that the torturous wait may just be over for me. Without giving it a second thought, I close the book I'm reading in bed and lay it on the nightstand. I remove my reading glasses and toss them on top of the book so that I can better focus on the vision of incredible sexiness standing before me. I close and open my eyes to make sure they aren't playing tricks on me, because if they are, I'm going to gouge them right out of their sockets. That's how pissed I'm going to be if what I'm seeing is just a dick-teasing mirage.

Only a few minutes ago, I was reading my book, minding my own business when I suddenly hear a knock at the door. "Michael. Stephen. Grant. Are you decent?" Raquel hollers from the other side.

Somewhat engrossed with my reading, I answer back nonchalantly, "Yeah, I'm just reading in bed."

A few seconds go by. "Can I come in for a bit?" she asks.

"Sure! The door isn't locked."

Almost immediately after giving her permission to enter my bedroom, I catch a whiff of the most alluring scent which makes me stop reading—cold turkey. I raise my eyes to look at her and I'm totally blindsided and enraptured at the same time. The first thought that crosses my mind is, *Man, I've died and gone straight to erotica heaven.* I swear, I don't think I've ever seen Raquel look so beautiful and tantalizing.

I'm not sure what I did to deserve this but, Raquel is standing a few feet away from my bed looking like—as the kids of today say—a delicious snack. One that I'd absolutely love to delve into—head and tongue first. She's wearing a scarlet-colored oriental-style silk mini-Kimono robe and matching high-heeled pumps which do a stellar job of accentuating her gorgeous, lean and muscular gams. The upper part of the robe has been left opened enough to show a hint of white lace underneath which has gotten my imagination running wild with all kinds of cock-raising ideas.

Looking at her is a job for more than one man, really. She's so goddamn radiant and desirable. This may be hard to believe but the one thing about Raquel that attracts me the most is her booming confidence. It projects in her countenance, brighter and stronger than most people in this world exhibit. I strongly believe it works as an aphrodisiac on most men. Something else about Raquel that I've liked from the start is her naturally wavy black hair that falls slightly above her waistline. I really appreciate the way it bungees effortlessly to the middle of her back when she walks. Right now, her lightly-roasted caramel colored skin and piercing almond-shaped eyes that look like sunlight is penetrating a jar of honey has gotten my penis all rattled in its cage. All I have to say is that she can't saunter into my bedroom looking hotter than a Victoria Secret model and not mean business.

Normally in a lucky situation like this, what comes next should be a no-brainer. Believe me when I say that I've had my fair share of women trying to seduce me while them wearing racy lingerie. But this is no ordinary woman before me. We're talking Goddess material here that most men are not heavily equipped enough to handle and satisfy. Have I hit the Jackpot? Is Raquel trying to seduce me? Is she coming on to me so she can *cum* onto me later? Because if I think what's happening is really happening, then there's absolutely no reason for her to stand on ceremony because I'm a sure thing. Still, perhaps it's best to tread carefully so I ask her, "What brings you by tonight, looking so, mouthwatering?"

Raquel lets out a sexy, almost diabolical laugh and suddenly I feel like the luckiest sonofabitch alive. But I'm also scared shitless that I'm going to do something to make her go away, so I wait for her to say something. Only she doesn't. She does something better, something totally un-precedented and out of character. With a come-hither look in her eyes, she adeptly unties her robe, slithers out of it, and lets it drop to the floor in one clean, dramatic sweep. And just like that the undeniable glory of God shines before my very eyes. Suddenly, I am possessed by the HORNY GHOST and I swiftly brush the covers aside and prepare to receive the offering that's being given to me. Except Raquel beats me to the punch and it's her who makes the first move toward me.

I know this is a silly question but, I have to ask it. So, I scoot over to the edge of my bed and let it out in one breath. "What are you doing?"

Undeterred by my stupidity, Raquel boldly struts over to me, reaches low and takes a firm hold of my manhood. "What does it look like I'm doing? I'm tired of waiting so I'm taking matters into my own hands." Then she follows that up with a sexy wink and I start to go bonkers right on the spot. "I'm tired of waiting, MSG."

"For what?"

"For you to fuck my brains out," Raquel says as she gently gets on her knees and squeezes her centerfold looking tits in between my legs. My cock is growing and hardening by the second, it's practically trying to poke a hole through the boxers I'm wearing. Raquel lets go of it and looks up at me with an incredibly arousing sultry look in her eyes. "I want you. Now! I just hope this isn't a one-way street. Please tell me that you want me as badly as I want you."

Her gutsy declaration makes me cave in and any composure I had left immediately goes out the window. In anticipation of great things to *cum*, I grab both of her wrists and together we slowly rise to our feet. I reach out for her pretty, dainty chin and pull it in close to my lips. As I look deeply into her spirited eyes, my fully erect penis spears her triangular erogenous zone which makes her flinch and smile.

"Oh baby! You have no idea how long I've been waiting for this moment to arrive," I admit.

Raquel reaches up and caresses my jawline with her index finger. "Really? How long?"

Before answering, I take her finger and gently plant a kiss on the pad of it. Then I guide it inside my mouth and, I start to stroke it with the tip of my tongue. It's my way of giving her a precursor of what I'm eagerly willing to do inside her wet pussy when the time comes. She starts to breathe heavily and bites her lower lip a little. I can tell she's warming up to the idea of letting me go down on her. As I continue to suckle her finger, my left hand slowly wanders over to that perfect mound of hers that's covered in sheer white lace and I start to fondle it. My unexpected touch makes her entire body shudder and that tells me she's mine for the taking.

I just know that if I don't slow down, Raquel is liable to cream her panties, so for the sake of prolonging what is surely going to be the new reigning fuck of a lifetime as long as physically possible, I stop fondling her pussy and let go of her finger. "Sweetheart, I've wanted you since the day I hired you," I tell her outright. "And that's not all."

She moves in closer and swallows hard. I can feel the tips of her bronze colored nipples come to life and start digging into my chest. It takes all the willpower I have to keep me from ripping off her bra which isn't exactly leaving much to the imagination and, one by one, start tasting and sucking on them. Instead of giving her that pleasure I focus on what I want to say next. "Raquel, I'm desperately in love with you. I have been for a long time now."

Raquel pulls back and studies my face. "Why have you waited so long to tell me this?"

"Well, for various reasons," I quip back.

"Like what?"

"For starters, I was dying. I didn't want to start something I wasn't going to be able to finish."

My first answer seems to appease her. "Then there's the matter of Dr. Adam Lancaster. I thought you had the hots for him. I figured as long as he was in the picture, I didn't stand a chance."

Raquel bows her head in silence for a moment. "I'm not going to deny that at first I was really drawn to him," she begins to say. "But the more time I spent with him, the more I realized something."

"Oh yeah? And what was that?" I ask, taking her hand.

She raises her head and looks me squarely in the eye. "That he's not half the man you are. That he's not you."

Her words spoken with conviction and sincerity instantly move me and I know with great certainty that I'll never be the same again. Feeling the need to pour my heart out to her, I pull Raquel in tightly. If I could swallow her whole so she can know first-hand how much my heart swells with love for her, I'd do it because I fear my expressions will never be enough. I undeniably love this human being before me more than I've ever loved anyone else in my life. But now is not the time for any more romantic banter. A man must recognize when it's time to give the woman that he adores the kind of immense pleasure that will reduce her to tears of indescribable happiness. And that's exactly what I'm going to do.

I scoop her up and she instantly wraps her breathtaking legs around my waist. Our lips meld together with a sense of urgency. I kiss her like my life depends on it and she responds with the same level of passion. She squeezes me even tighter with her legs and my dick rises up to the occasion and begins to tease the crack of her beautiful ass. Even though there is only a thin layer of lace keeping it from having full contact, the sensation I'm starting to feel is quite remarkable.

As we continue to kiss, Raquel starts to grind her pussy against my waist and I'm relishing every second of it. By the way she's moaning, I can tell the sensual movements are driving her to the brink of climaxing so, I pivot and slowly lay her down on the bed.

"Please fuck me! I can't take this anymore," Raquel says to me.

The words I thought I'd never hear coming out of her pretty mouth turn me on like you wouldn't believe. "Make no mistake. I will fuck you long and hard, like no one's ever done before. I'm going to give you everything I've got. There will be plenty of time for that. But first, I'm going to make love to you with all of my heart, body and soul," I explain to her.

In total surrender, Raquel lays her head back and relaxes her body. Then she gifts me with the most inviting smile I've ever seen plastered on her exotic looking face up until now. I remove her high-heeled pumps, grab her right foot and start massaging it. Then I do the same on the other foot. When I'm done giving her feet some tender loving care, I slowly and deliberately start planting a trail of kisses all the way up her legs. By the time I work my way up to her inner thighs I can smell and feel that she's ready for me to penetrate her but it's way too premature for that. I haven't even begun to pleasure her yet.

Much to her disappointment, I stop short of her pussy. I can't help but take a few moments to admire that enticing neatly-groomed thick, black bush of hers and how some of its stray hairs are threatening to escape through her lacy panties. Raquel reaches out and starts to tousle my hair with her fingers. I think it's her way of encouraging me to keep going with the foreplay. I strategically position my fingers over the crotch area of her panties and use one of them to trace the outline of her vertical smile. Raquel doesn't know it but I'm about to finetune and play her pussy like the fine instrument it is.

Knowing perfectly well that I've got her juices starting to brew, I lean in and start kissing her entire vagina area over the panties. They moisten in a matter of seconds and the smell of her is absolutely intoxicating.

Raquel lets out a deep guttural moan and says, "Take them off already. I'm begging you."

Realizing that I've really pushed her hot button I comply with her request but only because my tongue is dying of thirst and only her refreshing womanly juices can quench it. So, I help Raquel to remove her panties. As soon as they are completely off that plush raven black bush of hers springs to life. She lays back down and I immediately delve inside her vagina and start exploring it with my tongue.

Finding her clit and knowing exactly what to do with it won't take me long at all but I'm hellbent on pacing myself and taking my sweet time in gratifying her. "Oh baby, you taste so damn good. I want to feast on you all night long," I say in between my carefully calculated tongue strokes.

"Spoken like a true gladiator," Raquel manages to say in between her gasping and moaning. "You're starting to make me delirious."

"Good! That's the whole point. Now just lie there and brace yourself because my tongue is about to make you start speaking in tongues," I warn her.

Raquel lets out a soft chuckle. "Very funny," she says. "So, does that mean I should start calling your dick The Pentecostal Maker?"

"You damn straight," I answer back. Then I decide to up the ante by prying her vagina lips further apart with my fingers so I can deliver more far-reaching pleasurable results. Having more room to work with, I'm quickly able to pinpoint her sweet spot and I latch onto it like there's no tomorrow. At a well-synchronized steady pace, I start flicking my tongue back and forth inside of her and wait for feedback. It comes in the way of Raquel aggressively digging her fingers into my scalp and squeezing her thighs against my cheeks—hard.

"OH! MY! GOD! That feels so great," she cries out frantically. "Baby, you're driving me crazy. I can't take it anymore. I'm going to come."

Listening to Raquel while she's in heat makes me horny as hell. So, I start French kissing her clit and it isn't long at all before I start to taste the early secretions of her inevitable orgasm. There's no greater rite of passage than a man drinking the sugar wall juices of the woman he loves for the very first time. It's akin to having a born-again experience. And I'm ready to get on with it. Judging by Raquel's uncontrollable jerky movements, she is too. So, I kick it up a couple of notches.

"Ohh, yeah baby! Mmmm! Don't stop!" Raquel lets out unabashedly. Even though her breathing becomes more labored, she is still able to let me know what's on her mind. "Please, I want you inside of me."

Of course, I'm not about to give her what she wants. At least not right now. I come up for air just long enough to tell her, "Have patience my dear. Right now, it's all about you." Then I go right back to making out with her clitoris. A couple more flicks of the tongue is all it takes for her to have an explosive orgasm that fills my throat with her delectable tasting nectar.

"Fuck! Oh, Fuck! I'm coming!" Raquel whisper shouts. As the crescendo of her orgasm reaches its highest peak, her breath quickens and so does the beating of my heart. What starts out as merely a whimper of pleasure quickly becomes more of a guttural scream and that's how I know she's reached the highest note possible.

"Baby, you sound so sexy when you cum," I exclaim, totally out of breath. Right after I say that, I roll away and collapse to the side. Rendering earth-shattering cunnilingus requires a great deal of power and stamina. Having a good pair of elbows that can take a great deal of abuse helps too. I lie back and spread eagle myself so that I can replenish my energy. Raquel has no idea that I'm just getting warmed up. I plan on rocking her world, all night long. By daybreak we are both going to need stretchers and be admitted into the hospital due to sex exhaustion.

Before I'm able to resume normal breathing, Raquel lifts herself off the bed and stands near the edge of it. She goes ahead and undoes her bra and with a quick snap of the wrist, her beautifully sculpted breasts are dangling before me which makes my penis start to come alive—again. She gets back on the bed and positions herself comfortably on her knees. In slow motion, Raquel runs her fingers through that glorious hair of hers and then leans back and starts to play with her tits. As Raquel caresses them, she wets her lips with her tongue and bedamn if I don't feel like my dick has just gotten struck by lightning. After several minutes of teasing me in this entertaining way, she starts crawling on all fours and stops right over my cock which is about to catch on fire any second now.

Without using her hands, Raquel maneuvers her torso so that my hard-as-steel penis is nestled nicely on the rift that separates her majestic twin peaks. With the grace of a gazelle, Raquel moves back and forth and, I begin to go stir crazy. Every time she comes forward, Raquel kisses the head of my one-eyed snake and now it's me who is begging for more. I reach out and tug on a strand of her hair affectionately and say, "Oh please baby, suck my dick!"

"It will be my pleasure," Raquel responds without the slightest hesitation. "Close your eyes and enjoy."

As soon as I do precisely as I'm told, Raquel begins to swirl her tongue around the rim of my penis in a clockwise direction.

After making several rounds, she shifts gears and starts moving counterclockwise. "Your dick tastes so good baby," she remarks. Then she takes my inflamed head fully into her mouth and I can feel myself start to lose it. A small amount of ejaculation squirts out. Raquel realizes that she's gotten me overly excited and that if she doesn't slow down, her blow-job is going to make me, well, blow. So, she shows me mercy by letting the head of my dick see the light of day, but still continues to pleasure me by licking the entire length of my shaft with her tongue from every conceivable angle.

I try to say something but only a few gasps and moans come out. At this point, I've lost all control and so I gently force my fully erect cock inside her mouth. Raquel eagerly takes it all in and starts going to town with it. Immediately, I am bewitched by the beauty of her Native American-looking high cheekbones. "You are so fucking beautiful!" I blurt out in the heat of the moment.

Raquel pauses and pulls my cock out long enough to say, "I love you! And I want you to come in my mouth."

Again, I do exactly as Raquel orders, and it's such a high-intensity sweet release, the likes of which I've never felt before. To express how incredible my climax feels, I let out a resonate yell from way deep within my core that would have made Tarzan, King of the Jungle immensely proud. As I watch Raquel swallow my secretions, I can't help but think to myself: *Hell, it doesn't get better than this. Or does it?*

Now it's Raquel who collapses back onto the bed winded from having rendered an Oscar-award-winning fellatio performance. I snuggle close to her and start kissing her softly on the lips.

"You're so incredible," I whisper to her as I pull away a few sweat-drenched strands of hair that are stubbornly clinging to her forehead. "Give me a few minutes and I'll be ready to go again," I add playfully.

"Oh my God! You're unbelievable! A real freak of nature," she utters.

"I'll take that as a compliment."

"Yeah, you do that."

I move in again and this time I give her a long, drawn-out kiss on the lips. Then I say to her, "Listen honey, when a man's sexual appetite becomes boundless it's because the woman he's with is insatiable. That's you in a nutshell, sweetheart."

With lovey-dovey smiles on our faces we lie side by side holding hands. It takes a good while for our accelerated heart-rate and breathing to get back to a more normal rhythm. Eventually though, we are able cool down enough that we end up taking a short catnap for about twenty minutes or so. I'm the first one to come back to my senses. I look over at Raquel lying buck naked next to me and right away my penis starts aching to feel the softness of her baby soft skin again. What we did earlier is merely child's play in comparison to all the naughty things I wanna to do her next.

I prop myself up to the side and begin to softly paw her lovely ripe melons hoping it will awaken her in the mood for some more love-making. After groping them lightly for a while, I lean in closer and start to suck on her nipples. As I anticipated, she starts sighing and moving her head from side to side. I then take one of my hands and start rubbing her pussy and this really does the trick. Raquel opens her eyes and smiles approvingly. She then reaches for the back of my neck and pulls me toward her face and we start to kiss with wild abandon. The whole time we're sucking face I insert my middle finger inside her clitoris and begin to swipe at it delicately.

"You're going to make me come again," Raquel utters.

"You say that like it's a bad thing," I reply.

Raquel gently bites my lower lip and with a lustful look in her eyes she says, "This time when I come, I want you deep inside of me."

"That can easily be arranged my love," I answer in return.

Without exchanging any further words, we quickly get into the doggystyle position. Raquel is on her hands and knees waiting for some amazing G-spot stimulation. She even arches her back to make way for deep penetration. But before plowing my big hard-on into the very heart of her vagina, I decide to take a few moments to enjoy the magnificent back panoramic view in front of me. Suddenly looking at her sexy ass isn't enough. I grab onto her buttocks and start squeezing and kissing them. "Baby, you have such a great ass. It's making me so damn horny," I feel compelled to let her know.

Raquel wiggles her perfectly round apple-shaped ass and then rams it back against my erection. She doesn't know it yet but I'm taking this as an all-out declaration of war and this highly aroused dick of mine isn't taking any prisoners. In retaliation, I grope her tits forcefully and massage her genitalia vigorously. At the same time, my fully extended penis is locked and loaded—ready for rear entry.

"Slide it in. I want to feel you inside of me," Raquel manages to get out in between her huffing and puffing.

The notion that she's dying for me to be deep inside of her makes me go ballistic. Unable to hold out any longer, I grab onto the sides of her hips tightly. Slowly and gradually, I bulldoze my cock inside of Raquel as deeply as it can go. She lets out a sweet-sounding yelp and it's on. Filled with an all-consuming carnal desire, Raquel and I are able to harmonize our sensuous movements for our mutual benefit.

As I thrust powerfully, she easily glides back and forth and together we are able to create mind-blowing erotic friction. After a while of having smoking hot intercourse, Raquel and I come to the realization that we are right on target to climax together. I reach around with my free hand and cup her chin. "Baby, let's come together," I suggest. "Are you ready?"

Raquel gives me the green light by nodding her head. That's my cue to pump just a tad bit harder and deeper so I do and a few seconds later, we both scream out of pure, unadulterated ecstasy and it's the most beautiful symphony I've ever heard in my life.

"Wake up! MSG, wake up!"

Talk about a rude-awakening! Why in the hell is Raquel standing over me, with her hands on her hips, fully clothed? How did she go from Point A to Point B so quickly? And more importantly why isn't my nine-inch putz all over her cinnamon-colored ass. What kind of sick joke is this?

Since I don't react quick enough for her, Raquel bends over and shakes my shoulder briskly. "C'mon, wake up now! You fell asleep on the couch again," she lets me know. "I need to talk to you. It's important."

Even though I'm still feeling a bit disoriented, not to mention utterly disappointed that my having the most incredible sex in my life was all but a pipe dream, I can detect the sense of urgency in her voice. "Okay, give me a minute!" I tell her. Then I decide to make a formal complaint. "You just woke me up from the most beautiful dream."

Raquel scans me from head to toe and right away she sees that the entire crotch area of my sweatpants is soiled. Of course, she has to rub it in my face. "Oh, I see. You were right in the middle of reliving one of your past raunchy fuck sessions with God knows what woman. It was probably with one of those tiny, skinny Asian chicks you screwed while traversing the Far East doing motivational speaking. You know the kind I'm talking about. The type that tells you, 'I'll make you holla for a dolla!'"

Feeling a bit self-conscious about my ejaculation being on full display I grab a throw pillow and place it over the affected area of my sweatpants. Raquel scrunches up her face in disapproval. "Ha! Ha! Very funny," I comment. "It wasn't anything like that at all."

Raquel wastes no time in coming back with a snide remark of her own. "If you say so." She then asserts her authority over me. "Sit up so I can sit down. I need to tell you something."

"What's up? And where have you been all day long?" I ask her.

"I've been at the hospital helping Adam get things ready for his departure. He's leaving for Sweden next week."

"Oh, so he recruited you to help him pack up all his clinical trial shit."

It's apparent to me that Raquel clearly doesn't like the way I phrased that. "It's not like that at all. I offered to help," she replies defensively.

"So, did you two say your final good-byes?" I inquire. "By the way, he's a pussy you know. The fact that he hasn't tried to bang you yet makes him one."

Again, Raquel is quick to defend him. "Not every guy is a manwhore like you."

"Well, I'd rather be a manwhore than a pussy any day of the week."

"Can you be serious for just a minute?" Raquel pleads with me.

Seeing that there is something weighing heavily on her mind makes me relent and soften up a bit. "I'm sorry sweetheart. What is it that you want to tell me?"

Raquel takes a deep, cleansing breath and lets it all out. "Dr. Lancaster has offered me a job and he wants me to go to Sweden with him next week."

Damn! I wasn't expecting that. I feel like I've just been sucker-punched. "Really?" I ask, trying my best to downplay how much this bothers me. "What kind of job?"

"He wants me to be his Medical Scribe."

"What the hell is that?"

"Basically, I would accompany him during patient interactions and document all relevant information to be used as part of that patient's record. I'd also be performing other clerical duties so that he has more free time to focus on diagnosing and treating patients," Raquel explains.

"But you're a creative writer. In time, this kind of work is going to bore you to tears," I assert.

"Maybe, maybe not! I'd be his Medical Scribe the whole time he's conducting his clinical trials in Sweden. Then from there we will be traveling to third world countries doing humanitarian work. Adam has in mind to start writing books that chronicles all of his life-saving work and he wants me to be his co-author." Raquel pauses so that we can both let it all sink in. "Really, it's the opportunity of a lifetime for a girl like me," she adds.

The idea that she may be leaving me really stings like a motherfucker. "So, you've already made up your mind that you're taking the job?" I demand to know.

"Not yet. I have until early next week to give him my final answer," says Raquel. "You're doing great now. Adam says you've successfully completed the clinical trials and are living proof that this revolutionary method of treatment works. He also says you'll be in good hands with Dr. Campbell."

That sonofabitch! That's the first thing that pops into my mind. If there ever was a moment for me to open up and pour my heart out to Raquel, it's now. I just wish I was better prepared to tell her how I really feel instead of having to do this on an emergency basis. How am I supposed to come up with the right words on such short notice? Wouldn't you know it right when I'm about to start mouthing off my Don't-go-because-I'm-desperately-in-love-with-you spiel, my stupid cell phone rings.

Needless to say, I'm not in the mood to answer it so I just ignore it.

"Well, aren't you going to answer it?" Raquel asks.

"Nope! Why don't you answer it and take a message?" I counter back.

Raquel reaches over to the coffee table, picks up the phone and presses the accept call button. "Hello, you've reached the cell phone of Michael Stephen Grant. He's not available at the moment but if you'd like to leave a message, I am more than happy to pass it along to him at the first opportunity."

While Raquel handles the call, I decide to kick back and prop my feet up on the coffee table. I continue to deliberate whether I'm going to beg her to stay with me instead of running off with Dr. Lancaster. The thing is that I certainly don't want her to stay because she feels sorry for me. That's just not the way I roll. If Raquel does not run off with the hot doctor, I want it to be because she's in love with me. Somehow forcing the issue doesn't seem like the right approach to take. Perhaps I should just man up and roll the dice, let Raquel make up her mind without any outside interference from me. This is the only way I'll know for sure if I mean anything to her or not.

By the time Raquel ends the call, my mind is already made up. I'm not going to try to convince or dissuade her one way or another.

It's her decision to make! *Tout ce qui sera sera.* As heart-wrenching as it is to think that I may lose her for good, I have to be a man and suck it up. So at this juncture the best thing for me to do is to abort the dialogue we engaged in earlier and avoid any further sentimental talk.

"Who was that calling me?" I inquire.

"Uh, that was some woman with a charming Southern accent. Said she bought and read one of your books and wants to hire you to be her life coach," Raquel discloses. Instead of providing more details about the woman, she tries to resume the conversation we were having before my cell phone rang. "So, what do you think I should do?"

Playing dumb, I come back with, "About what?"

"Should I take the job that Dr. Lancaster is offering me or not?" she hollers out at me, clearly frustrated by my neutrality.

"It's totally your decision. Why are you asking me?"

"Because in a way you're my mentor. I value your opinion," she asserts.

"That's very flattering, Dear. But you're on your own on this one. All I can say is follow your heart and do what it dictates you to do."

Raquel throws her hands up in the air and then let's them drop down. "Well, you're no help at all." She grows silent for a few seconds and then asks me. "If I go, will you be okay?"

I answer her back right away with a downright lie. "Of course, I'll be all right. Look you still have some time. Meditate and pray about it."

"I guess that's pretty good advice," Raquel acknowledges.

"Did the lady who called me say what her name was?"

Raquel furrows her eyebrows and gives it some thought. "Yeah, I think she said her name was Diane. Her name and number registered on your cell. She said you can just give her a call back at your convenience."

"Wait a minute! Did you say her name was Diane and she had a Southern accent?"

"Yeah. Why? Do you know her?" Raquel asks.

I quickly delve into my memory banks and in a matter of seconds something comes to mind. "I used to know a pretty Southern gal named Diane. But surely it couldn't have been her. I mean there's just no way. What are the odds?"

Raquel laughs. "Let me guess, you knew her in the biblical sense, right?"

"How did you know?"

"I had a haunch," she says. "Hey, since we have some time to kill, why don't you tell me all about this SOUTHERN BELLE named Diane, who you got to know in a BIBLICAL SENSE?"

"Sure, why not! Make yourself comfortable kiddo!"

Raquel sits on the couch next to me and she rests her head on my shoulder. Before getting on with my erotic tale, I take a minute or so to savor having her close to me just in case I end up losing her next week. "Well, it probably won't come as a surprise to you that I've always been a sucker for Southern beauties with sexy accents. Listening to them speak always made me see pink," I start to say. "Of course, it never did take much to get me horny."

"I'll never forget my first trip to the south and my first encounter with a genuine Southern Belle. There I was in a small business meeting with about a dozen people in Birmingham, Alabama of all places. We were strategizing on how to improve the company's marketing efforts throughout the region. Participating in the meeting was a real looker. When she spoke, you could tell that she'd been born and raised in the South. She sounded so wholesome and sincere. Damn, she was so pretty, too. Every time she spoke it drove me crazy."

"Let me guess, her name was Diane," Raquel blurts out.

"Yeah, I really think it was. Diane looked like she was in her mid-twenties. She wasn't wearing a ring, which was surprising to me because it meant someone that charismatic, beautiful and intelligent hadn't been corralled by a man yet. If my memory doesn't fail me, Diane was the total package. I remember checking her out every chance I got without making it look too obvious. I could tell she was checking me out as well. Since this was only a half-day marketing strategy meeting, my time was extremely limited so if I wanted to have a crack at some Southern pussy, I had to act fast. After all, I was flying out that same evening. A part of me thought, *why even bother trying?* But what kept nagging at me was the fact that I'd never had a Southern Belle before. I saw this as a major challenge for my super inflated ego. I had to have her, but how? She was no pushover—this woman had her act together in every conceivable way."

"So how long did it take you to bust a move on her?" asks Raquel.

"During the meeting my wheels were spinning on how best to engage this girl and quickly. My flight was scheduled to leave in six hours and only two scheduled ten-minute breaks. An hour and a half into the meeting, the first break was called. I didn't want to come off as being too eager for her beaver so, I waited until she got up to leave before exiting the room myself. I immediately approached Diane and asked her, "Can I speak to you for a moment?"

"Sure," she replied sweetly.

"It wasn't like she could really say no. After all I had been flown in to be the subject matter expert. 'I have some ideas on how to better market your message. However, these ideas of mine are quite controversial and could be perceived as being highly political. I certainly don't want to raise them in this forum,'" I told her.

"I understand," she said to me.

"I saw an opening and so I decided to seize the opportunity. 'If I wasn't leaving for Montgomery this evening, I would ask you to have a working meeting over dinner,'" I proposed.

"Perhaps on another one of your visits we can schedule a meeting to discuss this further," Diane countered with a flirty grin.

"Okay, here is my business card."

"Here is mine." Diane handed me her card as well.

"For a good while, I actually thought I was going to strike out on this trip. After the meeting resumed, Diane and I were occasionally eyeing each other, more than before. There was an undeniable chemistry between us. Instead of throwing any more pickup lines directly at her, I opted to tease her and the others with a few suggestions on how to better market their core message and services, just enough to whet her appetite. She was intelligent, aggressive professionally, and wanted to go places in this company. Diane knew I had tons of experience and my recommendations would carry a lot of weight and be good for her career.

Unfortunately, time was running out for me. It didn't look like anything was going to happen. The meeting was adjourned and, everyone started to say good-bye. When Diane came up to me, I said to her, "Thank you for your gracious hospitality. I'm staying at the Marriott down the street. I need to go checkout and head for the airport."

"Have a wonderful trip!" she said to me.

"Thank you and good-bye," I reciprocated.

"Upon arriving at the hotel, I went to my room and started to get my stuff together. I was just about done when the phone rang unexpectedly. I simply thought it was the hotel operator telling me to check out already—it wasn't. It was Diane on the other end."

"I'm glad I caught you Michael. Would you like to meet for dinner? I'd like to know more about you and your plans," she asked with confidence.

"What about my flight?" I queried.

She replied, "I checked, there's a flight to Montgomery that leaves at 6:00 AM."

"I didn't beat around the bush in asking, 'Will you also keep me company tonight?'"

"You've got a deal," she confirmed.

"Naturally, I called Jenny that evening and instructed her to change my flight and extend my hotel stay for one more night. I had no clue this Southern Belle was going to be so aggressive. We made arrangements to meet for dinner at a nearby restaurant. When we met at the restaurant, there wasn't any reason to play the seduction game because Diane had already told me she was coming back to my hotel room. But still, she could have easily changed her mind in a heartbeat, especially if I didn't make her feel comfortable and special."

"Right off the bat I divulged to Diane, 'I like your personality, intelligence, aggressiveness, accent, charm, and looks.'"

"She replied in kind. 'Thank you. I think you're a genius. I'm also drawn to your demeanor and personality. Plus, I find you to be very handsome and debonair.'"

"The objective was to make her feel comfortable and relaxed around me as quickly as possible. In theory, the more comfortable she was, the less likely she would get cold feet and the more fun we would have later on. To seal the deal, I interjected as much humor as possible into our conversation.

There we were laughing up a storm. Initially, I sat across from Diane, but midway through our meal I moved next to her. We talked about our personal lives and careers. She already knew all about me because she had read several of my books."

"Do you like to travel?" I asked her.

"Yes, that's one of my goals, to travel the world."

"Have you ever been to Fort Lauderdale?"

"No, unfortunately I haven't done much travelling yet."

"Her answer gave me the opening I was patiently waiting for. 'What if I flew you over to this really cool beach resort in Fort Lauderdale? I will be there in a few weeks and staying through the weekend. Would you like to be my guest?'"

"Diane's pretty blue eyes lit up immediately. 'Are you serious?'" she probed.

"I'm always serious."

"Yes! I would love too," she blurted out animatedly.

"Okay, I'll have my assistant contact you with all the details. Her name is Jenny. You will love the resort," I elaborated.

Diane did not hesitate in expressing her gratitude. "Thank you, I can't wait."

"Let's order some desert and coffee to celebrate," I suggested.

"We split one slice of my favorite desert—New York style cheesecake. I turned on the charm by spoon feeding her small portions."

"I'm glad I didn't fly out tonight," I confessed.

"I'm happy you didn't fly out either," Diane concurred.

"We talked for at least another hour. It was around 9:30 PM when I asked her, 'Shall we go?'"

"Diane gave me the green light at once. 'Sure, you are quite charming and fun to be with. Why not?'"

"The Fucking Gods were definitely smiling upon me that evening. When we got to my room, I told Diane to kick off her shoes and make herself comfortable. I did the same. I also went into the bathroom to relieve myself. When I came out, she was sitting on the edge of the bed with her legs crossed—OUCH. She immediately took charge. Diane knew exactly what she was doing. Instead of me going down on her first, she unbuckled my pants and pulled them off quickly. Then she grabbed my cock and caressed it gently in her smooth hands. Not needing any coaxing, she started to lick the head. Within a matter of a few seconds, she took it to a whole other level by sucking my entire *unit*. Before I knew it, the time for the grand finale had come. Diane swallowed all nine inches of my *unit* and I instantly floated all the way up to Cloud 9. With a force I didn't think she had, Diane threw me back on the bed, took off her top, and pressed my dick in between her tits. She was teasing the shit out of me, rubbing my cock between her fairly large breasts.

Diane was wearing a business suit. She proceeded to unzip her skirt and removed it slowly but left her slip on. She flat-out refused to let me take charge. Damn, she was all over me like flies take to shit, kissing every part of my body. Since I couldn't reign her in, I just let her do her thing. Hot dog! Diane knew what she was doing. This wasn't her first time around the block, I can tell you that. She took my Johnson inside her mouth and swallowed it deep down her throat."

"She looked at me with a naughty look in her eyes and said, 'You are definitely special. If you're not careful . . .'"

"Before she was able to finish her thought, I moaned, 'Oh! Oh! OMG!' The ecstasy she made me feel was truly amazing. She kept smiling the whole time and didn't unlatch. There I was seeing stars and still the nymphomaniac wouldn't let go. She was driving me absolutely bonkers. My dick was so freakin' sensitive. Diane kept gesturing for me to push her away. Finally, I obliged. Now it was my turn to make her feel good.

I picked Diane up and placed her on her back. I kissed her entire upper torso making sure I didn't neglect her perky nipples. Then I started making my trek downward. When I got to the DANGER ZONE, using my nimble fingers, I tore into her pussy. Oh, it tasted so yummy! I continued to do my thing long after she had her first and second orgasm. Although she kept trying to pull away, I just wouldn't stop. It was my turn to exert my male authority. She kept begging for my dick to be inside of her but, I wouldn't comply with her wishes. I had to make it clear to her that she had finally met her match, that she had to succumb to Michael Stephen Grant.

After having her third orgasm, I turned Diane over and hiked up her slip. My intention was to penetrate her doggystyle. Once I got the operation running smoothly, she enjoyed every moment. At first, I thrusted my penis in and out slowly, then eventually shifted into slamming it hard. She absolutely loved it. Before climaxing, I pulled it out, flipped her over and forced it back into her mouth again. Diane did not disappoint. She swallowed it whole once again which made my head spin out of control.

Before calling it a night, there was one more thing I wanted to do—impale her ass with my almighty spear. I wanted another orgasm. We rested a bit for about thirty minutes. Then I started kissing the back of her neck again and gently caressing her cherry. As soon as my almighty spear got hard again, I positioned her facing away from me so that I could stare at her exquisite butt cheeks. After having my fill of them, I grabbed my trusty traveling Vaseline container and generously lubricated my revved-up cock and her ass. I even inserted my middle finger into her butt hole to loosen it up. Next, I made my arrowhead rove all over her rosy colored passageway in a circular motion. Before aiming and firing away, I decided to drive her wild for a while longer with my tongue. I inserted my tongue as far into her passageway as it would go. After slithering it in and out for a few minutes, I went ahead and replaced my tongue with the arrowhead. Slowly, I gained entrance and not long after that I started pounding her ass. It went on for at least ten minutes before I exploded for the last time that evening, only by then morning had already set in.

By the time all the smoke had cleared, Diane and I concluded that it was a draw between us. We agreed that I had met my equal and she had too. After this unforgettable encounter, Diane promised that she'd always have some fond memories of me. We both couldn't wait to spend the weekend on the beach in Fort Lauderdale. She really showed me some great Southern hospitality. Around one o'clock in the morning, we both passed out. She knew I had to get up in a few hours to catch my flight. When I left, I gave her a kiss good-bye."

"I can't wait to see you in two weeks on the beach," she said to me while half-asleep.

"You and me both. Go back to sleep, love."

"Later that day, I called Diane from Montgomery and thanked her for one of the most memorable evenings of my life."

"Next time we meet will be on the beach in Florida. I feel sorry for you because I'm going to suck you so dry, you're going to need plenty of lotion to prevent wrinkles down there," I warned her, fair and square.

"We both had a good laugh about it. Well, that's it," I conclude.

Raquel leans forward and stretches her arms outward. "That was pretty entertaining. Thanks! Now if you'll excuse me, I'm going up to my room. According to a friend of mine, I have a great deal of meditating and praying to do."

"That's right, you do," I say patting her knee.

As I watch her ascend the stairs to the second floor, I can't help but think, *she's going once, going twice, sold to Dr. Adam Lancaster!*

Chapter Fifteen

All Tied Up
(Bondage a la Duct Tape)

Where in the hell is that roll of duct tape? This morning I've been wandering throughout the entire house for nearly an hour looking for that damn thing and still no luck. I need at least a few feet to wrap around the worn-out extension cord of my beat-up vacuum cleaner. I've been meaning to get to the store to buy a new one but, I just haven't gotten around to it. I woke up in the mood to tidy up and make breakfast for Raquel. It's been exactly a week since she dropped the bomb on me that she may be fleeing the country with the Englishman who doesn't seem to have the balls to fuck her. Can you believe it? What's wrong with women these days pining over celibate men? Am I bitter about it? You bet your ass I am.

I must confess that I'm also still feeling aftershocks from that sexually explosive wet dream I had about Raquel and me. I haven't been able to stop visualizing our no-holds-barred lovemaking. It's been hard for me to be in Raquel's presence, let alone have a conversation with her without feeling like a dirty old Peeping Tom. Yet, day and night for the past week I've been plotting in my head, obsessing really, about how to make it come true. But since the timer is about to go off, I can't afford to continue to skirt the issue any longer. The momentous occasion for Michael Stephen Grant to take what he wants has arrived. Like one of my heroes Elvis Presley used to sing, *it's time for a little less conversation and a little more action, please.*

So, the plan is to find the duct tape and finish vacuuming. Then I'm going to prepare a delicious healthy breakfast for Raquel, take it upstairs, and serve it to her in bed. I even have a fresh single long-stemmed white rose waiting in the refrigerator that I'm going to give her. As she eats her breakfast, I will speak from the heart. I'll declare my undying love for her. Who knows, I may take the Jerry Maguire road and tell her that she completes me. I know, I know, this seems a bit melodramatic, especially coming from an extremist manwhore like me. The truth is I believe I very well could be a re-formed manwhore now and it's all because of the beauty sleeping upstairs who has saved me in more ways than one. Hell, there's no way I'm going to give her up without a fight. After I'm through working my magic on Raquel this fine spring morning, Dr. Lancaster is going to regret having saved my life. But first, I have to find the duct tape.

Now I have to ask myself, when was the last time I used duct tape around here. Nothing is registering in my brain right now so this must mean it's been a long time since I had a need for it. Wait a minute! I think it was back in late October/early November. Yeah, that's right. I used some to insulate some of my outdoor pipes to prevent them from freezing. I know exactly where to look for it now. I'm pretty sure there's a half-used roll of it in the garage. The funny thing is there's got to be a least a hundred different practical uses for duct tape. Heck, if you're creative enough, you can even use it to practice sexual bondage with the object of your desire. Trust me, I should know. I'm speaking from personal experience.

I must have been in my late thirties when I started fooling around with an incredibly sexy blonde named Jane from work. At the time, I was married and come to think of it so was she. Jane worked the evening shift, from 3 to 11 PM, in our computer room which we also referred to as the Data Center. It was where all the mission critical technology for the corporation was housed and monitored twenty-four hours a day, by an operations staff. Whenever I wanted to take a break from the corporate political battlefield, I would go into the Data Center and shoot the breeze with the gang—probably once or twice a week. The Data Center was where my career had started twenty years earlier. It was fun for the staff and it also gave me a much-deserved breather from my intense and long workdays.

To be completely honest, there was also an ulterior motive for my regular visits to the Data Center. I was making intentional pit stops just so that I could get to know Jane better. I quickly figured out that she was impressed by me. I could tell because she was always checking me out when I went there to talk with some of the guys. There were typically two to three people working each shift depending on which night of the week it was. On this particular evening, to my amazement, only Jane was working. When I asked where her co-worker was, she answered, "He called in sick tonight."

There she was, wearing a beautiful red dress. She looked so va-va-voom in it! "Why are you all dressed up?" I asked her.

"It's my birthday and I felt like going out afterwards for a bit," she said.

Naturally, I said back to her, "Happy birthday and have a blast after work. Good night."

Right before walking out of the room, Jane surprisingly flung a loaded question my way. "Aren't you going to buy me a birthday drink?"

My comeback was quick and easily rolled off the tongue. "I'm sorry. Sure, let's go get a drink when your shift ends. I'll meet you in the parking lot by your car around 11:00 PM," I proposed to her.

"Okay," she agreed.

I followed Jane to the bar at the Hyatt hotel a few miles down the road. We walked in together as co-workers, just talking and laughing. After she had one drink, we walked out as a couple—holding hands and I had my arm around her. When we got back to her car, I opened the driver's side door and suggested that we sit and talk for a bit just to make sure the alcohol was out of our system before attempting to drive home. She opened the passenger side door of her blue Volkswagen Bug so that I could get in. I looked at Jane and told her that she looked awesome in her red dress. The next thing you know we were kissing passionately with my hand roaming up under her dress. After making out heavily for about thirty minutes, we decided this session would be continued another night as our spouses were waiting for us.

A few nights later, we got a room at a different hotel and my first corporate affair was in full swing. I'll never forget the first time we went in the hotel room—Jane looked superhot. She was wearing some extremely sexy red and white lingerie under her work dress. It didn't take me long to know that. As soon as we closed the door to the room behind us, Jane and I started making out like crazy. We took turns taking off each other's clothes. Once the clothes came off, she wanted nothing more but to get on top of my nine inches immediately—you can tell she wasn't getting it at home. I teased Jane at first by letting her get on top of my cock and work her way into a frenzy. But before I had an orgasm, I pulled her off. Then I went down on her.

I tore into her pussy with my tongue, sticking it as far in as possible. Around and continuously it went until I latched onto her clit and she jumped for joy. I wouldn't let go until she exploded all over the place. Then I put her back on my dick and rammed it in with authority. Jane was loving it. We went at it for several hours. She was a natural blonde with pretty blue eyes. She had large perfectly-shaped boobs and a nice butt to go with it. Yup, she was definitely one sexy lady.

Over the next few months, we were having sex everywhere: in the car, at her house when the hubby was away on business trips, in the fields, in the pool, even during work in the back of the Data Center. Sometimes Jane would call to tell me she was wearing a dress in case I wanted to sneak into the back of the room on her breaks. She knew what triggered my hot button—knowing that she was wearing a dress would drive me bonkers—no way I could work.

We continued to see each other on a regular basis. As one can imagine our relationship blossomed and we started having real feelings for each other. The sex turned into love-making to the nth degree—our sexual appetite grew to a whole other level. I actually thought she had turned into a nymph that could never be fully satisfied. She wanted to meet before work, at lunch time, and after work—it didn't matter where—she just wanted it. I turned her into a sex freak of the highest order.

During one encounter we shared our deepest sexual fantasies with one another. For Jane it was tying a guy up so she could have her way with him without any restrictions. Of course, mine was what every hot-blooded man in the universe wants—a threesome with two ready-to-go chicks. Her request was simple so, I decided to grant her wishes. The next day I went to the local hardware store and bought some duct tape. When we met for another one of our unbridled passionate rendezvous, I surprised her by tossing her the roll of duct tape and saying, "Here you go."

Without saying another word, I started stripping down. When I was butt naked, I threw myself onto the bed and spread my legs and arms out. Her eyes lit up. I said to Jane, "Let's go! Do what you want. Have your way with me, just don't kill me."

Jane went into her closet, grabbed some lingerie and high-tailed it into the bathroom. For this special occasion, she put on a long, sexy burgundy colored night gown and jumped on the bed. She started kissing me while duct taping each of my wrists to the bed posts. Then she did the same with my ankles. It was all serious hanky-panky business to her. Meanwhile, I couldn't budge not even an inch. Once she had me all secured in place, then her fun began. Jane pulled up her nightgown a little. She knew I was a leg and ass man. As she continued pulling up her nightgown slowly, Jane turned around so that I could see her butt starting to be exposed. The dishonorable intention was to show me that she wasn't wearing any panties. Well, I was already going ape wild. I tried to release myself but, I couldn't budge. She was loving every second of it because for once in her life she was in total control.

Eventually, Jane raised her nightgown all the way up to her waist and she began to pull herself closer to my face. OMG! She sat right on it and immediately I started licking that beautiful pussy of hers. Within a few lickety-split seconds she had her first screaming orgasm. I was hard as can be and throbbing profusely. When she was done sitting on my face, Jane mounted my nine-inch erection and started to ride it like a professional rodeo cowboy. Oh man she was driving herself crazy. As for me, I was already delirious from not being able to take control of the situation. She pumped a few times then got off just to tease me. Then Jane really turned on the heat by turning around and nestling her butt hole close to my dick. She grabbed my super excited penis and started to rub it near her butt hole. To say that I was going crazy is a huge understatement. I was way beyond that point. I tugged so hard that I thought I was going to break the bed.

After teasing me with her butt, she came back up to sit on my face. *Here we go again* was the thought that ran through my mind. I hooked on to her clit and refused to let go, even after she had her next orgasm. In an attempt to free herself, Jane put both of her hands on my head and separated me away from her clit. Then she went down and took my pecker deep into her mouth. Jane could see that I was in ecstasy and about ready to cum. Right at that moment, she took it out of her mouth and sat back on top of it in a forceful manner. It quickly became apparent to me that she wanted me to release inside of her and within seconds I did.

Lucky for me, Jane wasn't through—not by a long shot. She left me tied up for at least another hour. She brought me some water and proceeded to lick my balls. Obviously, she wanted it hard again and quickly. I'm proud to say that I was able to rise to the occasion on command so she could sit on it again. Right before I had another orgasm, she abandoned ship which meant another round of teasing torture for me. Jane took her favorite position of sitting on my face again and waited for me to jam my tongue in as far up her pussy as it could go without gagging too much. This abuse was insane so to fight back I latched on to her clit and sucked it until she had another orgasm. I kept telling her to untie me but, she wouldn't. She knew I wanted her ass in a big way.

Jane started kissing me passionately as she started to untie me. It was a tormenting experience but, I couldn't let her see me in pain. I didn't want her to think I was a pussy. When she peeled the tape off my skin, a whole bunch of hair went with it. Now that was painful, but she seemed to dig it. Once she untied my wrists and ankles, I flipped her over so that she was lying down flat on her stomach. I pulled up her nightgown over her ass and I jammed my dick hard into her small brown hole. An entire constellation of stars flashed before my eyes. What a truly memorable night that was. I'm sure wherever Jane is right now, she can still picture the image of Michael Stephen Grant all tied up in bondage a la duct tape.

After I nailed her in the ass really good, she passed out for a few hours. The woman was a walking sex freak show who could never get enough. We ended up seeing each other for about a year until she moved out of town. During the span of time that we were together, she duct-taped me at least half a dozen times. She was hooked on it. My guess is she loved having full control of me. But little did she know that I was the Puppet Master the whole time. All I cared about was plugging that fine ass of hers all the time and I did!

Come to think of it, back in my younger days, nailing the most beautiful women I could get my hands on was all I cared about. I didn't give a shit what the cost was or who I hurt in the process so long as my dick was always inside a wet pussy. I honestly thought having promiscuous sex with hordes of women is what made me a real macho man, not to mention the envy of all of my male friends. It's taken me nearly three decades of maturing, a grueling battle with cancer, and finally meeting the one woman who I will never get bored of to realize that it didn't. All it made me was a demented, selfish bastard.

It is also very likely that I was a sex addict too. I would do or say anything just to get a girl to jump in the sack with me, including using the "L" word. Even married women were fair game to me. Actually, knowing beforehand that the woman I was about to fool around with was married turned me on in a huge way. It sure did pump up my ego to know that I was going to pleasure them in a way that their unattractive and overweight husbands couldn't. I engaged in this kind of reckless sexual behavior for years and years and didn't even bat an eye. I was the poster boy for that old adage that goes: A stiff dick has no conscience.

There's no denying that I was an immoral pig—a fornicator and adulterer—who dishonored women every chance I got. Until one day I woke up from my three-sheets-to-the-wind-like sexual stupor to find myself alone and dying from lung cancer. Talk about the worst possible rude awakening a man can have. Suddenly, the scent of a woman wasn't so appealing to me anymore. It finally took me receiving a death sentence to realize that: MAN DOES NOT LIVE ON PUSSY ALONE. For the first time in my life, I felt empty and defeated. I had spent all of my energy and physical prowess on meaningless sex and now when I really needed it, I had no fight left in me at all. But just when I had lost all hope of survival, an unex-pected miracle named Raquel Lopez happened. Now I'm ready to turn over a new leaf—to be a one-woman man for the rest of my life.

Raquel Lopez trumps everything! She is so remarkably beautiful. While it's true that her physical appearance attracts the eyes, espe-cially mine, what has really captivated my soul is her inner beauty. In retrospect, she's probably the only woman who has been able to stimulate me intellectually with her unparalleled wit and brilliance.

But the things that distinguish her from all the women I've ever known in my life and makes her the Queen of Queens is her irresistible charisma and caring demeanor. Then there's that sweet, sensual, compassionate voice of hers that I wish I could bottle up and sell. Most women have to really work it with their bodies to get a man aroused. All Raquel has to do is talk to a man and his temperature will spike up in no time flat. If I had to pinpoint the one thing that truly amazes me about Raquel, it's her humility regarding her sexuality. Either Raquel is playing us men or she's actually clueless as to the power she wields. She has a way with men that simply can't be taught to other women. Oh, if she only could, the world would be jam-packed with genuinely happy men.

While I am undoubtedly a changed-for-the-better man, there is still a small residual of me that continues to be a self-seeking egomaniac. There's no way that I'm going to share Raquel with anyone else. Doctor Adam Lancaster and all the other men in the world can just go fuck themselves. One of the things that my whore of a mother taught me before leaving this world is that anything valuable in life is worth fighting for. Raquel is a rarified, precious gem and I truly believe she is meant to be mine and mine alone. I woke up this morning with an entirely different outlook and thank God that I did. Actions speak louder than words. This is why I'm aborting my dumb "silence is the best strategy" game plan and embracing a more hands-on direct approach.

So, here you have me expeditiously preparing a breakfast platter for the woman I love. I've made all of her favorite breakfast items; freshly brewed coffee, a vegetarian omelet, yogurt topped with granola and blueberries. I even went the extra mile and arranged all the goodies on a platter as artistically as I possibly could. Of course, the long-stemmed white rose I've been preserving for her certainly adds the hint of romanticism I'm going for. Hopefully it's the first item she will zero in on when I present her with the platter.

While this is a grand gesture on my part, I can't help but wonder if it's going to be enough to close the deal with Raquel. Is it arrogant of me to think that she can easily be persuaded to pass up on a once-in-a-life time opportunity with a once-in-a-lifetime guy just because I bring her breakfast in bed? If I truly was a knight on a white charger, I should have come to my senses days ago and gone to Jared's or Tiffany's and bought her the most expensive diamond ring I could afford. Then I could have attached it to the long-stemmed rose with a piece of satin ribbon and when the perfect moment came along drop down on one knee and ask her to marry me. Considering that I haven't even gotten to first base with Raquel yet, if I had dared to play out the scenario I've just described, well that would have really blindsided her. Baby steps. I've always been a gambling man so I am going to start out by giving her my heart. If she accepts it, then the ring will come later. That's my plan and I'm sticking to it.

Carrying a fully loaded breakfast platter up the stairs was a lot harder than I thought it would be. Even though I treaded lightly, I spilled some coffee along the way. No big deal. I'll just clean it up later because right now I have some fishing to do and hopefully I've got the right bait to reel in the CATCH OF THE DAY—hook, line and sinker. I would be lying if I said I wasn't feeling like a nervous wreck, standing in front of Raquel's bedroom door, breathing heavily. It has just occurred to me that I didn't think the logistics of this whole man servant act all the way through. How am I supposed to knock on her door while holding a large-sized platter of food? I'm such an idiot. Well it may not be debonair of me but, I'll have to pounce on the door with one of my feet and wait for her to let me in.

Okay, something is wrong. I've been tapping against Raquel's door with my right big toe and calling her name for nearly five minutes and I still haven't heard a peep from the other side. From my perspective, there are two possibilities she's a no-show so far. Either Raquel has slipped into a coma or she's playing impossible to get. The longer I stand out here, the more foolish I feel. I can't take being ignored any longer. Trying to remain optimistic, I carefully lay the breakfast platter on the floor. I put my hand on the doorknob, twist, and hope to God that she didn't lock herself in. A gushing feeling of relief washes over me as soon as I hear that familiar clicking sound. As I'm pushing the door open, I think to myself, *maybe she's in the shower and didn't hear me.* I smile because coming face-to-face with a naked and wet Raquel would be the best-case scenario I could ever hope for. I mean how lucky could a guy get, right?

"What in the hell . . .?" is all I can think of to say when I finally gain full entrance into Raquel's bedroom and see that it's been completely emptied out. You would think a team of professional cat burglars cased the joint and cleaned it out. All of her personal belongings are gone and so is she. Just to make sure, I make a mad dash to her closet and open it in a hurry. Of course, there's nothing in there. There's no trace of her left at all. I'm such a love-sick moron. This whole time I've been playing it safe so that I don't blindside her and in the end I'm the one who gets sucker-punched in the heart. I'm too late. Right now, I really hate myself for procrastinating for so long. I should've told Raquel months ago that I love her. But then again, how could she just pack up her shit in secret and leave without saying good-bye as if I meant nothing to her? After all I did for her. What a fucking cunt! I'll never forgive her. I hate her.

I storm out of the empty room, slam the door behind me and proceed down the stairs wishing I hadn't beat cancer after all. What my next move will be, I have no fucking clue. It's hard to think when you have a knife deeply wedged into your back. In my mind I had made many exciting plans for Raquel and I. Now that I'm out of the woods, I was going to take her to see the world and show her a damn good time. But that's all shot to hell now. I tell you what, if you want to give God a good laugh, tell him what your future plans are. I should have known that a man really doesn't have any power over what truly isn't his. It will also teach me not to be so in love that I can't see when the shit is about to hit the fan. As I climb down the stairs with my broken spirit, all of these things come to mind.

When I get back down to the first floor, without the platter of food, I immediately go into the living room. I really need to lie down on my comfortable couch and process that Raquel is really gone. Maybe if I close my eyes for a while and then open them back up again, I'll discover that it's just another one of my harebrained dreams. As soon as the couch comes into my field of vision, I see it propped up on the coffee table—a sealed envelope with something written on it. When I'm able to see that it's my name in her handwriting, my heart does an aerial cartwheel. Suddenly the small amount of light left in me is overshadowed by a gloom and doom darkness which clamors that I'm never going to be able to survive Raquel's abandonment.

In a zombie-like state, I sit on the couch and stare at the envelope. I'm too afraid to reach out and grab it. I'd much rather be reaching out to embrace the real living and breathing Raquel, but no, all I have left to hold onto is this piece of rectangular paper. Of course, I know what's inside that envelope. It's a Dear John letter. What else can it be? The question is do I read it now or just put the damn thing in the trash and try to move on with what's left of my sure-to-be miserable and wretched life moving forward? Why in God's name did Raquel work so hard to nurse me back to health when all along she was planning to leave me on emotional life support? That just doesn't make any freaking sense. It isn't fair.

Against my better judgement, I finally reach out for the envelope. Like a lovelorn puppy, the first thing I do is raise the envelope up to my nose and I take a whiff of it. Just as I feared, her scent is still on it. I wish I had the backbone to not read what's inside the envelope but I don't. The curiosity is killing me. Unable to resist the urge for a second longer, I reach over and pluck the envelope off the coffee table. Using my right index finger, I gently break the seal and unfold the piece of fine linen paper that contains Raquel's last departing words to me. I inhale deeply and brace myself.

Dear Michael Stephen Grant,

By the time you get around to reading this letter, I will be well on my way to Stockholm, Sweden to start a new chapter in my life. The first thing I'd like to tell you is that I did not take this job because I'm in love with Dr. Adam Lancaster. I accepted it because I think it's a once-in-a lifetime opportunity for me. My gut feeling is that it's a step in the right direction toward fulfilling my dream of becoming a best-selling author one day.

In order to become the best writer and person I possibly can be, I really need to get out of my comfort zone and take a giant leap of faith. Experiencing and enduring hardships and uncertainly will make me stronger. I know living in Sweden under luxurious conditions won't exactly be roughing it or suffering. It is what will come afterward—traveling to third world countries, feeding and curing sick children—that will test my limits. This is the part of the journey I am most afraid of and looking forward to at the same time. I really want you to be proud of me.

Leaving you is the hardest thing I've ever had to do because I care about you so much, more than you will ever know. My feelings for you are genuine and truly run deep. You hiring me to take care of you was divine intervention. I know that now. What I didn't count on was that you were going to take care of me instead. I didn't save you. It was you who saved me.

Thank you so much for taking me in when I was at the lowest point in my life and didn't have any other place to go. You opened up your lovely home and heart to me even though I was a complete stranger and for this I will be forever grateful. Please forgive me for having left so abruptly, without saying good-bye. I didn't trust myself to carry-out my decision to move on if I had to face you in person. What I feared the most was that you would take me in your strong arms and my resolve to leave you would dissolve in a heartbeat. I never told you this but every time you gave me one of your bear hugs, the warmth of your embrace made me feel so safe and cared about. Being in your loving arms always made me feel like I was home. I hope that one day you'll forgive me for my weakness. In the meantime, feel free to call me every offensive name you can think of.

Something else you will have to forgive me for is meddling in your personal affairs. I just didn't have the heart to leave knowing you would be alone. Several weeks ago, I called your ex-wife Maribel in France and told her that you still love her. I suggested to her that she should return home because you need her. Maribel confessed to me that she has never stopped loving you either and she's ready to come back into your life. I know there is bad blood and a sordid past between you two, but everyone deserves a second chance to make things right. Please be open to rekindling your relationship with her. You have so much to offer a woman. If you accept Maribel back into your life and heart, she will be an extremely lucky woman.

Make no mistake, I will miss you terribly, especially your praise and generosity. I'll think of you every single day. Everywhere I go, I'll carry your presence with me. In return, I hope you will never forget about me and please don't ever stop writing books because the world needs the wisdom you possess. This isn't good-bye. Think of it more as until we meet again. Once I get settled in Sweden, I will send you my full contact information so that we can keep in touch. If you're forgiven me by then and are receptive, I would like to come visit you after completing my one-year stint.

Take care of yourself. I love you with all my heart and soul.

Hugs and kisses,

Raquel

Unbelievable! I've just finished reading Raquel's letter and someone is ringing my doorbell like it's some kind of emergency. Who is stupid enough to come calling right smack in the middle of the day? Man, I'd really like to smack whoever this intruder is square in the face for bothering me at the most inopportune time. I yelled at whoever it is to go away. I'm not in the mood to put up with any more shit. All I want is to sit on this couch and lick my wounds for the rest of my life. I can't remember when I've felt so heartsick. It's not every day that a man gets his balls cut off in one clean swipe by the woman he loves. How am I supposed to go on? Maybe I should ask the asshole still ringing my doorbell. Crap! I can't take it anymore. I better answer the door before I lose my fucking mind.

I get my ass off the couch and storm to the door feeling aggravated and emasculated. I don't care who it is, I'm going to give them a piece of my mind. I'll teach this person not to show up at anyone's door uninvited. With more brute strength than necessary I open the door, huffing and puffing. When I catch a glimpse of who is on the other side, my eyes immediately do a double-take. Sweat starts coming out of my pores and I can feel my blood pressure soar to new heights. The BAD KARMA GODS must have it in for me today. I mean what are the chances that Michael Stephen Grant gets bushwhacked by two women in the same day?

"Maribel, what are you doing here? I struggle to get the words out. Then, my mind takes me back to what Raquel said in her letter about reaching out to my ex-wife.

Looking like the Puerto Rican Goddess she's always been, Maribel drops her suitcases on the doorstep and practically leaps into my arms. Surprisingly, my loins react to the full-on contact. I'm not sure what to make of it. Maybe I should just chock it up to being on the rebound. Maribel takes it a step further and starts kissing me deeply. Again, I'm not sure what this means but I decide to just go with it for now. After making out with my ex-wife on the front porch for all the nosy neighbors to see, I finally pry us apart.

"I'm not going to deny that I'm enjoying the affection you're showing me, but what are you doing here in Texas?" I ask her bluntly.

Maribel doesn't hesitate to cough up an answer. "I've come to my senses, Michael. I'm still in love with you and I want us to get back together again. It was a mistake to divorce you. I don't want to live in France anymore. I want to live here with you and for us to start over."

First, I get an eyeful from Raquel, and now I'm receiving a mouthful from Maribel. This has turned out to be such a looney-tune day. What am I supposed to do? This is way too much for me to process right now. The midday Texas sun is really starting to wear me out so I'm thinking it's a good idea to invite Maribel inside. "Listen Maribel, it's getting really hot out here and you must be exhausted after your long flight. Let me help you with your bags."

Just as I'm about to pick up Maribel's bags and get them inside the house, a yellow taxicab pulls up to my driveway.

"Are you expecting someone?" Maribel asks me.

"No."

"Then who could it be?"

I scratch my head and say, "I have no idea. Let's wait and see."

Maribel and I freeze on the front porch and wait with bated breath to see who it is. A tall, athletic young man steps out of the taxicab with a large-sized duffel bag in tow. He walks over to the driver's side window of the taxicab, pays the driver, and smiles warmly at him. The taxicab driver cranks it in reverse and begins to back away. The young stranger picks up his duffel bag and starts making his way over to Maribel and I. As soon as he gets close enough for me to be able to discern his facial features, it strikes me that he's bi-racial. Actually, he's a great looking kid, with smooth caramel colored skin and piercing blue eyes. He could be a dead ringer for that popular actor on television. I think his name is Michael Ealy.

The handsome young stranger stops a few feet away from us and asks, "Is this the home of Michael Stephen Grant?"

"Yes, it is. I'm Michael Stephen Grant. How can I help you?" I answer him.

The young man lowers his head. I can tell he is conflicted about something. Suddenly, his head pops up again. He straightens up and flashes a beaming, confident smile. "Hello! My name is Terrell Grant. I don't know how to say this but, I believe you're my father."

My jaw drops down to the ground. Just when I thought this day couldn't get any worse. I am completely blown away. Then I remember that Maribel is standing right next to me. I look at her inquisitively, expecting her to go ballistic over this big reveal. But to my surprise, she maintains her composure which is downright scary. I'm talking Twilight Zone Scary. There must be a glitch in her system because there's no way that a feisty Puerto Rican woman is going to take this lying down. Instead of having a meltdown, Maribel just looks at me like she's never done before, as if I'm an extraterrestrial fresh off the MOTHER SHIP. She starts laughing and shaking her head profusely. Okay great, now I'm really stumped.

Maribel waves her hand in the air and simply says, "Never mind. I'm outta here!" Then, as if she was a refined lady, she bends down and picks up her bags. Without saying another word to me or the young man, she turns around and starts walking toward the street. The minute Maribel steps off of my property, she turns around, drops her bags and gives me the finger. Then what she was trying so hard to suppress inside comes rushing forth like an unstoppable Tsunami. "You're such a manwhore!!!!!"

TO BE CONTINUED . . .